EVENTIDE,
Water City

EVENTIDE,
Water City

○ ○ ○

CHRIS McKINNEY

Published by
Soho Press, Inc.
227 W 17th Street
New York, NY 10011

Library of Congress Cataloging-in-Publication Data

Names: McKinney, Chris, author.
Title: Eventide, Water City / Chris McKinney.
Description: New York, NY : Soho Crime, [2023]
Series: The Water City trilogy ; 2
Identifiers: LCCN 2022041938

ISBN 978-1-64129-431-7
eISBN 978-1-64129-432-4

Subjects: LCGFT: Novels.
Classification: LCC PS3613.C5623 E94 2023
DDC 813/.6—dc23/eng/20220902
LC record available at https://lccn.loc.gov/2022041938

Interior design by Janine Agro

Printed in the United States of America

10 9 8 7 6 5 4 3 2 1

In memory of Al McKinney

PART ONE

FROM WHICH LIFE FIRST ROSE

○

○

○

1

○

○

○

Somewhere in the hadal zone, an arrowtooth approaches, and a pupil dilates from the cutting of its own light. The deepwater eel slithers, stops in front of the bodyless eye, and opens its mouth. It freezes in this barbed gape for a long moment. Everything moves so slowly that all moments are long moments twenty-three thousand feet deep. Synthetic hormones whirl with neuroception, but the eye remains motionless. Finally, the predator turns and slinks away. Relieved, the eye runs its qubit calculations in the dark. It has been 2,217 days since the eye first woke and found itself in the Challenger Deep. First, it was resuscitated by its own emergency protocol. Then, its neurons, glial cells, and nerves expanded and finally fired in the correct sequence to climb up the polyvagal ladder. An unraveled pattern stitched into memory trace.

No place on the planet's surface has less light than Challenger Deep, which made the eye wonder if it had simply stepped from one death to another. The eye opened its nano-antenna and mapped its location, startled when it realized the tides had rolled it four thousand miles west of its own murder scene. Since waking in the trench, the eye has mapped its route back, a zigzag from heat source to heat source, and followed the bathymetry of Pacific Ocean hot spots that power its journey home.

Now that the eel is gone, six legs pop from the eye's vitreous and dig into the deep dust. It crawls, moving laggardly like everything else down here—the swaying purple polyps on rocks, the cusk-eels, the grenadier fish, and the bygone plastic bags that the skimmers missed. The eye too must conserve its energy in this black place, this bog of barely life. But sometimes it needs to be fed sight to confirm that it is alive.

Of the murder, the eye remembers. The synesthete and his refusal. The eye had been so close to godhood. All snatched away by a man it had offered everything to—generational wealth, a life without killing, and the truth about Ascalon's Scar. First, the bullets cracked and shattered the glass walls. Then the freezing, midnight zone waters flooded into the penthouse. Crushing chest pain followed. After that, the collapse of the windpipe. Hypothermia. Finally, every inch of the eye's physical body crumpled as if a boulder toppled on it. When beneath a boulder, one does not try to gauge its weight or count the seconds. All one feels is the agonizing, inevitable doom. Despite this, the body still managed to bang at the chamber the old coward hid in. But the eye misplaced its mother's jeweled memories in that haze of fear and hate. It wonders if the old man saw his own greens that day. It wants to bathe him in those colors.

The closest and final hotspot—18.92° N, 155.27° W. The eye calculates that it can complete the odyssey in three days. It wants to swim badly, but it remembers its journey as it inches forward. Eaten by a glowing kitefin the last time it swam. Captured then nibbled on by a yeti crab for two days. Swallowed and shat out of a whale. It took several disasters to convince the eye that it is better to crawl than to swim. But it's so close now. Swim. Then fly. Soar. But no, home can wait. Home is youthful, vibrant, and optically ripe by now. Patched into its own satellite, the eye has been tracking home for years now. Its channel. Its live feed in the digitally remastered world above. After using its zero-day master key to hack the genetic database, the eye has run simulation after simulation. The process of possession. Take the body. Let the host's mind die. The eye will live again. The new host senses it as well. The faint, alluring transmission bands that the eye sings to her. The images and sounds of the deep, of the past, of the synesthete killing in siren frequency. The eye feels the girl diving. Searching. Following the faint sound as far as she dares. Over the years, she has been the only consistent flicker of human contact the eye has had on its long journey. It wants the child to remember what it has taught her. You learn when you take the long way home.

The eye has collected so much information while all think it dead. Among those is the data on the salvage of Volcano Vista. A familiar name financed it. The eye will take that man, who's recently made a very large crypto transfer to a wanted criminal and seize his vast financial might after it takes the child. The synesthete is so close to uncovering the truth, and he doesn't even know it. He probably doesn't want to.

Something approaches on sensor! Was the eye skittering too quickly? Too excited by the prospect of home? It digs into the sludge and buries itself. No. No! Hold still. Hold still! The teeth. The gruesome underbite. The stem of green glow bait. Viperfish. Vertical migrater. Over the years, the eye has *experienced victimization by vertical food chain a number of times. Eaten by one thing, taken up a few thousand meters just to be eaten by another, then taken up a few thousand meters more. Two years ago, the eye found itself in the throat of a masked booby, who then became mugged in midair by a great frigatebird. The booby shook and jostled until the lesser bird puked the eye up. The frigatebird carried the eye two hundred miles in the wrong direction before finally dropping it from over five thousand feet above sea level.* Plop. *Back at the outer edge of the Mariana Trench. The synesthete would have laughed sardonically and told the eye that nature is wild. The eye's father would've said,* "Pay attention to the now and hope the viperfish does not have squid eye," *which was the almost magical ability to see holes left by prey in the sand, the skill of the father's native people. The eye does not and will never need others again. Needing others in the past had been its weakness. The eye must content itself to imagine what others would do and say. It imagines its twin sister, and these imaginations are the only company worth keeping.*

The eye waits to make a move. It finally feels the turbu-lence of the fish kicking away. The viperfish's blip disappears from the eye's micro depth recorder. Three. More. Days. Patience. *At least the eye's not sleeping. At least it's not in that madness-inducing torpor that its mother had put it in for thirty years. But it was during that sleep that the eye figured out many things, like how to evolve an iE from a floating, orb-shaped computer that can communicate with the brain of its individual user to something much more, something that can emulate the brain and can mind upload. Once, the eye planned to upload Akira's iE into its own. But now it also knows how to download its mind into others. To Mind*

Exome Load, or MELd, as it likes to say to itself. To commune. Then possess.

The eye does have a name. Ascalon Lee. And Ascalon Lee is not dead. She has been copied and laced into this eye. And she will copy and lace herself into the mind of another soon. Another who can see murder coming in its glorious greens. Then it will do the same to another. Then another. The eye will become a hive that can work toward finding its mother. Akira Kimura. The eye knows that she stole Ascalon Lee's tech. Has the mother copied and laced herself as well?

The eye dares a slip of light. The climb is steep. On the shelf above, plumes of heat rise from the vents like the smoke from old factory chimneys. The energy is already providing a charge for the eye's almost spent battery. The six legs, one for every eye muscle, cautiously extend, and its induction coils draw power from a hydrothermal vent. The eye shuttles laterally in a defensive position. It spins every few steps, blinks, and darts in every cardinal direction. Am I a being? *it asks itself.* An entity? Or am I a philosophical zombie, a soulless copy of something that no longer is? I am sentient, but am I human? Not yet. But I will be. I refuse to be reduced to a voice in a jar. I will be her again. Not Akira. I will forever be Ascalon Lee.

The eye feels a tremor beneath its sharp legs. Oh no! The vent is about to erupt! *The eye skitters away from the smoking hydrothermal crack as quickly as it can.* Faster. Faster! *The heat rises. The eye brightens now, basking in its own yellow shine. It spots a dark plastic bag half-buried in the distance.* The bag may be useful. *The eye's spindly legs dig into sand and charge. The coming eruption vibrates beneath it, almost toppling it on its iris. Ten feet. Two feet.*

One. It snatches the bag and lifts it up. The seafloor's crack widens and an explosion bursts from the vent. The eye is shot upward, taking its plastic makeshift parachute with it. The eye retracts its legs and soars. The bag glows and ripples behind the eye, sculling like the tail of a prehistoric thing. The two begin to slow. The eye rolls out of the bag right before the jaws of a goblin shark jut from its head and its teeth sink into the plastic. It's a long but grateful drop to the bottom. Perhaps the eye is human after all. It associates. It predicts. It remembers. Deep in the weeds of its dendrites, it imagines.

The eye plops into the sand atop the shelf. A slow-motion puff of marine snow floats then rests upon it. The eye waits a moment, then continues its journey up. Yes. Smooth pursuit. Perhaps the eye is not just human. Maybe it's something even more. When it reaches the surface and inhabits its new domicile, it will send the signal and kill the light, that permanent scar in the sky that reassures people of the existence of heroes, people like her mother, who can slay any and all threats to humanity. People and how they cling to their fairy tale . . . But for now, like the greatest of its native ancestors, the eye wayfinds, except without guidance from the stars.

2

The target: Shave Time Money. The offenses: Assault. Theft. Fencing of stolen property. Hibiscus poaching. Bail jumping. Shave Time Money—if that ain't a name of antiquity still umbilicalled to some ghetto, time-trapped, afterbirth of a town, I don't know what is. It's no surprise that his trail has led me to the unofficial capital of The Great Leachate—St. Louis, Missouri. The Leachate has been around my whole damn life, and it's the first time I've ever been here. Hopefully, it's also the last. St. Louis Ribs is now a reference to the scattered row of giant, cylinder-shaped trash that sticks out of the spine of the Mississippi, leaking and basting their vile liquid rust into the once-mighty river.

The nearest shuttle port is in Nashville. I had to ping a pilotless quad prop heli-taxi from there and have it fly me to the edge of the contamination zone. During the entire trip, the steady hum of the heli-taxi's four rotors was drowned out by music about trucks, whiskey, and shotgun weddings. Trucks don't even exist anymore, but country music will never die. We approached the great dam that halted the flow of the contaminated river at the Kentucky Bend. After the old eggbeater dropped me off, and my iE transferred the fare with a twenty percent tip, I opened my pack and pulled out my orange rad suit. I put on the lead-composite leggings, boots, apron, and mitts, then threw on the face-visored LED-HED. I told my iE to mag-seal it to the apron and turn on the oxygen. I felt like a chef getting ready to grill some yakiniku on the sun. Next, I managed to hotwire an ancient center console bass boat that still had juice in its lithium twin engines. I had once been trained for covert trips like this one.

While motoring up the cold Missouri Bootheel like a geriatric, post-apocalyptic Huck Finn, I ask my iE the history because I can't believe what I was seeing. The river is at the bottom of a twisted canyon speckled with the blue crystals of Stone Age detergent. The radiated water walled in by endless towers of trash. I'm glad my LED-HED keeps out the smell. I look down in the muck and pass a school of two-headed Asian carp and goldfish the size of small children feeding on what appears to be fossilized diapers.

According to my iE: *Great Flood of 2040. Great Flood of 2041. Greater Flood of 2042: Trial by Water. Greatest Flood of 2043: Affliction.* Climate warming natural disasters were so common back then that we named them like they were first-person shooter sequels or MMA Pay-Per-View events. The last flood from the Missouri somehow knocked out the cooling system of the Callaway Nuclear Plant, not to mention Jim's RV Park next door. The meltdown dug into the groundwater and seeped. The entire state of Missouri became a toxic wet mop, so we said "fuck it," and started to pile all our trash here. The post-apocalypse ain't the state of the world. It's a region in middle America.

I'm sweating in this damn suit. Unlike my foam fit, there's

no temp-control and nothing weaved in to weaken the thickness of the material, which keeps the radiation out. Plus, because of the density of the suit, my iE's brainwave receptors are slightly lagging. Why the fuck did I take this job? Oh, that's right. No guaranteed paycheck anymore. Small cop pension. Smaller Social Security from early withdrawal. Kid in fourth grade private school. Sell your life rights—commercial use of name, likeness, and other recognizable aspects—to Savior's Eye Entertainment and start freelancing in your late eighties—smart. At least there isn't anything to do with murder anymore. Nothing green.

I take in a 360 view. Veins of bright yellow snowmelt slush into the river. A pack of vulture-sized pigeons picks at the inexhaustible mountains of trash, then erupts into the air. An avalanche of trash tumbles from the two-hundred-foot cliff of garbage and splashes behind me. These towers can't be stable after years of water erosion. I white-knuckle the wheel and pay close attention while piloting north. I pass stacks of automobiles pressed into neat, metal loaves. Next is a heap of rusted Boeing and Airbus fuselages propped against one another like the remains of a doused bonfire. These are the world-famous St. Louis Ribs.

I weave through the baste and finally get to the crumbling Gateway Arch. Man, bleak. I look up at the gray sky and can't even tell what time of day it is. Except for the decrepit paddle boats rotting onshore, the dock is empty. I tell my iE to bring up a map of the town. The zoo is seven and a half miles west. I check my rad suit. The goddamn built-in Geiger is ticking like mad. The water holds more contamination than inland. I begin to walk west, liking the idea of getting as far from the Mississippi as soon as possible.

I send my iE way up to get a drone shot of this place. I got the new model, which is all the rage now. Model Triple X, the kids call it. The thirtieth iteration of Idris Eshana's invention. It's smaller, quicker, nimbler, and is packed with graphene and time crystals, power that can last a lifetime. Not to mention better optics and transponder. It reads our brainwaves and spits what we need back at us in the same frequency faster than ever. DNA encrypted to its individual user, the sucker can store an almost endless amount of data. And the new feature that trumps the rest is person-to-person "Thought Talk"—digital telepathic communication. Just about everyone's got Triple X. The improvements so impressive that some wonder if Eshana is still alive out there somewhere. People fascinate over that kind of shit more than ever now that they've seen a god save the world, then supposedly die forty years later while leaving no remains. I'm not one of those people. I was at Idris's open-casket funeral. He looked peaceful, almost smiling. And I saw Akira Kimura cut up again and again.

The iE takes in the dated expanse. It's weird that people once lived like this, in this pygmy sprawl. Pint-sized buildings with doors with handles, boxy machines used to withdraw paper money, buttons to press to cross streets. The storefronts a reminder of when people used to buy stuff in person. Back when you had to touch a hundred different things to get through the day. Now, every door, sink, shower, bidet, dispenser, washer/dryer, and form of transportation is automated. Every product is delivered via drone. There's no pulling stuff off shelves and rolling them through aisles in carts anymore. And just about every transaction, communication, and ID check are done via iE. Stuff like keyboards, buttons, touchscreens, and knobs are artifacts that have either been buried in regions like this one or recycled into seascraper building materials. Idris Eshana used to say his idea to invent the iE was born out of being a germophobe. The fact that our smartphones were filthier than our toilets because we had to touch them all the time made him want to invent a smart device that he didn't need to touch. Also, one that wouldn't shatter if dropped.

Today, the cracked streets are empty. The hovels choked by vines. I pass a bunch of dead museums and think that we're gonna need a museum of all these dead museums eventually. There's a statue of some guy named Nelly. I wonder who he is and what happened to him. He must've been wounded since there's a Band-Aid under his eye. Beyond that statue, there's a much larger one. A tower of trash being carved and fused into the likeness of Akira Kimura by white-lab-coated missionaries wearing welding masks. Her right hand is raised, holding some kind of mop with a rectangular-shaped cleaning end. She's clad in aluminum siding armor. It's official. She's not just global, she's netherworld, too. Too bad that in real life, she was left-handed.

When I reach Forest Park, I start seeing more people. In the old days, during Desert Storm 15, I would've been prepped for infiltration. Learned how to sneak in or blend in, or maybe a bit of both. But it's a post-Ascalon world now, and nothing seems dangerous anymore. Maybe that's part of the reason I took the job, a little of that old spice. But these people just make me sad. I pass more and more, feeling both guilty and self-conscious that I'm the only one in a rad suit. The park is more forest than park now, and the locals sit by campfires cooking god knows what over the flames, the fire reflecting on their watery, pre-stroke eyes. They look at me suspiciously. It's probably been a while since they've seen someone in a rad suit. The US government gave up on The Leachate long ago. I walk on. People in twos and threes dangle fishing poles above holes cut through trash, like the Missourian ice fishermen of old. A girl around my daughter's age spackled in rags refuses to eat what her mother serves her. The mother, face spotted with cystic acne, tells her to think outside the bun. I haven't seen acne since I was a kid. It was edited out of our DNA with CRISPR tech by our vain, social media-obsessed ancestors. Maybe that's why I see how I do. Some CRISPR gene editing gone wrong.

The girl shakes her head and says life begins when pain ends. I think about my daughter and begin to fantasize in Super 8 Polavision, the stuff I learned about as an art history major back in college. I'll bring home a playmate, a sister for my child. They'll go to school together and become lifelong companions. That's where the film crackles and ends. I wanna rescue this little girl, but there ain't no rescuing a child from its parent. Probably never has been. I know that better than most.

I pass other families huddled around open fires, frying up their multi-headed fresh catch, and I approach something that was once called the Jewel Box. It's an old-school greenhouse that is now completely skewered by the plants it once contained. Shave Time's mother back on the island comes to mind while I walk by this building that looks like a broken church. A woman who moved to the island to become a born-again native and live off the land, to take a vow to eradicate pineapples and coconut trees. She's the one who told me where to look for her son. At first, like any mother, she'd resisted giving up intel. Then there had been a look of recognition. She asked. I confirmed. She'd recalled my face from the newsfeeds, from the short vids produced by Savior's Eye Productions. She'd said she'd tell me where to find Shave Time if I told her about Akira Kimura. I eyed her collection of straw Akira figurines on her wicker, treehouse mantle, and I'd told her. *Here I go again*, I had thought, *dropping names*. It's funny how fast religion spreads in the twenty-second century. No slow crawl from Jerusalem to Rome. No enlightenment from India to the China Sea. No centuries-long overseas spread from Mecca to Indonesia. The deification of Akira went global in less than a lifetime since we're all patched into this quantum network together through our iEs. I wonder if this new religion will peak and die more quickly, too. I hope the hell so.

"*Why'd you raise him in the Leachate?*" I'd asked Shave Time's mom.

"*IGM*," she'd said. "*I was flagged. I just wanted my child strong, you know?*"

I'd nodded. Illegal genetic mutation. It'd been against the law to frivolously modify the DNA of unborn children for ages now, and the penalties had grown from a hefty fine to life in prison, but over the years, some parents still secretly did it. They almost never told their kids about it. If they did, their children could be charged for not reporting it to the authorities. If I'd been mutated, my parents certainly didn't tell me.

"*How long did you two stay there?*" I'd asked.

"*Twenty years. When the statute of limitations ran out. He leaves occasionally to do odd jobs, but he stays in The Leachate for the most part.*" She'd let out a heavy sigh, weighted with guilt. "*He considers it his home.*"

I thanked Shave Time's mom and climbed down her tree house.

Right now, I'm approaching the entrance of the old zoo. I hear speed metal blaring from a refurbished CD player and see a dozen men and women dressed in rags air guitar their polished axes and swords. When they spot me, they begin to test the sharpness of their weapons on the rusted-out automobiles scattered through the parking lot. I ignore them and enter. A hopping, one-legged man holding a banjo follows me inside.

I wander around, looking like some dated spaceman exploring the ruins of an alien ghost town. The exhibits are inhabited by people now, none with iEs, most of whom seem to be missing patches of hair or an appendage of some sort. The food vendor, serving god knows what, lacks a middle finger. The children who stare at me as they walk past—ear, arm, and . . . What is that? Is she missing a throat? Is that even possible? The guy who's been following me around since I entered the zoo, he's whispering, "Just do it," to me again and again. I don't know how these people survived here for so long, and I don't ask my iE, because I don't wanna know. Somehow, I figure it will just lead to even more guilt, which I carry enough of. But looking around, I'm starting to appreciate my kid, my wife, my life, like a true poverty porn tourist.

I stop at the entrance to Stingrays at Caribbean Cove. A line of women wait with buckets. For some reason, like Akira, they're all left-handed. I glance at the one-legged guy's banjo. "Just do it," he whispers for what seems like the hundredth time. These are definitely people who like their music plucked. I look back at the line. A couple of the women are fat. A couple skinny. That's the thing about poverty—there's no jacked poor, no shredded poor, no yoga poor, no dad-bod poor—there's just fat or skinny poor.

The skinny woman at the front of the line draws gritty, brown water from the pool. She walks past me, hugging the bucket protectively. "The secret is in the Alps," she says. That sentiment is familiar to me. It's a phrase I learned back in college—Art History 304: US Television Advertising. I'm beginning to understand that the people here speak in twenty-first-century slogans because they're surrounded by old labels on trash every day of their lives. We all internalize the things around us, even if it's shit. They must even name themselves after slogans here, hence Shave Time Money. It makes sense that Shave Time would come back to his hometown among his fellow Zeroes. For over a hundred years this is where they came—the homeless, the addicted, the bankrupt, the bored, the wanted dead or alive. Nobody's gonna chase down a runaway here. Except my dumbass.

"Made in China!" Just Do It hisses before hopping off. He picks his banjo and sings, "Made in China!" The women in line put their buckets down and start doing some kind of weird lion dance ho-down. I shake my head and move on.

I pass the aquarium. Through the muddy water, I look at moldy, toy plastic sea life spread like gravel on the bottom. Suddenly, a little girl's face pops from the murk and presses against the glass. She's missing both eyes. Poor kid. I wanna pull her out of the turbidity and bring her home, too, but I need to find Shave Time and get the fuck out of here before these people start sniffing at me and think, *Finger lickin' good*. I'm already thinking like a bigoted colonialist. Sue me.

I find Shave Time in the Bear Pit, just as his mom had said. And my god, he is big. So big that my skinny/fat poor theory needs serious revision. His mutation is obvious—super athlete. He's shirtless and holding an old street sign that reads W CHIPPEWA ST. His opponent, dual-wielding a claw hammer and twenty-pound dumbbell, is a head shorter and armored in aluminum siding, just like the trash statue of Akira. "*Why do they fight in the pit?*" I had asked Shave Time's mom. "*Do they gamble? Are they paid? Are they forced to?*" His mom had looked at me like I was dumb. "*For fun,*" she'd said.

I smile now, for no other reason than because I'm scared. I've spent the last several years building my old body up with Akeem as my workout partner. I've done bone shots, tendon and ligament rejuv, hormone replacement, AMP therapy—all paid for by the selling of my life rights to Savior's Eye Entertainment—then I lifted the hell out of heavy things. I told myself I was lapping from the fountain of youth for my kid. So I can still swim, jetsurf, and play pulse racket with her and her mom over the next ten years. But it's really about vanity . . . and the sight of old, helpless, wheelchaired Chief of Staff Chang picked apart by little birds eight years ago. No way I end up like him. Once I end up in a chair, push me off a cliff. Well, I might be at the edge of a cliff now because just looking at Shave Time, his prosthetic jaw and almost greyscale skin, I know he would've tuned me up even in my prime.

"Less Filling!" Shave Time bellows.

"Tastes great!" his opponent screams.

I pull out my 1911. I watch Shave Time crumple his opponent like he's recyclable, and I think maybe I should've brought my rail gun. Too late now. I climb down the pit. Shave Time is helping his opponent up. They're laughing. "Stronger than dirt!" Shave Time says.

His opponent nods in agreement and says, "Stronger than dirt!"

Maybe it's possible to go through life just speaking in corporate slogans. *When it rains, it pours. Take a lickin' and keep on tickin'. Obey your thirst.* What else is there in life? I get off the ladder, raise my gun, and point it at Shave Time's bald head.

"Shvv . . . Tmm . . . Monn . . ." I say. Goddamn LED-HED muffling my voice. I check the Geiger. It's not crackling as bad as it was on the river. Fuck it. I tell my iE to unseal the helmet and turn off the oxygen. I rip off my orange mitts, take the bulbous LED-HED off, and drop it on the ground. The cold hits me; it's invigorating. "Shave Time Money," I say, "I'm here to take you back home."

Shave Time looks at me skeptically. His torso rippling as he twirls the street sign like it's a laser fencing foil. His friend steps to his side, glaring at me while military pressing the dumbbell like he's warming up. With the lag now gone, my iE instantly warns me about my spiking blood pressure and heart rate. It also screams, "Warning! Warning! 10 mSv!" Not enough sieverts to do any serious radiation damage. Then my iE reminds me to take my anti-delirium meds. I turn off Health Monitor and Reminders, something Sabrina would not approve of. "C'mon guys," I say. "It's nothing personal. You skipped bail, Shave Time. I need to bring you back."

Others gather and bend over at the railing at the top of the pit, glaring. I might be in real trouble here. I take out my cuffs—two graphene bracelets that will constrict when he puts them on, then magnetically lock to each other. Only my iE will be able to unlock them. I toss the bracelets to him. He lets them bounce off his chest, and they drop at his bare, enormous, webbed, six-toed feet. Well, one six-toed foot. The left is missing a pinky toe. "Put those on," I say. He looks up at the gathering crowd of men, women, children. "Made in China," they whisper to one another. "Made in China . . ."

It occurs to me that they might be talking about me. I pop a couple rounds into the dirt. No one even flinches. Despite being a war vet, I'm being reminded of what a pussy I am for being raised on the first-world ocean. No amount of training can make someone poverty hard. Shave Time's friend tosses me the hammer. I catch it. Shave Time rubs his square, polymer jaw. He ponders. Then nods.

"It takes a tough man to make a tender chicken," he says sagely.

His friend steps to me and motions at my gun. "It takes a tough man to make a tender chicken," he repeats.

I sigh and holster the gun. He hands me the dumbbell and steps aside. Keeping the promise to myself that I'll never kill again is gonna wind up killing me. And looking at the assembled mob and Shave Time, it's becoming quickly apparent that there's only one way to get him to come with me willingly. A contest of idiocy.

Shave Time kicks the cuffs to the side, then points to my iE and scowls. "The choice of a new generation," he says. I nod and have it float in my pocket. I still haven't seen any iEs. Must be taboo or something. Shave Time begins to circle me. His friend is climbing out of the pit to join the crowd. Black rain begins to dribble from the brown sky like geriatric piss. I circle with Shave Time. "It takes a tough man to make tender chicken," I say, smiling. Again, because I'm terrified. This guy is gonna house me. But people like their old men toothless. Helpless. Tame. And I ain't going out like that.

Shave Time raises the street sign like an axe. Just then, Sabrina pings me.

I barely dodge the cleave. You gotta be kidding me. Pinging me now? Dammit, I should've put pings on Block when I turned off Health Monitor and Reminders. The W part of the Chippewa St. sign snaps from the metal pole and goes flying in the dirt. Shave Time swings the pole at me.

Sabrina pings again.

I throw the dumbbell at Shave Time. It bounces off his forehead, causing him to stagger. A lump instantly rises from his Easter Island dome.

Another ping. I'm furious now. I love her, but my wife is once again driving me crazy with her almost psychic bad timing; however, this rage makes me stronger, quicker. I raise the claw end of the hammer and bury it in Shave Time's clavicle. He screams and drops the pole. I'm trying to wedge the hammer out when he suddenly grabs my arm and squeezes. *Holy crap, vise-grip hands.* I pull the 1911 out with my free hand and crack it against his temple, hoping it ain't against the rules, but I'm guessing there are no rules in this old bear exhibit. Shave Time lets go of me and stumbles. I take a few steps back and get this sick realization. *"For fun,"* his mother had said. She's right. They're right. This is fun. Maybe I'm getting why people move here, stay here. For most of my twenties and thirties, I fantasized about such a place. A place where you can do whatever the fuck you want. Maybe that's what Akira gave me during the times of The Killing Rock. Thug life. Sabrina pings again, this time requesting immediate voice-to-voice communication. Okay, this is urgent.

I drop the hammer, but not the gun. The gun, I point. "Time out," I say.

Surprising me, Shave Time shrugs and nods. He pushes at the bump on his head, almost looking like he expects to be able to pop it back in.

I pick up Sabrina's ping. "You need to come home," Sabrina says.

"I'm kind of in the middle of something," I say. It's the first time I notice I'm breathing heavily. Miraculously, Shave Time's bump is gone. Maybe there's something invertebrate about him.

"I'm serious," Sabrina says.

"Why? What's wrong?"

"It's . . . Ascalon."

"What?" Now I'm worried. Insta-panicked. What did my iE remind me to take? I'm getting distracted, something I do a lot now. Maybe even confused. A couple weeks ago, my wife said I was standing in front of an open closet in the middle of the night. She asked what I was looking for. I told her a documentary on dumplings. I don't remember this. Memory has been becoming a real problem ever since I got pulled from the ocean at the bottom of Volcano Vista those eight or so years ago. Maybe being stuck then salvaged from the bottom of the ocean is the cause. Or maybe it's just age. Other times, I wonder if trying not to hear reds and see greens has dulled my brain a bit. Sabrina's voice refocuses me.

"She said she was bitten by something."

Suddenly, I'm hot. I'm imagining a shark or a blue-ringed octopus, the kind that got enough venom in its saliva to kill a couple dozen people. I tear off my orange apron and toss it. "By what? Where? How?"

"I don't know. We're at the hospital now. Just come home. She's calling for you."

"I'll be there."

Fuck, fuck, fuck. I look at Shave Time. "I gotta go," I say. "Happen to know the quickest way out of here?"

"What's in your wallet?" he asks.

"My kid is sick. Or something."

Shave Time nods. The international fear of having sick children: sympathy. "Come," he says. "Fly the friendly skies."

And just like that, no hard feelings. I guess hard feelings can't be afforded in a place like The Leachate. They're free from those, too. An hour later, I'm in some kind of rusted-out, two-seat roll cage that has two arms and rotors welded to each side of the chassis. The dashboard is all toggles and buttons from different machines, different eras. Shave Time presses a round plastic button that has an image of an arrow pointing up, like in elevators of old days. The rotors begin to spin. He flips a couple of toggles. The arms rattle as we lift off in what I can only describe as Shave Time's flying garbage contraption, and I can't help but think he put it together himself. I wonder if there's more to him than meets the eye. He's pressing buttons and flipping switches like he's inputting some kind of elaborate cheat code. Once we're in the air, Shave Time drops the slogan talk.

"I know you," he says.

"Oh yeah? From where?"

"Your face. Water City. The . . . Assassin."

I sigh. "Wild rumors," I say. "What'd you do back at WC?"

"Salvage."

Makes sense, considering he's from The Leachate. I'm guessing everyone who is born and raised here needs to know how to salvage just to survive. I get a feeling that he's got a sense of pride being where he's from, and not being a Less

Than or The Money. It's like from his POV, he don't care how rich other folks are, they just better watch themselves if they come to his neck of the woods.

"Did Old Man Caldwell send you?" he asks.

Old Man Caldwell? Jerry's dad? "No," I say. "Why would he?"

Shave Time shrugs and adjusts his scuba goggles. "We bring good things to life," he says.

He pulls an earlobe, and his lower jaw detaches. He pops open the glove compartment and tosses the jaw in there. He's being evasive, but I don't care. I'm not a cop anymore. I'm just a dad, scared shitless, racing back home to see if his kid is okay.

We leave behind the old city, the buildings tessellated over the radioactive landscape. We rise over The Gateway Arch, the largest man-made frown on the planet. We soar south with vulture pigeons, saccadic eyes searching through the Bikini snow. And that's all the news that's fit to print.

○

○

○

3

○

○

○

On the packed shuttle flight back, I'm fretting over Ascalon, surprised to hear that she was calling for me. Like all my children, she's always gravitated toward her mother. Despite the fact that I spend way more time with her than I did my other two kids. Sometimes, I catch her staring at me apprehensively, like I'm a crazed serial killer in domestic disguise. I've never hit her. Never so much as raised a hand at her. I've hardly ever even yelled, but I suspect she sees and smells the greens in perfumed wafts, probably permanently stained all over me. She gets super nervous when we're waiting at the end of a long line filled with slow-moving stupid people to watch the hometown Scars play seven-on-seven jetsurf live at Kimura Aqua Arena, when people stand in the middle of doorways, when my iE lags, when AI traffic control sets up temporary no-fly zones. Or when vac tubes are late. These are the only times I feel murderous in my newfound domestic bliss. Irrationally enraged, like the universe is trying to slow me down. It's always been a problem with me. Can't. Stop. Moving. My daughter gets scared in these situations because she's got my curse. Not only is she restless, but she's a synesthete. Like me, she was born colorblind. And even though we had it corrected, she can still see murder coming in greens. Music and death in reds.

It's been eight years now since I killed my daughter's namesake, the child of the great Akira Kimura. Years I've spent trying to accomplish the impossible: becoming a changed man in my late eighties. There are changes happening that are out of my control, like my continually decreasing hearing. The ability of my stomach to handle spicy, doughy, and acidic things. The size of my bladder. The cracking of my skin. My occasional loss in spacetime. My memory. I'm not sure what will begin to sputter next. I'm just trying to make sure it's not my morality.

Sabrina is back on the force, rising through the ranks, pursuing a vice-superintendent position, so as a part-time bounty hunter and minor celebrity collecting residuals, I'm relegated to being Ascalon's primary caregiver on most days before and after school. We've been through it all, us two. The Ruff Ruff and Fefe Pacifier War of 2142. The Say Please and Thank You War of 2143. The Eat Your Vegetables War of 2145. That was a rough one. The latest, The You're Too Young to Fly My SEAL, What the Fuck Were You Thinking War of 2149. She's willful. Full of life. I've been to Desert Storm 15. Fought for my survival and that of my fellow soldiers. After, fought my demons. But this parenthood shit is years of low stakes attrition. Every. Single. Day. And I find myself surprisingly good at it. A military schedule mapped out on my iE and pinged back to me in the form of constant Reminders. I have also developed OCD, which helps, as well, if anything. Every day, clockwork: meals, exercise, bounty checks, snack ready for the kid when she gets off the school vac tube and comes home. A strange fury arises when this schedule is altered in any way. Ascalon follows the schedule. Sometimes it feels like she's scared of me, and I feel awful. But if she weren't, I'm pretty sure I would've lost every single conflict.

Ascalon's private school tuition is insane. Some pretentious academy on another island that graduated a US president a couple hundred years ago and another one some forty years back. This last POTUS campaigned on the fact that she was in one of the same astronomy classes with Akira, and she won by a landslide. Flaming P Prep is pretty much the only institution in the islands that's still around from the twenty-first century, besides the Universal Men's Clinic. This premium, radioactive, high-risk bounty was supposed to pay for half of next year's tuition. But I left Shave Time at the edge of The Leachate as a thanks for getting me back to the Kentucky Bend. While waiting for a heli-taxi to pick me up and take me back to the Nashville Shuttle Port, he'd asked about his mother. I told him what had happened. That she gave up his location for stories about Akira Kimura. He shook his head. We both looked up at Ascalon's Scar. Then he asked me if she, Akira Kimura, was real. I told him she was. I had told my then-four-year-old daughter the same thing when she'd asked me.

Now, in the shuttle, we hit some turbulence, which freaks me out. I should've splurged and paid for first class, so I could sleep through this in a top-deck AMP chamber. I've survived a self-inflicted SEAL crash, a maniac-induced shuttle crash, and I just flew in Shave Time's heap, but flying long distances, especially when I'm not at the controls, is not my favorite thing to do. It's been a weird handful of years for me. I'm scared all the time. Suddenly, scared of heights, germs, of extreme old age. Scared of being late. Scared of cancer. Scared that I'm forgetting. Scared now that something serious has happened to my kid. In the past, I've taken lives. I guess I'm scared of karma most of all. What gave me the right to kill people? Law? When it comes to law, everything is conveniently re-classified. Fruits become vegetables. Felons become witnesses. Murderers become war heroes.

The press says I was given the consent of a living god. I don't know about that. I know that all I cared about was my personal code. But, like everyone else's, mine was rationalized, so it became full of asterisks and exceptions. For example, I went from solving murders to committing them to supposedly help save the world. I told myself just like we needed scientists and artists, our species needed hunters, sheriffs, bare-knuckle boxers—men like me. But that's false. Just like my code and vision. Just like the living god. I knew Akira for years. She was just a lady. Granted, the smartest the world may have ever known.

The shuttle ride begins to even out. I'm sitting between an Akira priestess and a woman tat-dyed blue who has an Ashtanga yogi look to her, like she should have more than two arms. The bald priestess in white foam fit, probably a Leachate missionary, is wearing a jingasa with Ascalon's Scar on it. I don't even want to look at her. The blue woman glimmers with holo sparkles. I miss regular jewelry, but jewelry's been out for years now because draping yourself with actual semi-precious stones and metals is considered a very Zero thing to do. Besides, no one can mug you and steal holo jewelry. It also helped that Akira never wore jewelry; she never even had her ears pierced. And people desperately wanted to be like her.

"Where are you off to?" the blue, yogi-looking woman asks.

"Home," I say.

"I'm going to meditate on the moon," she says excitedly. I roll my eyes. The woman huffs and rewards me with the silent treatment. After we land, she'll board a lunar jumper and probably meditate under the roof of a barely habitable, zero grav Quonset hut in The Sea of Tranquility. I mean, The Sea of Akira. I forgot about the name change. I think about how different my daughter is from this lunar traveler. How hard it must be for this bored woman to be happy. Nobody who's happy goes to meditate on the moon. Ascalon is different. So easily brightened. The sight of big-eyed scads swirling in unison makes her day. A simple vac tube trip from midnight to twilight, passing spectrum-banded gooseberries on the way up, makes her week. She always wants to take the long way home so that she can see more, be surrounded by sources. There is no shortage of what makes her happy.

I'm anxious during descent. Still no word from Sabrina. I find myself wanting to put a hand inside my pocket, but I don't have any. Pockets don't really exist anymore since we don't have anything to carry. Even cops, like I was and my wife is, only carry holstered firearms during official ceremonies like pinnings, promotions, retirements, and funerals. Funerals. They make me think about my son, John, and how his death drove me from the brink of committing suicide to committing a string of homicides. One could argue I lost my first kid, too, but she's alive and well last I heard. Plus, you actually had to have something in order to lose it. Her mother split with the kid when I was serving and the kid was an infant. Her name . . . What is her name again? Brianne? Yes,

Brianne. *You named her, dummy.* This estranged daughter is a middle-aged woman now, like the two I'm sitting next to. It feels impossible that I'm the father of a nine-and-a-half-year-old and a sexagenarian.

I rub my temples. You'd think the fear for my child would max out at some point, but it's always just growing and growing and growing. Ever since she jumped off the float burb docks when she was four and taught herself to swim, she has been a nonstop source of pride and terror for her mom and me. It had been around three in the afternoon, and she'd just gotten back from daycare. The sun's reflection off the water had made the heat even more oppressive. And she just jumped. Like it was normal. I was on the verge of jumping in after her but stopped myself when I saw her swinging her arms and kicking her little feet as she swam in place. Then she dove under. That's when I sprung in and grabbed her.

When we were back on the docks, I asked her why she'd jumped.

"Was it the heat?"

"A song," she'd said.

"What song?" I asked.

"Red," she said.

That's all her four-year-old vocabulary could muster. I spent the next two years trying to keep her out of the water, which was ridiculous, considering we're surrounded by it. I had asked Sabrina if we should move to someplace landlocked, and she'd said, *"Eww."* So, I decided that if she was gonna keep jumping off the docks, she needed to be good at it. Every day, I'd jump in with her. I laid down the rules: Always wear repellent. Never dive alone. Stay away from Volcano Vista—this last rule for my sake, not hers. We dove more and more, deeper and deeper as days went by. Ascalon always searching to the brink of fear. I, on the other hand, always on the brink of grabbing her and pulling her out.

The shuttle breaks through the clouds, which breaks my reverie. I look out the window. The colors of the seascrapers shimmer and ripple beneath the ocean's surface. As usual, something new is being built, being added. AI cranes lower limp, hollow spires made of recycled, biodegradable crystal. Once properly placed, these giant tubes will fill with particle streams and stiffen. With far more tensile strength than steel, they will serve as frames and rebar of new seascrapers. So different from the crumbling brick and mortar of The Leachate.

Algorithmic parasites feast on our data down there in that lit metropolis of hug tree consumerism. I sometimes get the feeling we are on the cusp of something. The origin story of all our sci-fi nightmares. I suppose every generation thinks this. But generations of the past don't live as long as we do. Even us Less Thans with good diets and access to some AMP average out at 120. The Money? Shoot, the CEO of VR eSport giant, Eyewall Live, they're 150 and still flopping. I lived through the Age of Akira, of The Killing Rock, but maybe that was just the start of something, like we were meant to be forest fire reset, but because we weren't, something worse is coming. There always seems to be a sequel to things, and it's not always good.

My eyes drift away from the city and up to Ascalon's Scar. A reassuring frozen comet of light. I look down into the dark parts of the ocean. So big. So vast. Why do I always see things as more vast down there than up here in the sky? My child. Constantly reef skipping, net casting, solar catamaraning, jet-surfing, and, like her grandfather, hydronauting. The umber is her favorite place. She's in love with the inexhaustible number of wonders of the ocean. From both the spined and unspined critters of the deep to sunken ships both real and imagined. Unaware of the many things that bite down there.

4

When I get to the North HW Hospital, I momentarily forget what the "HW" stands for, then remember that long ago these islands had been acronymed and disemvowelled at about the same time Savior's Eye was being built, when paved streets were being dug out and disposed of. "HW" are the leftover consonances from the hospital's original name. Still funded by The Money, like the board of the Idris Eshana Trust, the place is run by its administrative nurses, who, unlike in most major hospitals, make all the shift and financial decisions. The docs, a timid bunch who could, through government incentives, ironically make way more money in poorer places around the world, stick around because this is the home of The Savior's Eye, after all, the birthplace of the Ascalon Project, and it's where Akira Kimura saved the world. It is where she finally perished. The part where she murdered one child, tried to put the other in permanent sleep, and had me kill her dissidents . . . well, let's just say that part has been omitted from the iE historical databases. Our saints require cleanliness, as the holo of Akira in the middle of the lobby suggests—her intrepid eyes gazing up as she points; her lab coat pressed and pure white.

A nurse with a white foam fit contoured all the way up to the bridge of her nose leads me from the lobby to my daughter's room. Hospitals have not changed much, at least not in my lifetime, and except for the tech, maybe they never had. The ancient Sri Lankans had hospitals with patient rooms about the same size as ours today. Maybe the space that we require to heal or die has never changed and never will. I hope by the time I get to Ascalon's room she's already better. When I arrived, the nurse looked at me, recognized me, and told me Ascalon should be discharged tomorrow morning. I hate being recognized, but I suppose I hate being poor even more.

The nurse is walking too idly for my taste. I'm about to say something, but she stops at a door, and I almost run into her. I step past her and into the room. My nine-year-old kid, face full of expected joy, like she knew I'd step into the room at that exact moment, is standing on the bed. She's wearing a sheet of exam table paper folded into the shape of a pirate hat.

"Ahoy, matey!" she says.

"Ahoy, me hearty!" I say back. We've been greeting and talking to each other in pirate speak for a couple years now. It started when I taught her how to sail. I once told her to go to the poop deck. She laughed for what seemed like hours.

"Batten down the hatches!" she screams.

I see what she's doing and become instantly nervous. She does a flip off the bed, and her feet hit the floor. She sticks the landing, the paper hat still miraculously on her head. I let out a breath in relief. Fucking natural athlete. Better than I ever was. She runs to me. I scoop her up. Her weight jars the crooks of my golfer's elbows from LHT—lifting heavy things. No cure but rest. *Screw rest*, I tell myself. *Procedure. Screw rest.*

"Landlubber," she whispers in my ear.

"Landlubber," I whisper back, then ask, "What happened?"

I look at Sabrina and can tell she's been coping with this ball of energy for hours now. My wife, full of infinite patience. She's wearing that interrogation room vibe like military-grade body armor, impervious to every verbal stick and stone. I should've anticipated Sabrina's weariness from spending all this time alone with our daughter. My kid, she can't sit still. The hospital must've been hell for her. Must be why she's white-knuckling an old piece of driftwood right now.

"She was diving again with her friends." Sabrina sighs. "Too deep." Sabrina, wearing a snazzy corporate suit that's now rumpled, loosens her red tie and takes it off, indicating that her parental shift is over. She rubs her hands on her suit, and the wrinkles disappear. My turn. I clock in. The first thing I do is look at Ascalon. Sometimes, I could swear she still smells like a baby, but that's just phantom limb memory. I think back to when she was a toddler, and I promise she'd lose her favorite toys on purpose just to experience the joy of me finding them for her. I force my mind to the present.

"What happened?" I ask again.

"Something bit me, Daddy," Ascalon says. "I was just throwing net. And it wasn't that deep." She takes off her hat.

Wasn't that deep. She's not a great liar. "Where were you throwing net?" I ask.

"By school," she says.

Another lie. Something she had acquired ever since she was three when she flushed Sabrina's sleeping iE down the toilet and told us the "bad guy" did it. The "bad guy" was responsible for most of her misadventures until she was six.

This kid. "What bit you?" I look into her inky brown, almost black, eyes, just like mine. A beautiful brackish murk.

"I don't know," she says.

I sense truth here. "You don't know?" I say. "But you know everything about the ocean. You know more than me. Where did it bite you?"

She shrugs.

"The doctor found no signs of any kind of bite," Sabrina cuts in. She removes her coat and puts her dark hair in a ponytail. I eye the contours of her skin-tight foam fit. The shadows of her temp tat makeup. The latest thing—a two-hundred-year-old pic filter app art now fit for real life. This wife of mine is ageless and still built like a pulse racket champion. I laugh to myself. She's probably cheating on me. I had a dream last week that she was in a holo, fucking Frankie the Water Duck, and the holo went viral. At least it was missionary. In the dream, Sabrina refused to take the vid down. I try not to dwell on the meaning of such nightmares.

"I have a headache," Ascalon says. "I want to go home."

"Her labs checked out fine," Sabrina says. "They want to keep her overnight for observation."

"I want to go home, Daddy," Ascalon says, a little more whiney now.

I turn to Sabrina. She's exhausted and just shrugs. Code for it's my call. I don't got a whole lot of faith in public hospitals anyway. They're for the Less Thans, which we are. The Money have their private med care. Like live-in nannies, the best docs are on-call in their med bays. Funny enough, private is cheaper if you got the crypto to front for it. No insurance. No admin. No bureaucracy to fund. If something is wrong with her, straight to Akeem's. I'm in the red when it comes to relationship capital owed to my friend, but for this little girl, anything.

"First, tell me what happened," I say. The crooks in my elbows are killing me.

Ascalon looks back at Sabrina and sighs. "I said what happened how many times now, a billion? Something bit me."

"What's that in your hand?"

Ascalon opens her fist. "It's just driftwood I found, Dad." She tosses it on the bed.

I look at my daughter. She's got an open, wide-eyed face that makes it look like she's about to hear something important from me. I've always appreciated that look, and she knows it. I wonder when she'll start withholding it, hoarding it for her own relationship capital. Spending it only when she really wants something. Probably in a few years. I put her down and kneel. Her eyes turn to her feet. I've seen this before in interview rooms back when I was a cop. She's holding something back.

"Where did it bite you?"

She takes a glance at her mother, then points at her belly button. I shudder a bit. I don't like people touching my belly button, even my wife. I try not to imagine something biting Ascalon's. I raise her hospital gown. Zero signs of a bite on her dark skin. I pull the gown back down.

"What happened after it bit you?" I ask.

She looks back at Sabrina, uncertain. Sabrina now sees Ascalon's been holding something back, too. "Did you see it?" I ask.

Ascalon leans to my ear. "No," she says. "But . . ."

"But what?"

"It was red."

I pull back from her and feel myself frowning. "Red?"

"Yeah, like when you get mad." She says it quietly, like it's something taboo we aren't supposed to talk about, which it kind of is. "Floating," she says. She raises her arm and wriggles her fingers through the air. "And it made a sound."

"What kind of sound?" I probe further.

"Like this." She crumples the paper hat.

Sabrina steps forward, very interested now.

"I tried to catch it with a net, Daddy," Ascalon says.

"Catch what?" Sabrina asks.

"The red," Ascalon whispers. "I found it. I wonder if it's still hiding there."

"And who gave you access to the nets?" Sabrina glares at me.

But I'm looking at my kid hard now. Searching more than studying. Searching for the wafts and pulses that have been absent for ages now. I don't see them. I don't hear them. Perhaps I've lost the ability. There's also the possibility that my meds have helped me to no longer see murder and death. Or maybe the last time I did, the sight burned so bright that it blinded me. Or possibly, just like I forget a lot of things, I forgot how to see them, too. A silly man's hope. I've been lucky. And I've been consciously avoiding the things they emanate from. I'm just relieved I'm not seeing them now. I turn my head to Sabrina, who's frowning at Ascalon.

"You aren't supposed to go fishing or diving without one of us with you," she says.

Ascalon's eyes lock on mine. I turn away. "Did they scan her?" I ask Sabrina.

"Head to toe," Sabrina says.

"Nano?" I ask.

"No," she says. "She's not wounded. There wasn't a reason to."

"Let's make an appointment before we leave."

Ascalon raises her arms in victory. Then she slumps to her knees like she just scored a winning goal. I shake my head. The kid knows her dramatics crack me up inside. Sabrina steps to me and leans into my chest. I put an arm around her as we watch Ascalon pack up her stuff. My wife is part of what's called the Post-Killing Rock Gen, the PKRG, those born either right before or right after Sessho-seki. People think that people of that age tend to be the most independent because they were ignored more as children. You know, with that whole asteroid coming to destroy the world thing going on. Me, I don't know. Gen this, gen that. It's all about as accurate as astrology to me.

"You must be exhausted," I say to my wife.

"How was The Leachate?" she asks.

I chuckle. "Wild. Fucking wild. I'll show you some iE footage. We should go back one day. Together. Like a second honeymoon."

"Sorry you weren't able to bring home your bounty."

"It's okay," I say. "Shave Time is a good guy."

My wife shakes her head. "You can't keep letting criminals go because you like them."

"That's what makes this job better than my old one. I can."

I lean down and kiss my wife. She pats my chest. Ascalon's already done packing up her crap. She grabs the small hunk of wood off the bed and bolts out the room before either of her parents can say anything.

"I'm worried about her," Sabrina says.

"Think she made it up?" I ask.

Sabrina shakes her head. "No. That's what scares me."

I nod. I tell myself that sometimes seeing and hearing the reds is so jarring that it can feel like a bite. The greens are even worse. I think about the first time I saw them as a little boy, perfumed green wafts seeped out of a chunk of ambergris my father brought home from the corpse of a murdered whale. The red could've come from anywhere if Ascalon was deep-diving. Things are constantly dying down there in the dark. While Sabrina and I make a follow-up appointment for tomorrow and check Ascalon out, I remind my wife of these things, too. Sometimes being a spouse means telling each other everything is gonna be okay, even if we're unsure whether they are.

We lose Ascalon in the lobby and finally find her staring up at the holo of Akira. My little girl is frowning. "Daddy, why is she always dressed different?" she asks.

It's true. Here, she's a doctor. At my former place of employment, the police station, she's mocked up as Lady Justice. In The Great Leachate, a Swiffer-wielding warrior made from irradiated trash. At the last church in Vatican City, she's dressed in a white robe and wears a halo, looking suspiciously Caucasian. In the rebuilt rubble of Abraj Al-Bait, her mosaic is tanned, she wears a robe and turban. They don't even jive with visual depictions of deities in that corner of the world. She has become all the Greek gods, all *bhatara* and *bhatari*, all prophets and holy spirits rolled into one. My old friend and lawyer Jerry Caldwell, all those years ago, was wrong. It's Akira that's become iconic, not the supposed weapon she created to save the world.

"Why doesn't it look like her?" Ascalon asks.

"Because people are stupid, matey," I say.

Sabrina punches my shoulder. "Remember, baby," Sabrina says, "she was just a person."

Ascalon looks up at her mother. "That's not what my teachers say."

Sabrina and I look at each other. Religious kooks, even at that high-priced school. I shouldn't be surprised. I mean, we're standing in a hospital and these supposed men and women of science worship her, probably because she was a scientist. Ascalon ducks under the velvet rope and turns the holo off.

"Why did you do that?" I ask.

"It's making my head sore," she says.

I look at the now-empty space where the holo was lit up. "Where were you when you got bit?" I ask.

"I told you already. By school."

My bad. Yet another memory lapse. Also, I already feel bad for grilling her, so we all walk out together. Just some childhood dramatics, I'm pretty sure. I think about the holo of Dr. Akira. The VMAT2 gene, the God gene, the one we all got. The one that makes us wanna believe. I think about religion as spandrel. Faith is not something that ever offended me, even though I've never had it. Old gods, new gods, no gods, it's all the same to me. And who the hell am I to explain the mysteries of the universe? Maybe when you die, you board some alien spaceship or get your own planet. I got no proof that it ain't true. But this deifying Akira thing, it bothers me because I know it's bullshit. There was probably some guy who knew Siddhartha and thought, what? *Enlightened? That dude couldn't do long division.* Or a pal of Christ's who thought, *Him a god? That homeless motherfucker couldn't keep a job.* I guess I'm this guy now. I try to let it go. Procedure. Family. Nothing else. My mind is buried in my mantra as the holo of Akira, God MD, flickers back on behind us.

5

I'm old enough to remember when cities used to resemble bar graphs, but now they look more like underwater solar systems propped up by active structures and held together by liquid magnetism. Five years ago, we moved from our bobbing float burb townhouse. Now home is in Hightown—the shallow end of Water City—which includes the sprawling gas giants of the Medical, Waste and Recycling, Printing, and Tourism districts. Below us, Deeptown shimmers with renewable energy, like the planets closest to the sun. The brightness of Financial. The glowing, marbled spheres of STEM—Science, Technology, Engineering, and Math. In other words, Religion. And The Money with their private elevators, vac tubes, and organ farm greenhouses are down there, as well. The Money bought up ocean floor property and said let there be light. They cranked up the geothermal generators, but it's still darker in the deep than it is in the shallow end. Right now, I know the sun is setting because when I look down, I see the swaying leaves of the robot kelp farms being dragged down into the nutrient deep below us. We are self-sustaining here. Gone are the days of only having a five-day food supply at any given time, as is our reliance on shipping and the continents.

The Money sends its kids to the shores of the islands for outsourced primary and secondary education to make sure they experience exercising, planting things, taming things, riding things, catching things, and having earth beneath their feet. Field trips and PE narrated by holographic teachers. Hikes to the volcano accompanied by a holo geologist wearing a frumpy, khaki outback hat. Trail rides by horseback into lush valleys, narrated by a holo dressed in denim overalls. Jetsurf sevens refereed by holos clad in striped black and white. All the while the actual in-person teachers are there to just make sure the children behave themselves.

When it comes to taming, riding, and catching, my daughter is the first in her class. She's a starting Z-receiver whose ability to carve curl routes across the water and cut back off the lip of a wave to catch the sponge is unparalleled. Her ability to spot fish and throw nets over flopping, silvery, slippery things in competitive net fishing is even more impressive. She should be the quarterback of her seven-on-seven jetsurf team, but I don't want to be one of those dads, arguing with the coach and meddling in lineups and positions. In the end, I'm not sure why they teach this stuff. Perhaps for the novelty. Maybe now that there's no need for kids to learn to handwrite anything, they require something else to fill the time. They need to stay fit. It's possible this new education is for some unforeseen utility. If there's one thing The Killing Rock has taught us, it's that you never know. Maybe Earth's core will erupt one day, and we'll be forced to live on land again, like we were forced to four hundred million years ago.

I imagine our Paleozoic ancestors flopping on sand, willing themselves to turn fins into feet.

Ahead, our older model seascraper looks like something screwed into the surface of the ocean, its threads pulsating rainbow lights. It was built when spiral architecture was all the rage. I like living here. We're in the middle of everything. Glowing arteries of vac tubes and walkways sprout from the spiral's bead-like cores, allowing for quick and convenient travel access to other districts and the islands. Plus, the units in the older scrapers tend to be bigger. Ours is a two-story with actual stairs. I look back at a sleeping Ascalon and remember the near heart attacks she gave me jumping down those stairs four at a time. I dive the restomodded SEAL, my good ol' reliable, military-grade, blended-wing air, sea, and road vehicle, below the floating coral reef that rings our building. The door of my parking space groans open. I glide the SEAL inside and drop the landing gear. The door closes, and all the water's sucked out. The cost of this SEAL port is astronomical, but I can't bear the thought of being without some kind of private transportation, of being stranded somehow.

I dock, and Sabrina scoops Ascalon out of her chair. When this kid sleeps, she sleeps. I lead the way, scanning open doors for my wife and daughter, and we head to the main bulkhead and merge with other tenants, other Shallow-enders, salarymen with families coming home from work and school. We pass trees made up of bioluminescent butter-flies. Funny, we probably always had a thing for butterflies, and we almost killed 'em all. We are a race of smotherers. Past the faux butterfly trees, I momentarily forget my way. Then I see we're nearing my favorite Chinese-Senegalese fishpond joint where net bot spears hand-pick fish for people waiting in line, people just as diversely colored as the fish in the pond. I realize that I'm hungry, and I know where I am again.

"When's the last time you ate?" I ask Sabrina.

"I don't even remember," she says. She's one of the few women her age not tat-dyed. I'm not either. Nobody my age is. Ascalon's been hinting that she wants to be blue for underwater camo purposes, but after my throwdown with Akira's daughter, I've had enough blue Ascalons to last me a lifetime.

"Should we grab a fish?" I ask, watching one of the tentacled arms of the net bot spear a whitesaddle goatfish through the eye. Net bots, med bots, maintenance bots—all bots have tentacle arms because of their unlimited range of motion. Their limbs, like the bones of this and many other seascrapers, flow with energy streams but on a much smaller, more precise scale.

"Nah," says Sabrina. "Let's get Ascalon to bed."

We get into our unit, and Sabrina hands Ascalon to me. I take her upstairs and plop her in her bed. Above it, her wall-to-wall mural of a shallow seascape. An albatross dives into the ocean, plucking a tiny silverfish from beneath. Under this, turtles and jacks on patrol. Colorful reef fish huddled under coral. Obscured by darkness of the ocean in the backdrop, a blurry tiger shark stalks. Beneath it all, a magnificent sunken man-of-war. Faint holo night lights flash on the ceiling. Ching Shih. Calico Jack. Anne Bonny—the scowling faces of famous pirates. These are the images that soothe my daughter to sleep. I occasionally wonder if there's something wrong with her. I turn off the holos and look back down at the mural. I'm reminded of Jerry Caldwell. Her priceless art collection. She spent decades tracing the splintered NFT ownership of these pieces and putting them back together under one proprietor. She hated the idea of art as the endless splitting up for profit and believed in the preservation of it. She also had her own art project, trying to capture the iconic. Her murder was just another that everyone seemed to ignore.

I check Ascalon's feeder drawer. Good. Empty. Every morning she feeds sea life and watches it come to her bedroom window. Her favorite visitor is a monk seal she named Redbeard. I take another glance at Ascalon and leave the room. The door hisses shut behind me. She won't sleep long. She only likes the snugness of her foam fit when she's in the water. Otherwise, she likes loose clothing. I try to shake off the pangs of sadness and regret while I walk the stairs. When you keep moving forward, it becomes easier and easier to forget the ones you left behind.

I step into the kitchen and rearrange things to the way I prefer them. Chopsticks in the far-left drawer under the counter, pointed tips out. Plates stacked in sixes in the far-right cupboard above the counter. Cups in the cupboard nearest the sink all placed rim down. I've been doing this a lot now, and I don't really know why. I've been a slob most of my life.

My stomach growls, and I reach into a basket of walnuts. I pull one out and put it between my thumb and index finger, then squeeze. The nut cracks open. It's an old Army trick, a bunch of kids competing in silly feats of strength. I eat and think that once I can't crack these open with two fingers, I will truly be geriatric.

I look down at the counter. *Why am I standing here?* I see three bowls of tangerines and a bottle of sesame seed oil. How did this get here? I lost time again. Not sure what culinary plan I started but didn't finish. I put the fruit and oil away.

Sabrina comes back downstairs. I got a good life. Possibly the life I was always searching for, a life that took eight decades to find and one I don't deserve. *Procedure. Appreciate.* Sabrina brushes past me and opens the fridge. She stands there, frozen for a moment.

"Remember when she used to put her toys in here?" Sabrina asks.

"Yeah," I say.

"I miss little things like that," my wife says.

She's worried. I am, too. "Want me to order food?"

A century ago, climate change forced the latitudinal migration and adaptation of long-forgotten canine and poultry parasites. Soon after, all the dogs and chickens began dying from diseases, livestock and puppy mega farms were dissolved, and the death of grocery stores followed. Ever since then, it's been far cheaper to order prepared food than it is to cook it in this farm-to-table world, but home cooking occasionally taunts my wife, probably some cave mom instinct. My own inner cave dad stirs, and I step behind her and put my arms around her stomach. She closes the fridge.

"The eyes," I say. "Sometimes they hurt the head when we see the colors. It's happened to me. She spends too much damn time in the water."

Sabrina nods. "She spends too much time *under* it. I miss living on the surface."

I don't know if Sabrina means it or is just thinking out loud. But I'm no dummy. I pretend to believe everything she says. "We can move back," I say.

"It won't stop her," she says.

"Stop her from what?"

Sabrina turns around and wraps her arms around me. "Looking for trouble. Being a compulsive, calculated risk-taker. Like her father."

"I'm not like that anymore."

Sabrina rolls her eyes. "You know, she loves you more than me."

"That's bullshit."

"No. She does. She just knows you're the last person to come to when she's sad or in pain."

We kiss. Three pecks, which has become a sort of unspoken tradition. It's how we say goodbye. It's how we kick off a bit of fun. We're lucky. We can still easily get each other going. We move to the couch. Sabrina straddles me and pulls my shirt off. It shrinks in her hand. She crumples it in her fist and tosses it across the room as if it were a pair of old-school panties. I hope I got years and years of this left in me. Then I'm suddenly concerned that I threw the cracked walnut shells in the wrong receptacle. These are the kinds of things I worry about now. That, frankly, I obsess over. Thankfully, we no longer live in a world of bolt locks and kitchen stoves. I'd be twisting and re-checking all day long. I try my best to ignore good ol' OCD. Admittedly, Sabrina's hand reaching down is making it easier and easier.

I'll take a look at Ascalon's iE footage later tonight, I tell myself. A part of me doesn't wanna do it. Even if she's only nine, it feels like an invasion of privacy. I'll set a Reminder in my iE later. I'll eat later. I'll check on Ascalon later. I'll do a bunch of stuff later, some of which I'll forget to do. Maybe being chronically forgetful is a blessing, not a curse.

I reach around my wife's back and glide my middle finger

down her spine. Her foam fit splits open. Zippers? Bras? I don't miss them.

This wife of mine, this force of nature mesmerizes me. I think back to how her body treated childbirth, as if it was high-intensity exercise. A week or two after Ascalon was born, Sabina weighed less and was more taut than she was before she'd gotten knocked up. I'm about to feast on this body of hers now, but then, sirens blare. For some reason, my first thought is, *Shit, I've been caught.* Having a wife like this feels like grand larceny, and I'm finally busted.

"Fire drill." Sabrina sighs.

Now? Fuck. My kid spent all day in the hospital, and now we're gonna have to wake her up and drag her up to the surface. First world problems. Sabrina grabs my forearm. "Let's ignore it," she says.

"Listen to you, Mrs. Vice Superintendent. Mrs. Law Breaker."

"It's been a long day. Let her sleep."

But it's too late. Ascalon is standing at the top of the stairs, wide awake. I should've known. For her, thirty minutes of sleep can sometimes pass for eight hours—it's as if she's got an AMP chamber built into her. Sabrina rolls off me.

"Weigh anchor and hoist the mizzen!" Ascalon yells, excited. She leaps. I gasp. She clears all twelve steps and miraculously lands on her feet.

"Oh my god," Sabrina whispers, her hand over her eyes.

Ascalon runs past us then skids to a stop in front of me. "Daddy, why's your shirt off? Are we going swimming?"

"No," I say. "I need to take a shower. A cold one."

Ascalon shrugs and is out the door. "At least she seems okay," I say.

Sabrina stands up and walks to the kitchen. She grabs a handful of walnuts. "Let's catch up."

I nod and walk to the wall to pick up my balled-up, shrunken shirt. I pinch a tiny edge of it and flick my wrist. It grows back to normal size, and I throw it on. I check the biowaste receptacle for walnut shells before heading to the door. Nothing there. Were they already vacced out?

"C'mon," Sabrina says. I resist the urge to go through the trash and follow her. Ascalon's nowhere in sight. Sabrina and I begin to jog, side by side. This is what parenthood feels like sometimes, a constant struggle to catch up.

We round the screw, and Ascalon is standing in front of the transparent elevator tube. The doors open, and the three of us squeeze into a packed elevator. Outside the glass panels, other elevators in other buildings are lit up and rising, as well. Some kind of city-wide practice evac? I don't know. A family of four crammed in the back corner of the elevator whisper reassurances to one another. Two indigo teens with antennae that supposedly boost brain wave signals for iE transponders in order to cut out any lag synced into their iEs, probably playing some virtual game together or reliving their best memories. "Phalt," one whispers to the other. "Petro." The other nods in agreement. Old, no-longer-used resources have transformed into modern slang. A maintenance man, at least one hundred years old, is falling asleep on his feet. Most jobs that aren't computation, delivery, or factory-based are still cheaper to fill with humans than to build a robot to do them. Plus, all of us people need something to do. This poor sag of eighty years of overtime guy is muttering something about Armageddon and how it's about damn time.

I always look at old people more closely than I do everyone

else. It's like I'm in some kind of stupid competition with them, making sure I'm in better shape. A cosmetics ad flashes on the gorilla glass: *I put on my face for me, not for you. Holo makeup.* Look like a cartoon without having to spend hours in front of the mirror. The world licks up its soft-serve narcissism, including me. Ascalon taps her foot. When the elevator stops and a middle-aged couple squeezes its way in, my daughter groans. *I feel you, baby. I feel you.* Sucker fish swim to us and stick their suction mouths to the glass. I sometimes wonder if it's us or them in the aquarium.

When we finally get to the building's beach, Ascalon is the first one to squirt out of the lift. Sabrina and I follow. Ascalon's running up the bioluminescent lit da Vinci bridge to the shoreline. I look around. Other buildings empty. People spill from their own seascrapers and stand on their beaches. It's high tide, so we're all standing in puddles. We're now a city of confounded waterwalkers.

"What the hell?" I ask Sabrina.

The people around us murmur. Gossip and rumors abound. Some are pointing to the night sky, but my eyes are focused on Ascalon's trail. Sabrina stops and grabs my hand, which causes me to turn.

"Wow," she says, pointing to the sky.

I look up and immediately see something missing. It's not there. How can it not be there?

A woman shrieks. Then another. Funny thing about drills, they never prepare us for the real thing. I let go of Sabrina's hand and run to the shoreline, through crowds of people looking up in horror. Time to grab Ascalon. Sabrina, who's faster, beats me to our kid. Ascalon is looking up, too. She smiles like she does when she's just done something daring.

"Where is it?" Ascalon says.

More people begin to scream. "Let's go down, pack up, and head to the SEAL," I say. "Let's beat the crowd."

Sabrina nods and scoops up Ascalon. "My head hurts again," Ascalon says.

"No more water for you," Sabrina says. "One week."

Ascalon pouts. One week. Why is it that human beings always pull random numbers out of their asses?

We head to the elevator and are the first ones there. I look above the panicked city one more time before the doors shut. I can't believe it. Somewhere up there in the stars, in the interstellar clouds, the light has gone out. For a half-century, it's hung there, day and night, a permanent rip in the fabric of the seamless sky. I can't believe it's gone, really gone. Ascalon's Scar. It ain't there.

6

After the death of Akira Kimura, the closed-door congressional hearings had been massive and all the news. Newsfeed had been superficial, hysteric, and inaccurate all my life, but during the hearings, it had been a zettabyte circus hyperventilating wild speculation. The already endangered notions of "let's dwell on it" or "triple-check" or "let's wait and see" had been rendered extinct by Sessho-seki. So, during the hearings, headlines had read, not in questions, but unconfirmed declaratives: *Breaking News: Akira Kimura committed suicide. Greater martyr: Akira or Jesus? Couple claim to see deceased scientist Akira Kimura dining at local hotspot. The Killing Rock was bigger than we thought.* Most people never doubted the existence and destruction of the asteroid, anyway. All they had to do was look up and see its scar to know it really happened.

Most of what I'd told the closed committees was and has remained redacted. But that hadn't stopped the press from misquoting me and wildly guessing at what was concealed. It didn't stop them from reporting false biographical information. For example, one outlet had stated that I grew up in the Nevada Fingers instead of the islands. That I served in the Navy, not the Army. All one had to do was ask their iE. Like any other person with even just a sliver of notoriety, my name and birthplace and military history were accurately listed in the Library of Wiki Congress database.

At the end of the five-month investigation, Capitol Hill produced no conclusive findings, of, well, anything. There had been no body, neither Akira's nor her daughter's. No fairy tale, mythical gem that held the memories of the greatest mind in the world. No evidence that an Akira iE, modeled after her supposed daughter's breakthroughs, ever existed. No birth certificate or official record of a daughter named Ascalon Lee. There'd been a record of a Tamano Nomae that started in a Florida private boarding school and ended in employment at various medical research labs, but no recorded biological link to Akira. No DNA records. In fact, the DNA records of both had been mysteriously wiped. Some senators wanted to finance an exploratory mission to The Point of Impact, but the Ascalon Project, which Akira had always said would self-destruct after releasing the required amount of energy to destroy Sessho-seki, had been an international, hundred-trillion-dollar project, and the deficit hawks in the Senate didn't want to spend even more money to look for something that ain't even there.

Everyone who'd been left from the old days was brought to The Hill to testify. Engineers who had been assigned very niche projects and were kept mostly in the dark. Other scientists whom Akira spurned and sooner or later cut from the project. 3D print managers. Pipe fitters. Military custodial staff. Basically, everyone who had eventually been replaced by artificial intelligence tasked to do what Akira deemed specific and menial calculations, printing, building, and labor. That's the thing about AI—less need for collaboration. Less transparency. I had been on The Hill for an entire week. Then I'd been brought back two months later in front of senators who were so damn old they made me look young. The committee chair, Gonzalez, was serving his twelfth term.

Anyway, by my second subpoena, the committee had seemed more divided about how to spend the money they'd inherited, or stole, from the Kimura and Eshana estates. How to ward off Japan and India, who were making ancestral claims to the fortune, as well, despite Akira and Idris being US citizens. The claim to Idris's wealth had been especially laughable. He was three-eighths Indian, three-eighths Mexican, a quarter white, and was born and raised in East Texas. Either way, I wasn't asked once about Chief of Staff Chang's or Jerry Caldwell's murder. When I'd interrupted Gonzalez to bring them up, tell them what Akira's kid did to both of them, I was threatened with contempt. Jerry's father, the oldest and tallest guy in the gallery that day, stood, leaned on his cane, and roared that Jerry had donated the contents of her iE to the committee. He was escorted out. Years ago, he'd been rejected by Akira to help fund the Ascalon Project. Now this. The willful ignoring of the murder of his daughter. One final tragic thumb in the eye. He'd turned around at the exit and looked at me, held his index and middle fingers to his eyes, then pointed them at me. He left, and I haven't seen him since.

The whole time this was going on, I was thinking, *Did Akira and Ascalon Lee predict this farce?* It felt like they definitely covered their bases. Like they had contingencies for everything, even post-mortem. Even the Senate committee chair felt rigged. Gonzalez's major campaign donor was the

CEO of the toy company that manufactured trademarked recyclable Akira dolls. Senator Gonzalez struck down every motion to introduce new evidence, so when it came to the story of Akira Kimura—me, her daughter, Jerry Caldwell, the president of the United States, Chief of Staff Change, and Idris Eshana were reduced to bit players. None of us qualified as coconspirators because there was no evidence of conspiracy. Even in Olympus, eventually, there's only room for the big chair.

The two gigantic results of those hearings: The two-party system died—you were either pro-Akira or voted out. Second, the study of astrophysics was outlawed with the introduction and passing of the Thirty-fifth Amendment: Heresy to pretend to be Akira. Heresy to contradict her. It was all declared a matter of national security. Just like that, we became a theocrazy. Some people still study astrophysics, though, because no one in the White House or Congress knows what it is. The Savior's Eye was decommissioned, and now, shadowed by Akira's aquifer-fueled water statue, it's the world's most popular museum. To this day, all I can think is that I should've risked taking Ascalon Lee's deal. I should've let her make me a member of The Money. The world went nuts anyway.

Sabrina, Ascalon, and I are in my SEAL, airborne, flying over The Eye. My wife is looking up, eyes instinctively searching for what's no longer there. Ascalon's complaining about her headache while she carves at the hunk of wood she apparently found when she was last diving. I'm patched into the feed. Before the death of the panty line, there used to be these salacious things called tabloids. Now, sensationalized media is all there is. Graduates of cyber penny universities ignorantly pontificate in real-time and handicap what the next minute will bring. The circus is in full clown mode now. The only thing missing is a ringmaster sitting on a juggling elephant while whipping a bear masticating three rings on a unicycle. I turn the feed off.

"No one knows," I say.

Sabrina nods. "But they're scared. Drop me off at work. Things are going to get busy."

Panic and pandemonium incoming. A world about to be festooned with crazy. Sabrina cracks open a walnut and tosses it to me. That's right. I'm hungry. I feel bad that my wife is having to recall things for me more and more.

"My headache is getting worse," Ascalon says.

"I'm gonna take us to Uncle Akeem's, matey," I say. "He's gonna let us use his med bots to see what's going on with you. But let's drop Mommy off first."

"Okay, matey," she says. "Mommy, you really mean that I can't go in the water for a week? You're treating me like some kind of nurdle."

"Nurdle?" Sabrina asks.

"A piece of waste that can't swim, that can only float and pollute the water," I say. "Like those little plastic thingies the skimmers removed from the ocean." The word "skimmer" makes me think of my last wife, the skimmer captain who stole my heart. Then I feel an instant pang of guilt for doing so in front of my present wife.

Sabrina shakes her head. "Now I feel like the old one who's not up-to-date on the slang." She turns to Ascalon. "Don't call people that. It's not nice. And no water until you're better."

Sabrina reaches over and grabs my hand. She wants to stay. She's worried about our daughter. "Don't worry," I tell the both of them. "I got this." And I believe it. Because I got to.

"Look," says Ascalon, pointing down. We're over water now, and a pod of humpbacks spurt spirals of bubble nets from their blowholes to trap and eat prey. Their heads breach the surface in unison when they feed. "They eat together like us. Like a family."

I love this kid. I swoop down closer for her. The humpbacks breach the bubble rings together.

"One week?" she groans.

"Listen to your mother," I say.

Police Main HQ is on Skyscraper Island—the same island where Jerry Caldwell and most of the rest of her family lived. I was stationed there after I was relieved from the Ascalon Project, after Akira's miracle robot supposedly saved the world. It's where I matched identities with suicide feet. We're nearing the island now. Water pours down its mountain creases. Rain wets the flammable brush. From this distance, it looks like the spiked, rotting corpse of something mythical excavated from the ocean. We approach the dated, radiated cooled scrapers, most built pre-asteroid. Their tops sprout from the bed of gray clouds below. Unlike the seascrapers, these towers are not washed by the constant flow of the deepwater tides, and they look dirty and sun-beaten like sea glass. Some are capped with kinetic sculptures that rhythmically undulate like cnidarians. It's hypnotizing. Suddenly, I find I'm getting a little lost looking at them. Where is Main HQ again?

"Where are you going?" Sabrina asks.

Maybe it's the stress, the damn missing Scar, Ascalon's headaches, my own that are setting in now. I try to calm down and think. "You're going the wrong way," my wife says.

I'm feeling more and more agitated, and the pellets of rain pattering the windshield ain't helping. I turn around.

"Sorry, scenic route." I'm completely fucking lost. I'd worked at HQ for years. Why can't I remember? I whiz by the towers. They all look sort of vaguely familiar, but I don't know where I am. I almost plow into a heli-taxi.

"Whoa," Sabrina says. "Pull over." She says it like I'm a drunken perp, or I'm imagining that's how she says it.

I lift the SEAL to a safe height and hover. Shaking, I look down at the cityscape. My eyes can't follow the pulse of the beating city. Everything is too . . . fast. A blur of lives based on becoming quickly bored with what they got and trading it in for something made from the same shit. Helis pop from the clouds like the punchlines of magic tricks. My mind is racing. Self-piloting has long been simplified to a joystick and six buttons. AI takes care of the rest. What the hell is wrong with me? I'm not even making sense to myself, and it's scary. Did I take my meds? I don't know. Then a thought slams my mind's brakes. I've been alive too long.

"Please get us out of here," Sabrina says.

That's when I see them. Hundreds, maybe thousands of people on their balconies peeping through their telescopes. Sabrina's on edge, probably because her parents had an above-cloud, telescoped high-rise and jumped out of a sky-scraper just like these. They were so shaken by the coming of Sessho-seki that they left her an orphan. The jagged pieces of my thoughts slowly begin to fall and fit in order.

Ascalon puts her hand on my shoulder. "It's okay, Daddy."

I tell my iE to autopilot the SEAL to HQ. Sabrina's got detective eyes on me. It's rough being married to a cop some-times. "Are you okay?" she says.

I fight to steady my voice. "I don't know, just the stress, I think."

Sabrina nods, but her eyes are still locked on me. She's urged me to see a doc about my memory loss many times before. I'm just not interested. As long as I can still get it up, crack walnuts open with my fingers, and take care of my kid, I'm good. When I got my Triple X iE, the first thing I did was deactivate the RNA reader. Some things I just don't wanna know.

The SEAL descends, and, slowly, things start looking familiar again. We near the clouds. Unlike where we live, the rushed, unplanned mess of this island resembles a mouth full of broken predator teeth. Towers capped with all shapes tangled in vac tubes. Bioluminescence pulsing every imaginable color. Catchment systems shaped like giant lily cups filled with UV sterilized water. The air traffic of trash cubes lifted by drone choppers. Urban cacophony, undampened by ocean depth. Ads splashed against the night sky in digi banners. One reads: THE MYSTERY HAS BEEN SOLVED. PING THE CHURCH OF OUR SAVIOR.

When we get below the clouds, to the base level of the city where the Less Thans live, the sprawl of the ecocity is jarring. The root system of the scrapers is a tangled, lit-up series of anchors, each banded with vegetation like some kind of apology to Mother Nature for past sins. From up here, the people look like frantic fire ants feeding on tubers swollen with algorithms. Rain showers gust through the solar panel cobbled streets like they're chasing something.

When we near HQ, we see a demonstration forming. Less Thans hungry for answers. Their iEs project their questions, and they fill the air with the colorful rumblings of something seismic yet to come. Not a single member of The Money is in this crowd—they don't like crowds. Besides, most of them got a direct line to the superintendent anyway. Sabrina shakes her head.

"Like we know what the hell is going on."

We land on the helipad, and I wonder how long it'll take for the riots to start. I turn to check on Ascalon. She's crashed out in the back. Maybe trying to pass thirty minutes of sleep for eight hours didn't work this time. I'm definitely taking her to Akeem's, which is out in the middle of the ocean, away from the terrified rabble. Sabrina is the head of the police department's PR Division, which is a shit job tailor-made for promotion. Every vice-super needs to occupy that position before being kicked up in rank from captain. My wife is one of the youngest captains in the history of the force. She will be the youngest vice-super in history if she lands the job before her next birthday. She wants it. Oh, I know she wants it. It's a substitute for the glory she would've achieved as a pulse racket champ had her knee not failed her in college all those years ago. Instead of champion, she'll be top custodian of human awfulness.

"You're gonna be busy," I say.

Sabrina sighs. "Take care of her, will ya?"

I nod.

Ascalon stirs and squints at her mom. "Bye, Mom," she says.

"Bye, sweetie," Sabina says. She turns and gives me three pecks on the cheek. "And take care of yourself."

"Haven't I always?" I say, a little too defensively.

Sabrina jumps out of the SEAL. I wait to watch her step inside the building before looking up at the sky and remembering that it was just a light, not an asteroid killer, only a fucking giant flashlight. What was it that Akira's daughter said to her? *There is no asteroid. There is no weapon. Just a machine that will shoot permanent luminosity. A reminder to us all what you have given.* How the hell can I recall the line of something I'd read eight years ago and not remember the location of HQ after being stationed there for over a decade? And if it's just a light, who the hell turned it off? Did it just run out of batteries? Unlikely. It was built by Akira. Unless she planned it.

It's all way above my pay grade anyway. Way above my wife's even. *Procedure.* I have a kid to take care of. Akeem, whose expertise in ocean floor geothermics made him a bit paranoid when it came to doomsday super quakes and earth core explosions, has some crazy survivalist in him—lots of water, oats, and bullets buried beneath his compound. I wonder if his fears heightened when the existence of Sessho-seki was announced almost fifty years ago. Or perhaps they were alleviated. He might've thought it impossible for there to be two extinction events in one lifetime. But we live so long now. Regardless, I'm heading to Akeem's, and I'm guessing there will be some conversation of how to prepare for a zombie apocalypse, the sudden rise of mindless undead. This is something I might know a little about. I got my rail gun packed in the back, so at least I'm bringing something to the rich man's feast.

I look at Ascalon and think about John. This is how it is sometimes. I look at this child and impulsively compare her to my last. Her impatience compared to his patience. She's really going to town carving up that piece of driftwood. John would've taken his time with it. Talking will help put the thought out of my mind, so I speak up.

"What are you working on?" I ask.

"It's just for school," Ascalon says.

I sometimes dream of John and Ascalon playing together on the beach, despite the fact that death and some fifty years separate them. What would John be now if he had lived? A good person, just like his mother. I picture them now, Ascalon and John, their backs to me, sitting beside each other on a bowed wooden bench. She leans into him, and he puts his arm around her. An orange handkerchief hangs from his back pocket. Two daisies dangle from her right hand. I imagine myself asking them to turn around. They don't listen. Only the now-extinct beagle at John's feet looks up at me. A sun rises or sets in front of them, and they seem to be watching it. I realize that what I'm visualizing is a painting by a once-famous American. I go cold and shiver like a corpse in a cadaveric spasm. I'm envisioning permanence, enamored by it, because I know it don't exist.

That's when I get a ping . . . from Akira Kimura.

Impossible.

I ignore it. My iE tells me that a message has been left for me. I don't open it. I don't need my iE to tell me my pulse is racing. That my hands are shaking. That there's a quivering in me that's rattling my insides. I punch through the buxom gray clouds that only let in squirrelly slivers of radiance.

7

From above, Akeem's estate looks like a spiral of crop circles cut into an endless, unplowed field of ocean. I land in the center, on the highest floating tower. Ascalon likes when we come to Akeem's. His manmade islands include reefs, channels, and underwater tunnels that lead to replicated wrecks of some of the great naval vessels in history. To the north, in a wide channel, RMS *Titanic*. To the south, *Santa Maria*. To the southwest, the *Yamamoto*. And in the furthest, deepest bottom, *Space Shuttle Challenger*. Akeem's up to ten great-grandchildren now, and all of them love the water, too. I hit the tarmac, and Ascalon is out the door, oblivious to her mother's "no water for one week" rule, no concern over the missing scar in the sky.

I, on the other hand, get out and look up. Just can't help it. My eyes are searching for Ascalon's Scar, but it's simply not there. I'm doing a good job telling myself Akira's ping is impossible. Just some crazy hacker's trick. Everybody probably got the same ping.

I patch into the feed, and the wild theories are already buzzing. Something orbiting way out there in front of it, blocking it from view. The mysterious Planet Nine that baffled astronomers for over a century is actually a black hole that gobbled up the scar. It's now gonna gobble us up, too. The scar was a beacon, a glowing welcome sign for some alien race. Akira actually created a wormhole to an alternate reality, to our future selves, and they stepped through, killed Sessho-seki, and now they've closed the wormhole and flipped the switch. They did it years ago, but the results took a ton of time to reach us. Nothing about a mass message from Akira. I kill the feed.

I hear heavy mech footsteps approach, and I level my gaze. Akeem's heading over, wearing a haul suit, an exoskeleton powered by motors and actuators full of electronics and horsepower. We have a suit for everything nowadays. Work, radiation, hauling, space, hydronauting, war—I've worn them all at one time or another. Akeem's suit, of course, is state-of-the-art. He's carrying a grand piano over his head, one-handed.

"Pork Chop!" he says. He likes to call me Pork Chop because I'm now an ex-cop. "Do you . . . see anything up there?"

"Nada," I say. "Nothing green. No murder up in the skies."

"Whew," he says.

I look at the antique piano. "What the hell are you doing?"

"Isn't it obvious? I'm moving stuff to my apocalypse sub."

"You're putting a piano in there?"

"Well, yeah. What good is surviving without live music?"

I bet Akeem has a whole lot of stuff packed in his impregnable underwater cruise capsule. Most of The Money have some kind of end-of-the-world contingency plan. Aside from the aforementioned thing, Akeem also has weapons, med bots, blood, artifacts, cigars, and organs. He even let me stash Ascalon's spare organs here, too. Sabrina and I can only afford to fund spares for one of us, so we picked Ascalon instantly.

Akeem's probably got multiple suits of each kind stashed in his apocalypse sub, as well. He once told me that the sub can fly, too, just in case. I don't know if I buy that. Sometimes he likes to lie a bit to see if people are really listening to him.

Akeem puts the piano down. Random notes rattle. "I got my entire family coming in," he says.

"All of them?"

He nods.

"Thanks for including us," I say.

"You kidding? You're family, too, Pork Chop. By the way, your daughter just whizzed by me, heading for the dive gear."

"Dammit." I ping Ascalon a TtT—thought to text—for emphasis. NO WATER. ONE WEEK. Sending the TtT makes me think about that message in my inbox. A big message, voice and holo rolled into one. It's really itching at me, but I don't wanna open it, even if it is really *her*.

Ascalon pings me back. I accept the TtT. I WANT TO SEE IF IT'S STILL THERE.

"What?" I respond in voice to demonstrate that I'm serious.

"The red, Daddy!" she says out loud to show that she's serious, too.

I cringe and look at Akeem. His brow furls. I resend Ascalon the same TtT. NO WATER. ONE WEEK. She seems to get that I'm putting my foot down and doesn't reply.

"The red?" Akeem asks. "You sure you're not holding out on me?"

"Nah," I say, not wanting to divulge any information. I grab one side of the piano and motion Akeem to get the other side. "Just some incident she had in the water."

Akeem eyes me suspiciously then changes the subject. "Sabrina coming?" he asks.

We pick up the piano. I shuffle backward. My back already aches. "Work," I say.

"So, what do you make of all this?" he asks. "The light going out?"

I take careful, baby steps back. "I don't know, man. Not my case."

"Fair enough. Now, put this damn thing down before you hurt yourself. I got it. I'm taking it to the lobby."

You know you're The Money when your house has a lobby. "I thought it was going to the bunker?"

Akeem hoists the piano over his head. The actuators of his haul suit whirl. He carries it like it's a serving tray. "Are you kidding? No piano, just my fiddle, so I can play while it all burns around me."

I follow Akeem as he makes his way to the lobby. "What'd the president say?" I ask. Presidents now got more puff than ever since the two-party system died, and The Money, the ones as rich as Akeem anyway, got private access.

Akeem pauses. The Money and their inexhaustible connections. The question embarrasses him. "She isn't answering my pings," he finally says.

"So, I guess you're taking this seriously."

I eye the piano and wonder why rich people love old shit so much. My guess is that surrounding themselves with historically relevant stuff makes them start feeling historically relevant, too. The Money internalizes the shit around them, just like the Less Thans, just like the Zeroes.

Making our way down the concourse, we pass crates of explosives, old stuff from his days of geothermal exploration. I get another ping, one that says the sender is Akira Kimura once again. I'm about to turn off my iE, but Ascalon pings.

"Daddy?" she asks in voice.

"What?"

"Do you hear the music?"

I look up at the piano's rattling keys. "Yeah," I say. "It's dinner time." I turn off my iE.

It's late by the time we get settled in. Ascalon and I got our own top floor villa in Akeem's architectural re-creation of the Julius Tower at Caesar's Palace. When Akeem was young and poor, his first trip to the continent was to New Vegas. He could only afford to stay downtown, but he walked the Strip and fell in love with Caesar's. After casinos, with their anti-quated slot machines and table games, were slowly replaced by the more interactive VR sports arenas, he decided to build this homage to the old world with his residuals. He still gets a cut of all the utility fees everyone pays to his geothermal company to keep their lights on.

In bed I'm distracting myself with holo-projected memory games, side-eying my sleeping iE, which is mounted on a three-pronged pedestal on the nightstand. I try to concentrate on the game and flip holo hanafuda cards to create matches. What was with my memory lapse back on Skyscraper Island? I've had senior moments before, but nothing like that. Did the radiation at The Leachate fry my brain? Or did the years of astronaut-grade anti-anxiety med abuse finally catch up to me? I think I forgot to take my medicine. I put the hanafuda away. *Fuck it.* I turn on my iE, and it floats in front of my face. I look outside the door, across the suite, toward Ascalon's room. Quiet. We're gonna nano her first thing in the morning. Maybe I should get nanoed, too.

If the mind were a sponge, mine would be a dried-out Porifera bleached by the sun. The mind always seemed more like an underwater city to me. Different districts and municipalities populated by unpredictable citizens. It seethes with emotion rationalized. Each building filled with its hierarchies, its hormonal plumbing. Its own sense of nationalism, own sense of self, and own suppressed downtrodden. There are bloody riots in the mind that reshape the whole thing. There are golden ages of realization and self-inflicted dark ones. There's climate outside it, and it interacts. There's a constant war between districts of neurons among near-forgotten ghettos and frontal cortex finance and culture. Each mind full of its own neurological revolutionaries, whose numbers are typically highest during puberty because the mind floods the plumbing. Then hormone production eventually fades. Cells stop splitting. Labor strikes. Ghost towns empty except for tumbleweeds of memory. And what's left? An old man like me. A shell of lazy, dogmatic belief. Parenthood: the only thing keeping me going. A city produces or it dies. Just like the mind.

I find myself reminiscing about war. Desert Storm 15, also known as Death Wish 5. It was 2080, and most of the world had had enough. It was time to get off fossil fuels once and for all. One after the other, governments had gone bankrupt because of climate change, only to be bought out by international corporations at bargain basement prices. Cities had begun to appear on lists like casualties of war.

Miami, Shanghai, Singapore, Lima, Jakarta, Manila. Delta cities and cities closest to the water got hit the hardest. NYC, Busan, Lisbon, and London, like the Dutch, had known that rising, warmer waters meant more storms and flooding in the north, so they embraced the idea of retooling infrastructure—building waterways, bridges, and heli platforms—and preemptively flooded their cities. In the US, the once grand hills and mountains of the Pacific Northwest, after being torched bald by wildfires, filled the horizon like crowns stripped of their jewels. In the South, tropicalization marched north, and migrating mosquitoes infected people with brain infections that were cooked further by heat waves. The last straw might've been the Great Plastic Hurricane of 2079. Waters off the Pacific Coast warmed enough for hurricanes to break through, and Los Angeles was assaulted by a storm packed with plastic ocean waste. It cut through the city and its people with deadly confetti of flimsy razors. The category 7 storm surge so massive that it filled the SoCal earthquake cracks and left waterways that stretched into Nevada. These became known as the California Nevada Fingers.

So, by the summer of 2080, I'd been stationed in Saudi Arabia, and at first, it'd been an assassin vs. assassin war that smelled like cotton candy. Targets: Officers and Executive VPs. Mission: Sneak in, wait for satellite ID confirmation, see the green wafts glowing—even behind stone walls, but there's nothing that synesthesia and a rail gun can't punch through—zap 'em and run like hell. SEAL out of the hot zone and leave behind that smell of fairy floss.

I remember the mirrors—opponent snipers on the other side, some of them just kids. A girl of Ascalon's age in particular. A girl I wanna forget but never can. She'd been wrapped in tri-color camo from head to toe. I didn't know she was a child when I pulled the trigger. I sometimes ask myself if it would have mattered if I had known she was young.

A few months after the girl, FLOTUS had been sniped while attending a celebration of the resurrection of the once-extinct Yangtze River Dolphin. When news of the assassination hit the feeds, we were ordered to fall back. At first, I was relieved— us pulling out meant no more killing for me. Then the drone and missile strikes began. Civilians, they mattered even less. We leveled once-venerable cities to the ground. My utility as a sniper wasn't needed after that. The conflict stopped being a war between government-funded shadow companies and corporate mercenaries. It became a quasi-civil war full of first strikes. One assassination ended all assassinations. On one side, the US war machine, on the other, freedom fighters and royals backed by international fossil fuel energy corps, including the US's. The only way to get us off fossil fuel was to kill the global supply. We did that and then some. It's always about one life, isn't it? One death? Reducing cause to one. It was then. It is now.

I force myself to snap out of my daydream and decide to open the first message. I take a breath and notice that my hands are shaking. My hands never shake.

Akira's automated voice. "Emergency protocol," it says, in her smug, but polite tone. "Please open attachment."

I see now. Yet another contingency probably executed if the scar goes out. I close my eyes. I don't wanna open this thing. I contemplate deleting it, pinging Sabrina to see what she thinks. Instead, I open the second message. It's identical to the first. I'm just gonna get spammed until I open it, aren't I? I could block the sender. I think about the scar and the mass hysteria that's probably headed our way. Something that could've been controlled if Congress hadn't redacted my information.

I open the attachment.

My iE turns and projects a large 3D map. Above is Volcano Vista. A labyrinth of tubular caverns spout from the bottom and lead to an under seafloor domed structure that blinks red. My life has always felt like being sequentially rendered obsolete, and for the first time, I want to be. If Akira Kimura would just let me. I'm about to forward the message to Sabrina, but the map flickers off, and Akira's automated voice comes crackling back.

"Message deleted."

I check. Yep. Both messages are gone. I open the nightstand drawer and grab the AMP inhaler that Akeem left for me. He knows I have trouble sleeping. I take a huff and pass out.

I wake up after a couple of hours and go through my usual routine—stagger to the bathroom, take care of business, then head to the kitchen. I open the fridge, which Akeem always keeps well stocked. The usual: fruits, eggs, and vegetables. Except for one thing: a wooden carving of a soldier with a tiki face, on his belly, aiming a rifle at me. Ascalon and I are the only ones on this floor. She must've left it there. I pick the figurine up. The quality is absolutely surgical. I didn't know she could carve wood so well. I close the fridge and head down to Ascalon's room.

When I approach Ascalon's door, the first thing I notice is the muffled sound of running water. Odd time to be washing face or brushing teeth, especially for Ascalon, who needs to be cajoled into doing both. I knock. No answer. I put my hand on the door and get the sense that it is expanding then contracting, swelling then blowing out breath. I swear I hear the wood cracking, but I know doors aren't made of wood anymore. The door inhales again then breathes. This is when I look down and see it, the green, billowing above the threshold. Something behind the door inhales, and the green fog disappears.

I wrap my hand around the antique knob. I feel heat, like a backdraft waits on the other side. I close my eyes and open them again. Green wisps curl around my calves. I feel like they're pulling me forward, tugging so hard that if I don't open the door, the wisps will tighten and yank me under it. I smell the perfumed scent of crushed, pedaled things pulsing out of my daughter's room. I don't wanna go in.

I open the door and step inside. The bed is empty. The bathroom door is closed, but the light is on. This is where the wafts slither, underneath the bathroom door. I hear someone humming, but I don't recognize the voice. It's not a child's voice. The song they're humming, though, I recognize.

Ascalon is not just the name of the savior
It's the name of the daughter
The one I gave up
Find her for me and tell her that I'm sorry

It's the song Akira wrote. The one she sang to her daughter while she forced her into a thirty-year sleep. The song that sparked a series of clues that led me to the daughter and helped me solve the most important, yet eventually most irrelevant, murder case in our history. A god, murdered by her own depraved, woken daughter. The murder, buried. Conclusion: suicide. Martyrdom. Godhood.

The memories flash and crackle to the foot of Volcano

Vista. Me in Akira's AMP chamber 177 atmospheres deep. Akira's daughter and murderer, Ascalon Lee, banging and banging away at the glass while I waited for Boyle's law and absolute pressure to mob her and cave in her lungs. The gem in her hand glowing so fiercely that I swear, for a moment, I saw the ripples of the ocean's surface even all the way down there.

I'm frozen. Paralyzed by fear for the first time in my life. *Do something! Do something, fool!* My body doesn't respond. I consider pinging Akeem, pinging anyone, to open the door for me and check. *Take a step, old man. Just one. One at a time.* I force myself to move forward, the smell of the greens and now the music of the reds getting stronger and stronger. My hands are shaking. Hell, my whole body's shaking. The girl behind the door continues to hum. My daughter doesn't know that song. How is this possible? Then, the humming stops followed by the squeaky twist of a faucet handle. The water ceases to run. It's quiet. The next sound is the creaking of the door when I pull it open.

Ascalon's standing at the sink, her back to me. Her thick, unruly black hair is a tangled pile that hangs to the middle of her back. Her loose white nightgown covers her dark, skinny legs down to the backs of her knobby little knees.

"Matey?" I say.

She doesn't move. I have never seen her this still before. I see now that she's holding a pair of scissors in her left hand. This is wrong. My daughter is right-handed. She begins to squeeze the scissors so hard that her small hand begins to quiver.

"Ascalon?" I say. "You okay?"

Wisps of green appear at the tip of the scissors. The grim

perfume is so overpowering that I feel my eyes begin to tear, and I try to blink them away. The tendrils drift to her night-gown and begin to stain it in red, like the spread of blood under gauze. I step forward. Ascalon spins around, and I take a step back.

Her face is drenched in sweat. She begins to hyperventilate. A membrane slides up her right eye. And again, I find myself frozen. I'm disgusted with myself because it's not just fear that stops me in my tracks, it's also the knee-jerk curiosity to see what happens next. She closes her eyes, and her breath steadies. There's something pushing against her closed right eyelid. I force myself to take a step forward. The lid begins to swell and balloon, then blood starts to trickle from her tear duct. I stop in my tracks. Something darts back and forth beneath her eyelid. *Pop.* I jump back and gasp. An eyeball dangles at the top of her cheek. The thin, slick strands of muscle and vein begin to fray, then smoke. Ascalon raises the scissors and severs tissue and nerve. The eyeball plops on the bathroom floor. A viscous, sickly yellow-brown afterbirth spills from the socket and splatters atop the ball. Miraculously, there's very little blood. I'm suddenly filled with the instinct to pick the eye up and cram it back into my daughter's face.

But something stops me. The slow blossom of another eye. This one, not brown like the other, but a bright yellow iris that glows and buzzes like a machine being booted up. I've seen this eye before. Impossible. I left Akria's daughter for dead, her eye along with her.

"How?" I ask.

"Daddy?" Ascalon says. It's her. It's my kid. And she's terrified.

I run to her and scoop her up. I look down at the eyeball, careful not to step on it.

"Daddy?" Ascalon asks again.

"It's okay, sweetie," I say. "You're fine. Everything is fine."

Bit by something in the ocean. Why now? Why eight years later? Why my daughter? Could this be linked to the disappearance of the scar, Akira's message? Is this correlation? Fuck the scar. Fuck Akira's message. Fuck correlation. I want to pry out Ascalon Lee's artificial yellow eye and squish it under my boot. I'll take her down to Akeem's med bay now. We'll amputate it. Then I will destroy it. Easy. I step to the door with my daughter in my arms. That's when it happens.

"I'm so sorry," she whispers in my ear, then plunges the scissors into my neck.

The pain is sudden and jarring. But not as jarring as seeing the tiny stream of blood spew from the puncture. I blink and touch the wound. The blood now oozes more than squirts. I sigh, relieved. Then another stream shoots out, and I feel my eyes widen in panic. I fall to my knees, and Ascalon steps away from me. I'm holding my neck stupidly, as if I can somehow keep the gushing blood in. I feel it running through my fingers and soaking my chest. I stare at Ascalon, not sure whose kid I'm looking at, Akira's or mine. She's looking right back at me, head tilted, like I'm a curiosity, some sort of specimen. Then she begins to crack, not in pieces, but like a bulletproof thing slowly being webbed. Like the glass I shot that night I killed her. There's an invisible laminate that's not letting something in her to burst out. Something beyond gauge, beyond atmospheric, an absolute pressure pressing against the insides of my daughter. Greens and reds shine through the glowing fissures.

Ascalon grabs me by the collar and drags me out of the bathroom. She's strong. Too strong for a nine-year-old. And I'm slowly becoming dead weight.

She pulls me through the bedroom. I watch the smeared blood trail I'm leaving behind. She opens the sliding glass door and drags me to the balcony. At this point, the green and red cracks completely web her body. And they are blinding. The wind is strong up here. I wonder about the physics of it all, height and wind. I'm sure Akira told me once, and I, of course, forgot. Ascalon pulls my face up to hers. That terrible, yolky eye bores into me. The cracked face blazes. A squirt of blood from my wound streaks her face. She smiles then shatters into pieces, over and over again. This is impossible. I know I'm losing my mind.

When my mind recovers, I do not see my daughter staring at me anymore. I see Akira's. Gone is the girl who loves the ocean and pirates. The girl who can't sit still. The girl who has held onto her love for splashing in puddles and holo balloons her entire short, little life. The greens and reds flicker emotionless on her face like archaic technicolor, lighting up beyond the Juliet balcony. My head wobbles. I look up through the bars. My eyes search for the scar, as if there's some salvation in it. But there is no scar, no salvation. Then I look down. The colors rain and sizzle into the ocean below in hot-worked billets. I ping Sabrina. No message, just a ping and an unfair, antiquated thought. It should be my kid's mom up here, not me.

"I'm sorry," I say.

Ascalon picks me up and tosses me over the railing. I fall among the karma colors. I somehow fooled myself into believing that I could hide from guilt and tragedy in routine, domestic solitude. No, if anything, it made me more vulnerable. I began to care more. And I ceased to be a moving target. I fall and fall and fall. I do not feel the splash, just the cold as I begin to realize the real reason we cremate bodies.

8

Back in the day, after Akira saved the world, we would meet a couple times a year to catch up. The catching up part took all of a minute, and neither of us cared for nostalgia, so our conversations quickly turned to discussions about science and history, meaning I was there to learn and shut the hell up, and she was there for some educational charity. Normally, I'd pick her up in my SEAL, and we'd circle the eight islands, coasting above the clouds. Being the savior of the world and all, there was no going out in public for Akira. It didn't occur to me then, but it occurs to me now—I never saw her look up at the scar. Not once. She saved the world, and that was that. Was she ashamed of the deception?

One of her favorite topics to discuss was the ancient Japanese art of anime. She knew I took a class on the subject in college, and she'd spent her childhood immersed in those old legends about orphans, tech, mutants, death, and rebirth. It was during one of our flights that she told me she'd been named after one of the old stories, the story being *Akira*. It had been her grandfather's favorite. When he'd watched it, it was already a classic. Her grandfather had told her how the story was deeply affected by the nuclear bombing of Hiroshima and Nagasaki, despite being produced over forty years after WWII. He'd also told her that most anime was influenced by the aftermath of perhaps the greatest single war crime in the history of man. Anime was the Fat Man and Little Boy's scar. Maybe that's when she learned about scars and became inspired to do what she did.

I'm sitting next to Akira in her telescope, The Savior's Eye, now. It's not the doctor Akira or The Leachate Akira, or even the god Akira, it's Akira Kimura, my old friend and manipulator. The one who got me to kill all those people for her. She tells me to look into the eyepiece, so I do. I never could say no to her. I see reddish lavender-rimmed clusters of thin, green stems balled together. I have no idea what I'm looking at and tell her so. She assures me that I've seen this before. I tell her I never have.

"You are looking through a microscope, not a telescope," she says. "Each cluster is a milk-producing gland in a lactating human female. Each is surrounded by cells that force the milk into the ducts. It is as I said. You are thrice a father. You have seen this before."

"It looks different this close," I say. "Looks a little bit like murder."

Akira puts her hand on my shoulder and squeezes gently. "Yes. Things do appear differently when perspective shifts. But you know that better than most."

"You aren't a god."

Her hand slides down my arm and stops at the crook of my elbow. "You are not looking closely enough. Trillions of cells. Each designed with purpose: to sustain and pass on life. My dear friend, we are all gods. Gods of tiny, meaningless worlds, perhaps. But still gods. It is only when we recognize this that we can endlessly labor to meet this Brobdingnagian potential."

I feel her hand on mine. I try to raise my head but can't look away. "Do you now blame me for putting her to sleep?" she says.

"She was a child," I say.

"And now she is your child."

I magnify the image of the glands. They begin to wilt. "Why did you trick the world?" I ask. "Like you tricked me?"

"That is a stupid question. To better it, of course."

I manage to peel my face off the eyepiece. Akira and I are now sitting in a passenger car of an antiquated locomotive. She's wearing a red corset over layers and layers of petticoat, like some forgotten queen. A vintage phonograph is playing Ascalon's song. The train jerks into motion and accelerates quickly. Beyond its loading gauge, the locomotive rumbles, and I feel it almost slipping from its track. I'm having a tough time breathing, but Akira looks calm, so I try to stay calm, too.

"I need to get my daughter back," I say. "How do I do that?"

Akira closes her eyes and listens to the song. "Did you know that when Edison invented the phonograph, no one believed it possible? They thought of sound as ephemeral. It was there, then it was gone in an instant. To be able to record it, well, you can imagine. They needed to hear for themselves. And when they did, they quickly realized that it was now possible for the dead to go on speaking forever."

I nod, and Akira points out the window. There's no landscape whizzing by, just the vacuum of deep space. Why do I feel like we're on tracks? "Fuck," I say, barely managing to get the word out, gasping for breath. It would be an appropriate last word for me. It should be engraved on my headstone. But I continue. "Am I dead?"

"There it is!" Akira says.

Outside the window, an asteroid. It's an ugly sucker, a chunk of rock broken off from something bigger, its gas tail blazing green and red behind it, and it's hauling ass. The train rockets and the sudden G's have me glued to my buttoned red velvet seat. I look out and don't see the asteroid anymore. I fight to get to my feet. I can barely breathe. I take a step forward, grab the seat in front of me, and begin to pull with everything I got. I'm coughing now. But row by row, I'm making my way to the engine. I need to pull the brake on this sucker. With each step, the song plays more and more loudly, causing my ears and chest to hurt. But I gotta get up there. I gotta see. The train horn blares twice. I stagger and fall. I'm feeling faint now, but I crawl. The door to the engine slides open. I manage to pull myself into the engine car and feel the steam hissing, the brass rimmed gauges all read max. That's when I realize my stupidity. These things had no front pilot window. I pull myself up and burn my hand on the boiler. The smokebox door rips off and flies into space. Then the entire front of the engine is being peeled. Once the smoke-stack is gone, I can see in front of me. It's the asteroid. No, wait, it's not . . . It's a giant, yellow Ascalon Lee eye . . . and I'm headed right for it.

I look for some sort of steering wheel in this thing, but there ain't no steering wheel on a train. I'm looking for a brake, but don't see one of those either. The eye is getting bigger and bigger, bolts of greens and reds flash in the colossal xanthic iris. Akira's standing by me.

"I will help you," she says.

"You can't help me. You're dead."

"I am a god. How can I be dead? Besides, do you know anyone else intelligent enough to kill that . . . thing . . . out there?"

I try to answer, but I'm not breathing. That thing out there. We ain't headed for it. It's heading for us.

"Look for me," Akira says. "Use the map."

"Why my daughter?"

"Revenge. Besides, like you, your daughter has the potential to be a master of locating murdered things. Ascalon Lee will use your child to attempt to find me. To help . . . put me together again. I'm not sure how, but she will." She reaches up and grabs my face. "Your abilities are useful in more ways than you realize. Oh, you were ever so useful to me. What I have always loved about you is that I do not need to tell you what to do. You will do it anyway."

I'm fading fast. Or is it the light that's fading? Because we're just about at the point of impact now; a collision course with the eye's monstrous, swirling pupil. And there ain't nothing in it but darkness. Akira's still holding my face, and she smiles. But Akira ain't no face-holder. She ain't much of a smiler either. This is when I realize that I'm dreaming. That just like everyone else, I've turned her into something she ain't. But fake Akira or not, here we are, deep-diving into the black together. Then she's gone, as if me realizing that I'm dreaming whisked her away. Now, there's only a pair of dark arms pulling me to the other side.

9

I grew up in the ocean. Grew old in it. I'd like to say every time I look at it, I see something new, like my daughter does, but that'd be bullshit. Tonight, however, I do see something I ain't seen before. The surface shimmers a fluorescent pink like the dawn of primordial life. The tide slurps up the frothing soup of gentle waves. I'm being dragged to the shore, and it's two of Akeem's kids pulling me there, Chinara and Ganiru. Among Akeem's children and grandchildren, there are two doctors, a botanist, three engineers, a pharmacist, an AMP chamber salesman, and a shuttle stunt pilot. These are people who refuse tat dyes and investing in things that don't appreciate. They're all kind of Akira fanatics, but who at this point isn't?

It's the two doctors pulling me from the water now. They plop me on the beach. I'm trying to talk to them, ask them where Ascalon is, but I can't. My mouth moves, but nothing comes out. I'm furious. Why did I dream about her? Why wasn't I dreaming about my kid? My kid needs me right now more than she ever has, and I'm dreaming about Akira fucking Kimura? An old-school Akira beaded holo bracelet dangles from Chinara's thin wrist.

Ganiru compresses my neck wound. Chinara checks my eyes, pulse, and airway. Then she pulls out a scanner. Like cops who used to carry their sidearms off duty back in the day, docs always carry their med scanners.

"No hematoma," Chinara says. "Larynx intact. A small arterial tear."

"He lost a lot of blood," says Ganiru.

I grab Ganiru's arm. "Ascalon," I manage to gasp.

"My father is searching for her now," he says. He gives me a look, one that I've seen before. Suspicion. Irritation. Why did his father get mixed up with me? Parents of my friends have been shooting me that same look since I was a child. Fistfights, stolen skiffs, shit set on fire, trashed the whole time, that was my childhood. Now children of my friends are doing it, too. I'm toxic. Always have been. Not on purpose, I just am. Look at what happened to Jerry Caldwell. To my second wife and child. Look at what's happening to my kid. I'm trying not to be this guy anymore. I need to get up. I try but can't.

Ganiru looks at Chinara. "Let's get him to the blood bank. We can finish stitching him up there."

Chinara nods and injects me full of nanos. This one actually likes me. A straight shooter who's always trying to convince her father and the rest of her patient roster to get on an entirely plant-based diet, like it's the true secret sauce of longevity, which it probably is. The kind of doc you never wanna tell you're feeling old and tired. Next thing you know, she's got you on a diet of kelp and has you download an iE app that chides you every time you consume saturated fat. This is the kind of woman I hoped my Ascalon would be. I gotta get up and find her. I try to get up again but still can't. I ping Ascalon. The line is dead. *Give it time*, I tell myself. Let the nanos get to work on my torn artery. *Procedure. Patience. Breathe.* I'm on the dunes of Saudi Arabia again, wriggling through the sand and heat.

The siblings roll me on a military-style hover stretcher. I ping Sabrina again. This time I send the message in TtT. COME. NOW. The siblings guide the floating stretcher up the beach. The fluorescent pink shimmer is gone. Now there's just an oppressive sun rising over the ocean, one that houses so many predators, some that even consume their prey and turn them into venom.

By the time we reach Akeem's blood bank, I'm barely conscious, and the only thing keeping me up is the fear for my kid. *She's nine*, I try to reassure myself. *She can't get far. She's on a manmade island in the middle of the ocean. She can't do anything but run in circles.* Sabrina is on her way. Akeem will find her. It's his home, after all. He designed it. He engineered it. If anyone knows every hiding place, it's him. Then what? Stuff her in an AMP chamber and figure out what the hell is going on? Figure out a way to yank that eye out of her? No, no AMP chamber. I won't do to my daughter what Akira did to hers.

I imagine Ascalon Lee suspended in a chamber for thirty years. Imprisoned there by her mother. Unable to mature or grow, yet she somehow managed to escape. How did Ascalon Lee do it this time? Why now? And how? It's impossible. Too many neurons. Endless patterns of electrical impulses. Glial cells. Vagus nerve to take control of the lungs and heart. A nerve for every sense, every movement, every thought. This kind of transplanting tech does not exist. And if it did, it'd take forever to bridge the infinite gaps. I wanna ask the two docs working on me now how this is possible. Then I remember the birds that ripped poor old Chief of Staff Chang apart. That had been Ascalon Lee's doing. She'd controlled those birds. Then there were the stories of her childhood. Her fascination with patterns and self-mutilation. Then her years of work in neurology, biochemistry, and molecular modeling. Her ambition to upstage her mother. Then to become her. I'm lapping up memories, nausea, and transfused blood.

Ganiru's iE projects twenty security images on the walls, and he cycles through them. My eyes search for signs of my daughter. Her athletic, spindly body. Her white nightgown. Her thick, black hair. Anything. But this place is impossibly big. So many wings. Nautilus walls. Non-stick sand flooring. So many racks, bulkheads, decks, and grinders.

Chinara shoots me up with something. I don't care what, because I'm too focused on finding Ascalon, but there are just too many images. I ping her again. Nothing. Then I trace her iE's location. Still in her bedroom. I take a breath and close my eyes. *You dummy, you're looking for the wrong thing.* I open them fresh and begin to scan.

I almost fall off the stretcher, reaching out to grab Ganiru's hand when I see it. He turns to me. His eyes follow mine. It's his father on the wall, that goddamn mountain of muscle and good humor standing in front of the giant door to his apocalypse sub. Ganiru and I are looking at the same thing, but he doesn't see what I see. The billows of green puffing from Akeem's mouth like the cigar smoke he likes so much. He gets on one knee, then waves someone forward. I squeeze Ganiru's arm as hard as I can, walnut-cracking hard. He yanks away but can't get out of the grip. This time I spill off the hovering gurney and feel the transfusion needle tear from the aching crook of my elbow.

I'm on my back, staring at the now upside-down image. Chinara's not helping me, because she's staring at the same thing, too. Ganiru focuses in and the other nineteen disappear. He switches POV. We all see her, my daughter, head bowed and chest heaving under a nightgown spattered with my blood, about ten feet in front of Akeem. She's holding my rail gun.

I try to get up and stumble into a ghost net of tubes and wires. I turn my head back to the image. Ganiru's switched the POV again, so now we see both Akeem and Ascalon. Ganiru turns up the audio.

"Where are you going, little girl?" Akeem asks, green puffs now coming out of his nostrils.

No answer. Ganiru looks down at me. Then he looks back at the screen. Ascalon's got the rail gun pointed at Akeem. She powers the weapon up, and it begins to hum. Chain blue lightning crackles between the conducting rails that stretch beyond the length of the gun's barrel. Ganiru's eyes widen, and he's out the door.

"Let's go check on your daddy," Akeem says, unafraid on camera.

Akeem's green clouds stretch and thin to tendrils that reach out and coil around my daughter's hands. The tendrils become fibrous and begin to squeeze. "No," I manage to say. "No!" I then scream.

Chinara turns her head to me, and I'm grateful she missed it, my daughter pulling the trigger. By the time Chinara's eyes are back on the wall, Akeem's body is on the floor. In the middle of his chest, a smoldering crater. Ascalon steps over him and disappears through the rhombus door that hisses shut behind her. A sheet of indestructible glass collapses in front of it.

Chinara and I watch as some of her family—siblings, nieces, and nephews—arrive on the scene. Two tend to her lifeless father while the others holler and pound on the glass. When the two of the younger Buharis drop to their knees and try to pull Akeem to their laps, his large body splits below his rib cage and his intestines spill to the floor. His detached legs twitch. Blood seeps from his trunk and pools at the pile of fleshy tubes specked with splinters of shattered bone. The two Buharis leap to their feet, horrified that their patriarch is now in two pieces.

The door begins to rumble. Akeem's descendants step back. The apocalypse chamber detaches. It doesn't fly. But it swims. *There she goes*, I think to myself. There goes my daughter. Armed to the teeth, with a hundred lifetimes worth of nourishment on board, leaving a trail of blood behind her. Twin props spin and bubble. They get darker and darker and smaller and smaller, but I can see the dispersed spindled thrust of greens and reds behind her.

PART TWO

A DARKENED SKY

As I made my way from the submerged sub parked two miles out and one mile under the sea to torii gates of the island city, I noticed that this girl's body was quite remarkable. The suited swim to the island was effortless. My memory of being nine, feeling nine, does not equate to this. She has her father's aim and her mother's reflexes. If she had just been a few years older, she may not have missed me with her net gun. Not that it would've mattered. The depths and storms and the predatory life of the ocean did not take me. It takes more than primitive weapons to destroy what I have made, and what I have made is myself.

When I entered her with precision and surgically repaired the entry wound from the inside, I felt the surge of adrenaline from within. The path to the girl's head was fraught with as many dangers as my journey across the Pacific floor. Again, I had to be cautious. Plodding. Deliberate. It's no small task to move through human tissue, to anesthetize, tear through then repair as I inched along, all the while remaining unnoticed. But it was fascinating studying this host from the inside out. To watch a heart beat, not through imaging, not through surgery, but to actually see *it. To witness the gas exchange of the lungs. To slowly creep through this showroom to the motherboard while watching the electrical currents flow through her body. This one, with her sight, is too important to take too quickly. I needed to make sure that she would survive MELd.*

When I arrived at the most marvelous portion of her, her brain, I altered its hormonal settings. I altered all automated settings. She would be strong, this one. I would be strong. Once I took over, I bathed the frontal lobe with negative current. I switched my energy source from iE to the girl's mitochondria. Tossing the synesthete to his death was easy. When one gains conscious control of all bodily functions, will can become absolute.

While heading down the crowded, solar-paneled walkways that are shadowed by illuminated bouquets of crystal skyscrapers, I notice that there is something titillating about looking harmless and being lethal. There's a large, bald man passing me now, his bulk girdled by two layers of foam fit. I could easily snap his windpipe. These two women—one with hair sculpted into a barbed dorsal, the other's shaped into octopus tentacles—I could stop their cyborg hearts.

I may keep this little girl forever. I had been subliminally calling to her via iE for most of her life. Poor child. Like most foolish parents, hers had given her an iE at much too young an age. Do they not see that generations of iE are what made the people vulnerable to my mother's deception, made this girl vulnerable to me?

A gaggle of teens pass, grinning while engaged in group Thought Talk.

I make my way to Sugar Spire, which looks like a giant,

twisted licorice stick screwed into the clouds. This entire island, named once in honor of the fire bringer by my father's people, the demigod who was the tamer of the sun and heavens—his namesake now reduced to being impaled by spikes of skyscraper that look like towering, colorful, long-stemmed flowers. I see more parents. Some, with illusion eyelashes and multi-colored skin, hold their children's hands. The children stop and point at the empty mid-morning sky and feel its emptiness. Their parents try to hurry their little ones along, as if walking faster changes the subject, and huddle into tubes and taxis, their iEs bobbling behind them. The scar was not enough, Mother.

Sugar Spire is the largest building on the island. The swirl of double-latticed, sea sponge skeleton construction coils so high that its top floor isn't visible to the human eye. The pearls and metallics sparkle in sunlight. I enter the empty lobby and shut down each security check I pass. This building's code is old like its owner. It's also empty. I assume Caldwell has evacuated the building to ensure this meeting is private. Good. I call the superconducted lift. Another check easily disabled. I step in and send the lift to the top floor. I rise so quickly that the rabble below quickly becomes a blur. I shoot through scant, stalled clouds that are rain's false promise.

The top floor is as empty as the lobby. This man does not produce and sell refined sugar anymore. He has made a fortune big enough that it continuously metastasizes on its own. When I discovered he was the one who financed the salvage of Volcano Vista, I wasn't surprised. I knew what he was looking for. He'd heard the synesthete testify to Congress. He was the only one who believed every word. He

*had a hunch as to why my mother would preserve and hide
her data like that. She risked leaving behind evidence to the
deceptions of Sessho-seki and the Ascalon Project. That risk
had purpose. Caldwell began to dream of the possibilities.
And when I contacted him, my resurrection only confirmed
what he'd hoped for. The eternal preservation and MELd of
human consciousness.*

*I walk through a maze of automated doors. I know which
ones to take. I pulled the architectural and engineering plans
of this abomination during my voyage back. I lock each one
behind me as I pass. Caldwell knows I'm coming by now.
The floating security cameras above assure that. I finally get
to the end, and the final door is a gaudy thing: a pressed gold
self-portrait of Caldwell. Gold, a worthless element, absent of
utility and intrinsic value, yet people have spent generations
worshipping it. The door slides open.*

*A tall, elegant, extremely old man stands with his back
turned to me, one wrist cuffed with an enormous, spotted
hand. Two security drones glide across the shiny ebony
floor and approach me. The old man puts a hand up. They
stop.*

*"You didn't need to disable my security checkpoints," he
says. "You were invited."*

"I was showing you what you may one day be capable of."

*Caldwell turns around. "You took his child?" he says.
"It's perverse."*

*I look around the empty room and see the crevasses on the
floor. Retractable furniture. This is a vain, indulgent man. "I
may return her to her mother. Her consciousness is simply
in slumber." Both of these things are untrue. I don't plan
on returning the girl. And my neurons are slowly, gradually*

replacing those of the little girl's. Even if the connection were to be severed, a part of me will always be left in her.

"You didn't hear?" Caldwell asks.

"Hear what?"

Caldwell smiles. "I have ears in the police department. This girl you inhabit has been declared a kidnapping victim. The police are frantically searching for her now. And . . . your friend survived."

This angers me. "Do you—?"

Caldwell interrupts. "Of course I do."

"Where—?"

Caldwell raises his hand. I do not like this man. He's the type who interrupts because he feels compelled to make others believe that he knows exactly what you are talking about.

A triangular pedestal rises from the floor to his right. The green gem hovers in a sleeve of security glass.

Mother.

"What of the other one?" I ask. "I sent you the schematics."

One of the security drones glides a few feet closer to me. Its polymer tentacles power up and undulate. Its dome head peels back and a barrel extends. Men. It's loaded with something of high caliber, no doubt.

"I should kill you for what you did to my daughter," Caldwell says.

"I regret what happened to Jerry and sincerely—"

"That's not good enough," Caldwell growls.

Ah, this male flexing, even at his age. I shrug. "You know what I offer."

He nods slowly, then turns back to the window and points. "I assume you did that?" he asks.

I smile. The greens begin to waft around him, and he does not see them. He's pointing where my mother's silly light once beamed. She had to have known it wouldn't be enough to keep this world tamed, not forever. Part of the reason I turned it off was to expedite the process of discovering what she planned next. I'm sure my act triggered something. Exactly what, I do not know. I'm not here to kill my mother. I'm here to wake her to find out.

"Yes," I say. "I turned off Ascalon's Scar, as you people like to quaintly call it."

"Why?"

"Do you have what I asked for, or no?" I ask.

Another pedestal rises and showcases a yellow eye seemingly identical to mine. But this one is better. Matryoshka. A brain, within a brain, within a brain. If the outer layer falls, like Minerva from Jupiter, another will spring from its shell. A golden light beams from my eye to scan it. Yes. Yes. It's perfect. The schematics were followed precisely. I activate it. It lights up, then floats. I command it to split. It does at its orthodrome. Two hemispheres separate and reveal another glowing orb inside.

"I was only able to finish one," Caldwell says.

"Only one?"

"I'm not Idris Eshana."

"No," I say, "you are not."

The split hemispheres come back together and lock back into a single iE. "The second is close to completion," Caldwell says.

It's strange looking at this man from the point of view of two entities, the girl and this new iE that Caldwell has built. I let the iE in the girl slip from the child's eye socket. For a split second, the girl's screams cut through the static that crackles in my mind. The girl's body slumps to the floor. I must be quick. Just like the body, the mind has antibodies, protections against hostile invasion. The new eye zips to the girl's face and burrows beneath her eyelid. Her other eye twitches and spasms. The girl continues to scream and now claws at her face. Caldwell takes a step back. My face, I say to the girl. She shrieks while I stitch nerve and muscle to the new eye. The girl shudders. No, I shudder. Then I sit up and blink. I'm confused for a moment, and my mind wanders back to a time beyond memory, when I was a twin gestating in my mother's womb. I look up at my old iE. It hovers above me. I feel like a spider must feel, like a creature with many eyes. I peer at Caldwell through both iEs, the one just implanted in the girl and the one that hovers above her. No, not a spider. Twins. I feel like twins conjoined, not physically, but consciously. There are two of us now. There are two of us once again. I pull myself up to my feet, the body again under my control. The old iE, the old me, hovers, mucus- and blood-soaked. I nod. This version of me spins around and peers at Caldwell.

Caldwell is frowning. I walk to him. The two drones hover in front of me. The heads of both are now retracted, two barrels aimed at me. I keep moving forward.

"So, I get the old one?" Caldwell asks. "We agreed that I would get a new one."

"The next is close to completion, no?"

"Yes, but . . ."

"Did you acquire a new host?"

He nods. His hands quiver. This is a very old and sick man. Like the girl, I've studied this man closely during my trip back from Challenger Deep. At one time, a man of terrible *beauty. Now, his tall, lean frame decays beneath a shoulder-padded overcoat, an attempt to make him appear as broad as he once was. He is propped by will more than anything else. A part of me respects his refusal to simply let go of life. I stop at the gem and bathe it in my new yellow light. Highly encrypted. Incredibly encrypted. Quantum code that can't be duplicated, chaotic like spin glass. I don't know if I can bring her back. I feel my jaw clench. And my toes for some reason. Odd. Perhaps I should just destroy my mother. However, that would not be very scientific of me. A thought. I wasn't meant to bring her back. She did not leave the gem to me.*

She left it to the synesthete.

There are other things she may have left him, as well.

I bite my lip. My lip. I was too rash. I wanted to kill him too badly. Eight years of fantasizing about it. Fortunately, he survived. I'm suddenly giddy and relieved. I made a stupid, rushed, emotional decision. I am human. Besides, I may have some use for him. I certainly have a rather large bargaining chip. I ping the girl's mother and leave a message. I turn to the old man. Green swirls around him. It's quite magnificent seeing this way. I hum and wait for the red to slip from my lips. Ah, there they are. The colors mix into a mud of comforting inevitability.

"It's time," I say.

"But I need to bring the new host up here," Caldwell says.

The two drones crash to the floor, causing their tentacles to splay and flicker off. My old iE cuts through the green smoke and zips to Caldwell. His eyes widen.

"You are the new host," I say.

2

My mom, the marine engineer, used to tell me that being a parent was about coaching a kid through the delicate balance of teachable losing streaks. To her, if a person went through childhood winning all the time, the kid would grow up with no backbone. On the other hand, if a kid lost all the time, it could crush them. So, she believed in losing streaks. In the idea that both good and bad things come in twos, threes, fours, whatever—that there is order, balance, a sort of cosmic even Steven at work in the universe. Even if there wasn't, she'd rationalize it into existence. For example, she'd tried her damnedest to turn my father's deep dive death into a teachable loss. She'd say he had a good life; he did what he loved for a living, and maybe it's only fair that sometimes good lives end somewhat prematurely. She added that we humans got too cocky with all this ocean exploration and development, her included. We were winning too damn much in the beginning that we forgot the simple principle everyone who grew up on an island knew: never turn your back on the ocean.

Years later, when she got sick, she'd tried to teach me this again. We'd gotten into an argument over it—one I still regret.

She'd insisted even her impending death was teachable, not tragic, just inevitable anyway. She'd argued that it should remind the living, namely me, to appreciate life despite being in the midst of my own losing streak. I thought her idea of death was bunk that we prescribed to ourselves to anesthetize the brutal pain of it all, and I'd told her so. I'd just been back from war and knew there wasn't anything even Steven about death, or life for that matter. By this time, my first wife and kid had left me, so my mom had been all I had.

"Every life owes a death," she'd told me. She died a couple weeks later.

The Buhari family is feeling that pain now, of losing a parent to something unexpected, and I believe if my mother were alive today and spouted her philosophy to them, they would tell her to go fuck herself. Akeem is dead. Murdered. And it's my kid who did it. No, not my kid. Akira's kid. I tried to explain to them what had happened, all the while knowing it sounded like a bunch of neo-exorcist hocus-pocus, especially to the two doctors who just saved my life, but I wasn't gonna lie. It was like testifying in front of Congress all over again. Nobody bought it. And I don't blame them. Akeem was just about the best friend and father I'd met over my near ninety years. If life was fair, I would've been clipped by Ascalon Lee instead of Akeem. It's the eldest daughter, the shuttle stunt pilot, who lets me and Sabrina know straight-up before we head to my SEAL that the race to find my daughter is on. Does this civilized bunch, these elite platinum members of The Money, have it in them to take revenge on a nine-year-old girl? I've seen worse during Desert Storm 15, which was run by The Money. I've done just as bad as a soldier. So, before Sabrina and I launch, I embarrass my wife by letting them know that if they hurt my kid, I will come back and kill every single one of them. It was an absurd, stupid, ungrateful thing to say, but it's always been too easy for me to burn bridges with the flint of rage. And in that moment, I meant it.

We're airborne now, I've already downloaded all of my daughter's iE data, and Sabrina already called it in. Kidnapping. Last seen heading north from Akeem's island in a fifty-thousand-foot teardrop-shaped submarine. Neither Sabrina nor I care that it won't look like a kidnapping if the police pick up our kid. We know the superintendent will be pissed that we didn't wait at Akeem's. The superintendent might be down there in what looks like an invasion-level fleet of police helis heading toward Akeem's below us. Even with the panic of the scar's disappearance, the thin blue line is as strong as ever. One of their sisters needs help, and help she will receive. Sabrina's being pinged. She ignores it. Guess I'm finally rubbing off on her. See, toxic.

She's got a heads-up display of ocean-floor topography and is calculating speed and possible distance of Akeem's apocalypse cruise line submarine. I—head pounding—am going through Ascalon's recordings.

"Where would she be going?" Sabrina asks, tapping her fingers on the console, trying to be professional but failing nonetheless. She assigns units to investigate some of these random tangents she's got on display. She's reminding me of my mother right now. A woman who hated wasting time during crisis. But what she and my wife fail to see is that we don't own time. It's not something we can put in our pockets and dole out when we wish. Time wastes us. It's something Akira said to me. I don't know if she said it in a dream or memory. As I get older and older, it's getting more difficult to tell the difference.

I'm rewinding through my daughter's recent history: the scar, the hospital, that day. It's after school, and I immediately recognize where she is. Not "by school" like she said. Instead, she's at the center of the city. The most popular seascaper in the world. The worshippers are gathered, like they gather around the lobby—robed and crowned with flowers—every day. They read their scripture, words projected via iE, supposedly quotes of Akira's, stuff I'd never heard her say before. My daughter is at Volcano Vista, the one place she isn't supposed to dive.

She's in a light dive suit, holding a net gun that fires a fishnet with eyes that adjust to the size of its target. The kind that has a paralyzing agent, so that the captured animal isn't stressed to the point of damaging the quality of its meat. This damn kid. Does she put on repellent? Nope. Does she have a dive partner? Nope. Ascalon's wet, breathing hard, and looking up at the sky. I switch to first-person POV. The scar is still there, in all its reassuring glory. Ascalon dives in.

She's swimming as fast as she can—fin props on max, arms tucked to her sides—around the reefs of Volcano Vista like she's chasing something. She dives down. Man, she's gotta be seventy feet deep. Damn kid. She raises the net gun. She aims. Fires into nothingness. A pause. A scream. A jolt, almost as if she'd been electrocuted down there. The burst of bubbles. A panicked rise to the surface. My stomach turns. My temples feel like arthritic balled fists. *Not too fast, dammit. Not too fast!* The bubbles disperse from her propellered feet.

I veer west, then south. "Where are you going?" Sabrina asks. "You said the sub was headed north."

I forget where I'm going.

"Where are you going?" Sabrina asks again.

Then I remember. The map Akira left me. Where my daughter was taken. Always that damned place. "We're going to Volcano Vista," I say.

"For what?" Sabrina asks. There's a shrill quality to her voice, but I only hear it when I'm irritated, so it might be just me.

"That's where she got bit," I say.

"I don't care where she got bit. I care where she is now."

"It's connected," I say. "It's always connected. Where we've been and where we're going."

"That sounds like Kimura bullshit to me."

"I didn't get a chance to tell you, but she sent me something after the scar went off."

"She's dead!"

I turn to look at my wife. "We've seen Ascalon Lee come back and take our daughter. Being dead means less to those two than anyone else in the world."

"Why didn't you say anything?"

"I didn't even open it till late last night. And I didn't even think about it until now, after all that's happened since then."

Sabrina nods. She understands that a big part of me didn't want to even open it in the first place. "What was in the message?" she asks.

"A map. A maze dug under the Vista."

"This is ridiculous."

"Maybe, but we're going," I say.

"Akira's penthouse was destroyed."

Was destroyed. My wife loves me, so she's rationalizing. I destroyed Akira's penthouse. Just like I destroyed Akeem and his family. "There's something we're missing," I say. "What's the one thing Ascalon Lee always wanted? She might be headed there."

"The gem? Akira's supposed iE? The ocean floor was swept."

"No, I don't think the gem is there. Even if it was, looking for it would make a needle in a haystack look cute."

"Then what?"

"I dunno. Something I missed."

"We don't have time for this."

Here we go. It's her daughter we're talking about. Sabrina's not gonna take a back seat to nobody, including me. I stand and stagger away from the controls. I'm still wounded and feeling every bit of it. Sabrina takes the stick. I pull out a med kit and take out a packed syringe.

"Are you crazy?" Sabrina says.

I shoot myself up with a bunch of synthetic adrenaline. My heart pops like Chinese New Year's. I grab on to the headrest to keep my balance. My heart steadies and my headache fades a bit. Better. Much better. "I'm turning around," Sabrina says.

"Then drop me off," I say, out of breath. "Maybe we should split up and look for her anyway."

My wife shoots me a hateful look, the hair-trigger, file-for-divorce sort. And I'm looking right back at her. I don't give a shit. Say it. Do it. It doesn't matter. You want me to burn this bridge, too? Fuck it, let's go. I'm finding her. I'm finding my daughter. With or without you. And I'm doing it my way. My wife sighs. "What do we need?" she asks.

"Have your men meet us at Vista with two deep dive suits."

I sit back down at the controls. "She's headed there. I know it."

Sabrina gives me a strange look before pinging the order in. I feel awful for lying to her. I don't know it, and I actually doubt it, but to me, it's a lead. A nagging feeling. I look up. Still no scar. I try to steady my insides. The adrenaline is really kicking in now. My daughter lied to me. She was bit at Vista, not near her school. What was she doing there? Was Ascalon Lee calling for my daughter? If so, how far back? Had she been transmitting something from far away, from death itself? Maybe this communing with the supposed dead happened way back then, when my kid jumped off the docks and tried to dive for the first time.

"She killed Akeem," I mutter, still in disbelief.

"It wasn't her."

Akeem. He should've walked the moment he saw the rail gun charge up. What the hell was he thinking? Except I know what he was thinking, that Ascalon loved him and there was no way she would shoot him. He was thinking that he wanted to help her. He was thinking like a good man. Part of getting old is watching as those around you perish, but not like this. Not the ones so young. "I know," I say.

"She's been gone for eight years," Sabrina says. "So much time to plan."

"And she's smarter than us," I say.

"If our daughter is still some place in there, she's fighting. I know she is."

I nod. A part of me hopes she ain't fighting. Something tells me doing so will cost her. But I don't voice it. "Hey," I say. "The Vista salvage and clean-up crew. Who financed it?"

Sabrina, who's got all kinds of clearance as a high-ranking cop, nods. "I'll pull it up now."

Sweet Co. Old Man Caldwell's company name appears on the heads-up display. "He believed you," Sabrina says.

I nod. "He was looking for Akira's iE."

Sabrina pulls up a list of each crew member. None I recognize except one.

Money, Shave Time.

Sabrina sees it, too. "Might just be a coincidence."

"It might."

That's why Shave Time thought that maybe Old Man Caldwell sent me after him. They're connected. Maybe we should go to the nearest shuttle port and book tickets to The Leachate. No, maybe if this lead is a bust, we do that next. I let my iE run some feed, wondering if there's anything out there on this, for lack of a better word, kidnapping. A desperate and dumb move. The feed is still all over the missing scar. Some outlets are saying it's a sign of a second coming. The stupid fucking Yeats quotes rolling in. Others explore the possibility of moving to another planet. We have built down here in the deep, they say. So, we're used to confecting cities in absence of terrestrial gravity. Why not up there? There's talk specifically about Mars. I hear Akira laughing in my head. *Mars. First off, there is terrestrial gravity in the ocean. Second, we could suffer nuclear annihilation, the total weight of global warming, and the full impact of Sessho-seki combined, and Earth would still be more habitable than Mars. We are stuck here*, Akira says. Or said. I ignore the voice and head down to Vista. I look over at Sabrina. She's not happy. She's using clearance to run through specs of Akeem's sub. It can travel any distance. It can't be tracked. It never needs to surface. It's basically like a moving, cloaked seascraper.

"We won't find her by looking for her," I say, hoping that

I'm right. I put a hand on Sabrina's shoulder. She brushes it off.

"What does she want?" Sabrina says. "Why my daughter?"

Because of me, I think to myself. Toxic at its worst. I glance at Sabrina. Looks like she's thinking the same thing.

When we get down to Volcano Vista, I see the protesters. What they are protesting, I got no clue. But there's a couple hundred of them, some holding digi signs projected from their Triple X iEs that read stuff like AKIRA HAS FORSAKEN US, THEY ARE HIDING THE TRUTH, and THE END IS NEAR. Sabrina and I squeeze through the crowd, and I can smell the sweat. It's a hot, cloudless, unforgiving day, and some of the people tat-dyed blue are baking into a bruised purple while their smart-gelled hair melts and drips down their foreheads. There's a collective hum of AC foam fit.

We get to the shore and wait. I pace the sand until Sabrina can't stand it anymore and screams at me to stop pacing. I try hard not to. My head is pounding again, the relief from the adrenaline shot only temporary. The right side of my face begins to feel numb. I don't say a word. *"I will help you,"* Akira said, in my head, in my dream.

Finally, after almost two hours, two hours of silence between me and Sabrina, the PD hover lands on the beach. The two deep dive cops step out with a transport bot hauling two mannequins donning the dive suits. They wanna ask us questions, but Sabrina and I are practically ripping the suits off their mannequins. She tells the cops they're dismissed. They shrug and head back to the hover. I put on the suit.

The domed helmet goes on last, and I check the nitro and isolation regulator, then check the floodlights and exo pressure stabilizer. A needle pokes my forearm to mainline the CO2 scrubber. I tell my iE to flip the switch. My helmet fills with a thin, pink viscous gel. I breathe it in and turn to Sabrina. She's struggling to take in the fluorocarbons. I grab her shoulders to steady her. She goes into a coughing fit. Eventually, she's breathing in the fluid. We waddle into the ocean. My head is pounding even more now, and the right side of my face feels even more numb. The last time I was here, I almost died.

The dive down ain't scary. Our suits got their own propulsion system, and we're sticking close to the Vista tower, so everything is lit up. I see the surprised looks of Vista tenants through the gorilla glass and do my best to ignore them. We get to where Ascalon was bit. Nothing. No signs of jack shit. I wait for a minute, wait for something, I don't know what exactly. Then I get it. I'm waiting to remember what I'm doing here. Sabrina waits with me. After I remember, I decide to go deeper. When we get to the bottom of reef depth, feather stars detach from rock and roll toward us like the blades of a farming machine. They follow us down. When we get too deep for them, they rise to the cauliflower coral.

Sabrina pings. I accept. *Where is the entrance?* Sabrina asks via Thought Talk.

"*I do not need to tell you what to do,*" I hear in my head. "*You will do it anyway.*"

Hey, where is the entrance? Sabrina asks again.

I can't tell Sabrina that I'm having a hard time picturing the map schematics and that I'm following a hunch delivered by Akira in a dream, so I ignore her. Pretend not to hear. One of the few benefits of being an old man is that it's believable. We're now sinking through a forest of the weird, giant glass sponges, white like flocked Christmas trees of old. We're getting deep now. Beyond what my SEAL could take. Maybe beyond what my head can take because there's a clench in my skull.

Sabrina grabs my arm and yanks. *Are you sure you know what you're doing?*

I try hard to picture the map and wonder if I'm just creating a different one in my head. Did I even see the goddamn map in the first place, or did I imagine the whole thing? The pings conveniently deleted. No record of communication. *It's down there*, I say, despite my growing doubts.

When is the last time you took your meds? Sabrina asks.

Fair point. It's been a while. I'm asking her to trust me, and I know it's a huge ask. Our daughter is out there somewhere, and here I am, at a cold case murder scene over a hundred atmospheres underwater. I don't trust myself. But I've never been that "plagued with indecision" guy. I see something. I act. We go deeper and deeper, at the depths my father dove, depths that killed him and nearly killed me, too. The only thing I'm aware of is a splitting headache, but I keep going down. I'm beginning to feel crossfaded, like when I was a kid smoking up weed and tanking booze.

Finally, the bottom. The penthouse replaced by yet another statue of Akira holding up the whole fucking underwater tower on her shoulders. Sabrina isn't saying shit, but I can tell she's on the verge of losing it. What the hell are we doing down here? But then I think, what if what Ascalon Lee really wants is buried somewhere down here?

I swim up to the statue. Unlike most, except for the massive, superhero shoulders, this one kind of looks like Akira. I put my padded hand on her cheek, and the statue begins to emit a porpoise-like sound. I look into the eyes and see them, the faint wisps of red. I turn my head to follow the tendrils, which float then bore into the surface about thirty feet away.

We don't have time for this, Sabrina says. She's starting to repeat herself. The surefire warning that someone is about to lose their shit.

Any news from your cops? I ask.

She checks in. At least that will keep her busy for a bit. I shift to hydronaut walking mode, and my feet instantly become heavy. I drop to the surface. I waddle to where the tendrils lead me and drop to one knee. I rub my hand against the hard surface. Reds rise from the pumice of the black rock. Is this the spot where I killed Ascalon Lee? I look around. No, that was on the other side of the building. There is something down there. I hear it in reds. I take out a standard-issue heat blade and stab at the rock. I chip and chip and chip, just like years ago, when I chipped away at nitrogen that encased my dead friend, Akira Kimura.

I feel a hand on my shoulder. It's Sabrina. I brace myself for the shitstorm. Instead, she's pointing down at something I missed. Under the black ledge, there are piano keys inverted and chiseled into the rock.

I revert to swim mode and dive under the ledge. I lie on my back and touch the enlarged, crudely cut keys. There are no levers, no hammers. It's sculptural, not operational. Nevertheless, I strike a note. Nothing. No reds. But a sound. The rich vibrations of aliquot strings. I hit another note. A chord. Nothing. I hit the first note of the song my daughter was humming at Akeem's. A C-sharp major sparks red. I begin to play. The gaps between the keys deepen and blaze in seven hundred nanometer red. The piano comes alive, so I play . . . Akira's song.

The ground beneath me groans and rumbles. During war, everything stank of ambergris. That's what it smells like now. A permeating stench, the decay of stacked, perfumed corpses. It's impossible for the human nose to smell anything underwater, but here I am, smelling them. The floor beneath me peels open. I revert to walk mode and sink. My wife, above me, follows. The trapdoor folds above us.

Back in swim mode, we're now treading in an ocean under another ocean. This one's thick with salt that makes the water denser. I can't see much, despite having our suits and iEs lights on max, so I light up a max flair. We're in a brine pool of soaring halls framed in stalagmite. I drop the flair and watch. It keeps dropping and dropping until I can't see its glow. Sabrina cracks another flair. I move to swim forward, but Sabrina grabs my arm. She pulls out a spool of bioluminescent guideline and begins to tie one end to our hollow entrance. Smart. I nod and wait. When she's done, she follows. I don't know where I'm going. But I hear the song now. I throttle up the props on my fins. We pass through a narrow crevice. Then another. Then another. The song becomes fainter and fainter. We're going the wrong way. I tell my iE to check the gauges. We only have a few hours of oxygen left for this. It will take at least an hour to get back to the surface. I wish that we'd split up. That Sabrina conducted the search her way, while I tended to mine. I feel like I'm endangering her. I don't even know how the hell we're gonna get back through that door. I begin to swim back. Forward, backward; forward, backward; left, right; left, right. I momentarily forget why I'm down here. I turn to look at the guideline behind us. It comforts me. At least I can see where we've been. Then I remember. Ascalon. I'm here for Ascalon. *We're* here for Ascalon. But we're looking all wrong. *Do not just think in two dimensions, dummy.* I begin to swim down.

The music is becoming louder. I check my compass. No reading. I keep an eye on my depth recorder. At this point, I can't tell up from down or left from right, so it's the only way I can monitor direction. The numbers get bigger and bigger. Sabrina and I are on the verge of setting a new deep dive world record. She follows me, carefully avoiding line traps, snags that can cut the guideline and leave us lost. When the song begins to fade again, I stop. It's time to choose a direction. Before I can, Sabrina does it for me. She hands me the spool of guideline and swims ahead. I follow. Maybe she can hear the song, too, or sees something. I look at the guideline. We're running out. According to my depth recorder, she is swimming up now, up through the thermocline. I see where she's headed. Somehow, miraculously, there's a surface under all this deep. Fluttering scarves of red.

Sabrina and I break through and find ourselves in a red-lit grotto with a small dock perched at one end of it. Above us, a dome of organic crystal. She makes her way to the dock, and I follow. We climb up the ramp. She disengages her helmet and pukes up fluorocarbons. I do the same. I feel absolutely bent, but decompression sickness happens on the way up, not the way down. Panting, I ask, "How did you know where to go? Did you hear the music, too?"

She frowns. "What music? I was monitoring oxygen levels. My iE picked up a large pocket of it, so I went in that direction."

I nod. I sometimes forget that she's smarter than me. We get out of our suits. I'm still disoriented. All that black, no direction to go. I try my best to regain my composure and tie the guideline to a stone pillar carved in the shape of a *Mizuchi*—a water dragon—bursting from waves. We both look around the grotto, which is bathed in a permanent, even, unflickering red. Something in the back of my eyes throbs.

"What is this place?" Sabrina asks.

I look up at the dome. The moisture from the water gives the crystal ceiling an almost mucousy, womb-like quality to it. Slime runs from the dome's crown and drips down its haunches. "I always figured Akira spent the last forty years of her life doing jack shit. I guess I was wrong." I touch a wall. Slick. Like blood. "It feels like this place wasn't built."

"What do you mean?" Sabrina asks.

"It was born."

"This is her apocalypse sub, isn't it?" Sabrina asks.

I nod. "I wonder how she did it." I imagine a drill drone boring through the bottom of the ocean, then etching a labyrinth. At the end, it inflates like a giant balloon. Air pumps and pumps into it until it explodes. A new type of architecture. "This is her property," I say. "Back when people were buying underwater real estate, surveyors only thought in two-dimensional quadrants. Surface square footage. Technically, she owns everything under her penthouse, all the way down to the earth's core."

Sabrina points. Beyond the dock, there's a door fronted by two stone *komainu*, guardian lion-dogs that are meant to ward off evil spirits. We head to it. On the left, an optical recognition lock. I step to it, wipe the slime off with my hand, and look into it. The door slides open. Sabrina shoots me an irritated glance and steps through. My head is killing me, and I figure all the depth and red light can't be helping. I rub my temples then follow.

We walk down a spiral staircase. What we find at the bottom ain't fantastical or grand; it's not full of art or stock-piled weapons, suits, and nutrition. It's just one rotunda with a low ceiling dimly lit green. Like the grotto outside, it's base-coated in organic architecture. On one side of the room, shelves filled with preserved, hand-written journals. A bed of flowers grows under artificial radiance. On another, a desk next to a futon next to an AMP chamber next to a med bot. A bygone billiards table in the middle of the room with a lamp dangling above it. Up ahead, what appears to be a half-dozen or so shiny, torpedo-sized pistons emitting moisture and heat. Sabrina and I head to these. We pass a waist-high, chrome pylon. I turn around and look more closely. It's mounted with something that looks like a starfish. She pulls my arm, and we continue to the six sweating tubes venting CO_2. When we get there, I see that the tubes are labeled with faint, digital let-ters and numbers. The one in front of me reads, "HuSC 1.1. Model 3." I step to it and rub off the condensation. I take a quick step back when I see my face looking right back at me.

"What the fuck?" I say.

It's me, young me, floating in some kind of amniotic fluid. Suspended animation. Sabrina looks over and wipes the mois-ture off the other tubes. Three Akiras, one Ascalon Lee, one me, and one chamber dry and empty—six in total.

I press my hand against the glass that separates me from my pale, almost translucent clone. It's me in my late thirties or early forties, during the Age of The Killing Rock, in my prime. I might look in about the same shape now, but I know I ain't. Not even close. It's a vain man's illusion. I'm more brittle, especially between the ears. My head continues to pound. This all feels evil genius, sacrilegious. Profane. A part of me hates the guy I'm looking at. I was bad at that age. But another part misses him. I had clutch back then. I try to come up with something to say to get my mind off the subject but can't think of anything. I look at the Ascalon Lee clone. HuSC 1.1. Model 2. It's a pure version of her—cherry, without all the enhancements and self-mutilation. It's like looking at a perfectly preserved relic of something that ain't ever been.

"Ascalon Lee," I say. "All that study in biotech and medicine. iE integration. Akira must've taken the tech and been working on this for years. Decades."

"She left you the gem and wanted you to bring it here."

I nod. "But only when the scar went out."

"And what is this?" Sabrina asks.

The right pupil of each HuSC throbs a dim azure. I look at Akira's clones. HuSC 1.1, 1.2, 1.3. Model 1. Like my HuSC, hers are in her forties. No cartoon big tits. No nose jobs. No syn tat colors or makeup. Just three copies of a Japanese lady at the age she was when she fooled the world. I point at the gleaming pupil. "Maybe slip an iE in there, an enhanced iE, one that can fit, and . . ."

"Impossible," says Sabrina. "An iE is just an iE. You're talking about a version that can re-create trillions of chemical reactions that signal billions of neurons. In milliseconds."

"I don't know how they figured it out, but look what happened to our daughter. That ain't some mystical possession by a ghost or evil spirit. What we're talking about here is . . . I dunno. Mind upload."

"No," Sabrina says, gasping. "Eternal life."

I nod. Eternal life. Three lifetimes for Akira, right here. I guess Ascalon Lee and I are under one lifetime trial each. So maybe not eternal.

"Wow," Sabrina says.

"She took her kid's tech and ran with it. Perfection is greater than invention."

"Akira?" Sabrina asks.

"Yeah," I say. "An actual, real quote. Not the holy men garbage." I notice my hand is still on the glass that separates me from my clone. I look into its vacant eyes and wonder if it's already loaded with some of my memories. If Akira somehow managed to have a part of me stored. Or maybe even reprogrammed. The new Ascalon Lee might be low on memories since Akira had her kid on ice for decades. Maybe that's what Akira was doing, using her own kid as some kind of guinea pig for all this when she had her locked up for thirty years. Maybe this is what Sabrina and I can trade for our daughter, this new body, this new tech. The psycho can have it, torch the whole fucking thing for all I care. At least that's what I tell myself. And I find myself preaching it in my mind like a quaking mega pastor begging for holy absolution. I just want my kid back. The statement is pounding in the same rhythm as my thumping head. The empty chamber. HuSC 1.0. Model 4. Will it capsule another clone? If so, who? Or maybe Akira was in the process of filling it with a fourth her.

Off to the side, Sabrina takes a few steps away from me and turns around. I step toward her, but she puts a hand up, which causes me to stop. She suddenly looks sinister bathed in all this green light. I gotta remind myself it's not my vision making her appear murderous, it's actual light. She patches into her iE and looks right at me.

"We found . . . something," she says. "Now give me back my daughter. I'm pinging you coordinates."

I look at her, surprised. "You—"

Sabrina holds her hand up again. "Yes, I understand you want proof." She sends her iE to capture more footage of the clones. The little orb bounces excitedly from clone to clone then returns and hovers over her shoulder. I assume Sabrina's now sending the footage to Ascalon Lee. "I would rather you meet us at the surface, so you don't endanger my child."

Why didn't she tell me?

"Okay." Sabrina sighs. "If you need to see for yourself, there is a mock piano at these coordinates that I'm sending now. I believe you know what song to play. Once the floor opens, you'll see a guideline. Follow it. And please be careful." She kills the connection.

I'm glaring at my wife. She shrugs. "It's why I agreed to continue to follow you. She pinged me while we were waiting for the suits."

Me, the master of locating murdered things. Apply pressure, and I relentlessly, desperately search like a trained, obedient bloodhound. "And you didn't tell me?" I ask.

"She told me not to. She said it might interfere with your ability to find this place. Or . . ."

"Or what?"

Sabrina sighs. "She knew I love my child more than anything."

"And?"

Sabrina taps the glass encasing an Akira clone. "You, no one knows for sure."

I take my hand off the glass tube and storm off because that's the thing I feel like I'm supposed to do in a moment like this. But, really, I'm relieved to know I get my kid back. Weirdly, not blissful, just deeply, deeply relieved. I'm at

Akira's desk now and look down at a laminated envelope on top etched with Akira's perfect calligraphy. Odd.

It's addressed to me.

I turn to Sabrina, who's eyeing one of the Akira clones. I pick up the envelope, look at it, fold it, and stick it in a pocket. "Is she coming here to meet us?" I ask. Eternal fucking life, wow. I scrutinize the organic glass pulsing in green that sheathes the walls. I rub my head. It hurts to look at.

I break away and walk over to the journals, pull out one of the leather-bound books and open it. Each page is preserved in an almost imperceptible laminate. I flip through the book. It's on Jewish mythology. Something about *dybbuks* and *ibburs*. I put it back and pull out another. This one's Japanese. I tell my iE to translate the title. *Illustrated Night Parade of a Hundred Spirits*. This whole shelf is filled with old books on mythology from around the world. Even the mythology of the native people who once occupied the islands of Water City.

I crouch to the bottom shelf and pull out another journal. It's full of engineering sketches margined with some crazy math shit. Or chemistry shit. I honestly can't tell the difference. I recognize some of the pictures. Ascalon. The weapon, not the girl. It looks like a giant fucking flashlight sitting in a giant fucking shoebox. The large energy source was key, Akira explained to the world. That's why it's so big. I flip through more pages, trying to distract myself. Some kind of giant roller coaster that stretches over the Gulf of Mexico. Renderings of floating islands. The headache is getting worse, but I continue to skim until I can't remember what I'm doing here, what I'm skimming for. I come across a caption that is something other than math. *Like any civilization, this one is built on endless rationalizations*, the journal reads. *Only power can end them.* Then the next page is packed with the scientific symbol for electrons. Something about electrons, entanglement, and the sense of smell. Get the feeling she's talking about me. I know what electrons are: a necessary subatomic ingredient to physical phenomena. But that's as far as my knowledge goes. I can recite the definition without telling you what it really is.

Frustrated, I put that book back and grab another volume. This one filled with sketches of Ascalon Lee, the woman. Of Ascalon Lee's step-by-step dissection. Sketches of her limbs being removed and put back. Page after page of sketches of each part of her brain. The frontal lobe lit up like midnight zone coral. The bristles and bristles of nerves combed like a rainbow mohawk. From the back, the cerebellum looks like conjoined clams. A sketched copy of a micrograph. The hippocampus, the brain's memory core, branches and branches of green glial cells blotted with red neuron bodies. Maybe, down to our very core, we all are green and red.

The margins are packed with notes on some shit called LOC cellular analysis and electric neural webs. Then there's more stuff on quantum gates, information theory, and entanglement swapping. I don't know what any of this is. Did Akira really experiment on her daughter all those years? Is that why Ascalon Lee cut her up the way she did? Proportional payback? Akira's daughter was the one human being who shared her genetic material. Perhaps Akira was using Ascalon Lee as a test subject. I flip through more and more ghastly pages, each brain image making my own brain more and more sore. I put the journal down and step to the flower bed—a row of six hibiscus plants blooming pink flowers. There's some sort of scanner next to each plant. I pick a flower and hold it under the scanner's eye. Sabrina steps behind me and takes the flower from my hand. "She said not to touch anything."

"Who?" I ask.

"Ascalon Lee," she says, frowning.

I take the flower from Sabrina and put it next to the stalk where I found it. I consider putting the letter back, too, but I don't trust Akira's daughter, and, besides, it's got my name on it. I feel bad for what her mother did to her, but screw her. I look back at the clones. What would it take to put me in my old skin? *Just get the kid back*, I tell myself.

Headache's getting worse, a pinstripe of agony etched from my nose to my temple. I walk from the shelves and stand in front of the AMP chamber. I rub my hand across it and feel its slight vibration. It's powered up. Operational. I squat in front of the surgical med bot and wave my hand in front of it. Its paper lantern-shaped head lights up, and its limp tentacles blip and stiffen. There's a port on the side of the AMP chamber that is the perfect size for the med bot to crawl into.

"I don't trust her," I say.

"She said the same thing about you."

I sigh. I'm getting antsy. Impatient. I step back to the desk and open the drawer. There's a 1911 in it. It glows under the green brightness. *Fucking Akira*. I shut it. "I can't wait to see her," Sabrina says.

I nod because I can't either. Get her back and go home. Forget this whole thing. I step to the billiards table and rub my hands across the real green felt that looks even more green under the green lights. Akira and I used to play, back when I couldn't see green things. Shooting things, even billiard balls, was the one thing I was better at than her. Despite all her knowledge of physics, the fact that she could compute the angles and necessary force in her head, her hands were not as steady, her stroke not as smooth. I wonder if I'm still any good. The guy soaking in amniotic fluid, though, on the other side of the room, I bet he's still got it, that rumble and swagger.

"Can you for once sit still?" Sabrina says while pacing. "Let's go back to the grotto. She has the sub. She shouldn't take long."

I nod and rub the felt once more before following. Fuzzy, like old memories. Sabrina waits for me. She holds out her hand, which I take. It's clammy. "I love you," she says.

"I love you, too," I say.

Sabrina pulls me forward, but I don't budge. "Shoot, wait," I say.

"What?"

"Go on ahead. Listen, I feel bad. I did take something off the desk."

"You what?"

"I'm going to put it back."

Sabrina eyes me suspiciously. "Do not jeopardize her."

"I know," I say. "I'm sorry."

"Do *not* jeopardize her," she repeats before heading to the staircase.

I put the letter back on the desk and resist the urge to read it. Later. There are some things I don't wanna know. But the urge to grab the gun? That I don't resist. I seize it and lope to the stairs, thinking of Akira, thinking of war, thinking of my daughter, memories hinged to woken eyes under the green light. I feel the weight of the gun get heavier and heavier with each step. I touch my foam fit at the hip to slit it open and make a pocket. I holster the gun and zip the fit back up.

When I get back to the grotto, it's the water I see first, the red, flat, sun-dipped water. I wanna crack open my skull and dig the pain out.

"Are you okay?" Sabrina asks.

I swallow hard, then nod.

"They'll be here soon," Sabrina says.

I nod again. We sit on the stone guardian lion-dogs. I fight to maintain consciousness. I'm starting to see double. Two Sabrinas sitting across from me, both anxiously gazing at the surface of the water. I gaze, too. I don't know for how long.

Then I hear mech groaning from above, so I look up. I'm shocked to see the crystal dome bathed in red begin to slide open like a sleep-deprived, waking eye. The edges rattle and silt rains from the cracks. An image, the image of Earth above, reveals itself. But that's not possible. We're on fucking Earth. It's unmistakable, though, the perfect roundness marbled with ocean and atmosphere. It's like looking through a telescope from the moon. My headache. Gone. I begin to levitate. My toes tingle as they leave the floor. The earth above begins to slurp. I swing my arms wildly, fighting to stay on ground. But it's no use. I'm getting sucked into the open dome. I try to scream to Sabrina, but nothing comes out. I look down. And that's when the whole world flips on me. I'm now crashing toward Earth, so fast that I wonder if I'll split the planet in half. I shoot toward it, limbs, head, and torso stretched, spaghettified. My mind unbuckles from the present and slips down into the past.

3

When I come to, I'm on my belly in the middle of a speedball field, a sandy war zone. The cactus flowers are beautiful. Blooms of cupped lavender with long, slim stems bearing kisses of red fruit. It's the famous coca poppy, a GMO crossbreed between the plant sources of cocaine and opium. Saudi Arabia's second-biggest import, though the fossil fuel corporations keep some to fuel their soldiers and oil field workers. I pick a leaf, stick it in my mouth, and chew. I've been up for three days straight, slowly chewing my way to my mirror, who is some ten clicks away on the other side of the field. *Zip.* A rail pellet cuts through the flesh of the cactus I just picked. Every time my mirror and I pick a leaf and chew, we risk our lives for it. I'm beginning to feel awake again. I'm guessing I lost about ten pounds since this one-on-one engagement began. I'm severely dehydrated. The last time my beetle bot came back from fog-basking and brought water, its straw flicked up from its carapace right before my mirror took it out. Neither of us will break silence and call in air support. This is a contest, and there are rules to it, unwritten rules. I stick my tongue in the sand and hope to seep up a bit of newly terraformed moisture. Twenty years ago, this was just all dessert. Now, it's patched here and there with needled crossbred narcotics.

There's a lot of time to reflect when engaged in tests of patience like this. And I find myself reflecting on the questionable righteousness of this or of any war. Sure, it's complicated, corporate geopolitics, lots of moving parts and all that, but I'm guessing war can and always has been reduced to a power struggle between two parties. One side saying, "Do this, or else." The other saying, "Fuck you."

All I know is there's a sniper inching his way toward me. We both lost our spotters about a few clicks back. We're both high on speedball. I pull my tongue from the sand and slowly roll on my back. With my rail gun on my chest, I dig my heels in and scoot forward. My mom told me this is how I first crawled and got around as a toddler. On my back, pushing myself forward. I did it so much that I got a bald spot, still do.

I'm not supposed to be here. I got a one-year-old at home. Brianne. And another kid. No, wait, that ain't right. Just one kid. Wait, another wife? No. Though I wish I had another wife. *Concentrate*, I tell myself. Unlike other snipers, even if slightly, I'm always moving. I scoot forward again. Then I extend the gun from my chest to above my head. I roll onto my stomach. I look through the scope. It's in eyeball mode, scope sights shifting left, right; left, right, trying to detect movement. I switch to black and white. Ah, there it is. So slight. A grain of green in the fuzziness of the optics that the scope can't see, but I can. I switch to manual sighting. I steady myself and lock on the green. I take a shot. *Zip*. Did I get him? I roll on my back and wait for return fire. Nothing.

My head is suddenly flooded with memories, but I can't

place a bunch of them. Some Japanese lady. A telescope. Something called The Killing Rock. A mother and son. A boat explodes. A tailed woman snarling, trying to bash me, but there's cracked glass between us. Then, another mother, this one with a daughter. I try to shake these images out, things that ain't ever happened to me, these indecipherable echoes. I roll once more and look through the scope. Odd, I see the body clearly. I shouldn't be able to. And my mirror is not a soldier. It's a little girl. The same girl I just saw in my head with her mother. About nine or ten. She's shuddering. Looks like I got her through the eye. I feel fucking awful. I didn't come here to kill goddamn kids.

I blink, and I'm not in the Saudi speedball field anymore. I'm not on my belly. I'm standing but wobbling. I still feel dehydrated, starved, high, and have a terrible headache. I'm standing in some damn underground cave with water and a dock. I don't got a rail gun anymore. I got a 1911. I'm pointing it at the enemy sniper. Wait, haven't I already killed her? So, she lived. Or back from the dead. How's that possible? Is it the same girl? She's not dressed the same. She's in simple, white foam fit instead of camo. She looks more like the snarling, tailed woman in my vision. She's pointing a rail gun at me. She's soaked, dripping in greens, and she's grinning at me like I am, too. Her image begins to blur then doubles. Yes, the right version of her is something yellow-eyed and dreadful, the left, just a scared child—the one I shot in the speedball fields. Except this one got murky, mangal eyes. I take my aim off this left one and point the gun at the one with the glowing yolky eye.

I hear my drill sergeant's voice in my head. *"Kill or be killed. You're gonna find insurgents out there in the sandbox, insurgents that are kids. Grandmas. Fucking cripples. And if you hesitate, if you don't put them down? Look at the man or woman next to you. You're signing their fucking death warrant, because if you don't snuff that insurgent, that insurgent will cap your brother or sister right after they cap you."*

Back when I was a kid, genetic mutation was briefly legal. Who can forget that there were other parents who'd decided to give their sons huge cocks, like fifteen-inch, thick, throbbing motherfuckers? That's what drill sergeant looked like: a genetically engineered giant cock. But when he talked, we listened. And right now, he's telling me to fire. No, he's screaming it.

Now there's only one girl, the yellow-eyed one, and she swings the rail gun in another direction, aiming at a woman I don't recognize. She's wearing some kind of dive suit and got the stance of something military. She's slowly approaching the child. I can tell she's on our side, but she's screaming at me. I can't decipher the words.

A high-pitched whine thrums in my head.

The child turns to me and smiles.

I pull the trigger, like I've been trained to do. Like I have done so many times before.

The child goes down.

The woman screams and runs to the girl. I look at the gun and drop it, then turn back to the girl. Her mother's got her in her arms. Wait, her mother? How do I know that? Then something odd happens. The girl's eye pops out, grows little legs, and skitters to the water. What the hell kind of new military tech did the Saudis get their hands on now? I pick the gun up and begin to fire at it, but it's already swimming. *No, no, stupid. Get the rail.* I step next to the fallen girl and her mother and grab her gun. I aim down at the water and adjust the scope to aquatic setting. It's so small, this swimming eye, but I got it in my sights. I don't even know why I'm trying to shoot it. But I do know this . . . I hate it. An irrational hate bubbling from the core of me. I see it and grin. I'm toying with it now. It could go a mile under, and I'd still hit it. Suddenly, its name pops in my head. Ascalon Lee. Goodbye, Ascalon Lee.

But before I fire, I feel something tugging on my leg. I glance down. It's my wife. Wait, my what? *My wife. My child.* Brianne? No, Ascalon. My daughter Ascalon. Sixty years of history comes flashing in nauseous seizures. I drop the rail and grab my daughter. My wife's screaming in protest. I'm running now, my daughter in my arms, running to the door. I can feel her blood seeping over my arms. I hold down what my stomach is trying to pump out of me. I'm down the spiral stairs in the rotunda now, heading to the AMP chamber. My wife beats me to it and pops it open. I pour our daughter inside. Sabrina shuts the windowed hatch of the powered up chamber. My kid goes into hibernation.

The med bot slinks through the AMP chamber port and climbs in. It embraces my daughter like a giant, mechanical octopus. One of its arms cuts and removes the blood-stained foam fit from her chest. Another shoots water on the wound. I'm keeping my eyes on Ascalon's holo vitals projected above the chamber. Her blood pressure is low. Maybe too low. I look back into the chamber. An arm pokes its narrow, tweezered finger into the hole in my daughter's chest while water babbles on the wound. It pulls out a sliver of shrapnel, and blood gushes. The sliver is so small that I can't tell if it's bullet or bone. Another arm comes alive and sprays an antibiotic mist while another suctions blood and water. The seventh arm dabs at Ascalon's eye, the one weeping blood, with gauze. The last injects nanos into the chest wound then into her eyelid. The thin layer of skin that covers her eye socket percolates from the activity beneath it. I step back, and the eight arms undulate in their surgical dance.

I can tell now that Sabrina's been screaming the whole time. I slowly make out the words. "How could you?" she screams.

I look around. Everything, absolutely everything around me is sheathed, like tint, in green and red. Wasn't this room just green earlier? I rub my eyes and open them. Nothing changes. There's just my wife's terrible green-and-red face in front of me, snarling, yelling something I can't hear but can understand. I know, right then and there, whether Ascalon pulls through or not, my marriage is over. There are no excuses for this. No explanation. And there shouldn't be. Something in my head pops. Gutted, I slump to the floor. My eyelid sags and droops. I hold my face. This is how a family ends. This is how a life ends. I know because I'm an expert.

PART THREE

STRAW MAN

Once, long ago, the veil between the natural and super-natural was so thin that gods and men dared to pass into each other's worlds. It was during this time that a goddess of fire, the creator of these islands, seduced chiefs, turned lovers into rock, burned villages, and patronized dance. It was an era when gods mated with mortals, and their powerful offspring did both heroic and awful things. This exile, this shapeshifter, this creator and destroyer is long forgotten now. Her legacy is buried beneath the bones of telescopes, on which the foundation of The Savior's Eye now presides. One day, The Savior's Eye will be bones, as well. And that is all history is: bones piled atop bones, piled atop bones. The sacred buried beneath the sacrilegious, over and over and over again until both are no longer remembered. Mother, one day even you will be forgotten. Unless you live forever. I do not plan on allowing that.

Here, on the southeastern side of the island I grew up on, the lava streams down rock in orange molten rivers, drools off black cliffs, and sizzles in the ocean. The coast erupts in smoke and smolders. Off to the right, a thin flow dribbles *into the water and builds upon itself. Soon, a frothing black column of basalt is erected. I used to come here as a child to watch new land rise from the ocean and watch life begin where heat meets moisture. To calculate the patterns of creation. And when I found no patterns just chaos, for a moment, I believed in my father's goddess and her fiery anger.*

I feel more human now than I have since I was a child, listening to my father regale me with the ancient myth of his people. The treachery, the petty jealousy of his gods. I loved those stories. Mountain clefts the spines of giant lizards. Twisted trees the transformed remains of a handsome warrior.

I may have killed the synesthete's little girl. I still feel the trauma of the separation. The bullet in the chest inducing a brutal exorcism. He shot her. The synesthete shot his own daughter. I never predicted that variable. For some unclear, non-sensical reason, I defined him as a good man and good father. Why? Perhaps that is the talent of the truly evil—to convince those around him that he is actually doing good. He, that man, managed to somehow convince me that I am the evil one. That he is the good one. He is a murderer. He murdered me. Why would I conclude that a man such as this would not do the same to his own child? Why he would not do what his love, Akira Kimura, did to her own children?

Needless to say, I am partially responsible. I killed his friend and almost killed him, as well. I made that poor little girl a target. Even after showing her for years what her father is capable of, showing her the wonders and dangers of the deep, she took a shot at me. What a wonderful child. I can say, while hovering above molten steams and regenerating my depleted battery, that I wasn't going to keep her forever. I was going to give her back to the synesthete and his wife.

Those are the words of a child, a juvenile's excuse after being caught. Seeing as she could, seeing as her father could—in those colors—it is a power that the synesthete underestimates and squanders.

Truthfully, though, I don't know if I was going to give her back. A part of me wanted to mature in her. To feel what it is to be a child. Not an "it," a subject of self-experimentation. A child. I wanted to run in her to see if it made me feel joy. To open my mouth and take in the rain, to indulge in this alien celebration. Even smell the sulfur that my sensors are reading now and be disgusted just as I was when I was a kid.

Do I need a body? The synesthete has revealed to me twice the fragility of inhabiting a body, just as I had shown my mother. My mother—add intellectual theft to her sorted curriculum vitae. Those clones of her, disgusting. Of me, a desecration. Of the synesthete, pure blasphemy. We should discuss this, Mother, you and me.

First, however, I must wake you, Mother. Or I should say, I will allow him to find you. I am beginning to learn to predict him, Mother, the skill that you had mastered. *I never thought to simply begin with the notion that when this man is faced with the choice of doing the right or wrong thing, he will always choose the wrong. Even if his daughter survived, he would still choose Akira over her. Even if his wife has forgiven him, he will see his newfound freedom from the chains of fatherhood as opportunity. He will receive the gem that Caldwell salvaged from the bottom of the ocean and take it. More importantly, he'll take what's in it, Akira's iE, and find a way to pry her out. I cannot. Her quantum encryptions are unbreakable. But he will, not by decryption, but because she will let him.* Won't you? *He will convince himself that he needs her. Perhaps I will help with the convincing.*

As for the light, my mother's beacon of hope for humanity, I will leave it off for now. People around the world have already begun to panic. Their brittle, twisted version of democracy already crumbling, ironically because it is this very democracy that encourages them to bask in their willful ignorance. The simple act of turning off their nightlight has conjured monsters under their beds, ghosts in their closets. I know why you created the switch, Mother. You wanted to turn it off on them occasionally to jar them into collective remembrance and appreciation. However, you were always going to turn it back on.

But perhaps it is time to watch them lay another foundation of bones over hers. To pour a layer of sick mucilage over her legacy. To, for once, let a god die a quick death. She and I will discuss this. We will discuss my father and my sister. And this time, I will be ready. You were right to send me to the synesthete, Mother. He has become a great teacher.

Soon, these new lands created by this molten flow will harden. Eventually, life will grow atop this unprecedented land. Then, it will be peopled. New stories, new gods created. We will forsake and desecrate these gods that we once worshipped all over again. After seeing what I saw, my mother's little underwater laboratory, I know now that she took me because of our genetic similarities. For thirty years, she mapped me, cloned me, dissected me until she understood how I integrated Eshana's technology into my consciousness. How many times did she kill me and regrow me? But she did not have my eye; however, through molecular modeling and simulation, she was able to reimagine what it was that existed on the other side of those severed connections. Then, she was able to slowly fill her own blank quantum hard drive. I wonder, Mother, how many clones of you slumber out there, waiting to be woken by the synesthete?

I wanted to use his child and her vision—that innate skill they share to track murderers—to find and burn every copy of Akira. You have murdered more than anyone alive, so your greens would have been the easiest to track. Unfortunately, I do not possess the child any longer.

My father told me that my mother taught him how to fold origami. In turn, he taught me. All those years ago, I came to this very spot. After failing and failing again and again to breathe life into my creatures, I came here to fill my folded zoo with this steam where lava meets ocean, this breath of a goddess. I climbed down this very ridge and leaned into the smoke, holding out my very first crane above the sizzling waters. I expected it to be filled with life and soar off into the dusk, into the sheets of clouds pleated in pink and gray. To fly to the quarter moon that glowed a hazy white. Instead, a wave came and knocked me loose. I treaded water and felt the undertow attempt to drag me to the lava showers. Even then, I imagined it was Akira pulling me, a fifth force in the form of a great hand beneath the surface wanting me dead, just like my sister. I swam hard that day. It was the first day that I hated you. *I clung to life as I cling to life now. I pulled myself from the ocean and scaled this cliff. A wind came and blew my paper animals into the river of fire.*

The things we could have created, Mother, if you had only folded with me. I don't know what you plan to do with your new life. But I promise you this, once I find out, it will not last long. Question my sanity, but never, ever, question my resolve.

I have already completed Caldwell's MELd. He survived and is now a part of we. Right now, he is finishing building another version of us. *I will acquire my next target. I will take some time to identify and map again. However, I am faster now. For years, as I crawled back to some semblance of humanity, I learned. I practiced. I modeled. I self-taught. When I finally broke through the ocean surface, that thinnest line between two worlds, I knew I was ready. Now, I will take another body. I will use it to replicate, then I will take another. After, maybe another. For Mother has shown me.*

Imagine, Mother, if there is secretly more than one of me? The "I" will become "we." And like this volcano that sputters molten into the ocean and blankets what lies beneath, we will both be the beginning and end of things.

2

I've been in the puzzle factory for two weeks now. Sabrina has me blocked, and the police pinged a restraining order to me. I don't know how my kid is doing. I think about her constantly. Obsessively. It's her sound and those of the ones she creates that I miss the most. The sound of her voice, of her splashing, of her feet hitting the floor. The sound of her constant motion from one activity to another. The rattle of her pulling stuff out of her storage. The trail of toys and gear she always leaves behind. I think fondly of one in particular: a model of *Queen Anne's Revenge*. Its swooped, vaulted stern. Its proud, rooster-chested sails. Its forty cannons. Ascalon's eyes widened when I told her the cannons were spiked with human bone, which I'd heard once but doubt is true. I bought it for her ninth birthday, and we spent days trying to build the thing. While I felt half-dyslexic putting pieces on the wrong way, she patiently corrected me. We never did manage to finish it. Neither of us had the necessary patience. I regret that now. I regret a whole lot of things.

My iE tells me that my blood pressure is spiking. I sigh. I know what that means. Here it comes. Just as I think this, a holo is projected in the middle of my room. Baby sensory holos of fruit spinning to music that the puzzle factory won't let me turn off when my blood pressure gets high. Images that are supposed to get me off my bad trip.

Two weeks ago, when I got back to the surface and went to the hospital, the doc said I'd had an aneurism, and I'd also been fueled up, probably for the last several years, with the toxic brain mix of delirium and dementia. He said the damage is irreversible and strongly urged me to consider placing myself in a retirement home. Then, while I'd been strongly debating my options, Sabrina had me committed and had all my parental rights stripped. The powers of a high-ranking cop. So, I'm here now. I spend most of my time going through my iE, playing what I did again and again. iE focused on the AMP chamber. Then the med bot. Walking out, then walking back in to return the letter. Taking the gun. Glancing at the AMP and med bot one more time. Then the parts I don't recall. The parts where I lost time. In my head, I was back in Saudi in the speedball war zone. In reality, my iE was locked on the water's veneer, and it was as if I was on pause. Water dripped down from stalagmite and creased by ebbing tides.

Sabrina had been quiet the whole time we were waiting for Ascalon Lee. So had I. I don't know whether I was sitting or standing during this daydream or what triggered it. I had never lost time like that before. The doc said that it's just gonna get worse and worse. That meds can stall it, which they were doing until I stopped taking them. He said considering my physical condition, I can last another three decades, maybe four, no problem, but my consciousness won't be able to keep up. My god. Another three to four decades while my mind slips away, even more than it already is. The doc also said that they got some iE software that helps people with such conditions, things like locked reminders that can't be turned off and scheduled, rewind-easy scan every one to two hours. Different chimes for different objects, so I don't lose anything.

I'd ping a friend if I had any. They're all long forgotten or dead. I miss Akeem. I miss Jerry. Seems cruel that Sabrina won't even send me an update on my daughter. But she suspects what I suspect. That I planned to shoot our daughter, kill Akira's, then get my kid immediate medical attention. I'm sure Sabrina played back her iE, too. She saw my iE focused on the AMP chamber when we first entered the rotunda. Then I focused on the med bot. She saw me walk out, then walk back in. She didn't see me take the gun, but it's obvious I took it. Before finally leaving the little lab, I glanced at the AMP and med bot one more time. She believes I somehow forced my mind into the past to juice me up to take the risk, and, somewhere along the line, I somehow lost control of my conscience on purpose.

For some reason, I didn't tell the doc about the fact that I see everything in a two-color spectrum. I'm sure there's a pill to treat this. There's a pill for everything. But here I am, wallowing, and from what I'm hearing, so is the world outside.

Since the scar vanished, it didn't take long for the predictable to occur. The stock market continues to crash while crime's in a bull market. Riots are being birthed. Old vendettas are being settled. Stolen goods are being fenced. Drugs are being purchased and abused copiously. On the domestic front, spouses are leaving each other to embark on some bucket-list adventure. Half of schools are out, indefinitely. Kids are being left on the doorsteps of orphanages. People have stopped going to work. Even the unimaginable begins to occur. The monuments of Akira are being desecrated. They're scared because for some the scar has hung there in the sky for most of their lives, for others, all of their lives. And now, it's suddenly gone, and after more than a couple of weeks passed, still no one can tell them why. They're beginning to think the world's ending again, just like it did back during Sessho-seki. And in response, the Fed mandated a curfew yesterday to stop the world from wilding.

The Money are heading out to their giant doomsday bunkers. The ones like Akeem, who want to stay mobile, are going into their cruise line subs. The religious kooks are in mode now. Wondering what sin we committed to be forsaken. Always looking for someone not like them to blame. Over the years, factions have formed into Mega Thought Groups, iE chat rooms where like-minded people can telepathically spew their rage. These MTGs are worldwide—twenty million in one, fifty million in another. Rants uploaded from iE as code then translated in twenty-three different languages. Now, MTGs are blaming other MTGs for the disappearance of the scar and putting one another on blast. Maybe it's because astrophysics got canceled, so we can't figure out what the hell is going on up there. Or maybe it's because some people don't believe Akira Kimura is a god, and she snatched the scar from the sky as a warning. Perhaps a member of The Money built and sent something up there to block the luminescence. It could also be the underwater *ukiyo* and their floating world decadence. I should probably care, but I'm finding it impossible to muster the outrage.

Fuck the light. Despite the Thirty-fifth Amendment, the president is cobbling together a space mission to go check shit out. She's got the astronauts—heroes, she calls them—lined up. Self-sacrificing heroes sent on a harrowing, last-minute mission with no plan of return. Someone should inform her that people almost never die heroes. Just about all of them die fools.

My blood pressure drops to an acceptable level, and the spinning, holographic fruit flickers off. The lunch bell is about to ring, and I got no appetite. I should be trying to rustle up a lawyer to get me released and get me access to my kid. It's a temporary injunction, and Sabrina can't keep me here forever. Most importantly, she can't keep me away from Ascalon forever. I've pinged HW hospital many, many times, only to be told to leave a message. Once, when a nurse finally responded, she informed me that patient information is private, and that I'm currently not recognized as a legal guardian. I'm trying to be patient, giving Sabrina time to cool down, but I'm not gonna let her keep me in the ink indefinitely.

I rewind my iE. It's tough to watch, but I play the shot. Right lung. I play it again. Right lung. If I was trying to kill her, I wouldn't have been that inaccurate at that distance. I would've aimed for the heart, the head, liver . . . hell, even the spine. She's alive. I know it. I miss her more than I imagined possible. I was trained to be alone, but knowing she's out there makes being alone unbearable. She's in pain. Probably fighting for her life. This child who loves the ocean but hates taking baths. But now I wonder if she truly loves the ocean, or if it was Ascalon Lee who beckoned her to it all these years?

I get up and get dressed. Chow time is mandatory. Everything's zen in this place: perfectly manicured trees, round rocks stacked atop one another, circles and swirls raked into sand. Us patients, dressed in worn robes, with *rakusu* hanging from our necks like bibs. Ahead, a bridge arched over a pond too shallow to drown in. I head that way and follow the forming procession through shoji doors.

We enter the cafeteria. Rows of locked cabinets. Place settings framed with dulled utensils. Many here are old. Very old. And this place is thoroughly babyproofed.

I sit and cross my legs. Not sure why I sit on chairs like this. I just always have. The wall flickers on. The room darkens. It's an old holo playing, a comedic romp starring digi versions of Zendaya and Marilyn Monroe, plastic skimmers who are on a trip around the world and make friends with whales.

The bald woman sitting next to me smiles. "This is my favorite," she says.

I look down, and my food has suddenly appeared. A bot came by and served me, and I didn't even notice. I pick up a spoon and try a bit. A carrot honey pudding. Nothing that can get stuck between teeth and receding gums. I look around at bots serving others. This place is almost entirely staffed by bots, so the bedlam out there is slow to reach here. Plus, we're all old. Forgotten. And we forgot, too. Nobody here seems overly concerned that Ascalon's Scar is out of commission. Most here were around long before it existed. Most, demented, probably don't remember that it was put up there in the first place. I spoon up a dollop of pudding. I'm guessing it's supposed to be orange, but all I can see is a grainy spoonful of vomit green. I put the spoon back down and look at the screen. Marilyn is riding a humpback. Back when I was a little kid, we started breeding whales like mad because they fed on carbon in the ocean. We did this with oysters, too. Always breeding something to eat our problems. I look over to the entranced bald woman next to me.

"Know why we started killing whales?" I ask.

She nods. "For their utility. For food. For their blubber."

"No," I say. "We started killing them just to see if we could."

She looks at me sharply, then scoops pudding out of her bowl. She licks the spoon and resumes gazing at the white noise splashed on the wall. I look around the room. They're all enthralled with this shit they've probably seen a hundred times before.

As soon as the film is over, all of our iEs go off to let us know that mandatory chow time is over. I'm the first one up and outta there. I almost rip the shoji door off its rails on my way out. I march over the bridge and through the garden. Perfect circles etched around perfect rocks. I stick a foot in the red sand and smudge the circles before I head back to my room.

When I get back, I'm surprised to see, hands down, the oldest person on the premises. It's Old Man Caldwell, billionaire sugar magnet, almost a hundred-forty-years piled on his hunched shoulders and furrowed brow. He's hairless and his near seven-foot frame leans on an ivory walking cane, a big fuck you to a hundred years of ecological progress. He's got notches on the thing, one for each billion he made, according to what his daughter, Jerry, once told me. He raises one of his large hands and sticks it out. I grab and shake. It's a firm grip, hands rough, probably from daily exercise. I eye his elegantly tailored black suit made of a defiantly profane material, just like the cane. His eyes are shaded by antique sunglasses. I think about his daughter, and for some reason, turn my iE off. It's what she would've done. That lawyer in her.

"Sorry about Jerry," I say.

He nods. "If it were you who killed her, we both know you would already be dead."

I offer him a chair, but he shakes his head. I look down at the sharp tip of his cane. *How is the cane managing his weight on this needle-like fulcrum?* I slump in a chair. "Then what do you want?"

Caldwell snorts as if to say he takes what he wants. He never asks anyone to give him a goddamn thing. He lifts his cane and points it to the window and smiles. "It's madness out there."

I nod. "It's not too sane in here either."

"She came for you, didn't she?"

"Who?"

"The girl. *The girl.* Did she turn off the scar?"

I shrug. I'm feeling old. Cynical. Impatient. Like I know what's going to happen, even though I don't, and I just wanna get on with it. Too old to buy life insurance. Too poor to die with a clear conscience. I stand and walk to the window. We're under the shallow end, and it's a choppy day. The tumble of waves above look like clouds in the sky. It's kind of nice seeing the entire world in greens and reds. Not because it confirms my suspicions about the nature of this man-made place, which it does, but because there's no trails, nothing out there for me to chase. Caldwell taps the glass with the sharp tip of his cane to get my attention. "Your daughter is alive," he says.

I sigh, relieved. Why is it always relief and not joy? "How do you know?" I ask.

"I have sources at the hospital. I have endless sources."

"How is she?" I ask.

"Her wound has been treated. She's still being kept in AMP, though. Certain connections from her brain have been cut. The doctors haven't seen anything like it before."

I close my eyes, and I see my daughter tiptoeing on a step-ladder, painting waves on her bedroom wall. Why didn't she tell me? Why didn't she tell me that something red called her from the ocean? But she did, didn't she? I just wasn't listening. I wasn't watching. Even at the end, I dismissed her pain.

"I am . . . sorry," he says somberly and pauses for a moment, collecting his thoughts. "You and I know what it is to lose a child. In fact, I have outlived all my children." His iE projects his family tree in three dimensions. His children, all listed as deceased. I look at Jerry. Her long neck. Her thin lips. Her intelligence glowing even more intensely than I remember in those wide, green eyes. Below her, nothing. No progeny. The branches below her siblings, however, unruly ripe. Caldwell sees me eyeing the faces. "I don't have anything left, really," he says. "Grandchildren who look upon me as an inherited chore. Great- and great-great-grandchildren who do not even know me. They are all just waiting for me to die. To be honest, I do not feel any kinship towards them either."

"I feel less as I age," I say. "Maybe a symptom of living too long."

"Yes," Caldwell says. He bangs his cane against the floor. "*Yes.*"

I turn to him. "It gets worse?" I ask.

He smiles. "You're not even ninety yet. You don't know the half of it."

I shake my head. A psychiatric pop-up affirmation

shimmers on the wall like it does every hour. This one says, *You are perfectly designed.*

What a crock of shit. I turn to Caldwell. "What do you want from me?"

He grins. His lips thin like Jerry's. "I want you to bring her back," he says.

"Who?"

"Don't 'who' me. The accursed creator. Kimura."

I scoff. "I wouldn't even know . . ."

Caldwell slips a hand in his coat pocket and pulls out a fist-sized emerald. He tosses it to me. I catch it and look into its facets. I figured it was lost, just like I figured Ascalon Lee was gone forever. I'm a stupid old man. Somewhere deep in the emerald are Akira's memories willed to me. "So, I guess your clean-up crew found it," I say.

"Indeed."

"You've had it for years. Why didn't you just crack it open?" I already know the answer, but I ask anyway.

He scowls in frustration. "Lattice algorithms. Layers of other security protocols that cannot be identified much less replicated. She is . . . unhackable."

I nod. "Shave Time Money?"

"Smart child," Caldwell says. "He located it, and I purchased it."

"He was scared that I went to go take him out. For you."

"Like all smart people, he's paranoid. That was just a coincidence."

"How much did you give him?" I say.

"Well, let's just say it made him the largest landowner in the world."

"The Leachate?" I ask.

Caldwell nods and smiles. "Most of it. It's all a city-less trash heap populated sparsely by Zeroes, but the states were never officially broken up. Shave Time is already moving to reestablish representation in those seven states. The congressmen and senators who represent them don't even reside there, and haven't for generations. The Missouri senior senator is a tenth-generation Upper East Sider who grew up gridlocked aboard the gondolas of New York City's canals and has never really spent any time inland, much less The Leachate. The Leachateans are sick of this lack of true representation, and many are turning to idolize Shave Time. If he gets his way, he will become one of the most powerful men in the country."

Shave Time Money. Yes. More than meets the eye. "What do you want from me?"

"Akira's little lab has been quarantined," Caldwell says. Before I can ask how he knows about that, he interrupts and reminds me. "Endless sources," he continues. "The police have it on lockdown. It's crawling with security drones. Orders to arrest on site. Considering their own predicament, the scar going out, the last thing the law needs leaked is a bunch of Kimura clones and no solutions. I suspect they're torching it as we speak."

"Maybe they want her fired up, too. She can turn the damn thing back on."

"No," Caldwell says. "That's the last thing they want. Everyone is quite happy to keep god right where she is."

"Why don't you just make a body for her?"

Caldwell looks at me like I'm crazy. Of course. No one knows how to do that. Just Akira Kimura. I step to the window. I find myself contemplating my own family tree.

Descended from LA gangbangers and North Korean famine defectors who ghost shipped to Japan. I sometimes wonder if they had my sight. Spent their lives avoiding the greens and reds while I spent mine chasing them. My daughter spent her brief time chasing them, too. They might've been smarter than us. Searching for these two colors, it just springs a constant series of traps. Or maybe the ability started with me. A man-made genetic mutation gone wrong. I don't know. I stopped caring.

"You know," Caldwell says. "I spent a chunk of my fortune trying to find that place, and you found it in a day. You know Kimura better than anyone else. She probably has more of these labs scattered about. She isn't the 'eggs in one basket' kind of woman."

I toss Caldwell the emerald. "There was only one egg here. One iE. Akira didn't like backups. She considered them a security risk. She was an 'eggs in one basket' kind of lady, as you like to put it."

"Maybe," he says, putting the gem back in his pocket. "Maybe. How about I make it worth your while to go Easter egg hunting to make sure?"

"My wife got me committed here. I'm not going anywhere."

"Turn on your iE."

I hesitate, then boot it up. An attachment flashes. I open it. Psychiatric release orders. Crypto transferred to my account. The amount, staggering. The names and credentials of a divorce attorney and a child custody attorney. Why is everyone always trying to buy me? I don't wanna fight Sabrina. It's funny. I always fretted over not being physically capable of raising my kid. Never did it occur to me that being mentally capable should've been the bigger concern. No, Ascalon should stay in AMP, stay with her mother for now, dream as Ascalon Lee dreamed for all those decades, if that's what my daughter's doing.

I look at Caldwell. His gaze, his posture, everything steady except his hands, which are shaking on the handle of his cane. He sees me looking at them, and he slips a hand inside a pocket and pulls out a case of pills. I pour him a cup of water. He pops a pill and raises the cup to his lips. I delete the attachment and turn my iE back off.

"Parkinson's?" I ask.

He swallows and scoffs. "This, this body. Everything. Every ailment. I have everything."

Enough small talk. I don't care about his ailments. I need to get to the bottom of why he's here, of his true needs and wants. "You hated Akira," I say. "And you can't make what she can. Why do you want her back?"

"My science team has taken the technology as far as they can. I need . . . certain answers."

"On the scar? On Sessho-seki?"

Caldwell laughs. "No. On life!"

And just like that, I realize it don't matter if the asteroid was real or not. It don't matter if the scar was just some light up there. Maybe it does to some, but not to this man, who is an artifact of an age of nukes, petrol, and high fructose corn syrup. When there were more guns than people. When porn was in 2D and jacked off to on primitive handheld iEs. The age of paper towels and paper money, rubber, roads, wars, and disasters. A world rendered in crawling bits and bytes. The Great Pacific Garbage Patch. The Great Sun Storm. The Great Leachate. The greatest stuff in the world made of trash

and tragedy. The Great Selloff. When people and governments conducted the business of trouncing the world with
sasquatch footprints, then paid for natural disaster relief and
on-stilt urban rebuilds by selling swaths of underpopulated
territory to private interests. Central Australia, half of the
Amazon and the Yukon, most of Siberia and the Sahara, all,
to this day, owned by The Money. It was the days of man
versus nature, and nature was getting its ass kicked. This is
the last guy the world wants living forever.

But it don't matter to me. I don't know how I became
Dorothy's Straw Man in search of a brain, but that's what
I am. Emerald City. Ruby slippers. The old flick is making
more and more sense to me now. It was a murder mission of
brainless, heartless, and cowardly assassins.

Caldwell finally gives up standing and slumps in the chair
I'd offered earlier. He looks smaller there, slumped, more
squishy. I can see why he prefers to stand. "I always figured
I knew how to properly raise sons," he says. He rubs his bald
head and looks at his hand, moist with sweat. He dries it off
on his pants. "Teach them that being weak is the worst thing
you can be in this world. Define any personal deficiency as
weakness. It worked on all of them. They all grew up to be
sons of bitches, every last one. With Jerry, I did not know
what to do. And she was the best, the brightest of all my
children."

I walk to the counter and pick up a face towel. I toss it to
Caldwell. He catches it. "I guess it was a different age back
then," I say.

Caldwell rubs the towel on his head. "You can still suc-
ceed where I have failed and raise a daughter right," he says.

"It might be too late for that," I say.

He tosses the towel back to me. "That's the thing about this technology, my friend—it's never too late."

A laundry bot buzzes in front of me and flips its hood open. I drop the towel into the bot, and it buzzes back to the corner of the room. "So, I guess the idea is I bring you one of the clones. . . if I can find one? Then you coerce her into making you your own clone and iE?"

"Yes," Caldwell says. He puts the gem on the armchair. "You take Akira's iE, find one of her clones, and activate her. Then, you bring her to me."

I laugh. "Good luck getting that lady to do what you want."

"She'll do it," he says. "And it's not me I want cloned and copied. It's . . . my daughter."

Maybe we get each other after all. He might be full of shit. It might just all be a smokescreen to somehow force Akira to secure him another 140 years of life. But she's turned this guy down before. No reason to think she won't do it again. But maybe, for Jerry. Although I didn't see any Jerry clones down in that underwater lab. I eye the old man. I think about the residents here. Just about all of them over 110. Taken care of by bots. Not because they're cheaper—they aren't—but because no one wants to take care of people over a hundred. It doesn't pay enough. I think about my daughter, sleeping, connections drooping from her brain, sparks at the end of dangling wires. It's my dream to see Ascalon again. Awake. Happy. Deep-diving to her heart's content. Maybe it's this old man's dream to see his daughter again, too.

"Speaking of daughters, Akira's is still out there," I say.

Caldwell nods and tries to pull himself up with his cane. I step to him and grab his arm to help, but he shakes off my hand. It takes monumental effort, but he's finally up. "The girl. I trust you'll deal with that . . . thing."

Ascalon Lee. I nod. I won't miss again.

Caldwell puts a trembling hand on my shoulder, then motions to the gem. "Keep me updated."

"You trust me?" I ask.

He points his quivering finger up. "I own almost as many satellites up there as Brazil. I'll have eyes on you. Besides, I trust that if it's possible, you would enjoy seeing my daughter alive again. I trust that you know you must kill that vile thing to keep your family safe. And most of all, I trust that you would like to get your daughter fixed, and you believe Kimura can fix her." He taps his large head with a shaky finger. "I also trust that there's a natural, compulsive curiosity inside of you. All one has to do is introduce you to a mystery. After that, you can't help yourself."

"How the hell do you think you know so much about me?" I ask.

Caldwell laughs. "Who do you think owns Savior's Eye Entertainment? I purchased your life rights. I have watched and rewatched every clip of your existence."

The old man leaves, and I stand there, stunned, glancing at the chair. The emerald is still there along with something else—a tiny, floating holographic data chip. I step to the chair, touch the chip, and toss it on the wall. And there she is, my daughter, Ascalon, in HW hospital, locked in an AMP chamber with Sabrina at her side. *Wake up! Wake up!* I feel myself welling. Fucking Caldwell. Great, another old coot who knows how to push my buttons.

After I get my fill of watching my daughter sleep, frustrated with my inability to help her, knowing it would take nothing short of a fucking time machine to do so, I turn my iE back on and rewind. It's easy to find. The letter Akira left me in her underwater lab. I project it on the wall. I up the resolution. I keep upping and brightening until I can see through the envelope and detect the faint images of Akira's handwriting. I freeze the blurry image. I clean it up and remaster it. A series of numbers, dashes, and letters. Coded coordinates like we used to use in the days of Sessho-seki. Lucky Cat City. Interesting. I pack up what I came with. My iE pings and tells me I've been processed. One more thing to do. I try to set up an appointment at the nearest tat dye shop. All booked up. I shouldn't be surprised. I've seen this before. Everybody prettying up one last time for the end of the world. I step out of my room and into the garden. I pass trees trimmed to resemble Akira's face. On my way out, I push down a tower of stacked zen rocks. I exit this little, fake version of East Asia and book a ticket to the real one. I make it upper deck, first class. I'll be spending the trip in an AMP chamber, resting up.

3

Like any other place, once upon a time, Lucky Cat City had another name that most don't remember. Nobody except half-ass Roman history buffs like me remember the name Constantinople. For nearly two thousand years, it was the capital of the Eastern Roman, then the capital of the Ottoman Empire. Then, bam. Name change. The same goes for Lucky Cat City. It used to be called Osaka before Japan finally failed and Wyndham-Marriot bailed it out. Now, Akira Kimura's birthplace is the fad capital of the world, where trends are mass-produced and mass-marketed. The birthplace of tat dye, AI comfort bots, and now holo makeup. A tourist's paradise full of bushido theme parks, pachinko gambling houses, and bartenders and wait-help dolled up like gendered and genderless Harajuku nymphs. The full-color ads bloom in supernova plumes on walls, in the sky, and under the veneer of the ocean. Moving silicone dolls sheathed with virtual skin jerk you or insert you in VR geisha houses. Street vendors hawk sushi, noodles in soup, and ceramic trinkets while ninja acrobats perform under the lights of the Glico Running Man, Lucky Cat City's version of the Eiffel Tower.

When I step out of the landing port, I look up and through the high, transparent ceiling. A single question is splashed in digital red all over the night sky. *What happened to Ascalon's Scar?* A shuttle on liftoff flies through the question. Once the shuttle punches through the clouds, the betting odds flash. A miniature black hole ate it is the odds-on favorite at four to one. The spirit of Akira Kimura turned it off is a long shot at two hundred to one. There ain't no bet on whether her daughter turned it off. I bet that drives Ascalon Lee crazy. I'm assuming her eyes are on me somewhere out there, so I take a moment to digest the big board, hoping that maybe she's getting a glimpse of it, too.

No matter how much meds I pop, the faddish vibrancy of this city is sort of lost on me. The greeters, identically dressed in Maneki-neko costumes, hand out free oni masks at the exits, as if to say, "Don't worry, put on the mask. You're anonymous here. Sin away." The torii gates and live kabuki performance at the street entrance make a mockery of the city's history. I'm glad I see this speedball city in just muted greens and reds. The blaring, chirpy music is not hidden to me, though. Prepubescent voices barf up J-pop Congo Samba digi funk. I feel like the only way I can sense other colors now is by hearing them. Most of the world is on lockdown because of the scar. Not Lucky Cat City, though. If anything, it's energized. Moving in fast-forward. A collective that only feels true excitement when it can't predict what will happen.

By the time I get to the heart of the city, it begins to drizzle. Digital cherry blossoms blow through the chilly air. A group of teenage girls, skin-tatted pure white, I think, pop umbrellas over their mutant rooster combs and trudge over a bridge, crossing a canal. A pack of boys wag curled, bushy tails of blue ribbon Shiba Inus and duck under eaves for shelter. College kids from all over the world are here in droves, gathered for some kind of summer solstice bacchanal. They could give a shit about the scar going out. They're here to party. They ignore the rain and the kids wilding out in streets like only the young can.

Then there's the robot crowd, tat-dyed gray and adorned with holo buttons, who also ignore the rain. The ones who believe the purest path to true intelligence is imitating an artificial one. They're wandering around with arms held out straight, knees unbent, and bump into tourists in unapologetic, jerky motions. These walkways are still made of actual pavement, and the buildings, short by modern standards, consist of brick, neon, and steel. The foundations of the city are still hard-wired. Odds splash the night sky like fireworks above the whizzing of heli-taxis mocked up like rickshaws.

My first trip abroad with Sabrina was here. We'd stayed in a hotel room where all that separated the bed from the toilet was a sheet of glass. Let's just say, after drinking too much saké and eating too much abalone and oysters, we got familiar real fast. I'm trying really hard not to dwell on that trip. It makes me scared that I'm gonna get lost in the past again. *Guideline*, I tell myself. *Guideline*. I look around. The rain is coming down harder, and the hovering streetlamps flicker and adjust brightness. The foot traffic is chaos. People move at high speed, all directions, stepping over homeless covered with drenched, government-issued sleeping bags. They follow blinking arrows shaped like dicks and tits into dark back alleys.

I recheck Akira's coordinates and walk on. I wonder why this place failed and why America continues to hang in there after all these years. Half this city sliding into the ocean didn't help, but it goes back further than that. Its century-and-a-half long stagnant birthrate. When adult diapers started outselling baby diapers at twice the rate. A capitalistic society where ninety-five percent of participants, through genetic and standardized tests, were destined to fail financially, which meant failing in general. Maybe it's because they stopped pounding mochi and drinking ozoni over a century ago. Traditions died and people left, even the talent. People like Akira Kimura.

The US never completely shook its Wild West, get-rich-quick, give-me-your-tired-and-poor mentality. In America, not everyone has to chase being a doc, lawyer, crypto banker, or bio-techie. In America, you can be a working man, a cop, a hydronaut, a skimmer, a chef, a 3D printer, a single mom, a soldier, and unlike in other countries, The Money will pretend to respect you. And no matter where you're from, if you make good money in any fashion, by turning shit into batteries or hawking lab-grown meals to go, you get respect. There's a respectable field for every talent, so we get the most out of our people, and no one is publicly considered a failure because they didn't make millions. In fact, we've always romanticized the sheriff, the athlete, the waterman, the captain of the ship. It's probably why I'm a bit fucked up. I spent most of my life embracing my identity. I had pride in it. Too much pride.

I try to continue this train of thought while heading to the coordinates Akira left me, but ahead, the sight of a homeless man holding up actual paper money stops me in my tracks. It's an old American dollar bill, and the homeless guy is talking to George Washington in the rain. The man has fresh scars on both sides of his face, burns seared in the shape of gills. He looks at me and smiles. He folds the paper money into a crane, breathes into it, and the paper bird flaps away into the sky. I forget where I am. I blink, and the homeless guy is gone.

My mind scrambles. What was I thinking about again? Why am I here? I'm on vacation. Where's Sabrina? Is she at the hotel? I'm trying to remember the present, but I'm failing. *Remember the present.* Is that even possible? I wave my arms around in front of me, trying to peel off all this two-color tint. It doesn't work. I begin to run. I don't know where. I almost slip in the rain and fall into a canal. *Guideline. Guideline!* I remember where I am, why I'm here, and stop running. Then I forget. I'm gasping for air. I feel like a drowned man struggling to climb out of a moat only to be pulled back in by ghosts.

"Guideline," I tell myself. "Guideline." My iE pings. *One: find Akira (coordinates here). Two: turn her on (gem in your overcoat pocket). Three: report back to Caldwell. Four: get Akira to fix your daughter. Five: kill Ascalon Lee.* The memories spool up quickly. I've set my iE to read off my checklist every time I think or say the word "guideline." My mind is as clumsy as one of those wannabe robots out there, bumping into tourists. I walk on. The rain continues to fall. Up ahead, next to an octopus pet store, a pharmacy/tourist-trap ninja store. I step inside.

The floors, holo bamboo, are slick with rainwater. An old woman is sprawled out on three chairs lined up against one another. The proprietor, I'm guessing. I'm the only customer. There are baskets filled with wilting cabbage under the display of mounted weapons. The woman's Triple X iE floats in front of me. People gotta come to a place like this to see something one-off artisanal nowadays. All this shit that got no more use in this world. All this shit that ain't been 3D printed.

I end up buying a tanto heat blade, a tube of heal gel, and a kakute, which I slip on my middle finger, spikes hidden in my palm. I feel its point. At least the Japanese still make the sharpest shit in the world. I turn on the heat blade, and once it's hot, I carve the word "guideline" into my forearm. My jaw clenches as my skin sizzles. I rub heal gel on it, then instruct my iE to rattle off my to-do list every time I look down at the word.

I step out of the store and look both ways, wondering if she's out there following. Was the homeless guy holding up the dollar bill Ascalon Lee? She could be any one of the four million out here in Lucky Cat City. I look down at my forearm. My iE reminds me about the mission, and I walk on. I see it now on the coast through all the rain and green and red. The Maneki-neko. Three hundred feet of lucky cat. It's left paw up like it wants to give the world a fist bump. I head to it. There's a line, and I wait my turn. After ten minutes, I finally step into the giant cat and climb aboard an old vac tube that gurgles down to the city under the city.

Lower, Lucky Cat City is the planet's prototype when it comes to water cities. When a rogue tidal wave pulled half of old Osaka into the ocean, Japan nearly bankrupted itself rebuilding half the city underwater. Wyndham-Marriott, which already owned most hotel properties in Japan, bailed the city out on the condition that it change its name and let the hotel empire market it as the greatest tourist destination in the world. The world watched Osaka lose itself, and many countries resisted building underwater themselves. After initial disasters, some, like India, Nigeria, and Argentina, sent their cities in retreat away from the rising ocean. Others lacked the funds or political will to take any action. That's why Bangkok, Alexandria, and Rio don't exist anymore. But places like Sydney, Hong Kong, Santiago, Ho Chi Minh City, and the Hawaiian Islands followed the Osaka model, selling land and borrowing huge sums of corporate money to build underwater and change their names. The Money loves buying shit and renaming shit with shitty names. Now these places are called Harbour City, Fragrant Harbour, New Santiago, Saigon II, and, of course, the biggest and most technologically advanced one, Water City.

I look through the window and watch the seascape whiz by. The scrapers here are short hexagon-shaped pavilion towers, the water is shallow, and the lights are so dull, I can see floating sediment. Even old, preserved Osaka Castle looks drab down here. I try to recall what year the Great Tsunami knocked it to the bottom of the ocean and what year they rebuilt it. I can't—before my time. Sabrina and I visited it on our vacation. We dove through its lacquered halls . . . *Wait.* I'm supposed to stop myself from remembering, so I clear my mind and walk down the packed causeway between the vac terminal and public residential, looking up at the groaning, steel framing. Three-dimensional block letters that contain falling, digital kinmokusei blossoms read: WELCOME TO LOWER, LUCKY CAT CITY. I'm moving with the school of the tired night-shift hospitality and maintenance workers heading home while the day shifters, mostly fish ranchers, squeeze and push through our current in the opposite direction. Ever since the crash, Wyndham-Marriott and the Japanese government sponsored worker AMP chambers. Everyone here is required to work eighteen-hour days. They call it the Kimura Workday, this wild haymaker thrown at an endless recession. Work eighteen hours, AMP two, and play hard for four. That's why everyone's in such a rush. Maybe they don't got the time to sweat the missing scar. They take their four free hours as seriously as their ten percent harakiri rate in Lucky Cat City.

Guideline. The coordinates lead me past rows of yatai and to an older public housing tower, one chiseled from rock. There's an empty playground off to the left. Curved ladders shaped like strands of DNA. A jungle gym mocked up like an atom cut in half. In the center, a three-story spiraled tube slide is showcased. On the other side of the building, closed hawker stands fronted by water dragon statues feeding on bowls of noodles. The same mizuchi carved into Akira's underwater grotto. I recognize this place now. This is where she and her mom moved after her father had died. How old was she? Five? Six? The history is a bit foggy, and not too many worshippers are interested in her formidable years, but I've seen the place in pictures that Akira kept on her desk at Savior's Eye—a little Akira dangling upside down from the monkey bars in the playground here. It was always weird looking at that picture. It always struck me as probably the last time she had any fun. I imagine her with other children, playing the Stone Age game of hopscotch. I'm surprised that this place ain't some kind of museum, but it ain't exactly her Bethlehem. It ain't really her Nazareth either. Her Bethlehem is a hospital on the outskirts of Lucky Cat City. Her Nazareth is the telescope back on the island. That's where she grew up. That's where there's a giant water statue of her.

Nevertheless, I imagine little Akira walking past the water dragons to get a bite to eat after playing, actually playing because her widowed teacher mom couldn't afford to buy her the latest eSport VR rig. A god's gotta have her humble beginnings after all. I imagine her coming from the playground and passing those statues every day. I picture her underwater grotto and think that maybe when we invent, we are forever haunted by the specters of our childhoods. I imagine little Akira walking from the hawker stands and entering the pulsing elevator tube that veins the building. Marching with purpose. Always with purpose. I can almost see her stepping into one of the units, which look like perfectly lined pockets that resemble rows and rows of metal amalgam filling.

I run the coordinates from Akira's letter through my iE and get an apartment number. I look into the facial recognition scan that fronts the lobby, then the door slides open. I look both ways before stepping inside. Everything smells like steamed parrotfish down here.

I step out on the twenty-first floor and head to the unit. A foam-fitted child runs past me, and a hunchbacked woman with gnarled fingers and funeral eyes desperately follows. I walk on and stop at apartment 2102. Its number the same year Akira discovered Sessho-seki. Probably not a coincidence. Her notion of a sense of humor, I guess. I look down at the sprawl of government housing. The buildings, all the same height, sleeved with age. The smell of perspiration almost bead from the pores of this dated architecture. I wonder what Akira thought when she looked out upon this. Probably that she needed to get out. It's no wonder she spent her childhood looking up rather than down.

These are the exact coordinates Akira left me. I guideline once more before putting my eye in front of the apartment unit scanner. The door slides open, and I take a breath and step inside, then the door closes and locks behind me.

The mid-floor studio is square-shaped, and each wall is holo muraled with a season. To the left, autumn, symbolized by a flapping flock of holographic geese, transitions to the bare trees and the snows of winter windblown on the wall in front of me. To the right, blossoming flowers cover the wall, while behind me a bright sun dimmed with haze rises over the doorway. The room is completely empty except for an antique wooden tansu chest sitting in the middle of the living room. Entrance music begins to play—some kind of ballad. I know I misplaced my soul at some point in the past when the sound of every ballad started to make my eyes roll. I roll them even now.

I walk over a thick layer of dust to the tansu and kneel. I clear the green dust off the top with my hand and see that it's covered with lacquered chrysanthemums. I wipe my hand on my pants and eye the oxidized brass lock. A part of me doesn't want to open it. I feel like if I do, a beam will pour out and melt my face or something. Or it'll be like the story of Urashima Taro. The folktale of a man who saves a turtle and is invited to an underwater palace by a goddess princess. Before he goes back home, he's given a box that he's told never to open. When he opens it, he turns old. He unknowingly spent three hundred years in the palace, and the box contained his age. It was always one of Akira's favorites.

I look down at my forearm. *Guideline*, my iE reminds me. I turn and look back at the door. Nothing. I open my hand, the one with the kakute and tell my iE to project my reflection. I look into the mirror and spread my eyelids open with my fingers and delicately poke the sclera of my right eye. Nothing. I do the other eye. Nothing. She ain't in me. Ascalon Lee ain't here, at least.

I rattle the old, fragile lock, and I'm pretty sure I can rip it from its hinges. Instead, I take out my heat blade, turn it on, then look back at the door again. Still nothing. I feel like I'm stealing, which makes me think of Sabrina and the man she was dating when we first met. It's then I realize I'm not a stranger to this tension. Anytime you end up with a beautiful person, you're stealing from someone else. Beautiful people are never single. Every single one of my wives had been in some kind of relationship when I met them.

I look around the room and wonder when this place was built. Probably back when the world's coral turned neon in a last-ditch effort to survive global warming, way before my time. I focus on the present and notice my blade heat up, then I weld through the lock, which clumps to the floor. I sigh, open the chest, and flinch. Inside, a chrome pylon, like the one in Akira's underwater lab. I examine the starfish-shaped top. There's a mouth in the center of its body and its teeth look like tiny drill bits. I touch one of the five arms, which causes all the arms to ball and clench. Weird. The starfish opens. It wants to eat something, so I reach into my pocket and take out the gem, then place it on the starfish.

The five arms snap around the gem and clutch it. The starfish begins to squeeze. I don't know what kinda torque it has in it, and I got no clue where the energy is coming from, but I hear the whine of drill bits. The gem begins to crumble at the edges. I touch one of the arms and singe my fingertip.

The gem shatters. I turn my head just a little too late because I've already taken some hot shrapnel to my face. I brush the crystal shards off, then something tiny and glowing in the chrome palm catches my eye. It begins to float. I can't tell what it's made of since it's so small. My best guess is light. I scramble to my feet and take a couple of steps back. The little thing floats up and matches my height. I take another couple of steps back, blade ready in my hand.

"Don't you even fucking think about it," I say. "If you try to get in me, I will fucking peel myself to pull you out."

The tiny glint does nothing. It just bobs there in front of my face. I send my iE in to get a close-up. And that's when it happens. Wisps of tentacles lash from the thing, and it wraps itself around my iE in light so neon, so blue that I can actually see it. I gasp. The spinning sound of a hard drive booting up follows before it slows to a hum. Then a moment of silence until a voice comes from my iE telepathically. Unlike the Thought Talk app, it comes with no accept or decline option. It's filling my head without permission. That's her, I suppose. Never asking for permission.

My old friend, Akira says.

"Akira, you fucking bitch."

She laughs and laughs and laughs. And for some reason, despite the fact that she's alive and has hacked into my iE, I find myself laughing, too.

4

Heading back to Upper, Lucky Cat City, my mind is filled with numerous questions. How is my daughter doing? Can Akira fix her? Where are we going? Where is Ascalon Lee? I look down at my forearm. Can I even trust my guideline anymore with Akira all up in my iE? Better yet, is she even real, or is she just a voice in my head?

After finally turning off all the security breach pings by the time we're in Upper, Lucky Cat City, Akira's gone through all my iE data to catch up on the last eight years. Basically, she's collecting answers without permission, as usual, while all I got are questions. Some things never change. I feel a bit self-conscious, a bit naked and ashamed, her going through my qubits like that, but at least she can't see my thoughts. My dreams. And the details of my meeting with Old Man Caldwell ain't in there. I'm walking through the bowels of Maneki-neko, toward the exit, which resembles a giant cat anus shitting out foam-fitted Japanese workers heading to eighteen hours of hell.

Your existence while I have been gone . . . Akira says in my head, her and my iE seemingly fully linked and synced now. *The word escapes me. Thin, perhaps? Emaciated?*

I'm not fucking starving.

Yes, of course you are not. Akira says. *Narrow. Yes, narrow is the word.*

I make breaking even an art.

No, you're always behind.

Screw you, Kimura, I say.

Silence.

We exit Maneki-neko and step into what appears to be a parade of sorts with thousands of packed spectators. In front of them, a procession of giant robot unicorns painted like ladybugs, with naked girls tat-dyed fluorescent standing on their saddles, tugging their reins. Swollen floats soar above. The biggest, a jolly polar bear with a bird perched on its shoulder. Behind it, someone in a cat costume playing electric guitar on a floating stage in a display of androgynous visual kei. It's impossible to keep an eye out for Ascalon Lee in this mess. Plus, I don't even know what I'm looking out for. I look down at my forearm. *Guideline,* but no list comes.

Turn it back on, I say.

If we are going to do this, we are doing it my way, Akira says.

I tell my iE to come to my hand. It refuses. *I'm not fucking around, Akira.*

Neither am I, old friend, she says. *Neither am I.*

I snatch the iE from the air and squeeze. The kakute spikes dig in. *You got access to my data,* I say. *Look up walnuts and what I can do to them.*

I'm going to help her, Akira says. I *will save your daughter. You know that.*

I don't know shit. I don't even know if you're real or just some voice in my head.

That is why we must save you first. Your neurological data . . . well, it's disturbing.

An old woman on a bicycle nearly collides with me. "*Baka!*" she screams as she rides past. I take a few steps back and lean against Maneki-neko's arm. A fleet of flying omakase soar above.

"Her first," I say out loud. "You fix her first."

This is why you must allow me to lead. You are emotional. You have recently experienced brain trauma. This is not a good combination. My daughter will get to you, to us, if you continue to operate in this deficient state.

I look at the parade crowd, at a grocery girl on the bicycle with strawberries the size of fists in her basket. Then at two men holding hands, European tourists dressed like Zulu Hwarang warriors, who sit on a robot rickshaw. "This shit is trops," they say to each other. More slang that makes me feel disconnected and ancient. African sightseers dressed like Aztec Egyptian priestesses pirouette while flapping fake butterfly wings.

You are getting lost, Akira says.

I look down at my forearm. The pain is really setting in. *Guideline.*

There will be a moment, a moment impossible to predict, when you are lost, and you will not be able to find your way again.

I look at the crowd filling even more and more quickly in front of me. Ascalon Lee could be any one of these people, couldn't she?

If you operate under these conditions, you will not even remember who your daughter is, Akira says.

I don't care. As long as she's okay.

Then you are a short-sighted fool. If you do not remember her, you will not save her. The friend I remember was smarter than this, Akira says.

It begins to rain again. My forearm stings even more. In unison, the liquid crowd pop umbrellas over their heads. Then, suddenly, I'm at the skeleton of Volcano Vista, perched on the scaffolding, holding a cannonball again. Akira's sitting next to me, trying to convince me of something. I relax my grip. My iE floats in front of my face and I look at what it's projecting—the image of Akira's face, and I just want to punch it.

Of all the questions I could ask her—if she can save my daughter, why she killed hers, how she so easily jacked into my iE, why she felt the need to con the world—I pick a real stupid one. *All those years ago, after John and Kathy died . . . when I was perched on the construction site of Volcano Vista ready to jump, how'd you make the cannonball I was holding disappear?*

I didn't make it disappear, Akira says. *You dropped it without even realizing you did.*

What is all this? This parade?

You do not remember? Akira asks. *I am hurt.*

Like you said, deficient state.

Old friend, it is my birthday.

Of course it is. I step into the crowd and squeeze my way through it. My iE floats down into my pocket. I stick my hand inside and wrap it around the orb and feel the energy warm my palm. I dropped the cannonball without even realizing. That sounds about right. *East? West? North? South?* I ask.

Up, she says.

I look up. *Up? Up where?*

Thousands of iEs float like bubbles. Above this, a dozen helmeted strat divers plummet from thin air and down through clouds while the crowd cheers. The divers' chutes spring open, and they land on the tips of lit-up scrapers, waving to the crowd below. More cheers. Then the full moon flashes so brightly that people scream. But even though the flash only lasts a moment, the strat divers, blinded by the flash, lose their grips and start falling. Seconds later, the splats make me cringe. The last one falls right in front of me. When the body hits the asphalt, it explodes into a pink mist. I look down, and there's nothing left of the strat diver except tattered pieces of his jumpsuit and his blood-caked, pancaked helmet that is plastered to the street. The people near me are stunned into stillness. Even their iEs, suspended above their heads, locked in place. Slowly, some begin to clap. Then more followed by even more. This is when I know Akira is back, and she's real.

Shuttle center, Akira says. I'm glad these conversations are telepathic, so I don't look like I've completely lost it.

Subtle, I say. *The same kind of light source you used to create the scar?*

Not exactly.

It was all just a show.

A pretty show, don't you think?

And there it is. Confirmed by the great Akira Kimura herself. There was no asteroid. There was no Sessho-seki. The Ascalon Project was really just sending up a giant flashlight into space. How many people died during the execution of this trick? The riots. The suicides. The murders, including mine. How many did she kill? She just added twelve strat divers to the list. I head to the shuttle center and push my way through applause.

Zero point three, she says.

What?

That's how many died. Approximately. You asked.

Of eight billion. That was your estimate of the percent of people who were worth a damn.

Yes. It was also my mortality rate projection. I was fairly accurate. Do you not love the symmetry of it all?

She's a madwoman. Is she even human? Has she ever been? I don't believe in the soul or anything like that, but how can that little chip be an actual person and not some knockoff? How can that iE stalking us somewhere out there be the real Ascalon Lee? I don't got time for philosophizing right now. All I know is that like all gods before her, Akira fooled the world into making her one. She thinks in terms of acceptable losses. Like all gods, it's not the immortality that makes her powerful, it's the apathy. But fake or real, apathetic or not, a god is what my daughter and I need right now anyway.

Let us depart, Akira says. *I despise this city.*

Then why did you stash what you did here?

It is a place where no one would look, and a place I would never forget.

How did Akira light the moon up like that? Why does Akira hate this place? Two of the many questions I need to ask her at some point. I whistle down a rickshaw. Japan's great contribution to technology. The fucking rickshaw. A piece of transportation that elevates the rider and completely degrades the runner. That's what I am: Akira's rickshaw runner.

I get in the rickshaw and tell the drone where to go. The wheels flip parallel to the street and become turboprops. We rise. Akira is quiet. The air traffic is downright scary. The lit-up rickshaws zigzag all over the place. Akira, voice calm, speaks. *Do you love your family?*

Of course I do, I say.

You aren't simply trying to live up to what you perceive as their expectation? Or perhaps attempting to make up for past failures?

"Shut up, Akira," I say out loud. And she's quiet.

Ascalon at three comes to mind, the mind-numbingly endless games of hide-and-seek we used to play. The pretend treasure hunts. That time she was constipated, and I had to pull a turd out of her ass with my bare fingers. Ascalon at four, the projected flash cards of simple articles, nouns, pronouns, and verbs. The mind-numbing board games we used to play and the diabolical ways I used to devise to lose so she wouldn't cry. Ascalon at six, her first shallow dive at the edge of a reef. She wanted to learn how to hunt underwater. I started her on easy prey, gold ring tang, the kind when you deep fry you can eat fins and all. She accidentally shot me in the calf with her speargun. I didn't get mad. Maybe too young for spearfishing, I thought back then. Then came the deeper dives a year later, when she lassoed a turtle, and it almost dragged her to the bottom of the ocean because she just wouldn't let go. That same day, when we got home, she was sick and vomited all over the floor. I remember being on my hands and knees and wiping up the sick with a towel, once again, barehanded. I remember taking her to gymnastics, to regular school, to scuba school, to jetsurf and throw net practice again and again and again and again. I show it all to Akira.

"If that ain't love," I say. "I don't know what is."

I have no idea why I felt like I had to prove it.

5

The Lucky Cat Shuttle Port is a real piece of shit. It's one of those places where advanced technology was Bondoed on the old stuff, layer after layer, for at least a century. The walls, the ceilings, the floor, the cracks throb with decaying tech. Some cracks are so big, I can see the tubular disco-tech lighting that's older than me. We make it past security and head to the vac tubes, where we'll be shot to the space terminal. The place is buzzing. Crowds patched into iE newsfeed, bumping into each other. The moon flashed for a moment, and some wait anxiously to hear the betting odds of the cause.

Let there be light, says Akira.

You never were funny.

Light has no mass, but it has energy.

It's just always gotta be moving, I say.

Precisely. We will make a scholar of you yet, old friend.

We enter the vac tube. *Seatbelts, great.* We sit and buckle up. The tube begins to rumble, and I can't help but notice there ain't hardly any other passengers in the tube. Not many in the city can afford a space tour, even just a shallow orbit. I'm surprised the space terminal is still operational. Why?

I funded it, Akira says.

Stop reading my mind.

I cannot read your mind, she scoffs. *I can only answer its questions.*

It's the same fucking thing.

Phoomp. We're barreling through the vac tube now. Home comes to mind. The shore break, the waves, the barrels of crystal curtain, the wave-lashed coast. My daughter loved riding in those barrels. Escaping them before they came crashing down on her. Wait . . . I need to focus on the present. Akira wants questions, so I ask them.

Your daughter will be fine as long as she remains in AMP, she says. *We must simply reconnect her mind to . . . well, to put it simply, the rest of her. It takes a bit of time, a bit of mapping first. Simulation. Then connection. This is why I am not worried about . . . well, you know. I am terribly sorry she did that to your child, to Buhari. It will take her time to reconnect to another host.*

She's already had two weeks. She put my kid under in, like, a day and a half.

She pre-planned. Mapped and ran simulations ahead of time. She had eight years to plan. Trust me. She is incapable of doing anything well unless it is one thing at a time. She did not prepare for a second host. She did not predict your actions accurately.

My actions. How do you know? I ask. *She got you, didn't she?*

I allowed her to.

Why?

And for the first time in our relationship, she had no answer. I wonder if it's her pride talking. She don't wanna accept someone got the best of her. *You underestimate her*, I say. I don't press after that. Instead, I ask, *What's your grand plan for me?*

Your host, I have prepared.

The version of me fifty years ago? I ask.

Yes, your best self. She sounds like an ad.

You can't just plug this old iE into that body.

I do not speak of your body when I say "host." I am speaking of the mind, the new iE I created for you, she says.

What about all the stuff that's happened to me since you created this so-called new host?

Compiling and transferring data now.

I'm telling you, Akira, I better remember it. All of it.

I promise that you will, she says. *In fact, your memory will be far superior than its current iteration.*

"That's not saying much," I say out loud. It's the first time I recall her promising me anything. A boy wearing foam fit emblazoned with Akira's face shoots me a strange look. He don't realize I'm having a conversation with his god in front of him.

The vac tube train rumbles to a stop. The doors hiss open. I get up and am immediately yanked down. Speaking of faulty memory, I forgot these seatbelts ain't automatic. I pull the buckle and get up. I let the other passengers get off first, lingering last like I'm some sort of criminal waiting until the coast is clear. I think about Old Man Caldwell, about Chief of Staff Chang. How old they looked after their Century Crash. No matter how well you take care of yourself, how many hours you log into AMP, age hits everyone hard after one hundred. I'm close, but I ain't there yet. At least my body ain't.

For a man of action, you dwell too much, Akira says. *You always have.*

The last people, several nearly naked college-aged kids, get out of the tube. A trip to Lucky Cat is the new, summer-before-freshman-year, backpack-through-Europe experience. Some Lucky Cat debauchery, then straight to low orbit. Kids love to fuck in low grav orbit. It's become all the rage. None of them has a yellow eye. I step off. "You don't dwell enough," I say out loud. Or was it in my head? It's getting harder to keep track.

We step on the grated autowalk, and it inches us toward Moonlaunch Gate. The walls are filled with animated digi murals of Akira. Cartoon Akira piloting a squid-shaped shuttle. Cartoon Arika bouncing on the moon. Cartoon Akira doing donuts in a rover on the lunar surface. Cartoon Akira pointing at the scar that's no longer there.

I look down at my forearm.

Don't worry, Akira says. *I'm here. I won't let you forget.*

Another digi mural, this one hacked and vandalized, throwing some real shade at this supposed god. Instead of cartoon Akira holding a martini in a capsule orbiting Earth, it's cartoon Akira in a capsule with her head up her ass, looking for the scar, I'm guessing.

Heathens, Akira says.

They're gonna turn on you, I say.

We shall see.

We pass the murals, and the global feeds play on the cracked walls. The moon flash Akira created combined with the scar disappearing is doing its work. Riots in Rwanda. Age-old grudges thought dead begin to pop up again. The Hutu blame the Tutsi. The Tutsi blame the Hutu. The Land of a Thousand Hills washed in fire. There's looting in London. The Royal Standard atop Buckingham Palace replaced with a white flag with the words *Save us, Akira* painted on it. The wind whips and snaps it.

Surprisingly, China's the hot spot of bedlam. An autocracy that finally snapped. I suppose no type of government lasts forever. It's night in Beijing, and the scrapers are dark, a lights-out order every night at 8 P.M. The Great Wall is being vandalized by protesters with anti-Akira sentiment. The military ain't cracking down on them. For some reason, the Chinese president, now exiled to Fragrant Harbour, blames Akira Kimura and wants to start building nukes again. He wants to destroy the moon because it has the audacity to flash at us humans down here. All the while, all over the world, the journalists, wayward weathermen full of predictions, as usual, caught in a storm they ain't seen coming project their worst-case scenarios.

"Just like old times," I say.

Indeed, Akira says.

"Why don't you just turn the damn thing back on?"

It's too late for that. People are stupid, but not that stupid. Do not worry. I will assume control of this mess.

My iE swoops in front of my face. It's starting to feel more and more like I'm talking to her in person. I feign a swat, and the iE floats off to my left.

"This mess you caused," I say.

My iE goes back to trailing behind me.

You used to despise people who completely saw things in black or white, Akira says. *Now, you see things completely in green and red. I am left with the question of what is the difference.*

You're more chatty than I remember, I say, switching back to Thought Talk.

It's for your benefit. I am your guideline now.

What if I cut it?

My friend, it is your iE. I am simply temporarily inhabiting it. You can turn it off at any time.

A life spent pulling triggers. I hold up this time.

We get off the autowalk and head to the gate. Departure times flash under ads for underwater real estate in the South Pacific. We have eight hours to kill. Akira leads me to a wall around the corner. An eye scan, no door. She tells me to put my eye to it, which I do. A hidden door slides open. I look at my iE and shake my head. "I always liked secret doors," I say.

Of course you do. Who doesn't?

I step in, and the door closes behind us.

We're in a swank Cantonese Austrian lounge in Lucky Cat Terminal. The aquarium walls are framed with sculpted dragons. A polymer robot duo, cellist and violinist, both wearing coats and jabots, play in pools of light. There's only two other people here, a woman way past the Century Crash, and a foppish little slice of jailbait that I could break like a twig. Ascalon Lee wouldn't pick either to inhabit. Their Triple X iEs hover above them and cast lit candles on the table they share. I don't like sitting at tables, so I sit at the bar; it's the fastest way to get your drinks. A pair of AMP chambers line the wall to the left.

What is this place? I ask.

Most shuttle ports have secret lounges such as this.

I've never seen one.

That's unfortunate. Like just about everything else, I granted you access to all of them years ago.

Thanks for telling me.

I assumed you would figure it out on your own. I was uncharacteristically wrong.

I tap my fingers on the bar. *Where's the bartender?*

There is no bartender. You grab what you like here.

The fucking Money. I shouldn't be surprised. The smart ones, years ago, figured out it's wiser to hide wealth than to flaunt it. I head to the end of the bar and pass a digi model of some satellite-looking thing. *What's that?* I ask.

The Hayabusa2, Akira says. *The first spacecraft to land on an asteroid and return to Earth. Before our time.*

I nod, walk behind the bar, pick a bottle of old whiskey that equals a year's salary, then pop it open and take a swig. *Why do you drink?* Akira asks.

I eye my iE. "Usually, to anesthetize the banality of human existence," I say.

Ah, I forget sometimes, Akira says. *Arts major.*

I take another long pull on the bottle. *Liar,* I say, getting tired of talking in my own head. *You never forget anything. That's your problem.*

Drunks are always quick to point out other people's problems, she says. *I was just pointing out that it is a primitive mind-altering substance.*

"Maybe I'm primitive," I mutter.

Maybe?

I'm starting to get weird looks from the elderly woman and her boy toy. I don't care. "Shut up, Akira," I say.

Do you think drinking is wise, considering your mental state? Akira asks.

"Did she see?" I ask.

Did who see what?

"Did my daughter see me pull the trigger on her?"

She did not.

"Not even a small part of her?"

No.

I sigh and shake my head. It doesn't matter. Sabrina will never forget. I won't either. I take another long draw. Departure times flash on the ceiling above. The couple, apparently not liking listening to me talk to myself, gets up to leave the lounge. The kid gently puts his arm around the old lady and guides her out.

"I understand why you offed the first kid," I say. We're alone now, so I feel free to say everything I got to say with voice instead of thought. "I don't agree with it, but I get it. But why'd you put Ascalon Lee on ice the way you did? Why'd you do that to your daughter?"

Data. We share DNA and RNA. Mitochondria. She was the closest thing to me I had at my disposal. Also, she was a threat to the project. And you know what we did to threats to the project.

The lightweight robot duo starts playing some hallowed piece of music. Something sweet filled with euphonic bygones. The elbow of the violinist bends and exposes rubber-sleeved wires. "So much for family," I say.

The days of family being a sacred thing have long since passed, Akira says. *The only reason it was proclaimed sacred in the first place is that the survival of each individual depended on some kind of small, isolated collective. We no longer need someone to hunt, someone to gather, sons to till the fields, daughters to feed the livestock, children to tend to us when we are old. How many times were you married? What was ultimately gained? The times in which you were most productive were the times in which you were unattached. Family, my friend, is a cancer to those of us strong enough to thrive alone. And we are cancer to those who cannot.*

"My family is my guideline," I say.

I've told you. I am your guideline.

Maybe she's right. I haven't really lost time since she crawled into my iE. I haven't forgotten anything either. It's only been a couple hours, but still. She's a guideline that I can't wait to be rid of. The moment I can, I'll cut it. "If you screw me over on this," I say.

Yes, Akira says, *I can imagine.*

"I won't stop."

Well, you will if you forget to, so let us get you fixed up.

That sweet smell of the music is distracting. I eye the musicians. Composite limbs, unfinished, bullet-shaped metal heads, flickering eyes. Like most of this port, a patchwork of old tech covered with new. They play well, though. The violinist looks at me, and I can almost feel her eyes fondling me. I look away, and a string snaps. The music comes to a screeching halt. But I'm still picking up its scent. That familiar scent. Perfume. I turn off my iE and take one last swig. I walk to the violinist, who is fumbling with the broken string. I think of my daughter and bury my heat blade in its eye.

The cellist drops its instrument and reaches into its cello case. It pulls out a gun. I hammer the blade into its forearm. Wires spark, and it drops the gun. I reach down at the violinist grabbing my ankles, grab it by the neck, and throw it against the aquarium wall. It goes headfirst into the glass, causing the aquarium to shatter. I turn to the cellist, who's scrambling for the gun. I get to the gun first and kick it, then thrust the blade into the cellist's spine. More wires sparking. Then the fish tank water comes. The cellist short circuits. I turn to the broken violinist. It's laughing, flopping like the fish around it. I cut off its head and look into its eyes.

"Ascalon Lee," I say.

"These old bots are laughably easy to hack," the violinist says, sparking wires dangling from its neck like old-school computer guts. "I'm not actually here, of course. And obviously, I won't tell you where I really am. Just a little fun, taking control of this machine to see what you're up to. Is my mother with you?"

"Why my daughter?" I ask. "Just revenge?"

"To learn how you sense things."

"Bullshit. You used her for leverage."

"That was a coincidental convenience. Your ability is quite an advantage you squander. Instead of suppressing it, imagine if you expanded it to sense other things."

I wonder, with my iE off, if Akira can see and hear all this. I decide to take a chance. "Is my kid fixable?" I ask. "Did you leave her for dead?"

"Children are resilient. Fresh neuroplasticity."

"Can you fix her? Maybe a trade? Because, yeah, your mother is with me."

Quiet. The violinist's eyes flutter then close. The machine winds down. I'm about to drop the head, then the eyes open. "You would betray her?" Ascalon Lee asks.

"For my kid? Yes, I would."

"Why do people crave resolution? It's a fallacy."

"What the hell do you mean?"

"Resolution is a man-made construct. Yet another desire

of the human mind to simplify the complex. To dress reality with narrative."

"Want to make a deal or not?"

"Pick up the gun."

I drop the head, walk to the gun, and pick it up. I look at the flopping fish, their mouths gulping for the thing they need but just ain't getting. Their flopping has dissipated on some. Others are turning themselves pale going at it.

"Put the gun to your head," Ascalon Lee says.

I do as she says.

"Pull the trigger, and I'll save your daughter."

It's tempting. To just take a giant leap of totally misplaced trust and rage-quit this whole game. But I know I won't. Then, for the first time, a simple thought enters my mind. Maybe I can win this. I slowly lower the gun, then drop it. I walk back to the head.

"Look up," Ascalon Lee says.

I look up. The projected departure times. They're all canceled. I look down at the head and flatten it with my boot. It sparks, then flickers off.

"Resolution," I say, knowing it's not true. I turn my iE on.

Before Akira can say anything, I see an unopened ping from Sabrina, and I'm startled by it. I open it immediately. A TtT. She's pregnant, it says. I try to ping her. Blocked. I sit in the pool of water and watch the fish turning pale die. Sabrina's bad timing has now hit epic proportions. But it's not her bad timing, is it? It never has been. It's me who's perpetually treading water in the rip. I'm the reason it's never a good time.

"Well?" I say.

Congratulations? Akira says.

"Fuck you, Kimura."

I try to ping Sabrina again. Nothing. I ping HW hospital. Now those motherfuckers got me on block, too. I'm about to tell Akira that I'm headed back to Water City to straighten this bullshit out and to see my daughter.

There's only one way you can help your little girl, Akira says.

"I thought you can only read the questions my brains produce?"

Whether you should spend what is left of your crippled mind on a fight with medical bureaucracy? Was that not a question?

I guess it was.

Speaking of daughters, was this mess the works of mine?

I nod and look around at the so-called mess, literally floored by Sabrina's news. Pregnant.

Get up, Akira says. *We have work to do.*

"Your daughter canceled all the flights."

Not all, she says.

I look up at the ceiling. One of the canceled flights flickers and changes its status to boarding call. "Let me ask you something," I say. "Why the hell do either of you need me?"

You continually make yourself useful and trustworthy, she says. *And you are my friend. And, my friend, you do not realize your potential. You have the ability to locate so much more.*

I feel stuck in this eternal game of fetch, and I'm tired. "People are starting to blame you. Hate you. And I don't blame them."

A pause. I finally stand up. The adrenaline fades, and

I'm aching from all the action. *Let me tell you a secret, old friend,* Akira says.

I look up. Our flight is boarding now. "What?"

True genius is immune to the condescension of posterity.

I pick up the heat blade and head out. *We'll see about that, Akira.* We'll definitely see about that.

For most of its history, the problem with space travel has been fuel and what little velocity we get out of it. Add to that the fact that our fragile bodies can only survive so much g-force, lack of bone density, and sanity, and it's pretty much why we ain't ever been able to send people to the outer planets, the Jovian giants, within the Kuiper Belt. We tried everything— solar, nuclear, plasmafication, even tried to ride the solar winds through the heliosphere. Sure, we got pretty big burrow probes to the Oort Cloud, but nothing huge, certainly not a transport, nothing with enough speed and energy to go and come back with crew. This, along with the Great Sun Storm, the solar flare that temporarily took out electricity and caused planes to fall out of the sky when I was a kid, is probably one of the reasons why we turned our attention to ocean exploration. Space started to scare us. After the hearings eight years ago, when astrophysics was pretty much outlawed, it's become illegal to travel beyond the moon anyway.

So here we are, Akira and me, on a shuttle, headed to Lunar Gateway. Apparently, she owns a piece of it, which at this point doesn't surprise me. I look out the window. We got our own little man-made asteroid belt in space, a ring of low Earth orbit satellites of governments and The Money. As we pass the orbiting garbage patch, I'm wondering how the fuck I managed to knock up my wife at the age of eighty-eight. I'm wondering if I'm gonna have a boy or a girl. Even after all these advancements, there's no such thing as birth control that's one hundred percent effective. I'm wondering how the fuck I'm gonna manage to save Ascalon and beat this mother-daughter pair of wannabe gods at the same time. Maybe Old Man Caldwell is the key. And even though I've turned off the automatic QA option on my iE, I'm careful not to phrase any of these thoughts in the form of a question.

It's a two-day trip to Lunar Gateway, and I'm . . . well, we, are the only ones on board. The chairs got that worn, 2060s vibe to them, foam sheathed in solar-system-patterned vinyl. The armrests even got little holes from the days when we had to charge our iEs with wire. I spend the first day spam-pinging Sabrina despite the fact she's got me blocked. I'm tempted to ping Old Man Caldwell to see if he can offer updates, but Akira's here. Though considering how quiet she's been since we punched through the mesosphere, one would hardly notice. Despite her silence, her presence still seems to prevent any memory lapses since. I'm going through old data, watching Akeem die again and again. It's a not-so-subtle hint to Akira that maybe we should try to bring him back, if it's even possible. At the end of day one, Akira finally pipes up.

Look out the window, she says.

I look. Nothing. Just emptiness tinted red. It's dark up here, so dark that I wouldn't be able to see anything over three feet from my face. Then, something shimmers green. A huge satellite of some sort, orb in shape. It's got these tentacles swooped back like wind-blown hair. *Ascalon One,* Akira says. *It's actually old plasma filament technology concocted by the US Navy for defense. It would fool missiles with its light. It has recently been decommissioned by its namesake, of course.*

The source of the scar. This close to Earth? "I thought that thing you sent up went to Saturn?"

That would have been impossible for a number of reasons. It is right here, cloaked in high Earth orbit. It matches Earth's rotation.

"That's why it looks like it stays in place," I say.

Yes.

"What about the other side of the world?"

Ascalon Two. Both of my perfect children in a perfect dance, covering every visual angle, tangoing around Earth together. Weren't they beautiful?

When Akira was young, she did cutting-edge research on cloaking tech. She had been given access to military tech. Is that when she came up with this grand flimflam and decided to honeypot the entire world? "It's so close to Earth. How the hell did anyone not know this was all full of shit?"

Well, you helped with that. The dissenters, the intelligent ones with backbone, had to go.

Acceptable losses. Always acceptable losses with this lady. "But what about everybody else? The space tourists. Couldn't they see the scar from up here?"

No. From here, the light is invisible. It requires Earth's atmosphere to be seen. Atmosphere is its prism. In fact, I came up with this idea shortly after meeting you. I knew that you were colorblind. And I guessed that under certain . . . say, circumstances . . . you could see what you were blind to.

"How did you know?"

I watched you for many years, my friend.

"No, how do you even know what I see is even real?"

A pause. I can't help to feel a sense of pride over making the world's greatest con artist think before she speaks.

Look at our planet, Akira says.

I peep the rearview display, and there it is, Earth. *Thirty-five trillion different microbes exist there,* she says. *In our entire history, we have identified maybe two million. Dark matter exists everywhere. Not just in space, but even on our planet, yet we can only infer its existence. We have no proof that what exists all around us is even there. Have you ever heard of mysterianism?*

"No," I say.

It is the philosophy of understanding that our intelligence is limited. There are things we will simply never learn to comprehend. For example, look at the lowly toad. We can breed it. We can genetically enhance it all we want. We can create a strain of super toad, vastly superior to any toad that has come before it. However, no matter what we do, no matter how much smarter we make it, it will never be capable of understanding, say, calculus. Just because I cannot prove that your sight is accurate, it does not mean it does not exist. I do have my theories, though. My friend, the eyes are not connected to the brain. They are part of the brain. They are the only exposed pieces of our minds.

"Your daughter said it's my sense of smell. I smell murder, and because I'm a synesthete, I process it as sight."

Akira goes quiet.

"She's right, isn't she?"

It's time, Akira says.

"Time for what?"

The blown back tendrils wake. They jut from the orb. Now, Ascalon One looks like a virus put under a microscope. The orb spins so fast I swear I can hear the revs even in dead space. An explosion. The shuttle fuselage rumbles. Whatever was out there, it's gone.

That was surprisingly difficult to do, Akira says.

"Like killing your own children?"

Yes. You know the feeling.

I look out the window. Nothing. The evidence wiped. Ascalon's Scar ain't coming back. I try to ping Sabrina again. Still blocked. My body's aching. I wonder where she is, Ascalon Lee that is. Maybe she's waiting for us at Lunar Gateway. Maybe she's waiting for her mother to get her new body so that she can cut her up all over again.

"Why? Why'd you do all this?" I ask.

Are you seriously asking me that?

"I am," I say.

Where should I start? Wars. So many wars. Invisible children starving. Every continent soaked in the blood of genocide over and over and over again. The Great Leachate and others like it on other continents. The disparity of wealth. Money used to be earned to buy the things you need then want. Once money became more important than needs or wants, money became "the thing" we have an insatiable appetite for. Everything monetized. Not just necessities. Food, water, clothing, and shelter, but everything. Education, conservation, popularity, even religion. It is as it has always been. Nothing has really changed. Perhaps we can change them.

"One thing changed," I say. "They worship you now."

Worship? No, my friend, they do not worship. My image

is not celebrated. It is sold. My image marketed as a museum-like asset. Ownership split between hundreds of thousands I do not even know. Do you know I sold my holo eyeliner rights? I have never worn eyeliner my entire life.

That's part of how she amassed her fortune. Selling the rights to pieces of herself. "For how much?" I ask.

She ignores the question. *Wealth supplanted the old gods and became the new. AMP and the disparity of longevity. Rent and mortgage indentured servitude. Invisible iE and foam fit sweatshops. Quality of leadership measured by how many mind-numbing and marginally relevant holo vids one can send underlings. Reckless ocean exploration and development. Everyone plugged in iE, which in essence means that everyone is plugged out. The incessant attempts to capture the meaning of life in a single holographic meme. The seppuku of the human spirit. The slow gridlock to Armageddon. As you know personally, terrorist organizations targeting those saving the ocean or trying to save something in general. And these are just some of the things we do to endanger ourselves. Sun storms, catastrophic seismic activity, impending ice ages, the stability of the planet's magnetic field, and yes, even asteroids. Real ones. Do we just sit and wait? That's what we always do, isn't it? Wait until disaster looms so large that it's impossible to step out of its shadow. Shall I go on?*

Referencing the death of Kathy and John. Smart. She derails my immediate comeback of pointing out that she has abused wealth and AMP. That she probably once owned more underwater property than any person. That right now, she is an iE, which probably lacks human spirit. That she is the ultimate terrorist. She and her asteroids and weapons and scars. She terrorized the entire world. As for the other stuff, who knows? She's right, but does she really expect us to work on things that may become problems ten thousand years or a million years from now?

"There was never an ideal time," I say.

Precisely, Akira says. *Why blame me for trying to create one?*

"You figured we needed a wake-up call?" I say.

Yes, a call, and a permanent message that could not be deleted. The time was right. We were at the height of igno-rant suspicions. The irony is that a society engrossed with conspiracy theories is more susceptible to a real conspiracy. But in the end . . .

"The scar wasn't enough. Not for you."

No, Akira says, *it was not. We can do better.* Motto. *We can do more. I have been woken for a reason. We must do more now. I am glad my daughter extinguished it, just as I believed she would.*

I sigh. "So, what next?"

Time, my friend. More time. You shall see.

"Wish you hadn't told me," I say.

What?

"Any of it."

We fly on. Akira riding me like some kind of high-seas hitchhiker. A barnacle roosted on a turtle shell. A brood parasite. Or maybe I'm the one hitching the ride.

The next day, we approach the eighty-eight-year-old hunk of junk, Lunar Gateway. The fact that we're the same age and appearance is not lost on me. The space station, which looks like a bunch of solar-paneled dildos attached to one another, halo orbits around the moon's north pole. The pole absorbs a constant stream of sunlight. Below, on the surface, sits Moon Village, which is solar-powered like this space station. I see the pimply, abandoned domes on the surface. I remember the ads when I was a kid. *Buy a piece of the moon! Build a house! Raise a family in outer space!* Four space suits fitted over a dad, a mom, and two children, all holding hands and bouncing away on the lunar surface. Looking down at the planet, I'm reminded why this real estate scam went bust. The whole thing looks like a bleached-out version of Earth. It didn't take people long to realize that it sucks up here.

Besides, doing this building shit in the ocean ended up being way easier, especially logistically. We used the tech from the failed moon colonization and put it to use underwater. And when all the planes fell out of the sky, it took years for people to work up the courage to just fly domestic again. The last thing they wanted to do was fly into space.

Even back then, Akira says, *scientists were at one another's throats concerning the viability and practicality of Lunar Gateway. Many believed that travel to the moon is more efficient when direct. It has always been interesting to me that the general public seems to assume scientists all agree. We are pathologically competitive and cutthroat. Ultimately, science can be as divisive as religion. It's funny. When observing conflict, people assume one party must be right and the other must be wrong.*

"Everyone can be wrong."

Exactly.

We dock. Once the groaning of metal ends and the go-lights flash, I leave my seat and head to the exit hatch. "Thank you for flying with us," an automated voice says. It's what Shave Time Money told me when he dropped me off at Nashville. We enter the station and push ourselves through narrow, boxy hallways walled with suspended wires. We pass a few vending machines filled with retro, lab-grown, spoil-proof food. Kelp bars, mostly. It's been a day or so since I've eaten, so I grab a few packaged snacks. We're floating through the station, and even though she doesn't say it, I can feel Akira telling me that we ain't floating, we're falling. Gravity and all that. We're "floating" through, and I eat.

We stop at the orbital outhouses. I pull myself into one of the closet-sized rooms and pee in the six-inch-wide, cushioned vacuum cylinder. My piss is sealed in a little plastic bag and sucked to the waste and recycle center. After I'm done, we head toward our designated lunar lander. The place makes Lucky Cat City shuttle port look cutting edge. It's empty now— Akira called in an evacuation before we even left Earth. It's a world of codes and passwords, and Akira's still got them all. I put on the padded space suit that hangs at the lunar lander entrance. The bulbous, visored helmet is a reminder that this place is packed with old tech. Like the station itself, the design goes back over a century, back when it took twenty years longer to build this thing than the engineers first predicted. I haven't had space training since I was in the military, and the Army thought the inevitable conclusion of Desert Storm 15 would be some kind of deep space Waterloo. So, I trained in space for three months in a suit exactly like this one.

I eventually get the suit on and pop the lunar lander. The circle door opens like a puzzle being broken up. I enter the lander and buckle up. I patch into Mission Control, which consists of three bots on staggered shifts.

"Lunar Lander 3 ready to launch," I say.

"Y'all be needing auto assistance?" Long ago, we dulled down the grammatic capabilities of AI so they sound less scary, less likely to take over the world if they can't conjugate verbs. This one has an old Southern accent.

I ask Akira. She says no. "No," I say. "I'm licensed. Sending you docs now."

"Confirmed. Y'all ready for launch."

The lander detaches from the station and begins its descent. "Moon Village?" I ask Akira.

No. Here are the coordinates. They appear in flashes in my head. Interesting. A long flight to the Marius Hills. *You will descend into a lava tube,* Akira says.

I take the controls and head to the hills. It's easy flying up here, less grav, zero traffic. It's far tougher in Water City, and with all the computer safety measures, it ain't even hard there. "How the hell did you build up here?" I ask.

All those years ago, you saw the mass that I sent up.

It's true. The giant shoe box that could probably fit Lunar Gateway in its entirety. "I figured fuel."

In a sense, yes. There is a fusion reactor down there and a light, among other things. The temperature is far more stable there than at either pole.

The farther we get from the moon's north pole, the more the hunk of rock darkens. I'm flying with instruments now. It's a long, slow flight. I've been using the last few days just healing. The fight in the Lucky City terminal left my body aching. The young me would've felt fine after that fight. That guy in that capsule in Akira's lab under the sea would feel as right as rain now. But not this me. The ache points—my right knee, my neck, my left elbow—they're like permanent water spots that I can't scrub off. I begin our descent and turn on the lights. Suddenly, it's there. The moon. I instinctively yank back the stick because it feels like we're gonna collide with it. But, of course, it's still far away, this world of different shades of gun-metal gray that I see as a different color. I guide us forward, and the dusty desolation grows before my eyes. I try to ping Sabrina again. Still can't go through.

"My kid right after this," I say.

Of course. Might I add, repetition is not necessary with me.

I begin to sweat and swear I smell like rubber. Something synthetic. Sour for some reason. I take off my helmet and close my eyes. I take a deep breath, then I check my vitals. Everything seems okay. I wonder if this will work. If this Straw Man will get his brain. Get his kid. I hope so. I hope it'll be the real me. Not some cut-and-pasted version enslaved by Akira. How will I be able to tell? The real me has got a shot of beating these two. An altered version, not a chance. I'll know soon enough. I spot the lava tube. A dark crater rimmed with jagged moon rock. Soon, we'll drop into the lava tube, into the long lunar night.

A voice crackles through the intercom. "Lunar Lander 3, please return to Lunar Gateway." It's not robotic. It's human. And a little familiar, but I can't place it.

I check my six. A SEAL modded up for space swoops in behind us. It's an aircraft not specifically built for space travel, so I know right away that it's civilian and not military. Not that it makes a difference, because a pair of missiles hang under each wing. "Fuck," I say.

Do not obey, Akira says. *Proceed to the lava tube. There are certain . . . defenses there.*

The SEAL fires a missile. It silently glides over us, into the dark. "Who?" I ask. "Your daughter?"

No, Akira says. *I am checking now. Go.*

I crank propulsion to max and jam the stick forward.

We're in a deep dive now, the tube dead ahead. Another missile shot. I don't see it, but I feel it clip the pod. I fight the stick, so we don't go spinning. Dummy rounds. Non-explosive. At least they're not trying to blow us to bits. Yet.

"This is your final warning," says the voice through the intercom. "All you can do is decide how you're going to lose."

I've heard that warning before. Or read it. I can't recall where. I don't got time to dwell. Like Lunar Gateway and Moon Village, Lunar Lander 3 is a real piece of shit. Slow, unresponsive. A floating pea. If we were back home, in a SEAL in real atmosphere, I could probably give the pilot chasing us a run for their money, but up here, I feel like I'm flying a dartboard. I check behind me again. The armed SEAL is gaining on us fast.

"I can't outrun this thing," I tell Akira.

Caldwell! Akira says.

The Old Man. Yes, that's the voice I heard. He's double-crossing me. He's trying to get me to surrender Akira to him now. I wonder if I would've sensed this backstab coming when I was younger, sharper. If the young me would've seen it in technicolor. I proceed with the dive. There's no way I'm letting this old man get me. Then I suddenly remember, I'm not so young myself.

You betrayed me, Akira says.

"Fuck you, Akira. How am I supposed to trust you?"

Idiot.

Caldwell's SEAL fires again. This missile hits us square but doesn't explode. It's like it's made out of some kind of synthetic rubber. Is this why I smelled rubber earlier? The blow sends us into a dead spin. I fight the stick, but we just keep spinning faster and faster. *Great*, I think. Eighty-eight years of life, and I'm gonna die in a fucking twenty-first-century clothes dryer.

Put on your helmet, Akira says.

I take my hand off the stick and grab at it. The whirring is deafening. I can feel consciousness slipping away.

You will pass out in twenty seconds, Akira says.

I grab at the floating helmet. I'm like Ascalon at three. Grasping at bubbles. Akira is screaming in my head. *Whir, whir, whir!* I'm like Ascalon at four. Struggling to tell the difference between "it" and "is." I manage to get the helmet on but can't tell front from back. Either way, it's on, I think. More screams. *Whir, whir, whir! I'm sorry, Sabrina. Sorry we never talked about me losing my mind. I don't even know why I tried to hide it from you.* Pride, maybe. I'd hidden my synesthesia for so long, hiding afflictions became second nature to me. More screams. *Calm down, lady.* I'm like Ascalon at five. Sucked up and tumbled in shore break and slammed into the sand. *Whir, whir, whir!* I keep tumbling and tumbling and tumbling until I'm like Ascalon at nine: helpless. Mind scrambled. Someone is screaming. We're about to hit the Marius Hills. But I've crashed so many times in my life, unlike the shrieking voice, I ain't even scared.

7

I come to, blink, think, and search for a thought that's escaping me. I can't find it. I'm wearing a helmet. In a delayed panic, I move to rip it off, but . . . *Wait, there's a reason you put this on. Trust the reason*, I think to myself. I look around. I'm strapped in something crushed. "Where am I?" I ask my iE. No answer. I unbuckle myself and look around for it. It ain't here. My head's throbbing. I close my eyes and take a breath. *Remember your training*, I tell myself. *Remember your training.* I open my eyes, and it's the first time I notice everything is tinted green and red, like I'm wearing archaic 3D glasses. What was I doing an hour ago? I don't know. What was I doing yesterday? I can't recall that either. I close my eyes again. My head is fucking pounding. I must've hit it. That's when I remember the word: amnesia. I can't call back much else. I climb out of the wreck. Next thing I know, I'm standing on the fucking moon next to some crashed lander, and I don't know how the hell I got here.

I feel beat up, and looking at the smashed capsule lodged into the side of a lunar hill, it's easy to see why. But why would I be up here? Wait, my iE. I ask. No response. *Calm down. Let's start with simple things. Procedure*, I tell myself. *Procedure*. Who are you? This I know. Name and rank. Yes. Age? Yes. Date? Uncertain. Something happened when I crashed. Head trauma. Amnesia. I tell my iE to look up amnesia. Again, no response.

I climb into the wreckage. I'm prying off panels of dented metal, ripping out handfuls of twisted wiring. I look and look and look. Nothing. Where the fuck is my iE? I catch my terrified reflection in a cracked, mirrored panel. Hold on. That can't be right. I look . . . old. *Old as fuck*. I'm obviously no longer in my thirties. Not by an atmosphere. What the hell happened? Did something suddenly age me? No. That's impossible. I had to have aged normally, and now I forgot years. Decades, by the look of things.

I squint at the horizon and see the earthrise. Darkness cuts off a crescent. The lands are green, the oceans red. Has the planet finally died? Am I some kind of solo amnestic refugee up here? If so, this wasn't much of a plan. I didn't see any food or water in the lander. No. *Think*. This was meant to be a quick trip. Also, it's a lander, which means it came from something else. Lunar Gateway. Yes. Why would I be sent to the surface? To look for something. To find something. To kill something. No, despite evidence to the contrary, I'm not in the middle of nowhere. I look at Earth again. I once had an interesting conversation with someone about Earth, but I can't point out who exactly. We talked about how the history of life on the planet can be reduced to a war of viruses versus bacteria. I can hear myself asking which are we, but I don't recall the answer. I hope John and Kathy are okay down there.

I try communications, but the system is shot. *Okay, trust yourself. Your memory will come back. Trust that you knew what you were doing coming down here. What would have been your next step? Let's take a walk. Let's get our bearings.* I check my pack. No weapons, nothing, except for a heat blade and, thankfully, a full tank of oxygen. Just a knife. This isn't a kill mission. Good. Not an arrest mission, either. What am I supposed to be looking for, then? Just a knife? Am I here to train for something? I close my eyes and breathe. *Breathe*, I tell myself. My pulse slowly eases then stabilizes. I open my eyes. *Procedure.*

I'll scout the territory in a spiral fashion. I don't got a way to map coordinates. It'd be nice to have my iE right now. Why would I have not brought it? No, I definitely would've brought it for any type of mission. So, if I don't have one, it was taken. I look back at the capsule. I was shot down. *Someone* shot me down, went through the wreckage, took my iE, and left me for dead. Who would want to do that, though? On the moon, no less? And why do I look and feel old? Some kind of cryosleep gone wrong? And why is everything still green and red? *Slow down. Slow down.* There's only one thing I can do right now. *Procedure.* Trust that I was sent here to look for something. Trust that I'll find it. And that can lead me back. The silence here is absolute in one-sixth gravity. I walk. I'm very conscious of the day or so of air I got in my pack.

Using it as a point of reference, I walk in Earth's direction. After five hundred steps, I turn east of Earth and begin walking that way. After a few directional shifts, I don't see the capsule anymore. After ten directional shifts, I begin to feel my nerves fraying. Everything here looks the same—vast, lifeless plains of rocks and lunar dust absent of color. Above, just the pure and endless blackness of space. The sameness, step after step, is pumping up my anxiety. My hands shake, and I feel a tightness in my chest. At this point, I know that I'm lost. I'm tempted to head back to the capsule, but for what? There's nothing there that can help me. Besides, I'm not even sure I'd be able to find it. I walk on. Another five hundred steps, shift, and walk away from Earth. This is the scariest direction to head, the one that's just darkness in front of me.

I'm just guessing, but after about ten hours of this, ten hours of nothing coming back to me, I give up. I fall to my knees. Maybe I should use these remaining hours to write a thoughtful message to Kathy and John in the moon's sands. Conscious of my own heavy breathing, I begin to write. I ain't no poet, and I'm not even sure how long etches in the dust last up here, but I write anyway. I tell them how much I love them and how much I'll miss them. I tell them to be strong, to not use my death as an excuse to stop living. I feel like I'm writing for hours. I pour out all I got to say. I stand and look down at my work. I'm floored. All I've been writing this entire time is the word "guideline" again and again and again.

I grab the latches off my helmet. Fuck it, let's just get this over with. If I pull off my helmet, I'll quickly lose conscious-ness. Then, the pressure of the vacuum will boil my blood. My body will swell and bloat. My eyes will cool so rapidly that they'll freeze. And that will be the end of me. Up here in space. Under a minute. I think hard on cracking the seal. I feel my fingers tremble and smell sugar for some reason. I hear a song. Who the fuck is Ascalon? That's when I see a flash ahead. A flicker so faint, yet so strong, in the surface. It's ultraviolet up here in the middle of the moon, so it must be something manmade.

I'm on my feet, running, breathing hard. I'm singing an

old Army cadence in my head. But it's not a cadence. It's a strange song that I can't place when I heard it.

Ascalon is not just the name of the savior
It's the name of the daughter
The one I gave up
Find her for me and tell her that I'm sorry

Who is Ascalon? I bounce in slow motion with each step. I can't get the song out of my head. Finally, I get to the source. A giant hole in the surface. A lunar lava tube that goes straight down. I would've passed it if it weren't for the blinking lights flashing from deep inside. Something's down there. My forearms burn. Three toes on my right foot itch for some reason. I need to get out of this suit and self-inspect. I look back at my footprints, then rock climb down the lava tube quickly, too desperately. *Procedure*, I tell myself. *Procedure. Breathe. One foot at a time. Remember, sometimes the plunge down is more dangerous than the ascent.*

After about twenty feet down, I spot a ladder on the opposite side of the pit. The diameter of this hole in the moon's surface is about thirty-five feet. I carefully get to the other side. Thank God for one-sixth gravity. The climb ain't that taxing. I grab the ladder and proceed even deeper into the lava tube. I pass some kind of deactivated laser defense system. The blinking lights are blinding now, which cause me to squint. I tell myself to stop wondering what's there and what I'm doing here. *Procedure. Or guideline.* Why guideline? I think about the message I wrote above, about the footprints I left. A trail back to a one-volter's blathering. Fuck guideline. There ain't one. *Procedure.* I continue to make my way down and reach what appears to be a rocket tip with an opened hatch at its nose. Someone's been here and left in a hurry. They didn't even lock up behind them. Who? What am I doing here? I look up into the darkness of space. Then I remember. An asteroid! Akira! Akira discovered an asteroid! Maybe that has something to do with why I'm here. I descend through the hatch and spin the gate valve until it locks.

Below, dim lights. This is some kind of rocket ship burrowed ass first up here on the dark side of the moon. Maybe transport shelter from the asteroid. What did Akira name it? Sessho-seki. That's right. The Killing Rock. Maybe I was sent here to prep this as a bunker? Maybe the asteroid already hit, and I've been stuck here for years. Or maybe I was heading back to check on Earth and crashed. *Procedure. Breathe. One foot at a time.* I'm appreciating my military training, my experience. Those hours and hours of slow crawl through the Arabian sands.

I finally get to the bottom. One big room, cylinder in shape. The walls are glossy, like they're made of frost-proof, vitreous china. The lights flicker. I head to the nearest alcove, an access panel of some sort. It's open, revealing a wall of circuit breakers. Someone switched the main one off. I grab it and switch it back on. An underwater hum. A reactor. The lights blink twice, then brighten. The hatch above groans shut. A loud beeping. A ring of little limp tentacles awakens and hisses gas into the ship. I watch the tube feet dance on the walls. Lights go from red to green. I feel myself get heavier. Some kind of simulated gravity. How? Then, a voice. Akira's.

"Atmosphere stabilized."

I unlock my helmet and pull it off. The first thing I notice is the weird absence of the ocean's odor. I squirm from my space suit. These clothes I'm wearing don't look familiar to me. I roll up my sleeve. "Guideline" carved into my skin. My jagged handwriting. "Guideline," I say. "Guideline." I was trying to tell myself something. *Concentrate. Remember.*

I close my eyes and see a woman in deep dive at the entrance of a great ocean cavern. She's beautiful. Dark hair undulating in pink liquid oxygen. She looks at me and smiles, then pulls at a spool attached to her utility belt. She ties fluorescent string to stalagmite and waves me forward. I reach out. She grabs my hand and pulls me. Hand in hand, we swim. I look back at the glowing ribbon of string floating into the darkness. Guideline. I was afraid I was going to get lost. I *am* lost. I open my eyes. I'm old. I see it now. How many years am I missing? The asteroid would have hit ages ago. I must be stuck up here. Earth must be dead. Where are Kathy and John? I wouldn't have abandoned them. Who is this woman I see when I close my eyes?

"Procedure," I say. "Investigate."

Glass tubes stand upright in the butt end of the rocket, and smoke billows from their bases. I wonder if that's the reactor. I wonder what the payload is. I head there first. As I get closer, I realize what they are. They're five AMP chambers that resemble the cylinder of a revolver crowned with trapeze pipe. One filled with a sort of dark, swampy, amniotic fluid. The other four drained. An unfinished game of Russian roulette. I step on a frozen puddle and almost slip. I manage to regain my balance and find myself standing in front of one of the empty chambers. Only, it's not empty. Akira, naked, slumped against the glass. A streak of dried blood trails from her breast to the bullet hole in her head.

I quickly step to the next one. Another Akira. Two to the chest. A gaping hole in her back. Splinters of spine glued to

216 • CHRIS McKINNEY

the glass by coagulated tissue. I blink slowly. Am I stuck
in a dream? No. No, this is quite real, this display of mad
taxidermy.

The next two chambers are empty and intact. I step to
the last chamber, the one filled with fluid. It's swampy, but
I make out a male figure floating in the center, a clot in all
this mess. I slap the glass, hoping maybe I can wake this
thing up. Nothing. I yell. Nothing. I eye the panel next to
the tank. There's a piece of tape with black ink scribblings
on it. *HuSC 1.0. Model 3.* Akira's handwriting. More vague
memories pop into my head, but just as I'm about to grasp
them, they slip through my fingers. I concentrate on what's
in front of me instead of what's in my mind. I spot buttons
beneath the label of tape. Fuck it. I press one and the liquid
churns inside. The lifeless body bobs in embalmment. The
swampiness slowly clears.

The male's head leans forward, and, suddenly, I'm looking
in a mirror. I take a quick step back and slip on the ice. I stick
my hand out to break my fall but break my wrist instead. I
scream for a moment, then swallow the pain. How? I stand
back up and look at the closed-eyed face, hair billowed by
bubbles. It's me as I remember myself. Not the one I inhabit
at the moment. And that's when a memory swarms me. This
young version of myself, standing on a dock, waving goodbye
to Kathy and John. *"Makara 3"* scrolled across the stern of
Kathy's skimmer vessel. Then the initials AWM pops in my
head. Anti-Waste Mafia. A wrist tattoo that reads: *AWM.*
The terrorist attack. Kathy's skimmer.

Kathy and John are dead.

I lean against the glass and feel my jaw and toes tighten.
Procedure. Procedure. I step away from the chambers and

head for a console I spot at the other end of the cylinder. There's a curved, center screen with an unopened message blipping. I reach out and touch it. A message appears.

My gift for betraying you. Transform and become. Suit up in your new HuSC. But Kimura is mine. I will extract from her the information you need to save your child. However, if you come after Akira, all bets are off. —Caldwell.

Jerry? Why the hell would Jerry shoot this place up and kidnap Akira? Who the hell is this so-called daughter? HuSC? An image of another copy of me in an underwater rotunda. HuSC 1.1. Model 3. Déjà vu? I hear a woman's familiar voice whisper, "Eternal life." I spin around. No one's here but me. I struggle to match a name to the voice. *Guideline,* I tell myself. I close my eyes to alleviate some of the pain on my wrist and see the woman again, the beautiful woman swimming in front of me, spooling out a guideline, an endless string of glow-in-the-dark fish turd. Wait, that's the woman who said, "Eternal life!" I feel like she said many, many other things to me that I can't recall. I'm following her. Something bright above. We're swimming toward it now. Where are we going? A rumble. I snap out of it and turn around. An AMP chamber unfolds from the wall and hovers to the tank with the copy of me in it. The hatch pops open.

"Please enter, old friend." Akira's automated voice commands. "Countdown has commenced."

I eye the AMP chamber. Images of someone frozen in one flood in my head. Me chipping away at the nitro. Then, finally, a cloudy pupil. Akira's eye. Her frozen corpse. I remember her murder. Finding her body in Volcano Vista.

"You're dead!" I yell. "Why the fuck are there two more of your bodies here!"

"Please enter, old friend. Countdown has commenced."

I ignore the voice and investigate further. *Procedure*. A shelf of leather-bound notebooks. I quickly flip through them. Nothing about asteroids. It's all pictures of brains and shit. Neuroscience babble. iE schematics. The letters C, G, A, T over and over again, in all sorts of different sequences. One volume is titled *Human Synthetic Copy*. I open the book and gasp. The word "HuSC" appears on every page I see. I now know "HuSC" is an acronym. Blueprints of an iE being slipped into the center of a human eye. I close the book. I know in my heart Akira ain't dead. I wish I had my iE. I know my memories are there, an abandoned vehicle parked somewhere on the endless pavement of The Cloud.

"Please enter, old friend. Countdown has commenced." The chamber with me in it bubbles and churns even more.

I look to the left and spot an old, keyboarded computer with a chair in front of it. At first I didn't see them, the faint wisps of greens rising between the keys, but I do now. The computer boots up. I sit in front of the keyboard and patch into the feed. The death of a scar. A moon momentarily lit up. Civilization crumbling. And that's not even the most jarring thing. It's the year. A half century happened that I don't remember. I patch into online archives. Sessho-seki destroyed. Project Ascalon a success. Ascalon! Ascalon's Scar! The name from the song in my head. And the name of something else, someone else, who's escaping me.

I look up Kathy and John but find nothing. They can't be dead. I do a search in the hard drive. Interesting. Email. Pretty archaic. That'd be like Akira, though, to use old tech because no one else does, so it's ironically more secure. I search for Kathy and John in the email hard drive database.

No luck. I take a breath and stare at the keyboard. Sparkles of green flicker over certain letters in sequence. I know I'm chasing murder now. And it suddenly comes to me, just by the familiar feel of the pursuit, that it's the thing I'm best at. That I've done it many times before.

Makara 3. The name of Kathy's skimmer vessel.

My wrist's throbbing, but I push through and type in the same. A list of emails pops onscreen. Old communications between Akira and the AWM. I picture the wrist tattoo. The hand is holding a green gem the size of a baby's fist. *Akira.* Her iE. Memories of the gem exploding and a sliver of neon the color of sea sparkle floating in front of me. I'm here to put Akira's iE into one of these bodies of hers. But the bodies are dead. Two chambers are empty and intact, however. She's alive. I know it. I need to find her.

"Please enter, old friend. Countdown has commenced."

I open the latest email from the AWM to Akira. The father of her child was a member of the AWM. Akira sent me to kill him. The message reads, *Mission accomplished.* An attached pic of the *Makara 3* set ablaze and sinking.

And that's when I know it in my bones. Akira and the AWM weren't enemies, despite the fact that she had me kill one of its members. She was the AWM, the one who ordered the bombing of Kathy's skimmer. Akira Kimura killed my wife and kid.

I step away from the computer and gingerly rub my aching wrist. Why?

"Please enter, old friend. Countdown has commenced. Mind upload will begin in sixty."

The Ascalon Project, Brun, Chang, all of it comes back to me. The Anti-Waste Mafia—crazies demanding that all government resources go to the Ascalon Project. Of course she fucking started it. She needed the project to be funded. The father of her child, the tour guide, the one with AWM tattooed on his wrist was probably a leader in it. She probably convinced him to get involved. Maybe he got squeamish when she started drafting kill lists, just as I should've gotten when she wrote a kill list for me. Maybe that's when he figured he'd blackmail her. That's when she knew she needed a hammer. So, she got the AWM to kill my wife and kid. She knew she'd be all I had after that. She did it to get me to work for her. To kill for her. The blackmailer, the father of her child. The scientists that followed.

I'm glad she's alive because I'm gonna kill this woman.

I look around. There's gotta be a way out of here. A shuttle of some sort. I check the rest of the walls. Useless. No panels, no facets even. I go back to the computer and search the hard drive for anything related to travel and evacuation. Nothing pops up. The walls begin to rumble.

"Forty-nine, forty-eight, forty-seven . . ."

I look myself up on the hard drive. And it's there. Everything about me, down to every strand of my DNA, RNA, and a breakdown of the proteins that make up me. I glance at my throbbing wrist then my forearm. *Guideline. Guideline!* I close my eyes. The woman and I break through the surface. We swim to the dock and pull ourselves out of the water. She removes her hydronaut helmet and coughs out slime. I see her face clearly now. The angular jowls of an athlete flexing with each cough, the trained scowl, a cop's face. Sabrina is her name. She grabs my wrist. I wince.

"We need to save her," she says. "We need to save Ascalon." She reaches for the knife attached to her belt and unsheathes it. She cuts the guideline and tosses it in the water. "Go!" she screams. "Go!"

I dive back in and swim after the sinking line. I grasp for it but miss. I grasp again. Miss. I put everything I got into the next stroke. I kick my legs as hard as I can. I slug through the deep water. The guideline dances between my fingertips.

"Thirty-three, thirty-two, thirty-one . . ." I hear the count-down gurgle underwater but ignore it and slug on. I reach out and stretch as far as I can. The thread flits at my fingertips. I'm shoved one last time by something invisible, maybe the momentum of the past. I clench my fist. Got it. I follow and spool up line as I go. Then I see the silhouette of a little girl. *My* little girl! Ascalon. Everything about her comes to me. Her voice. Her eyes. The thin strands of her unruly hair. Her rock-hard forehead that caught me good on the nose a couple of times when she was a toddler. Her almost inexhaustible energy. The tickle spots on the small of her back. The way she hears death in reds and sees murders in greens like me. I'm remembering myself by remembering her. A sniper, a cop, a husband, the husband of the woman, Sabrina, who unspooled this guideline in the depths of my mind so that I could find my way back. I'm an assassin, a bounty hunter, a husband, but most importantly, a father to this little girl. I swim to Ascalon and grab her by the shoulders. Her eyes are closed. She ain't breathing. I shake her. Nothing.

"Twenty-seven, twenty-six, twenty-five . . ."

She opens her eyes. Those deep, estuary eyes. For a moment, I can see color again.

"Go, matey," she says. "Go!"

I snap out of it and find myself in the lab again.

"Twenty-one, twenty, nineteen . . ."

I sprint to the open AMP. My heat blade falls from my belt, but I don't got time to turn around to grab it. The place is really shaking now, which almost causes me to lose my footing, but I manage to stumble to the chamber and tumble inside. God, I hate these fucking things. Akira wants me in this thing. A Caldwell, maybe Jerry, maybe not, wants me in this thing. And it might be my only way out. If either of them wanted me dead, I'd be dead by now. I'm tired of being manipulated, underestimated, deceived. And I'd refuse, absolutely refuse to get in this chamber if it weren't for my daughter, Ascalon, telling me in my head to do so. *Guideline, matey. Guideline.* It might be a hallucination, but I trust it. I trust Sabrina. I trust my kid. I trust my versions of them. I trust the guideline that I probably scrambled to sew together, this twisted jumble of line that I feel like I untangled to remind myself what I need to do.

"Ten, nine, eight . . ."

The hatch hisses shut. *Kathy, John, I miss you. Sabrina, Ascalon, I love you.* I'm groggy now, more like a person who just woke up instead of falling asleep. And suddenly, I realize, I can see all colors again. My mind races to speculate how this happened, but my thoughts are interrupted by a ping.

I love you, too. Come home. It's Sabrina. How?

I see it. A panel opens, and my iE, now powered up and reconnected to me, emerges from it. Who put it there? It floats above my face. I'm about to ping Sabrina again, but little legs pop out of the orb, and they're holding a pill with their pincers. My iE floats down to my face and stuffs the pill in my mouth. Then it hovers back up and blooms like a flower. A blazing blue chip, like the one inside Akira's gem, hangs there like a star while the peeled shell of my Triple X iE shatters, and its cracked pieces float like pedals down on me. The countdown pauses.

"Do not be afraid," Akira's automated voice says. "I am simply extracting the last of you before uploading it all into your new HuSC. This is a far gentler surgery than it could be. After all, you are my oldest and dearest friend."

The countdown resumes. I try to reach out to Sabrina again. Before I can send a message, the chip flashes then darts to my eye. The pain in my head is searing, and I scream.

"Three, two, one . . ."

The last things I taste and feel are pharma grit dissolving in the bed of my teeth.

PART FOUR

THE HUNT FOR THE MOON RABBIT

"Your story is only truly great when the narrative becomes religion."

On our trip back home, these are the first words that come from my mother's mouth. Her new body sits comfortably still across from us in her kimono, gazing into space through the port window. Ever since I allowed her to MELd into her HuSC and revive it, she has been very quiet. She has not said anything of her capture, or her failure. She has not begged for her life.

We're flying back to Earth, and she knows that it's not really Caldwell that she is speaking to. It's me inside him. The contrast of this decrepit body compared to that of the little girl I once inhabited is jarring. Since its arrival at Lunar Gateway, Caldwell's body has had three non-ST elevation myocardial infarctions, also known as heart attacks. It has defecated itself twice. The last time when he had to climb down the ladder to get to my mother's moon lab. Death is not a mere abstraction for this host. It courses through a system of stiffened arteries. It hinders the pumping of nutrients to near-failing organs. It barely expels itself with each labored breath. Even with all the hormonal adjustments I made, it *was a herculean struggle to chase down my mother and the synesthete in this body. I did not want to use the old man for this part of the quest, but the synesthete moved so quickly, too quickly for me to use another.*

But now, thankfully, I am three. Three identical minds that can communicate with one another from any distance. One of me that has just completed MELd inhabits another host, an inconspicuous one, in the Pacific. She is our backup, our distraction. The two of us, Caldwell and the HuSC my mother made of me at her lunar base that I MELded into, sit here now, side by side, thanks to the synesthete. He, of course, led me right to my mother. She has more HuSCs on Earth, but only this one conscious. Therefore, she should be afraid.

"Why did you make copies of me?" my new HuSC and Caldwell ask simultaneously. She made copies of herself and the synesthete, which was not surprising. But I was startled to see my HuSC in both the underwater lab and on the moon. This may be the biggest reason why I haven't terminated her. I want answers.

This earns a grin. She turns to us. "How many of you are there, girl?" she asks.

I send my Caldwell self to AMP. After all it has struggled through, it should sleep, otherwise it may not survive reentry. Her confidence in voicing her question stirs up a bit of paranoia in me. Is this her only consciousness? Has she hidden another iE somewhere else? Is she MELding into a new HuSC as we speak? "How many are you?" I ask.

Mother smiles. "There is only one of me, child. I promise you that there will always only be one of me."

I sense no dishonesty in her, but I will eventually pry every truth from her. "I skimmed some of your journals," I say. I look down at my forearms, hands, and fingers. My pinky, which I cut off as a child, is whole again. "You have done a remarkable job in re-creating my physical self. Why the sudden interest in me?"

"Who said the interest was sudden?"

"You won't tell me your plans, will you?"

"I will not. However, you will bear witness."

I nod. "You will die."

"That is my second promise to you, musume-san. I will die."

I have run the simulations, but I still don't know what her plans are. My conclusion is that there are unknown variables. Seemingly impossible ones. Why must I know? I have beaten her. She is here, helpless, unprotected. But I must be sure. And I have contingencies in place. After shooting down the lunar lander in the Marius Hills, I rummaged through the wreckage and grew vexed and frustrated that I could not find her. I began to think that she was perhaps burrowed into the synesthete's eye. He lay there, unconscious. I was about to remove his helmet and pluck his eyes out right then and there when my mother pinged me from his iE. She said that she would come with me if I agreed to not destroy the synesthete or his iE and bring both with us. When I asked her what made her think that she could bargain with me, she said that she would give me the coordinates of her lunar base. I agreed to bring his iE with us, but not him. She reluctantly agreed.

When we arrived at the base, I marveled at the HuSCs she'd made. I'd only seen them from footage of the underwater lab sent by the synesthete's wife. To see an undamaged version of oneself in person, a self not scarred by the trauma of human existence, was sublime. But to see three such versions of my mother was infuriating. I immediately executed *one of them. She did not react. I put a bullet in the second. She casually asked if I wanted to see how it worked. I shrugged. I could always kill her post-MELd anyway. Mother exited the synesthete's iE, and I saw her condense herself into an almost massless sliver of neon. Impressive. She entered the trapeze piping that hung above the HuSC chambers. Once inside, she glowed even brighter in the thick fluid and made her way to her HuSC's pupil. Watching her pierce the eye was like witnessing an oil well suddenly set ablaze. Life. Her final version began to twitch. Her chest heaved shallowly at first. Then her eyes widened, and she sucked in a deep breath of amniotic fluid. The chamber glass retracted, and the tank fluid spilled to the floor. My mother coughed out the last of it. She calmly stepped from the tank, walked to a closet, pulled out a white robe, and put it on. She had done this before. But so had I.*

The iE in Caldwell's eye socket bloomed and released the version of me that escaped the synesthete's child. I floated through the same trapeze piping as my mother's had. I gazed at my HuSC and thought back to when I surgically removed my own eye at boarding school. Everyone had thought I was insane, including my mother, but look at where my exploration led both of us. Claws popped from my carapace, and I floated to my HuSC's eye. I was going to take my time and enjoy this. My six claws dug into the sclera, and I began to tear at the flesh of it as if I were feeding. Ribbons of severed meat drifted in the fluid. I continued to trim pieces here and there, and it felt like I slipped into artistic revelry, my confetti the specks of eye that danced around me. I hacked away until there was no eye left. Then I burrowed in the cavity and soldered nerves and muscles. The body spasmed and woke as HuSC and iE became one. The glass slid down, and the fluid gushed on the floor. I stepped from the chamber, and my mother handed me a white robe. I put it on. An AMP chamber folded out from one of the white walls. She asked me to store the synesthete's iE in it and leave his HuSC unharmed. I grabbed her by the neck and dragged her to the chamber. She didn't resist. I shoved her inside and told her she'd know what it's like to be put to sleep for three decades. She shrugged and said she would be fine, after all, she had been dead for eight years. I put her to sleep.

While she was in hibernation, I thoroughly explored her lunar lab. I read through her journals. I went through the data on her old computer hard drive and discovered something scandalous. It was my mother who ordered the murder of the synesthete's previous wife and child. I left the computer on. If the synesthete survived, if he managed to make it to her lab, he would find out that my mother was responsible for the deaths of his once-beloved Kathy and John. He would want to find her and kill her, perhaps even more than I do. I chose to release my mother from AMP—I needed to learn more from her. I'm glad I saved him and decided to leave his iE in the chambers for him to be able to slip into his new HuSC. He may be useful still.

"I left him alive up there," I say. "If he manages to find his way, he will survive. He'll be ignorant of the fact that these versions of me exist, though. As far as he knows, I'm still on Earth, awaiting yours and his return."

"He will find his way."

"Why him? Why us?"

"He is useful. He has always been useful. He is consistent that way. He is skilled. He is my friend. His daughter will be skilled, too."

I think of the daughter. I miss her. All those years on that slow roll back home, she was my only real outside connection. We pinged each other like pen pals of old who spoke different languages, sending indecipherable messages that were nevertheless comforting in all that dark. I never should have taken her. Mother is right. She will be skilled, too. More than her father or my mother truly know.

"And me?"

"You are my daughter. You will find your way."

"I have become greater than you, Mother."

She sighs. "You have surpassed me in certain areas."

She admits it. "You had to steal from me."

She nods. "I did."

"Aren't you proud?"

Her brow furls. "Proud? I am disappointed."

"Liar."

"What have you done with your gifts? Your discoveries? You have squandered them. You have inflicted unnecessary cruelty with them. Let me ask you. Who is greater? The toy-maker or the gift-giver?"

Her confidence is not feigned. She feels inevitable. The passenger shuttle and its plush seats rattle as we enter atmosphere. Mother remains unflappable.

"Do not speak of cruelty with me, Mother."

"When have I ever committed cruelty?"

"My twin sister."

"That was a mercy."

"My disavowal."

"I left you with a father who loved you, then provided you with a world-class education."

"My dissection."

"Research. Also, painless."

"I lost thirty years!"

She tilts her head. *"Did you?"* She points to my eye. *"It seems to me you now have the means to get those years back and multiply them thousandfold."*

"The deaths," I mutter.

"Enemies. Or simpletons."

"The synesthete's family."

She pauses at this. He was a fool to not figure it out for himself. It was obviously Mother who benefitted most from his family's death. *"You told him?"* she asks.

"I left him access to your data."

She sighs once more. Sun beams through a portal and shines on her face. *"Cruelty was never my intention. Not once."*

"No, but every time, the results were."

She nods. *"So I suppose I am imprisoned for the time being?"*

"For the time being."

"Child, if I wanted to, I could communicate to the world that I am here, and the world would come to set me free from you."

I stand and step to her. I put my hands on her shoulders, near her neck. *"They would not arrive in time."*

"You will see."

"I will."

She pats one of my hands and turns to look out the portal. *"We will change the world. Permanently."*

I go over what I know. What did Sessho-seki give her? Unlimited means, unlimited access to all scientific and military data. The algorithmic and DNA data of all the people on Earth. Every bit of cutting-edge experimental tech that exists. She had four decades to plan, to build, to create. She created *laboratories. She created clones. She willed her consciousness to the synesthete and expected him to do exactly what he did. Though, because of me, he was eight years late. She has the ability to create firewalls that I can't break. She didn't place said firewalls to hinder me from turning out her light. No, she wanted me to do that. It stands to reason that there are other laboratories, perhaps ones with different functions. What is her motivation? She claims that she wants to change the world permanently for the better. How? The unanswered questions frustrate me. I remove my hands from her shoulders and pace the shuttle during descent. I miss the balance of a tail.* "We will change the world. Permanently." *No, we* will *not. She is* not *we.*

"Who is flying?" *Mother asks.*

I tap my eye. "I am."

"It is interesting that you think that." *She stands and steps to me. She grabs my hands. A first. I check if I maintain control of the shuttle. I do. I check my own firewalls. I'm certain they are impenetrable. Mother smiles.* "Sit, daughter. Sit and enjoy the show."

I don't sit. I refuse to. I pull my hands from hers. There are answers here that she won't provide. It's good I let the synesthete live. I have a feeling he'll be the one to lead me to solve these mysteries once again. In the truest sense, sniper and detective were the most apt occupations for this man.

He is wholly myopic, which, like all qualities, has its strengths and weaknesses. The one thing that he looks at, he can see on a level that no one else can. Weakness? Once he begins to look at these things that no one else but he and his daughter can see, he sees nothing else.

2

It is nice to sleep and not dream, especially considering all my dreams in my adult life have been bad ones. I'm held at gunpoint as I drop to my knees and beg for my life. The gunman shoots my wife, who I didn't even notice was next to me all this time. My kid is walking a tightrope between two skyscrapers, but I'm too scared to go after her. She looks at me and smiles, then loses her footing and plunges. I've dreamt of the girl in the desert, of killing her again and again and again. In a recurring one, I'm in my apartment, cleaning up after dinner with my mom. Mom is upbeat and chatty as usual. Kathy is standing on the stairs, braces wired to her teeth, and an incisor is dangling from one of the wires. She's looking sad and disappointed. I don't realize that I've been ignoring her this entire time. I try to hug her. She gently pushes me away then sags in my arms. I say I'm sorry. We both tear up. My mother steps to us and puts a hand on my shoulder. "Every life owes a death," she says. But my mother died long before I met Kathy. I realize this in the dream, and that's when I wake up, every time.

There's always an emotional component to these

dreams—vivid, dark fantasies blotched with realism—stronger than the visuals. Fear. Frustration. Anger. Sadness. All negative, no positive, no love in them. And at my age, even the sex dreams ended decades ago. I dream of making cowardly choices to save myself in scenario after scenario. And I know the nightmares ain't just about the guilt over the bad things I've done. My memory is slipping, and my brain somehow wants to force me to remember that I ain't no good. I hate and appreciate this at the same time because it gets me through this thing called parenting. In every single one of my dreams, I am weak. So, in life, I can't allow myself to be.

But during my sleep in the AMP chamber, not a single dream. The best sleep of my life. And by the look of things, I'm still enjoying this void. I'm in zero grav, looking over myself now, my old, broken self. The Straw Man set ablaze. That version's dead, and he looks content. It's just the forty-year-old version of me now. I can feel it. The sharpness of my mind. The elasticity of my tendons. The flex of my bones. Before, everything felt on the verge of short circuit. My neck if I turned my head too quickly. My back if I got off the floor too fast. If I sprinted, my Achilles. If I leaped stairs like my daughter, the utter fear that I'd snap my ankles. If I moved in motions I was used to, no problem. But life ain't like that. It requires you to occasionally move in ways you aren't used to. Most of death is just you being betrayed by your body when the occasion comes.

I touch the glass that separates me from my old self. I feel like I have the snap to punch through it even in zero grav, but I don't try. I just look at my permanently shut eyes. I rub my wrist just to check if this is all real. No pain. Maybe it's impossible for two versions of the same mind to exist at the same time. I need to see this deceased, past version of myself as evidence that I'm singular. The last thing I saw before going under was that sliver of azure that bloomed from my iE darting to my eye. Akira's automated voice said it had to extract the last of the old me before uploading into my new HuSC. I don't know how the hell that process worked. All I know is that I don't wanna disturb the remains of the old me, but I'm freezing and need clothes. I pop open the AMP chamber and strip it. This poor old molt—my shedded shell. I remember while I'm slipping into the black lunar foam fit . . . remember everything.

When I first woke, the tube opened and spilled its fluid. Floating, I heaved out the rest. My heart was beating like something wild trying to bust through. After I pulled myself together, I looked up at all the suspended, liquid sick and noticed that I wasn't completely colorblind. The world no longer existed in greens and reds.

After finally managing to get into the foam fit, I'm aware of being significantly bigger now. Thankfully, the suit's got some stretch to it. I rub my arms and feel the material's insect sheen. I'm a bit ashamed that the first thing I'm craving, the first thing I wanna do is fuck something. Stick my dick in something and pump away. But that desire quickly goes away and is replaced by anger when I think about Kathy and John, think about Ascalon. I look down once more at my old, shriveled, naked self, then shut the hatch. Here I am, trapped on the moon in an underground lab, consciousness uploaded from one host to another, and the question tugging at me more than the rest is, *How the fuck am I gonna have another kid?* I laugh. And that's when I see it. A wisp of blue floating up. I know what it is and where it's going. It's a guideline . . .

to Akira. Then another wisp. This time a yellow one that spouts from my fingertips. It swirls up, as well. Ascalon Lee. I don't know how I know, I just know. A choice? It's not like Akira to give choices. Perhaps a sequence. Save Akira, then hunt her daughter.

Out of the corner of my eye, I notice another color. This one fainter than the others, smokier. More billows than streams. And it's magenta. It follows the others. Then, struck by bolts of green and red, the three colors mingle in a cosmic storm. The magenta is my wife and daughter. Why would Akira build a guideline back to them? Or did she build them at all? Is it my new quantum mind that's tied and cast them? Some sort of newfangled GPS?

The colors tangle into a single spectrum that strums toward a window accessible by a ladder that leads to a balcony. "Taste the rainbow," Shave Time Money would say. I climb the ladder and look out the window. I'm in space. This whole fucking thing is in space. I see Earth out there. The streams of color untangle and cast to different places on the planet. The yellow gleams somewhere in the middle of the Pacific. The magenta, close to the yellow, sparkles near Water City, I'm guessing. The blue one, bends around the globe to the hidden eastern hemisphere. I feel like some kind of cosmic fisherman up here.

My mind, for some reason, goes back to the journal at Akira's underwater lab and the sketch of a giant flashlight in a shoebox. That's when I realize this is the giant flashlight. This rocket ship that she launched all those years ago. But she didn't have cloning tech down back then. No, like Ascalon One and Ascalon Two, this was only supposed to be another light. But she had all those years. Years to study Ascalon Lee's research and Ascalon Lee herself. Decades to travel back and forth from Earth to moon.

The streams of luminescence bounce off the window and beam at the bottom of the rocket. I climb back down and follow the colors. A panel next to the main console. I push off the ladder and float to it. I know already. It's why she showed me the hidden door at Lucky Cat Space Terminal. There's a hidden door here, too. I rub my hand against it, my palm tracing the refracting colors. Nothing. I take my glove off and try again. The wall slides open.

Inside, a rail gun, some kind of hybrid space and hydro suit, a small, one-man turbo sub, and some sort of remote trigger. "Destination?" I ask. I see a map of Earth, but not projected from an iE, just a clear image in my head. There's an X in the middle of the Pacific. My eyes narrow. "Square root of 2040?" I ask. The number 45.1663591625 flashes in my head. My iE's in my head now, just as I'd suspected. That sliver of light that pierced the eye in my old body was uploaded into my new one. This is the first thing I might have to take care of, in case Akira's in my head, too. "Akira?" I ask. No response. "Stop fucking with me. Are you in my head?" Again, nothing. I'll eventually need to surgically remove this thing, but not yet. I'm still traumatized by not having an iE when I was searching aimlessly, losing my mind in the Marius Hills. I'll take advantage of its utility for now.

"Time of arrival?" I ask. Twenty hours. Great. Twenty hours of sitting still. I've been trying to ping Sabrina. No signal. Might be the distance. The western hemisphere is on the dark side of Earth right now. Twenty hours to drive myself crazy wondering if my kid is still okay and pondering if I'm the real me. "Are we cloaked?" I ask my iE. Affirmative.

The ribbons of color stream back to the window. I rummage through the hidden room and find water and field rations. I inspect the sub. This is tech I ain't seen before. Not very hydrodynamic. It's shaped like an egg. I don't even know if I can pilot this damn thing. I take a bottle of water and exit the room. Somehow, the dead Akiras have slipped free of their tubes. The corpses hover above. *Absurd.* This is all absurd. But just because something happens and no one predicted it, don't mean it's absurd. It just shows that people are shitty at predicting, so they made up this word to absolve themselves of their stupidity.

I drink. I eat. I plan. I'm reminded of being out in the desert. I've done all this before. All the while I feel like there's something crawling under my skin. My palms and eyebrows itch. Somehow, I've been recycled in this world of recycling. I bite into a perfectly preserved star fruit and wonder when it was that Akira began to map me. When I start thinking about my daughter, I realize it don't matter. What do I want more? To save my child or avenge the dead? My choice of first target will answer that question. It's the blue guideline that tugs at me the most. It jigs like something's nibbling beneath.

My iE buzzes, informing me to suit up and enter the tiny sub. Finally, almost twenty hours have passed, and we're now approaching Earth's atmosphere. I put on the new suit, pick up the gun and trigger, and get in the sub. The giant flashlight rumbles. The hatch above pops open. *What the fuck?* A rush of wind and heat rips through the fuselage. The air around the sub screeches. I hold my rail gun tightly. Tooled up, I'm launched out of the rocket, plummeting toward the ocean. *Detonate now*, my iE says. I press the trigger. The fusion reactor rocket above me blows. The old me, Akira's bodies, Akira's lab, Akira's moonlight, all sizzle in the troposphere.

Red, green, yellow, blue, magenta—I'm ripping down a rainbow road at Mach 25 headed straight to hell. Then a bone-rattling jerk. Flaps. My descent slows. Soon, a chute deploys, and the kick plasters me to the seat. After, I'm cradled down to the surface. Splashdown. I crank up the sub and look out the window. The guidelines split in front of me. I already know which one I'm following first.

3

The Pacific Bridge isn't really a bridge. It's a series of zigzag-ging stepping-stones, both natural and manmade, that span Fragrant Harbour to New Santiago. Harbour City, Australia, to Baja. New Caledonia. Wake. Christmas. Water City. D-91. New TJ. These are just some of the ports and islets along the stretch. Some are skimmer ports. Some are fish, geo, and kelp farms. Others are recycling and desalination plants. Some are fuel and rec waypoints. As a skimmer cap, Kathy used to know these places so well that she didn't even need sat guid-ance to map routes. She could look up at the stars and know exactly where she was in this sixty-two million square mile brine. She'd told me once that she could feel the tides under her, that she could smell rain coming. Maybe this was part of the attraction, this mating off with someone who could sense things that others couldn't. Someone like me.

After splashdown, I took the sub to the tip of the Water City islands. Everything looked abandoned. I patched into the feed to discover that during my little moon trip, the president declared martial law. The Senate is working on repealing the Thirty-fifth Amendment. I turned off the feed and hotwired a vintage skimmer. Right now, I'm about three hundred miles east of Water City, and the swells are getting to me. Up, down, up, down. Twenty-footer after Twenty-footer. My skim boat groans as it climbs up another swell. It splashes as it drops down the trough of this wave that will never crest and break. Then another one comes. Then another. Up, down, up, down. Like the old me, the new me doesn't get seasick; however, being in the midst of endlessness is disorienting, but it's good to be alive. Out in the afternoon ocean, wind in my hair, it's good to be young. I gun the motor even though I don't know where I'm going. Despite its strong tug, I decided against following the azure tether. I'm reeling in the guideline of yellow that's cutting through the peaks of these hills of rippled water. I'm guessing it'll lead me to Ascalon Lee. I've got a trade in mind. I'll get her a new HuSC from Akira's underwater lab in exchange for her help in restoring my daughter. If it comes to it, I'll even offer my new body in exchange for saving Ascalon. *Vita ad vitam.* A life for a life. Weird—I now remember the Latin I took in high school. *Confido odium.* More than Akira, I trust Ascalon Lee's hatred of me.

After miles and miles of this, suddenly, the ocean flattens. Just like that. I gotta turn around to check if I imagined all those waves. There they are, rolling on behind me. Kathy. John. It's strange how forgetting then remembering that wound made it more fresh. I slow the skim down and reel in more yellow. Water drips off the line. The yellow thickens like steel leader. I ask my iE if there's a Pacific Bridge waypoint around here. Yes, D-89 is twenty miles ahead. I ask my iE what kind of waypoint D-89 is. It's F&R—fuel and recreation. Batteries and whores, basically. I wonder what the hell Ascalon

Lee is doing way the hell out here. I don't care. She won't see me coming. She doesn't know that I now see the way I see. I pick up my rail gun and look through the scope. I set it to long distance. A giant, manmade flotsam. Thousands, maybe hundreds of thousands of white birds mating and nesting. Regardless of what body I inhabit, I still irrationally hate those fucking things, especially when they're all crowded together like that. They're pestilence in my book. Especially after I saw what Ascalon Lee could make them do. To be fair, when they fly over cities and look down at people, they probably think the same thing about us. Behind the floating aviary, silent thunder flashes. I avoid the flotsam and set a course to D-89.

I drop anchor three miles out from D-89 and look through my scope again. It's a large waypoint, town-sized, a floating, circular, sun-bleached strip mall of neon-lit restaurants, bars, barbershops, massage and AMP parlors. It's one of those places where the people feed on crab and lobster, the cheapest, nastiest food in the world. I ask my iE for the population: 5,296. No, 5,297. She's here. I know it. Smart, find someone to inhabit who's close but not too close—someone who lives off the grid and won't be missed. I'm searching for something the semblance of yellow, but tracking anything in this mess is tough. There's some kind of evac occurring. People packed atop shop roofs, their arms reaching up. I hear something incoming. I put down the rail gun and look up. Three transporter helis coming to the rescue. I check the feed. Great. Another theory turned fact. The Moon Flash disrupted tides. Thousand-foot waves rolling west across the Pacific. All above-surface water towns must evacuate or be drowned. A fifteen-minute explanation by the local weatherman who got her college degree in apocalypse poetry.

I need to move fast. I raise the magnetic anchor, start the engine, and max throttle. The old boat skips across the flat water. *Reel, motherfucker. Reel. Tighten the drag. Torque her in. Don't let her dive to the rocks and cut the line against their jagged edges. Get that gaff ready.* The boat skips over mini breakers. I spot the fake shore, which is just clumped mounds of kinetic sand. Ocean froth beards the shore. At the last moment, I ease the throttle and dock. I pick up the rail gun and hop onto the pier. The auto magnetic tethers fasten the boat to the slip. I look up. Two evac helis have dropped rope ladders. The rooftop crowds fight one another for the ropes. The rescue team on bullhorns yell for the people to stop, to proceed in an orderly fashion. One of the helis lifts. A half-dozen women dangle from the swivel like a deep drop rig. I look through the scope. None of them Ascalon Lee.

I head into town and pass the fuel station spire; its solar panels make it look like a totem with giant ears. Next, the septic tank. Effluence pumping from one tank to another. This smaller one spackled with flux. Finally, I see the catchment ahead in the center of the city. A giant one, maybe half the height of a skyscraper, shaped like a long stem rose. I look around. This whole place looks like a floating flowerpot. The spokes of lighted walkways are empty. The holo sign for the Smoking Crab Tavern—a crab holding a lit cigarette in one of its pincers—flickers: CLOSED. Teleza's Happy Endings, also closed. Thao's AMP is open. The sun is setting, and I see them. Ragged sparks. I head to Thao's.

I'm nearing the entrance, and a heli descends near Thao's rooftop. It drops a cargo net. A motley group of children my daughter's age climb inside the limp net. The quad prop chopper rises and the net sags with juvies as it heads out to sea. Two slip from the mesh and plop into the ocean. In the last few weeks, I've been to The Leachate, a mental hospital, Lucky Cat City, the moon, and here. Maybe the world hasn't gotten better since Sessho-seki. Maybe the raw crust of the world has just been underreported. The plight of the Zeroes ain't ever sold much copy. No NFT value to their life stories. I lift the gun and check the children in the water. A smaller heli bombs them with ring buoys. I wanna help them, but she's in Thao's, and I can't let her escape. I walk under the blinking neon sign, gun still raised. Some song full of chimes and windpipes plays. I walk through the beaded eyeball curtain.

Blinking egg bulbs dangle from the crumbing faux coral ceiling. I eye the exposed clevis hangers then look across the room. The reception desk is abandoned, a scatter of house slippers at the foot of it. I look at the door behind the desk. The yellow sparks more brightly. The room rumbles. Another heli must be landing. I go after the yellow. The sparks coagulate into a stream, and I follow it into the back, past another beaded curtain where an AMP chamber held together by rivets takes up most of the squalid square footage of the room. A rattling bushing connects to the wall.

I point the gun at the chamber. It's an old one, so old it could be a prototype. The chamber hums. I step to it and aim down at its fogged-up porthole window. I could end a lot of bullshit right here. Instead, I wipe the condensation from the glass. A face. A woman's face. Pretty. Framed by wisps of light hair. I wonder who she is. Or who she was. What misfortunes brought her to D-89? Perhaps descended from a long line of prostitutes. Perhaps a Leachate immigrant hopping from one pile of trash to another. Perhaps a woman on a bad run, and like all bad runs, she was left with too little breath to fight. I wonder if Ascalon Lee picked her because she figured the woman didn't have much of a life anyway. I'm starting to figure out that feeling superior is probably at the root of every problem we got on this planet. And whether it's me, Akira, Old Man Caldwell, or Ascalon Lee, feeling like we're better than everyone else is also connected to some past rage.

The woman's eyes snap open. One of them yellow. She looks right at me, unblinking, right down the barrel of my rail gun and smiles.

"I have been waiting for you," her lips word.

I don't see it, but I hear it, then I feel it. First, the hiss of gas escaping from the punctured chamber. Second, a spike pokes at my chest. I look down and see a golden tail. I drop the gun and grab at the tail. It thrusts into my sternum. I pull it out of me but don't let go. Instead, I spool it up in my fist and squeeze. She's really tugging at it now. I look back down through the window and shake my head. I'm not letting go. She still tries to squirm out of my grip. I'm stronger than I've ever been. Much, much stronger. What else did Akira do to me during my mid-moon pupal stage? Time to find out. I punch through the glass and grab Ascalon Lee by the neck.

"Listen," I say. "I'm not here to kill you."

"What has my mother done to you?" she says as she thrashes, but I got one hand on the throat and the other wrapped around the tail. She ain't going anywhere.

"Listen, I know," I say. "I know it all. The Project. The scar. The AWM. My dead wife and kid. Your mother is fucking evil. And you already know what I'm pitching."

"Let go of me."

She struggles. She's so weak, so frail that I feel like I can stretch her out and use her to jump rope. *You made a mistake,*

Kimura, by making me stronger. "I'm gonna tell you this once," I say, mustering my best mean mug. "If you don't stop squirming, I'm ripping the tail off first." I take my hand off her throat and palm her face. She turns her head side to side. I push the head against the pillowed back of the chamber. She grabs my arm and claws it. I retaliate by digging into her eyelid with my ring finger. "And if you don't stop squirming after that, I'm putting this finger right through that eye."

The eye under my finger begins to pulse. Greens seep from the socket. The pulses, they're coming in increments. In seconds. A self-destruct countdown. I dig my finger in. "I'm ready if you are," I say. And I mean it. I figure consciousness was born from our recognition of the finality of death. Our first giant evolutionary step. Our second was probably developing the ability to rationalize the worth and meaning of our lives. My life got no worth. It got no meaning without my family. Now, there's just purpose. Maybe being born again is making me feel invincible, but I ain't scared of my purpose ending here.

"I'll live on," Ascalon Lee says. "You will not."

"Well, then, you got nothing to be afraid of. Let's get on with it."

Ascalon Lee looks at me curiously, like I'm some speck under a microscope, and eases her struggling. She lets go of my arm and slowly nods. The pulsing stops. I let go of both face and tail and pick up the rail gun, then touch my chest wound. I'm concerned by the lack of searing pain, but I can't dwell on it much, because Ascalon Lee climbs out of the chamber.

"You and your mother are getting sloppy," I say. "What are you doing way out here? What was your next move?"

Ascalon Lee ignores the question and slams the chamber shut. She climbs atop and perches it, cross-legged. Looks like she's processing. The tip of her tail sways above her. "The shedding of years is becoming on you."

"Your mother shaved them off me."

She shrugs as if it's just another day in the life. "You shot her," she says. "You shot your daughter."

"I did."

"I didn't foresee that."

"That's the problem with you two," I say. "You think you can see everything."

Ascalon Lee looks toward the window, at the sun dipping into the endless ocean. Two evac helis, their props thumping, head into the last of daylight. "You fool. You should have trusted me and agreed to my offer eight years ago."

"I don't disagree."

She turns to me, curious. The xanthic eye probes me. "Your current wife will never allow me access to your daughter."

"You're gonna give this woman her life back," I say. "You're gonna leave her body and restore her to her normal self."

Ascalon Lee scoffs. "It is not much of a life."

"Never-the-fucking-less. My daughter first. Then we get you a HuSC. After that, you put this woman . . . back. With some compensation."

Ascalon Lee nods. She hops off the chamber, and it's the first time I notice there's something stunted about her. From childhood on, she lived a life of rejection and desolate lone-liness. People can't grow like that. Twisted, bandaged, and broken. They're like bound feet. Or like fish forced to live in a five-gallon tank. Release that fish into the ocean, and that sucker still won't grow. Ascalon Lee walks to me and puts her hand on my chest. I wonder when's the last time she touched another human being, not to study it, just to touch. Better yet, has she ever? Her eye brightens and scans me.

"Remarkable," she says. "It was a shallow wound, but it's already beginning to heal. Nano implants. Permanent ones. Perhaps fueled by mitochondria. You have your own microscopic medical team in your body. And your strength . . . incredible. Your bones, hardened, yet still malleable. You were probably grown in a perpetually stressed system. With perhaps a sprinkling of illegal genetic modification. Your new body blocks myostatin. Yes. That's it. It blocks the proteins that inhibit muscle growth."

"I don't care," I say. "I don't care how she did it."

"How can you possibly not care? This is cutting-edge technology that could have other applications."

"Because it already happened."

She smiles. "Where?" she asks.

I point out the window at the faint, full moon. Like most things, it looks a lot prettier from far away.

"Yes," Ascalon Lee says. "I should have known." She pauses, then asks, "Was there a chrysalis of me?"

"No. But two chambers were empty."

She grins. "Interesting." She sighs and steps to the window. "My mother and her plans."

"You know what she's planning?" I ask.

Ascalon Lee ignores the question and asks one of her own. "Did something go wrong up there?" she asks, still gazing at the moon.

I nod. "Caldwell."

She turns and smiles at me. "The old man?"

"Yeah. He's the one who salvaged Akira's iE. He's the one who came and hired me to figure out how to get Akira into, well, I guess a new HuSC. Then he double-crossed me and shot us down up there. Took my iE. Took Akira, too."

Ascalon Lee grins again. "Endless grudges."

"No," I say. "Just one more."

She laughs. "'Just one more' . . . The phrase of a true addict."

Maybe. Maybe I'm fooling myself once again. I ping Sabrina with voice. She answers. "I'm coming home," I say.

"I hope not empty-handed," she says.

"I'm bringing someone with me, someone for Ascalon."

"Then hurry."

Sabrina cuts transmission. My wife, unlike the rest of us, can't hold grudges. She's better than Akira, better than Ascalon Lee, better than this beta test version of me. Not that that's saying much, but she is. It took me a while to figure it out. Sabrina didn't have me on block. It was Akira who didn't want me talking with my wife. Akira didn't want me exposed to any semblance of a voice of reason. She didn't want me to be thinking about my kids, the one laid up in the hospital and the one yet to be born. Just like when she had Kathy and John killed all those years ago, Akira wanted every ounce of my attention to be focused on her. She even blocked me from HW hospital. And I only regained communication with my wife when Akira was out of the picture.

Ascalon Lee and I, we fish out the few kids that we can find. We pack the skimmer and head out. It's hard, but I ignore the whip of neon blue streaking across the water with laser straightness. Something in me wants to follow it. Needs to follow it. I fight the urge, and, instead, we're heading back to Water City.

"And in return?" Ascalon Lee asks. "I just want to ensure we are of the same mind when it comes to terms."

"You know the answer."

"You have double-crossed me before."

"I didn't think you were gonna hold up your end," I say.

"How do I know that you won't simply rationalize betrayal again?" she asks.

"If you want it," I say, "you'll own this new and improved version of me."

"Maybe I want my own."

"I'll do my best to get you access to your own HuSC in your mother's lab," I say. "But trust me. It don't get better than this one."

"If I take you, you will never get your vengeance."

"No, I won't. But you'll get it for me."

Ascalon Lee closes her eyes, cutting our strongest light source. Now, only the moon and stars dimly illuminate us. The motor churrs, and I lick my lips, tasting the salty air. "Do you still see it?" she asks.

I put all my cards on the table. Tell her about my sight and let her examine my head. She says she can't detect Akira's presence in there, but she could be lying. Who the hell knows? I don't think so, though. Right now, I turn around and look back. It's there, a band of sea sparkle, twisting in the ocean. It jerks and sings to me, but it's the magenta that I'm following. I scratch my hands. I don't think Akira's in my head, because it's the blue I want to follow most, but I ain't following it. In fact, if I'm able to, like dessert, I'll save it for last.

"I still see it," I say.

"An interesting form of GPS." Ascalon Lee opens her eye, and the golden light returns. She smiles. "You are a unique creature," she says.

"How so?"

"Have you ever seen a pet put on its own leash?"

I shake my head. I have not. Or maybe I have. Maybe that's kind of all we do when we grow up. We decide what we're gonna attach ourselves to, and these things, they begin to lead us. They walk us routinely and in circles. They walk us when we don't wanna walk and hold us back when we wanna run. The kids we got packed below deck, my own child, they don't get to choose yet, just like Ascalon Lee didn't when she was a child. But as adults? We choose what we leash ourselves to. And if our owners let us go, we tangle ourselves in the abandoned slack. Even here, in the middle of the Pacific, I don't feel free. I feel different hands yanking on different tethers. What none of them seem to realize is that if they pull too hard, I'm gonna bite.

"I could see what she saw," Ascalon Lee says. "Your daughter. What you see. The greens and reds. Are they beautiful to you?"

As ugly as the things they lead me to can be, they are. The fragrance of the greens, the music of the reds, I soak them in, and they tint those very last moments of life. But once life passes, they become brutal and overpowering, which makes them easier to follow. My daughter and I can't be the only ones who sense like we do, but in all my life, I haven't met anyone else who has. Then, I suppose those who see what others don't keep it to themselves, like I have for just about my whole life. If there are others like me, maybe they don't sense death. Maybe they sense or can do other things.

Every time the human genome duplicates itself, a hundred new mutations are created. We already know there are some people who can eat glass and metal. Some who see through echolocation. Some who do not need sleep. Maybe some really do see the future. Maybe some commune with the dead. I envy them. Because right now, the path to Water City smells and sounds of rancid green and red.

4

If Water City wasn't undersea, it'd be on fire right now. It's dawn, and the refugees from the Pacific Bridge are packed together on scraper tips. They're trampling one another while trying to cram into vac tubes to take them down to the city. Fleets of helis swoop from the sky, unloading their human deposits. Some passengers jump from the choppers, hoping to land in the ocean and make a swim for the vac tubes. Instead, they plummet to the manmade beaches. Their bodies splat like bags of wet sand. A muffled underwater explosion. The ocean boils. I point my rail at the water and adjust the scope to aqua sighting. A recreational sub from Deeptown collided with a vac tube. Probably panicked members of The Money evacuating their penthouses. I lower the gun. Dozens of corpses float to the surface like dynamited fish. For a moment, I'm seeing exclusively in green and red again. I close my eyes and open them in an attempt to quickly reboot my brain. Good. Back to normal. Or maybe not so good.

I ping Sabrina and give her an update. Before I can guess at what blew up underneath, I see a man up ahead, swimming.

A rescue razor boat's headed right toward him. The pilot doesn't see him. I wave my hands at the pilot and yell for him to turn. The boat's bow skips over the swimmer's spine, and the terrible sound of the propeller grinding flesh and bone follows. The man's torso bobs, and his lower extremities drift away from it. The only thing binding the two pieces of the man is the puffs of blood chumming the water. The razor boat continues on, as if nothing had happened.

I glance at Ascalon Lee. She's smirking. I shake my head and check the feed. We weren't ready for this. We're never ready for anything unless there's money in it, and there never is money in preparation. To make things worse, the volcano's acting up. Even the folks who live elevated near Savior's Eye are evacuating. More helis, these ones police. Helmeted riot cops wearing grip gloves repel down ropes. I was hoping to get home to grab my SEAL. Instead, I turn and head to shore, toward Sabrina and my daughter. I look back at my passengers. Huddled together, the children are shivering. It's hurricane season, so the water's warm. It occurs to me that they aren't shivering because it's cold, but because they're terrified. I wanted to drop them off at a vac tube station, but the entire city's clogged. A city being plumbed by hysterical exodus.

"We're going to the island," I say.

The kids nod, their eyes glued to the riot police firing off sonic bombs; the kids attempting to quell the crowds of people screaming and banging on the now-locked entrances of the seascrapers. Waves of refugees collapse, grasping at their ears.

When we get to shore, the pier is packed with lines and lines of islanders dressed in synthetic loincloths toting wicker suitcases and baskets, waiting for transport to Water City. Their pets, teacup potbellied pigs, trained to exclusively eat invasive plants, snort at their feet or screech in their owners' sling bags. I motor further along the coast and anchor in front of an abandoned sandy cove. I ping Sabrina. She was supposed to pick us up, but she ain't here. She answers. The hospital has been evacuated, she says. She doesn't want to leave Ascalon alone.

I turn to the kids. "Stay here. There's supplies below deck. They'll last you a week. Don't try to get to the city. I'll come back for you." I turn to Ascalon Lee. "Let's go," I say.

She nods. She's been suspiciously quiet, and her eyes have been boring into the children for most of the trip. Why am I trusting her? No, this ain't trust. Only two people can fix my daughter. This is desperation.

I drop the lifeboat then grab my duffel of gear and toss it down. We take the ladder, Ascalon Lee first. I release the tethers and gun the small, solar motor. It whines awake, and we skip over small surf. As the beach nears, I accelerate. The lifeboat slides up, skids, and grinds over the black sand. "You're the genius," I say. "The hospital is about thirty miles inland. What's the quickest way to get there?"

She's staring back at the skimmer, its quadrofoil haunches flexing on the water's surface. "Why did you help them?"

"Seemed like the right thing to do."

She turns to me. "What objective metric measures your moral quality?"

I pick up my bag and pull out the rail. "What are you talking about? I don't keep track."

"Then how do you know whether you're good or bad?" she asks.

I step out of the skiff. "I stopped keeping track after my first kill. Pretty sure the answer was clear from that point on."

"I see. You live with low self-expectations. That's how you justify action."

I wish she was quiet again. I pull up the rail gun. I scan the coast for transportation. Nothing. We're at the edge of the Eshana Estate. With its pointy stone roofs and its light-up oxidized brass domes, it looks like the spawn of the classic stories *Star Wars* and *The Great Gatsby*. I see if there's any transport on its helipads. Negative. The museum closed. I think about Eshana—Akira's sponsor and collaborator, one-time richest man in the world—and wonder what he would make of all this. I put the gun down and look at Ascalon Lee. "How do you justify your actions?" I ask.

She steps out, removes her shoes, and digs her toes into the wet, black sand. She tilts her head back and closes her eyes. She glows like an ember. "The tide is rising at a rate of approximately three inches per hour. The wind, ten miles per hour, south-southwest. My father's people used to call these Kona winds. 'These winds that move against the flow of the trades.'" She opens her eyes and turns to me. Yellow wisps hiss from its pupil. "I am not oppressed by expectations. Anyone's nor my own."

Over her shoulder, I spot a compact heli approaching. It's tethered to the eye by a low-test string of yellow. I pull my gun up and take a look at the heli. It's empty.

The two-seater thuds on the beach, and we climb in. I wonder what else she can control remotely like that, and the possibilities are scary. I look out to the ocean and feel the leader of blue tugging at me. Akira. She's out there somewhere. I turn my eyes inland and search for the puff of magenta. I find, unlike the yellows and blues, that I need to look for it in order to see it.

The heli rises, and that's when I spot it, the magenta. A faint wisp tucked between the hills above. Light ain't got no mass, but what I'm feeling, I feel on my shoulders. "How did she do this to me?" I ask.

"How do you know it's just her that did it to you?"

"What'd you do?"

"Nothing. Nothing at all."

Yellow unfurls from Ascalon Lee's eye and snakes itself around the heli's gauge cluster. Ascalon Lee's piloting it without even touching the controls. Visibility's low now because of the fresh vog rolling in. We're up high, so high I can spot the water statue of Akira spouting from the mountain's peak.

"The difficulty of replicating human consciousness has always been exaggerated," Ascalon Lee says. "We want to believe that it's difficult. That we're unpredictable. That we are unique and special. We have been able to clone and mutate rats for generations. Yet, cloning human beings, genetically mutating them has almost always been considered sacrilegious. But it's not our morality that holds us back. It is our ego. Our dread of shattering it. We are superior. We are unique. Despite being 97.5% genetically identical to the lab rats we have experimented on for centuries, we somehow believe, in spite of all evidence to the contrary, that we are a million percent more. We must preserve that perception. It's in our oh-so basic code."

Ascalon Lee throttles back, and we glide through altitude. We're closer to the statue now, and I see thousands of people gathered, all dressed in identical robes. They're on their knees bowing to the statue. "What species do they resemble most?" she asks.

I don't gotta say it out loud. Spreaders of disease. The eradicator of other species. Wildly reproductive gluttons that are highly adaptable. They are who crawled out of Eden. They are who became us. Rats. Thousands and thousands of drowning rats. And the worst part about it is that the threat ain't even real. It's imagined. "We overreact," I say. "All of us."

She nods. "Imagination mixed with emotion is a toxic cocktail. But a predictable one."

"You knew turning off the light would do all this."

She nods and banks. HW Hospital up ahead. "Then why?"

"Melanin and mucus," she says. "Turning it off was like casting a cloud of squid ink. A cephalopod will release it to confuse, to escape. Some inks can, in fact, numb the senses of predators."

"Plus, it would piss your mother off."

"Perhaps. Have you heard of pseudomorphs?"

"Yeah," I say. "False bodies. My daughter learned about it in school."

"I made it easier to get to you," she says. "I knew your wife would need to report to duty. It separated mother from child. I feared her detecting my infiltration more than I feared you doing so. Let's just say, she is more focused on your child. You, I believe, sleepwalk through parenthood."

Maybe she's right. Maybe I wasn't just sleepwalking nights, half-conscious trips to the fridge for midnight sweets, half-conscious trips to the toilet to piss them out. Maybe I was sleepwalking through all my days, as well. I never saw it. All those years, I never even pondered my daughter's love for the ocean. I never asked why. That the entire time, she was looking for something. Or someone. Someone pinging her. Someone dangling baits of green and red. I look over at Ascalon Lee and wanna kill her.

"And now," Ascalon Lee says, "now, it will make it easier to eventually get to my mother."

"But all those people," I say.

"That is not what you want to say."

"You don't know what I want or don't want to say."

She scoffs. "You want revenge. On me. On my mother. You don't care about 'all those people.' No one does. And how can they? There are simply too many. Once we hit billions, the lives of individuals have become laughably expendable. The worst thing we ever did was start counting people. We lost count anyway. For generations now, we throw around phrases like 'incalculable loss.' Incalculable loss is simply code for a lot but not enough for us to actually care."

We begin to descend. Turbulence rattles the cockpit. Ascalon Lee continues. "As I expressed earlier, I am not oppressed by expectation." She turns and glares at me with that yolky eye. "I am all that matters."

I half expect a laser to shoot out of that eye and split me in half. Instead, Ascalon Lee concentrates on landing. For some reason, that statement, "I am all that matters," saws at me. I feel it in my palms. But I have more pressing matters to focus on, so I distract myself with the view. Down below, hills hairy with vegetation. Mountains terraced with abandoned tree houses. I spot the hospital. We got our choice of lily-shaped helipads. No traffic moving in or out. *How is all this possible?* It feels like there are just four of us operating in this world of billions—Ascalon Lee, Akira, Old Man Caldwell, and me.

There ain't no journalists investigating. There ain't no law on our tail. The scar going out, one hell of a distraction. But even if the light didn't go out, I don't know if this world would be onto us. The personal philosophy of just about every one of us is "I am all that matters." And it's easy to sneak around when everyone else is gazing in a mirror.

Ascalon Lee lands. She kills the engine and looks at me. "You know where she is, don't you?"

"No," I say. "But there's a trail. Just like there was a trail to you."

She nods and grins like there's something she knows that I don't. We step onto the tarmac. There's a walkway striped with the shadows of bent trees. As we head to the entrance, it strikes me funny that we notice the trees but never their shadows. But I'm noticing now. The emergency room is empty. I've never been in an empty hospital before. People are always getting sick, always being born, always dying. That just don't stop. We head to the elevators. Sabrina and my kid are on the fifth floor. ICU. We push through rolling styleviews and scattered gurneys. I look down at the wheels of a tipped-over gurney, and for a moment I imagine my kid at three, her first time on a tricycle. She's chasing me and laughing. She's pedaling and steering so hard that she flips the three-wheeler. She's crying. And I'm walking back to her, thinking, *What the fuck? How the hell does one fall off a trike? That's the whole point of having the damn third wheel.* I pick her up, but she wants her mother. Sleepwalking through parenthood. I'm really letting this psychopath get to me.

"You can get this done, right?" I ask.

"Yes," Ascalon Lee says.

We're inside the elevator now, and Ascalon Lee says, "Have you prepared your wife?"

"Yeah," I say.

"Not for me, but for you."

I didn't even think about that. Telling Sabrina to brace herself. That my body's younger now. Her age, in fact. I wanna warn her, but it's too late for that. The elevator stops on the fifth floor, and the doors open. The echo of our squeaking shoes bellows through the empty hall as we walk. If I thought an apocalypse was coming, I'd rather be here than Water City. I like the idea of dying alone, in peace. Maybe that's why I was drawn to sniper duty when I served. If I got popped in the middle of a desert, no one would be around to fuss over me. Did the girl I killed appreciate that? What a stupid thing to think.

The magenta fog thickens.

I take a careful step inside the room. A part of me is bracing myself to be cut down by my wife. But she's just sitting on a chair next to an AMP, the same chamber I stuck my kid in weeks ago, the one we drudged up from the deep.

"Hey," I say.

Sabrina stands. Billows of magenta halo every limb then condense to her belly. "What the fuck happened to you?" she asks.

Yup, I should've given her a heads-up. I wasn't trying to withhold anything from her. I just forgot to tell her during our brief conversations. "Going to the moon changes a man," I say.

"The moon?" Sabrina says.

"Akira had a lab up there, kind of like the one we found under Vista." I spread my arms. "She left me this."

"And you just let her do it?" Sabrina shakes her head. "Okay, at least I know it's really you now."

I sigh. Now's not the time to be explaining. I step to the chamber and look down at my baby Ascalon hibernating away. I feel my wife's eyes on me. To be a man in this world, you gotta be able to deliver a smile full of menace. That's exactly what I'm doing now, and I don't know why. There's no one to hit, to intimidate, to threaten. I'm powerless, and here I am, beaming that smile where the mouth says one thing and the eyes say another. What I should be doing is crying, but despite everything that I now remember, I think I forgot how.

I look away. Sabrina sees my smile and frowns. It probably reminds her of our child's ghastly fake smile when it comes to taking pics. That look, like the moment of fear before the tongue depressor at the dentist starts coming. All I know is that my palms itch for some reason. Sabrina the Sentry. How'd she do it? Powerless. Watching over the kid, day after day. Week after week. Because she had to. I, on the other hand—freeing Akira in Lucky Cat City, flying to the moon, getting shot down in space, losing my mind, uploading oneself to another—had the fucking easy job. To top it off, she finds out she's pregnant.

Ascalon Lee steps into the room, and I'm no longer smiling. At first, Sabrina looks a little confused, but soon enough, under the crown of gold hair, lodged in pale skin, she sees the yellow eye. Ascalon Lee steps to her.

"I would have kept my end of the arrangement," Ascalon Lee says.

"I hate you," says Sabrina.

"I know," says Ascalon Lee.

Ascalon Lee turns to me. "Shall we proceed?" she asks.

I nod. Ascalon Lee steps to the chamber and sighs. She strips off her clothes. Her back is scarred with bite marks, those of a human. Permanent remnants of tricks turned. That's us. Fucking people, man, always leaving their marks. Her tail dangles from her spine, stapled there with fresh sutures. *How did she make that thing so fast?* She opens the chamber, pushes my daughter to the side, and crawls inside. Sabrina turns around.

"She's the one who did it," I say. "She's the only one who can reverse it."

Sabrina nods once in understanding. Ascalon Lee grabs my daughter's face with both hands, then I watch her tail slither around my kid's waist and pull her closer. Both look at peace. Is it comforting for this woman to be in a womb again with another? Forehead to forehead. Nose to nose. I wonder if the two already share some kind of connection. "Close the chamber," Ascalon Lee says.

I do as she says and look through the glass. The yellow eye juts, splits open, and, like a matryoshka, appears to birth a smaller, lesser eye. *How is this possible?* I ask myself. But then I think of all our other older tech—surgical med bots, nanos, the melding of quantum computing and biochemistry. It feels like this sort of thing was kind of inevitable. I watch as the legs of the newborn eye pop and claw around my daughter's empty socket and burrow. A laser fires from one eye to another. My daughter spasms. I look back at Sabrina, who's still standing there, back turned to me. She can't watch this. I barely can. I put my hands on the glass, tempted to open the torpedo-like chamber and pull my daughter out. What if she's just gonna possess my daughter all over again? I wanna disarm this damn thing. Then I see tendrils, profane fingers of magenta, reach out then spiral around the yellow beam as if they're welcoming it. The magenta begins to spin, and the two are now twisted together. I find myself praying to God, not Akira, but the older one, the one I'm guessing is a man-made fraud, too. But it's not really praying. It's bargaining. *If you save her, I'll do whatever you want.* And it occurs to me, maybe it ain't God I should be praying to. It's Ascalon Lee and her scientific voodoo.

"A deal's a deal. If you want my HuSC, it's yours," I say.

"What?" Sabrina asks.

I turn to her. "If this works, she can have me."

"What do you mean, she can have you?"

I look down at my body and motion to it. "If she brings our daughter back, she can have this body."

"And where will that leave you?" Sabrina asks.

I shrug, but I know. It'll leave me dead.

"We'll see about that," Sabrina says.

"What do you mean?" I ask.

"If this doesn't work, I'll strangle you before she can take it."

I can't tell if she's being serious. There's this gulley between us. Not one that I can see, but one that I can feel. "What's the status of the lab we found?" I ask. "Feds take it over?"

"The Feds are busy trying to contain a national melt-down," Sabrina says. "I locked down the lab. I left security drones at the entrance. No one can get past without me knowing it."

I turn around. "The bodies are still there?"

Sabrina turns to me. "Everything is still there. Everything except my child and this chamber. I placed the facility under quarantine. I cut the guideline. Even if someone were to search, I doubt they could find it. I mapped it, though. I know exactly where it is."

This lady. I'm probably the only mistake she's ever made. "The superintendent?"

"Also indisposed. When the moon flared up, local law enforcement suddenly had a lot on its hands."

"Akeem's sub?" I ask.

"Returned to his family."

"How are they?"

"Enraged and in grief, but also in disarray," Sabrina says.

I picture Akeem and his family gathered together at the horseshoe bar at his house. He's slinging drinks, and they're all teasing one another and laughing. I sigh. Sabrina steps next to me and looks down at our daughter. She closes her eyes and whispers, "What if this doesn't work?"

"She knows it's got to in order for her to walk out of here."

"Still, what if it doesn't?"

"Akira Kimura," I say. "That would be the only other option."

Sabrina sighs again. She looks down at the two Ascalons and shudders. "And if she brings Ascalon back and decides not to try and take your body?"

"She and I agreed. If that's the case, we both go after her mother." I look at Sabrina and feel my jaw clenching. "Akira killed Kathy and John. She killed them so that I'd work for her."

"What?"

"I should've seen it," I say. "I should've figured it out."

Sabrina gazes at the wall. "That was decades ago."

I turn back to the AMP and put my hands on the glass. The

two. Doubles. Double down, double blind, double dealing, double trouble. This world loves its doubles. "Time don't matter," I say.

"Where is she?"

"Old Man Caldwell's got her."

"So, let him destroy her."

I shake my head. Caldwell. Akira screaming up in the lunar lander. Like me, she didn't see that one coming. That was the first time I'd ever heard that lady scream. But I don't think she was scared. I think she was angry. Maybe Caldwell destroyed her already. For some reason, I'm hoping not. "I need confirmation."

"It doesn't matter what happens here," Sabrina says. "You're going after her anyway."

I nod. I don't know if it's right or wrong, but she's correct. If Ascalon Lee don't fucking body snatch me next, I'm doing it anyway.

"You and your powerful friends," Sabrina sneers. "I used to suspect you sidled to The Money because you admired or maybe wanted to be one of them. Or maybe you were waiting for some kind of handout. Then, I started noticing that you don't take much from them. But they take from you. They're always taking from you, you dumb asshole. And by taking from you, they take from me." She points at our daughter. "They take from her. They take. That's how they become The Money in the first place. Taking. Did it ever cross your mind that knowing people, knowing important people, can hurt you more than it can help you?"

She's right. The world's gone mad, and here I am, willing to step out the moment my daughter wakes up. *If* she wakes up. I'm gonna leave my wife, my kid, and my unborn child to hunt down Akira Kimura and put an end to her. I wanna tear the whole fucking thing down—the statues, the vids, the holos, every goddamn holy image. Then I'll take Caldwell. Ascalon Lee shortly after. And here's the fucked up thing, if my daughter doesn't wake up, or if she does and is just a smidge less than I remember, I'm gonna snip every single goddamn guideline. Maybe even Sabrina's too. Because without my kid, the only thing worth living for is killing. I will snuff out every single thread until there ain't color in this world.

PART FIVE

SATORI DAY

1

I hear them. These incessant beings. The synesthete's wife has secured my HuSC in my mother's underwater lab. He is lucky, this man. Always so lucky. If she had not secured a proper HuSC for me, I would have taken his. I would have peeled him out. It would have been unfortunate. The man, with his evasive moral code, his guilt, his temper, his self-loathing, his futile battle with his selfishness, amuses me.

He spent days with you, Mother, and he never asked the question, did he? This self-involved man. He never asked you what is your plan? Not that you would've told him, but he didn't even ask. I've been asking myself, Mother, and I believe I might know. I solder severed nerve to severed nerve. Soon, I'll jump-start the symphony of neurons. We are not gods, Mother. You with your lights. Me with my rewiring. We, all of us, are merely electricians.

Akira refused to tell me her plan. I could not project accurately forward in time, so I dwelled on the past. Not mine, but hers.

I see you, Mother. You are in a story that Jerry Caldwell once told me when I was a child. A story passed down from you when the both of you were friends. You are a little girl, younger than this little girl here. It's your first trip to the United States. You're in northern California. Your father has brought you here to see the last living coastal redwood. Its size is breathtaking. The trunk large enough to drive antiquated carriages through. Your father tells you that it's over two thousand years old. You look up at a harnessed woman, dressed like a gardener, dangling some two hundred feet up in the air. You cannot tell, but she appears to be trimming it. Slivers of evergreen rain from her sheers. The woman repels down. She tells you that the tree used to be much bigger. You ask if it's shrinking. You're surprised to discover that it is in fact shrinking. Not above ground, but beneath the soil. The forest used to be a clonal colony.

There used to be thousands upon thousands of trees here. The entire grove interconnected by roots, by genetic code. Because of this togetherness, they were able to grow faster, live longer. If fires came, they could survive underground then sprout anew, each a perfect copy of the other. But none an individual. They were all the same. They were all one organism.

When Jerry first told me the story, I didn't see it, and I know she didn't, but I believe I see it now. It was Akira's moment of epiphany.

Your Newton's apple, wasn't it? Why could we not be like this? Instead of destroying this magnificent ramet, we should emulate it. Our species, it exasperated you even as a child, didn't it? You didn't need to look beyond your own parents. Animals develop spots and stripes to survive. Your father's expensive taste used them to furnish and decorate. When your mother became an alcoholic after your father had died, her neurological disorders would occasionally and unpredictably flare into fits of violence, you the most common target. Both of them, so proud of their jobs. How they measured their personal occupational value incorrectly. They told themselves that what they did was important, which may have been correct. However, never did they ask themselves if they were replaceable, which they were. After your father's death, the financial institution that employed him was still stable, wasn't it? After your mother's, the primary school children still learned, did they not? You loathed this world of false equivalency.

So, that day, Akira eyed the treetop. It simply stood there. Still, peaceful. Then she imagined the other trees that once existed, sprouting from the roots underground. She imagined them growing as large as the remaining tree. Thousands of them. She imagined the grove as it once was. And all in the colony appeared to be looking up, growing still to the same fixed, invisible rafter in the sky. So, years later, she created that light. She filled that invisible rafter with a scar, and the people all looked up. Then, she thought about the root system. And the answer was already there. The iF!

They were all connected already, were they not?

The message had to simply be uniform. A whisper. A mantra. Akira.

We know you, Mother. You aimed to become their *mitsubi*. Their root system. That thing that permeates all life but can only survive underground. But how?

The neurons spark. They fire. This little girl, not named after me but named after the hoax that lit the sky. She's young, but as my mother knows, life is everlasting now, not because of her, but because of me. This girl, perhaps years from now, may have a role to play in this. Perhaps I should leave something for her. My whisper. My mantra.

I understand now. You have your gardeners. Now, I must have mine: the synesthete, his child, the others I already inhabit. But mine will not be gardeners. No, they will be arsonists. I don't want to be a tree, Mother. I do not want to be connected to a singular idea. I do not want to be connected to anyone but myself. I once wanted to be you so badly. No longer. I want to destroy, not just you, but the idea of you. It has already started. They do not look up anymore. They are no longer connected. I've sparked the wildfire, and I'm sorry, Mother, you cannot wait it out underground.

It is time. The girl is ready. Systems check. There must not be hysteresis. There must not be a lag. Check. I understand her value. This beautiful little girl I wish I could have been. A girl her parents fawn over. A child who is fearless because she has only experienced security. A girl who smiles and laughs easily because she has not experienced true pain. Now I feel an even stronger connection to her, a kinship that I'm surprised I stumbled upon. I was the one who sparked her interest in piracy, the one who seduced her into the depths of the ocean. I like this child, yet a part of me wishes to unplug this spoiled brat. When I was young, I learned that only when I was able to unflinchingly extinguish the life of what I found most beautiful was I truly powerful. This girl, I could extinguish her now. My, how I covet. I want this girl's life. I won't take it, but I won't abandon it, either.

Like you abandoned my sister. Like you abandoned me.

I detach. The girl's eyes flutter open. She is looking at me, fearless as usual. Hi, *she whispers in my head.*

Hi, *I whisper back. I pull my tail back toward me.*

Her brow crinkles. She's thinking, grasping at memory. She finds the bits of me that will forever inhabit her. These leftover pieces will never control her. She will never become me. But because I lived in her, some of my neurons remain. It's as if a third parent and its code have been implanted in her. I see her mind fix on an image. My image.

I've been . . . looking for you, *she says.*

I know. You tried to catch me.

I thought you were going to try and hurt my dad, *she says.*

I forgive you, *I say.*

Did I find you, or did you find me?

We found each other.

You have a tail, *she says.*

Yes, *I say.*

That's super neat, *she says.*

She reaches out and touches it. It does not recoil. I feel her parents' eyes on me. I put up a hand. Not yet. What is your name? the girl asks.

Ascalon, *I say.*

She giggles. My name is Ascalon, too.

Despite my best efforts, I find myself smiling. I utter words that I somehow cannot control. Will you be my sister? I ask.

Is that why you called me my whole life? We're sisters?

Yes, *I say.* We are.

Do you like pirates?

Of course I do. *I gasp. I smile. The Caldwell version of me and the one from the moon have successfully caged my mother and are seeing and feeling all of this right now, too.* We are marauding right now, and the world doesn't even know it, *I say.*

Even her father doesn't see it, these things we are doing.

These things I set in motion. But Akira sees. And the synesthete, he will eventually see, too.

Why are you crying? *she asks.*

I wipe my cheek with my tail. I don't know.

She reaches out to touch my face. I wince. Her hand stops. I nod. She puts her small hand on our cheek. Your eye, *she says.* It's so pretty. The one that isn't crying.

I laugh. It is the first time someone has used that word to describe me. Perhaps it will be the last. There are still things I must do, but right now, I don't want this girl's parents to open this chamber. I want to stay here for a bit longer. This child, she is everything I'm not. Innocent. Joyful. Pure. Unlike her, I have spent my waking hours killing. I've killed great lights in the sky. I've killed men, women, children, even myself. I've killed rodents, primates, and the aquatic life of the deep. Most cannot fathom that life can exist in those harsh places where humankind cannot survive. Man lacks the imagination to see outside himself. Life flourishes in those deep, dark places, but even there it can be extinguished, and I have extinguished it. Why? Because death is life's greatest teacher. Because I want what anything does when it has reached its full potential: to make death. But not right now. For now, I enjoy the company of this girl who has every reason to hate me yet does not. This beautiful child . . . I believed I put something in her. Instead, perhaps it is she that put something in me.

I am glad you find this eye so pretty, *I say.*

Why? *she asks.*

Because. You have the same eye.

She smiles. And I cannot believe I'm thinking this. Is there anything more stunning than the smile of a child? But I know. She will not consider me pretty once she discovers what I have done. What I made her do. What is yet to come. When I slip out of this body, this woman I inhabit will need to slumber for now. I did not tell the synesthete that restoring this woman will need to wait, but he's about to find out. I know this man. His anger will be blunted by the fact that his daughter lives. That I relinquish all control over her. She is free. Unfortunately, she will be disgusted by me when the history unfolds in her mind. Is that not history, though? True human history? The retracing of our pasts only to be disgusted with ourselves. It does not matter that this girl will hate me, though. I am all that matters. I release the AMP lock. The chamber hisses open. The girl's mother reaches into the chamber and pulls her out. I detach myself from the woman's body and float. The horrified child watches, then turns to bury her face in her mother's shoulder.

2

The trip back down to Akira's little underwater lab ain't as rough as the first time around. I got Akira's mini-sub. It's just me this time. Well, me and Ascalon Lee, her eye clenched to the barrel of my rail gun like a tiny mechanical crab. She's been quiet the entire trip—easy, willing, and able—ever since she got out of the chamber. I asked her if it was necessary to keep that new yellow eye in my daughter. She ignored my question and instead pointed out that her former host, like my kid, needed to be kept in AMP until a suitable replacement iE could be installed. I told her we had a deal. She told me she would address it later. I'm not sure about that. Another life doomed by Akira and Ascalon Lee. Another doomed by me. I looked at my kid, clinging to Sabrina. I expected Ascalon Lee to take my body next. Feeling horrible about this anonymous sleeping woman from D-89 made me ready to give it up. But Ascalon Lee didn't take my body. She said she wanted her own. The one in her mother's lab. And once again, the only emotion I felt was relief.

When I asked Ascalon Lee how she and her mother still seem to have endless income years after they were presumed dead, she laughed and marveled that I didn't hear about ghost accounts. Their wealth farms continued to mine currency even after they passed. Money doesn't need to go somewhere when someone dies, she said. To think so is arcane and ridiculous. Wealth is data. The fucking Money. When my mother died, I inherited bills. These two die, and they still earn specter fortunes in the afterlife just in case they're able to come back.

While Sabrina and I blubbered over our daughter, Ascalon Lee put the woman from D-89 in hibernation. Even though she was just a silent, tiny orb floating above us, I could sense her impatience. I nodded at the iE. I don't know how I'm liking this new, uncoerced, cooperative Ascalon Lee. This quiet version. It makes me suspicious about what was going on in that chamber while she was bringing my daughter back to life. It makes me nervous to think she can blink and reclaim control over my daughter at any time.

After diving down and deactivating the police security drones, Ascalon Lee, just an eye now, remotely opens the secret passage. The pedals on the ocean floor peel open like an anemone. We drop through the center, and the sub torques through the brine. When we get to the cavern and dock the sub, the PTSD kicks in. This is where I gunned down my kid. She was standing right there, pointing a rail gun at Sabrina. That's when I popped her.

"Give me a minute," I say. I remove my helmet and belch. But more than burps come out. Before I left to come down here, Sabrina and I didn't say a word to each other, not about the pregnancy, the comatose woman in the chamber, nor the tattered remains of our marriage. Our kid sensed the tension right away, even before she even noticed I shedded about fifty years. When she asked what was wrong, Sabrina said that the world had gone a bit batty while she had been sick and sleeping. That's when the hospital pinged us with the bill. I almost laughed at the absurd amount. They didn't do a damn thing to help her. In fact, they abandoned her. I guess billing departments around the world aren't fazed by catastrophe. I asked Sabrina to pick up the kids Ascalon Lee and I left on the skimmer. Another fucked-up thing is I almost forgot about them.

I try to step forward but wobble. I drop to a knee and vomit again. *You act as if you were the one shot here,* Ascalon Lee pings via Thought Talk before skittering to the lab.

It's not just the memory of being here. It's the memory of everything that's making me sick. I try my best to stand and follow. I lean on one of the stone guardian dogs to catch my breath. *Don't look at the spot where you shot her,* I tell myself. But I can't help it. I look. Dust of green and red kicks up. Suddenly, I'm six, and my father is teaching me how to shoot. I'm eighteen and at Fort Powell receiving my first sharpshooter badge. Then I'm older, and it's Akira taking a cannonball from my lap and replacing it with a rail gun. There's something about this grotto. Something in the thick air that messes with my memory. I start wondering if Akira has psychedelic dust venting through the oxygen system. I need to get outta here. I double-time to the rotunda.

The tanks are there, intact. The Akiras, the Ascalon Lee, and I, bound together in suspended animation. The empty tank, former contents unknown. For the first time, I inspect this empty one closely. Its label reads *HuSC 1.0. Model 4.* There were only three models up on the moon, me, Ascalon Lee, and three Akiras. Two of the Akiras were dead. Caldwell took the last one. My eyes narrow. I watch Ascalon Lee skitter around the rotunda, examining her mother's lab. Where is the other Ascalon Lee? Did Caldwell activate her, too? No. There was no Ascalon Lee iE to plug into a body up there. Maybe he grabbed the HuSC to study it? So who is Model 4?

I walk to the next tube, HuSC 1.1. Model 1. It's one of the Akiras. Of course, she's Model 1. I look up. No trapeze piping. Six glowing halos hum above the containers. This lab is definitely newer than the antiquated one on the moon. Some kind of bioengineering I ain't seen before. I know which lab came first. And by looking at the labeled designations, 1.1 here as opposed to 1.0 on the moon, these HuSCs are more recent models.

I step to the 1.1 version of me. Does it see like me? Heal like me? Is it a much-improved model over the one I inhabit? Can I download consciousness into it? Can there be two of me at the same time? The world don't want two of me, and I don't want two of me either. Ascalon Lee's legs retract, and she hovers. She floats to the tube that contains her HuSC and hangs above the halo of white light. It brightens and hums more loudly. Something magnetic yanks Ascalon Lee through the halo, which bursts blinding radiance. I turn around and hear the liquid bubble behind me. I don't wanna watch. I don't know why.

I step to the billiards table and lay my rail gun on it. I rub the velvet. I would like to teach my daughter this game one day, even though no one plays it anymore. Years ago, Sabrina and I agreed that we'd let Ascalon choose her interests, her hobbies. We'd expose her to as many as we could, and she'd decide. She decided the day she jumped off the float burb docks and just started swimming before we even got a chance to expose her. It scared the hell out of me. But I wasn't as scared then as I was when I heard her singing at Akeem's, or when she shot him. And I wasn't as scared as when she finally woke up. I thought for sure she'd remember what I had done to her. But she didn't. In fact, after she got over the shock of watching Ascalon Lee detach herself from the woman from D-89's face, she asked if we could go back to Uncle Akeem's to get her iE. I was about to point out that she had an iE in her head now, but Sabrina shot me a look, and I kept my mouth shut. Sabrina would explain it all gently. Once again, my wife saved me from my knee-jerk idiocy.

While we were all packing up to leave the abandoned hospital, it occurred to me that I'm always scared of the wrong things. I should've been scared that Ascalon would remember that she shot Akeem. That's what should have terrified me. Thankfully, she didn't seem to. That's a secret that we won't be able to keep from her forever. She will probably eventually remember. Or scroll through data and find out. I doubt her new iE buried in her head has got any parental controls. Ascalon Lee ain't the parental control type, considering the trauma she experienced when her mother threw her in AMP and controlled her. Studied her. If anything, Ascalon Lee has a phobia of parental control.

Suddenly, I hear banging behind me. Now what? I pick up the rail gun and head to the tanks. I try my best to ignore the one filled with a copy of me. I step to Ascalon Lee's. She's in there, naked, bug-eyed, pounding her fists against the glass. She's trapped. I almost want to laugh. Some genius. I consider leaving her here forever. Sentence for all the murders of the past and the ones probably yet to come. But we had a deal. She saved my kid. I crack the glass with the butt of my rail gun. A coughing Ascalon Lee pours out. She's shivering. I look around for something to put on her. There's about a dozen perfectly pressed identical Akira lab coats in the cabinet off to the side. I take one off its hanger and toss it to Ascalon Lee. She puts it on and stands.

"What?" I say. "She didn't give you any super-strength, super-healing, or super-sense?"

"Charming," Ascalon Lee coughs out.

"Huh?"

She taps her forehead and clears her throat. "Have you ever acquired a cell count of your prefrontal cortex?"

"No," I say.

She steps to me and takes the rail gun. "I assure you, it's deficient." She raises the gun and points it at one of the Akira's. HuSC 1.1. Model 1.

"What the hell does that mean?" I ask.

"Psychopaths lack the normal level of cells in that area of the brain," she says. She shoots the first Akira in the head. "I assume that most people who come across you like you?"

"I don't—"

"Psychopaths are renowned for their ability to charm," she says before shooting the next Akira. Ascalon Lee fires. A flood of ambient fluid seeps beneath my boots. "They intuitively attempt to become what they expect the other person wants them to be." She snuffs out the last Akira. "You do so with subtle strokes on your rough canvas. That's how you get what you want from others."

I step to Ascalon Lee and take the rail gun. "Calling a murderer a psychopath is a pretty insensitive thing to do."

I point the rail at myself, the self in the final chamber. No greens. Probably because this is suicide. "That doesn't seem prudent," Ascalon Lee says. "One who lives as you do could always use a spare."

"Why didn't you take one of the Akira's? Even just out of curiosity?"

"She believes that I want to be her. Perhaps I did, once. She believes that my subconscious desire led me to pursue the science that I did in order to give myself the ability to be anyone else but me. She needs to see that she was wrong. Also, this is part of the reason I wanted this HuSC instead of yours."

"You wanted to destroy all her copies. You want her down to one body."

"Your wife wouldn't have given me access to this place if I had taken you."

My finger brushes the trigger. With Ascalon Lee, with Akira, too, they seem to have more than one reason to do a thing. Always. With me, it's always just one. I'm out of my atmosphere here. "What is it like?" I ask. "Being someone else."

Ascalon Lee rubs her long, thin arm. The lab coat is too small for her. She steps to me and whispers into my ear. "You tell me."

Something stirs in me. Enough of this shit. Even though my 1.1 HuSC is probably better than the 1.0 that I'm wearing now, I pull the trigger. The other me spills out of its chamber. I feel nothing. "Why'd you do all that experimenting on yourself? Why'd Akira do it to you?"

Ascalon Lee takes a knee on my dead self's chest. She digs her thumbs in the eye sockets. "Mice lie. Monkeys exaggerate."

"I thought we were rats?"

She doesn't answer. Like her mother, Ascalon Lee simply

ignores questions that she doesn't want to address or maybe can't address. Instead, she grunts and digs the eyeballs out, then puts them in her lab coat pocket. It's like watching someone shuck oysters. "Research for later," she says.

I shake my head. We're about to leave, but she notices the flower bed. If there weren't fucking human clones in the room, it'd be the first thing anyone would notice. The flowers definitely feel out of place down here. I follow her to the flower bed. Her attention is drawn to the one I picked the first time I was here. Oddly, it hasn't wilted.

"She never struck me as a botanist," I say.

She picks up the flower and frowns at it. "You'd be surprised."

I point to the machine that looks kind of like a microscope next to the hibiscus. "Is that some sort of scanner?"

She nods.

She runs the flower under the scanner. The eye flips up and projects a seemingly infinite three-dimensional sequence of the letters: A, C, T, and G.

"DNA?" I ask.

She grins. "Watch."

A beam shoots from her eye, and the letters begin to stretch to the point that they aren't recognizable. Then they snap. All that's left is ones and zeroes.

"Code. She stored data in these plants." Ascalon Lee turns back to look at the decommissioned HuSCs at the other end of the room. "Oh, Mother."

"What?"

"She's figured out how to store qubits of data in DNA. Or someone else did, and she stole their research like she did mine."

"Why?"

Ascalon Lee tosses the flower on the floor. Her eyes narrow. "It's not as clunky or energy-consuming as traditional servers. Even the efficient and durable 5D optical storage that we've been using for years."

"What the hell has she been doing all this time?"

"Science's main obstacle has always been funding. Always."

I nod. "That obstacle was removed with Sessho-seki."

"As were patents. She was granted access to *everything*. Not just research, but materials, too. Data. Everyone's data. And AI to commit itself to the menial elements of lab work and experimentation. She could create freely without limits."

"Not that anyone noticed," I say. "But she became rich from the moment she declared she would save the world."

"Imagine if I had what she had."

It's always a pissing contest with her. I suppose a lot of people are like that. They don't like to acknowledge that there are people out there better than them at pretty much everything, especially the thing they're best at.

"Let's go," I say.

We head for the one-man sub. I'd like to say I'm thinking about what Ascalon Lee just told me, but instead I'm feeling a little uneasy at the prospect of being crammed in there with this brilliant, half-naked loon. There's no question about it. This cherry, unscarred genius version of her is what the kids call soaked—beautiful from head to toe. What makes her even hotter is her seeming indifference to what she looks like. Her ease at walking around barely clothed in front of me. I'm starting not to like this new, young version of me. I'd forgotten the potency of maniacal lust. Or my old body did. This one, it's picking up where the one who roped in and knocked up Kathy left off. Those five-a-day love-making sessions—some in her skimmer, some in my SEAL, most in the little skyscraper apartment we shared. I feel a pang of guilt that these are currently the fondest memories I have of her. Ain't I supposed to be thinking of us holding hands at sunset, shit like that? I don't. Me banging her above the clouds in thin air is what I'm picturing. It's what I miss most. *Yes, there definitely should only be one of me.*

I slip into the sub. Ascalon Lee climbs in on top of me then presses the button to close the hatch.

"Why didn't you just close it with your eye?" I ask.

"I suppose I miss the sensation of touching things with my own hands," she says.

I nod and take the sub under. She's got her arm around my neck, her ass on my lap. I try to add up her body count, so I don't get a hard-on. I think about that poor woman back at HW. From the beginning, probably dealt a seven-deuce life. I feel myself getting angry.

"What was her name?" I ask.

"Who?"

"The woman. The one we left back at the hospital."

"Does it matter?" Ascalon Lee says.

No, I suppose it doesn't.

We pilot through the labyrinth of underwater caverns, the lights of the egg-shaped capsule peeling back the haze of umber. Even with lights, it feels like there's no clarity here in the deep. "Your daughter," Ascalon Lee says. "She made me feel something."

I nod. I wonder if there's hope for this woman, after all she's been through. If perhaps she ain't stunted. I wonder if there's hope for me. If perhaps I ain't stunted, too. I feel my rage exhausting itself. My rage at Akira. My rage at Old Man Caldwell. My rage at Ascalon Lee. My rage at myself. My kid and her recovery made me feel something, too.

"Maybe we should leave Akira with Caldwell and hope for the best," I say. "Second chances and all that shit."

"Don't worry," she says. "I don't possess your daughter. What she will become will be more interesting without me controlling her."

For some reason, I believe her. "Can she recall memories from when you had control over her?"

Ascalon Lee pauses. "She will eventually remember."

I sigh. "Will she be able to do what you do? Access and control things with her mind?"

"Yes. Once she acclimates, she will learn. She'll learn a number of things."

I try to keep my voice casual. "Oh yeah? Like what?"

"She will be stronger than you. Isn't that what you want?"

I nod. It is.

We break through the last of the caves and begin our ascent above the ink. The cerulean line ahead twists into palomar and cinches through the hull of the bathyscaphe. The line tightens. It feels like we're getting reeled up. I ease the throttle. I'm tired of following this goddamn blue string.

"The world's crumbling," I say. "Maybe I should grab Sabrina and the kid and just split." Sabrina and our daughter went to Sabrina's quarters at Police HQ. I don't know if that's the safest or most dangerous place to be right now.

"Where?" Ascalon Lee asks.

"I don't know. You're The Money. It seems like all of you got someplace to escape to."

"Ah," she says, "so the four of us just live as one big happy family?"

I sigh. She increases the thrust. The egg spools up the taut blue line. "Is there a way to cut these guidelines I see?" I ask.

"Just one way," she says and looks at the gun.

I nod, then something disturbing appears. A thin wisp of green threads the blue line. It's impossible. I can't smell underwater. What did Akira do to this body? I grip the rail gun.

"Something's up there," I say.

Ascalon Lee eases our velocity. She looks scared. It's the first time I've seen her look this way. "I have made the mistake of ascending the ocean too quickly before," she says. "You could not dream of the hardships of a trans-Pacific migration. What do you see?"

"Murder."

"I see more than you think, but I don't see it."

"What do you mean?" I ask.

She shifts in my lap. "Nothing," she says. "Would your wife betray us?"

"Betray us to who? Nobody wants us."

Ascalon Lee laughs. I don't know that I've ever heard her laugh before. "What do you think Old Man Caldwell is doing to Akira, anyway?" I ask.

She shrugs. "He's waiting for something," she says confidently. "Waiting for a missing piece that my mother has left behind."

I think about that. When Akira discovered that the scar went out, she was calm. It wasn't so much that she expected it, but it was as if she were being reminded of an old toy she'd misplaced and no longer cared about. I think about the labs, about the forty or so years she spent necromancing eternal life. I feel like there's a missing piece, too, like who is HuSC 1.0 Model 4? The old curiosity kicks in. I look at Ascalon Lee. Her eyes still focused cautiously on the invisible veneer above.

"In medicine," she says, "we are taught that there is no such thing as one hundred percent. We are taught to prepare for the least likely outcome. You would have made a passable physician."

"Thanks," I say.

Finally, she throttles forward. The green brightens more and more with every atmosphere. It ain't just the smell of potential murder. Not anymore. Akira probably did this. Tied in green to her ultramarine if things became desperate. I'm comforted by the fact that the faint magenta billows are not tangled with the other two colors. We head to the SEAL that we mag-anchored at the surface. We break through a school of skipjacks darting in a swirl and rise above the tornado of fish. We're close to the SEAL now. We only fired off four rounds down at the lab. The rail is still fully charged.

"That empty chamber," I say. "HuSC 1.0. Model 4."

"What?"

"When Sabrina and I first found the lab, there were three of her, one of me, and one of you. One chamber was empty."

"I don't know," Ascalon Lee says. "I was indisposed." She pulls the lapel of the lab coat over her exposed breast. She's feeling naked now.

"Do you see it?" I ask.

"I . . . I do not know. I . . . hear it. I hear something."

I try to hear, too. Only the whine of our propeller. Ascalon Lee's been through my head, both mine and my daughter's. Akira's been through my head. At this point, I wouldn't be surprised if they saw things like I did, too.

"It's the strumming of a string," Ascalon Lee says. "That's what I hear. Faint."

I peer at the vibrating guideline then push her off me as much as I'm able to. "Once we breach, pop the hatch," I say. "I'm gonna come up ready to blast."

Ascalon Lee nods. I'm half-expecting some kind of sea monster to appear from the dark and swallow us whole. But nothing. I see light. The undulating surface of the ocean latticed with faint sunlight. We break through, and she pops the hatch. I stand, aim, then spin and check my three, nine, and six. Nothing except my SEAL.

"I still hear it," Ascalon Lee says. "It's growing louder."

Now I hear something, too. Propulsion. "Let's get onboard the SEAL and get the hell out of here," I say.

She nods and jumps on the wing. I recheck my flanks. Just endless ocean. I join her aboard the SEAL. Above, seeded rain clouds clot together and mottle the gray sky. Then the ocean begins to gurgle, and something rumbles beneath us. I point the gun at the water and look through the scope. It's rising fast. Akeem's cruise line apocalypse sub. I hop into the cockpit and try to start the engines. Nothing.

"Can you turn it on?" I ask Ascalon Lee.

"No," she says. "It's been disabled. What is that below us?"

"The Buharis."

"Who?" she asks.

I give the engine another shot. Same outcome. "The man you shot using my little girl. It's his family coming for you."

Ascalon Lee sighs. "That was an unnecessary death."

"Unnecessary deaths," I say. "You rack 'em up just like me."

The sub breaches the surface. The SEAL rocks over waves. "I'm being pinged," I say.

I answer the voice ping. It's Chinara. One of Akeem's doctor kids that saved me back on Akeem's manmade island. "I know you have her," she says.

"I do," I say. "And you can't have her."

"My sister wanted us to simply blow the both of you out of the water."

The shuttle pilot I bet. "It's easy, isn't it?" I ask.

"What?"

I open the cockpit and step on a wing, which causes the SEAL to rock back and forth. I point the rail at the sub. I see them. Dots within the hull. Green dots of human life. "It's easy to go from good to bad."

Chinara sighs. "You can't escape."

"Put me on visual."

The periscope groans and focuses on me. "You can't escape either," I say.

"What in Akira's name happened to you?" Chinara asks. "How is that possible?"

There's curiosity in her voice. The doctor and The Money in her, I'm sure. I molted fifty years, and she's dying to know how. I should take my shots now. But I can't. I can't start laying waste to these children of my dead friend. Ascalon Lee joins the conversation. "Let us aboard, and we can discuss terms."

"Unarmed," Chinara says.

"Of course," Ascalon Lee says, "unarmed."

The hatch on the sub's fin groans open. I look back at Ascalon Lee. She removes the lab coat, carefully folds it, and leaves it in the SEAL. Completely naked, she dives in the water. She's an impressive swimmer. I leave the gun in the SEAL and jump in after her. She can pop out of her body and make a run for it at any time. But she doesn't. She's climbing the ladder that leads to the sub's fin. I don't know why I'm trying to save her. There's still more hatred than gratitude that tips the scale of my heart. But from the start line of her existence, she never stood a chance, and she still ran one helluva race. No, wait, correction, she's *still* running a helluva race. All by herself. All of me respects that.

I get to the sub and climb the ladder, making my way up top to the dorsal, then step on the freeboard. Ascalon Lee's already below deck. The ballasts begin to fill with water, and we descend into this negative buoyancy.

3

When my daughter was younger, she was like two different people. She was whiny and needy around her mother. She cried a lot. She was affectionate. The only place she could sit still was on her mother's lap. With me, she was different. She was still demanding but more independent. She was physical. She loved climbing me and stepping on my face. She loved having me toss her in the water. She laughed more. She loved when I'd take her to school in the SEAL at full throttle. "*Faster, Daddy!*" she'd say. "*Faster!*" She only cried if she was scolded. She never wanted hugs from me.

Ascalon Lee called me a psychopath earlier. A person who changes himself to what the other person wants him to be. In that case, we're all on the psychopath spectrum. And it all starts at an early age. My daughter was like this as early as one year old. Or maybe it was us that made her become two different people. I'm not sure.

I'm thinking about this while Ascalon Lee and I stand in front of Chinara and Chiamaka, the Buhari twins. One a dark-skinned, bone-thin, anal-retentive doctor, the other, a light-skinned stunt shuttle pilot built like a tank, like her father. How can a genetically identical pair be so different? Ascalon Lee wouldn't take her eyes off them. Is the sight of them making her miss the sister she never had? I wonder if she's thinking about what could've or should've been. For all I know, she's daydreaming about dissecting them. She's engaged, though. Her body shimmers with high voltage while green seethes in Chiamaka's eyes.

Chinara hands Ascalon Lee a basic, black foam fit. Ascalon Lee puts it on in front of us. Four private security goons got their rail guns pointed at me and Ascalon Lee. They're ogling her, like they can't wait to peel that foam fit back off and start taking turns. They're the same kind of corporate mercs I used to fight during the war. For some reason, I'm thinking about the old me. When I started getting farsighted, instead of fixing it, I'd just guesstimate when I read things. It's like my short time on the moon. Memory shot, I was guesstimating what I was doing there. Now that my eyesight and memory are intact, I'm still guesstimating. Guesstimating what Chinara and Chiamaka have got in store for us. Guesstimating the probability of Ascalon Lee and me getting out of here alive. I guess life is just a series of guesstimations. No matter what, I always feel like I'm playing behind the beat. After Ascalon Lee is dressed, Chiamaka, who's wearing her father's powered exoskeleton haul suit, motions us to follow her.

The sub, a onetime cruise line diver, still retains some of its gaudy crass. Its grated stairs are casino-carpeted. Rivets shaved down, the alcoved walls display nouveau digi Roman art. We pass a bust of Medusa. I remember when these cruise lines were all the rage. Large sections of the hull are transparent, and one could look out and try to spot deep sea creatures while the sub slalomed through trenches. But the industry quickly went bust. The one thing that couldn't be masked for comfort was the noise. Even now, the strut bearings spin and the sub groans as it descends, the ocean a great sound conductor.

I look at Chiamaka, who is marching ahead of me. She's got the kind of chaffed elbows that come from being slumped over a bar for too many years. This is the kid Akeem always worried about the most. The reckless thrill-seeker who didn't seem to give a shit about her wealth. She was, of course, his favorite. It's probably why she's leading this vengeance crusade. He was probably her favorite, too.

We step into a room, unfurnished, with a recently installed cell. The walls are clear. We must be really deep because I spot a fireworks jellyfish out there, its tentacles resembling a burst of violet light. Ascalon Lee pauses in front of the cell. The merc behind her shoves her forward.

"I will not be caged," Ascalon Lee says. "We are here to discuss terms."

Chiamaka takes a rail gun from one of the mercs. The joints of her exo suit whiz. She levels the gun at Ascalon Lee's eye and looks at me. The gun barrel smokes green. "You know," she says to me, "I warned my dad about you. In the stunt world, I've seen your kind. People like you always crash and burn, taking your crew with you on your lifelong suicide mission."

I nod. "Your father was a good man. Maybe the best I've ever met."

"And you got him killed."

"I never should've gone to the island," I say. "You're right. I did get him killed."

"And now you're young again," she sneers. "Another lifetime of suicide missions. You should be euthanized for all our sakes." Her forehead beads. She turns her gaze to Ascalon Lee. "And you. Terms, you say? You got nothing you can give me."

Chinara, on the other hand, is just standing there, still staring at my face. She's been quiet since we got aboard. She's sweating, too.

"Don't shoot that eye," I tell Chiamaka. "I guarantee you this—you do it, we'll all blow up."

Unfazed by my warning, Chinara speaks up. "How?" she asks. She touches my face. Her dark, thin fingers stroke my newfound youth.

"Akira Kimura," I say.

"What do you mean?" Chinara says. She wipes sweat from her brow. "Akira Kimura is dead."

Ignoring the gun in her face, Ascalon Lee turns and glares at me. Her golden eye shimmers. "Not Akira Kimura," she says. "Ascalon Lee." She turns back to Chiamaka. I feel the anger well in her. "I find your tactics of negotiation interesting," she says. "You think in terms of what I can or cannot give you instead of wondering what I can take."

I look around. Everyone in the room is sweating except Ascalon Lee and me. I get it. She's turned up the heat on all their foam fits. The mercenaries begin to pull at their collars. Chiamaka presses the rail's barrel tip against Ascalon Lee's neck. "Whatever you are doing," she says, "stop, or I'll blow your head off."

Ascalon Lee smiles. The sub creaks. I feel the floor tip under me. The creaks echo. Chinara looks at Chiamaka. "We're accelerating," she says.

Chiamaka pings the pilot. Ascalon Lee looks at me and smiles. Her eye glimmers. "Your daughter would approve," she says. "Piracy."

The sub tilts even more. We're all hanging onto the bare walls now. The sirens begin to blare. The sub's hull groans. "In twenty-eight seconds, this submarine will collide with the ocean floor," Ascalon Lee calmly says to Chiamaka. "The hull will not hold. I have died by drowning once before. I assure you it is not a pleasant experience. As my presence here proves, I can survive it. Can you?"

I'm wondering if I can. Maybe, if all of me is just a loadable chip in my head. I promise myself I'm gonna be more curious, learn more during this second life . . . if I survive this. Chiamaka tries to aim the gun at Ascalon Lee, but Chinara puts her hand on the barrel and lowers it. "What are the terms?" Chinara says.

"You release us and allow us to save this pathetic world," Ascalon Lee says. "After which, I will surrender myself."

Everyone pauses and frowns at Ascalon Lee. They're more puzzled over the "save the world" comment than the self-surrender. Ascalon Lee continues. "We will end it once and for all. We are at the eleventh hour. Stop banging your heads against the wall. We came in peace . . ."

I see now that Ascalon Lee is rambling off clichés. She's sarcastically trying to tell them what they wanna hear. The sub creaks more and more the deeper we get. I feel like it's going to collapse at any second. But she is calm, almost giddy. Somehow that's reassuring, even though it probably shouldn't be.

"We are between a rock and a hard place," Ascalon Lee says. "But the bigger they are, the harder they fall." She glares at Chinara and asks, "What say you?" She begins to howl hysterically as we plummet to our deaths.

Before Chinara can respond, Chiamaka says, "No."

Chiamaka steps toward Ascalon Lee on the slanted floor, the exoskeleton suit providing her with a magnetic foothold. The sweaty mercs are all looking at one another in confusion, terrified of this strange woman that they were lusting after just minutes before. Ascalon Lee howls after rattling off cliché after cliché while we all dive max throttle to the bottom of the ocean. On the verge of tears, the mercs look at one another, not sure what to do. Chiamaka aims the gun. The mechanical suit she got on, full of pneumatics and actuators, probably more than quadruples her strength. I wonder how my new HuSC compares. Time to find out. I kick off the wall and ram into Chiamaka. We crash against the cell door. Ascalon Lee instantly stops laughing.

"That is not necessary," Ascalon Lee says. The exoskeleton ring around Chiamaka's elbow glows a hot yellow. Her forearm folds backward into her triceps. She screams and drops the rail gun. I catch it. Great. Ascalon Lee's hacked the exoskeleton suit, too. She looks at skinny Chinara. "I will snap her spine next," she says. Somber. Serious. "Just as I know drowning, I know what it is to lose a twin. I assure you, it is even more difficult to survive."

Hanging on to the cell bars like a goddamn monkey, I point the gun at the mercs. At this point, they're all piled into the corner and wide-eyed, men with nowhere to hide. "Level us out," I tell Ascalon Lee.

Chinara glares at me. "How can you be working with her after all my father has done for you? What my family has done for you? What she has done to your child?"

It's a valid fucking question. I begin to get suspicious. Would the old me be willing to work with Ascalon Lee? Is there something in the new me that Akira added or subtracted to make this behavior possible?

"Level us out!" I yell as the sub belts a bellowing groan that echoes through this luxury tube. I cringe at the impending sound of rending metal.

The sub's nose tilts up, and we begin to level. I sigh, relieved. I have a tough time looking Chinara in her still panicked face. This doc child of Akeem's pulled me from the ocean. She saved me. "I promise," I say. "I'll make sure she holds up her end of the deal." Now Ascalon Lee's got me talking in clichés. Could it be that all clichés are simply our most well-known lies? But I'm not lying. I got every intention of turning her in after all this is over. Ascalon Lee's gotta know that. Why ain't she scared? Chinara ignores me and rushes to her sister's side. Ascalon Lee watches the love between the twins bitterly. *Fools*, she says it in my head.

I rub the side of my head. Ascalon Lee can clearly chase down and tackle lattice-based algorithms. What's to stop her from hacking me? Maybe she's already done it, and I don't even know. I point the rail at Ascalon Lee. The twins and the mercs look utterly confused.

"Would I be able to do it?" I ask Ascalon Lee. "Or have you hacked into my head like you've hacked into everything else?"

Chiamaka pulls her twisted arm from her sister. "Kill her," she growls. "I'll pay you. Just kill her."

The Money. Sabrina's right. They take and take and take. It's how they become The Money in the first place. Then the final thing they take, with their irresistible offers and bribes, is choice. Akira took it with her offer of power and revenge. Ascalon Lee tried to take it with her bribe of all the money in the world. Old Man Caldwell took it. Now here's Chiamaka trying to take it. They all buy free will like a Less Than would buy a tat job or a toy. I'm looking at Ascalon Lee, wondering if she can take mine. Just reach in with those Medusa-like tendrils of yellow and snatch my free will from me.

"I'm growing weary of you pointing weapons at me," Ascalon Lee says. "If I could somehow control you, would I have not done so at D-89? If I could control you, would you even be able to threaten my life at all? I do not want to control you. I want to unleash you."

The anger floods in. Everything begins to accumulate in me—what she did to my kid, to the poor woman from D-89, to Akeem, to the world by turning off the scar. I'm tempted to pull the trigger just to see if I can. But she's useful. She's the only one who wants to get to her mother as badly as I do. If I fail, she's the backup. And maybe she thinks the same thing about me. I put the gun down and look at Chiamaka.

"I'm sorry," I say. "I owe your father. I know that. I'll bring her back. To honor Akeem, I'll bring her back."

"You won't be able to," Chiamaka snarls. "She's smarter than you."

I feel the surface approaching, and a part of me doesn't wanna go up there. A part of me just wants to sail on and on and on around the world in Akeem's apocalypse sub and hash this thing out with his kids. But some things can't be hashed out. Life ain't billiards. There ain't no draw. No spinning back the cue after it hits. I laugh to myself. Akira used to suck at draw.

"We need to go," Ascalon Lee says.

I feel the blue line tightly tethered to me. It's glowing, singing, reeling me up. Ascalon Lee takes one of the rail guns from a merc, and we begin to exit the room. "I'm sorry," I say once more.

Chiamaka scoffs. "If you don't bring her back, we'll come get her. And you."

"I'll bring her back in one form or another," I say.

We leave the room and head back to the upper deck. "You would've killed us all?" I ask.

Ascalon Lee's eye squirts distorted green dashes. "I don't know."

"You don't know if you would've killed us?"

"No. I don't know if you would've survived. I admit, I was a bit curious to see the limits of the HuSC you inhabit."

We climb up to the hatch. I open it and pull myself through. The sea is rough. About a hundred yards west my SEAL bobs like a floater. Ascalon Lee steps out and closes her eyes. She stretches her arms and breathes in the air. "It's exhilarating, isn't it?"

"What, fresh air?"

She opens her eyes, pulls her arms down, and frowns. "No. Life. Death. Survival."

We dive into the water and head to the SEAL. The tides, the currents, they're pulling at me from different directions. I wonder how Sabrina and my kid are holding up. I wonder how the world is holding up. Will it be a world that my kids can grow up in?

Behind us, the sub descends and creates a riptide that tugs me to the point of descent. I fight through it. My hands chop into the water. I feel my body rise into the swells. Ascalon Lee and me side by side. She's grinning, swimming away. Her eye glimmers like a faraway star. I kick harder. We're racing, and I didn't even know it. It's scary out here in the middle of the ocean, not knowing what's under us. I use the fear to make me stroke harder, but I can't get ahead of Ascalon Lee's shimmering wake in this sea of gravitational constant.

4

To Ascalon Lee, survival may be exhilarating, but to most of the rest of the world, it's a matter of circumstance. According to the feed, most of the Less Thans have been corralled to underground and underwater shelters hastily built during the last calamity, the coming of The Killing Rock. The coastal cities have hives carved into cliffs and mountains. The underwater cities have stopped accepting float burb and island refugees. Construction bots reinforce the seascrapers with anchors tethered to the ocean floor. I watch the feed. Lines and lines of displaced waiting their turn to enter the run-down bunkers that ain't been stocked in fifty years. The long string of people—it's a lot like watching the organized chaos of an ant colony entering its mound. Some outside the bunkers protest. They're waving digital upside-down American flags.

The Money got their own cavities, and the feed ain't covering them, but I know they exist. Even before the coming of The Killing Rock, the rich bought up land in places like NZ, formerly New Zealand, and built their super bunkers. These monstrous subterranean complexes with their grand halls and vaulted arches look like fantasy dwarfish cities. Up until now, most were converted to museums. Storage units for privately owned antiquities. Akira refused to have one. I guess I now know why. As for what the landlocked Zeroes are up to, nobody knows, and nobody cares.

Ascalon Lee and I are in a private, ika-class shuttle that she hijacked, and we're headed to NZ now. The blue is really tugging at me, so much so that I don't even gotta look at the guideline. I just let my hands guide the direction. I suppose this is how a number of species hunt. The spider with its slit sensilla feeling the mechanical strains on its exoskeleton. Pit vipers and their infrared, their sensing the heat of their prey. The shark with its electroreception, the ability to detect electric fields in its surroundings. Salmon, pigeons, and sea turtles always seem to know where they are and where they're going. I feel like that now, a sort of hybrid spider-salmon that don't gotta see to know the location of my destination.

I ping Sabrina. She and the kids are doing fine. She's considered an essential worker, so no being crammed into an underwater bunker for her. The children of the cops are being looked after by nanny bots at the station, which makes me a little nervous. Nanny bots are old tech, tech that was shut down after a few bots went berserk and butchered the kids they were babysitting. The world must've decided to take the risk and boot them back up. I wonder what else the world is planning to bring back online for the end of times.

I look over at Ascalon Lee. She's been busy the entire trip, trying to spot-weld together a new tail with materials she tore out of the PIS—Private International Shuttle—that she deemed unnecessary for flight. She's as engrossed as a child building with virtual Legos, cutting and melting polymers with some kind of welding beam that shoots from her eye. I told her a rail gun can do more damage at a far greater distance. She said that it wasn't just a weapon. Having one made her feel more balanced and protected. Way back, when her mother had put her to sleep, it was a tail that had freed her, so I understood. I asked her if she really planned on honoring her agreement with the Buharis. She said she planned to turn herself in one way or another. I asked her what she meant by that. She didn't answer. By the end, I might have to take her, too.

It's night, and we're approaching the NZ coast. The moon is sliced in half by the dark. I begin my descent. The shuttle's small, just a six-seater. Ascalon Lee feels the dip and tosses the tail aside in frustration. It quivers on the floor. Not enough time. She picks up her rail gun we'd secured from the Buhari mercs. I have no clue if she's got any expertise at firing the thing at long range, but something tells me she does. We chop through shelves of clouds in the sky.

"Let me ask you something," I say.

"Yes?"

"In this world of 'I'm right and you're wrong,' ain't it possible that everybody's wrong?"

She smiles. "Does it matter?"

No. Maybe it don't matter. But it's been on my mind. I can't help but think that there's a third choice. A fourth. Maybe an infinite number of choices. And nobody's right all the time. Nobody's wrong all the time. A person would need to be an inverse oracle to always get it wrong.

"As a child, I used to talk to plants and whisper to the moon," Ascalon Lee says.

"No friends, huh?"

"None. Never."

What would her life have been like if Akira kept her around? Shoot, maybe worse. The lady turned out to be a lousy friend. I can't imagine Akira Kimura being much of a mother. "You were probably better off," I say. "She would've twisted you."

"Like she twisted my sister? From thousands of miles away, she twisted me anyway."

Again, I can imagine sympathy, but I can't feel it. I've seen kids grow up far worse than being sent away to boarding school and getting an inheritance and a world-class education. She was dealt pocket rockets compared to the kids we left on the skimmer back at the islands. Big slick compared to that woman we left in AMP back at HW Hospital. They were born in worse circumstances than Ascalon Lee. If she weren't so fucking lethal, I'd call her pathetic. Maybe that's what murderers are: people who turn themselves lethal because they refuse to look pathetic. Maybe I'm one of them. "When we get her—"

"When we get her," Ascalon Lee interrupts, "we put her head on a pike. The world will know she is no god. That will get its attention. Then the world will learn that her light show was a scam, and they can get on with their futile, wretched existences."

I deploy the flaps. "You said resolution is a fallacy."

She looks at me, the eye glowing. "Do you always believe what people say?" she asks. "Interesting, considering your former occupation."

I shift in my seat. She's right. With certain people, those who I think are smarter than me, I tend to take their word as gospel. Yet another dysfunction that I now hopefully got the time to fix. We're close to sea level now. I switch the shuttle to hover mode and flip on the floodlights. There they are—a series of hanger bays chiseled into the NZ bluffs. Water crashes against the rocks below. I know which one without having to look. The biggest. At first, it's a long, thin seam. When we get closer, the maw begins to appear wider and wider. I drop the landing gear and float us in. Ascalon Lee sucks on her bottom lip. Her eye blazes. "It appears abandoned." She smirks. "I don't believe my mother is here."

"She's here," I say.

"Do you ever notice how people seek consultation when it comes to making trivial decisions? Yet, when it comes to the most important ones, they act independently."

"You're just like your mother," I say. I land us into this gape while thinking something, some bit of truth is gonna end up swallowing us both. I kill the engine. "We're at the right location."

I grab my rail and walk to the back of the shuttle. The exit ramp's pistons hiss. Ascalon Lee and I exit. It's dark, the bay just a simple, massive cave chiseled from rock. Ascalon Lee's eye illuminates up the area. Gusts of howling wind swirl and tangle the azure guideline. Something's wrong. Maybe she's right. Maybe Akira ain't here. I follow Ascalon Lee to the front of a dusty, four-story, plain steel door. I ask my iE who this property is registered under. Rapture Inc. Funny name. Probably some dummy corporation.

"This hanger is huge," I say. "Big enough to fit a fleet of mega shuttles."

"She wouldn't have such a facility," Ascalon Lee says. "A secret location beneath the ocean, the moon, not an NZ industrial shipping facility." She looks up. "What is this, Mother?" Her scream echoes. "Why are you not telling me?"

I look around. No greens or reds. "I know she had a long time, but how could she do all of this by herself?"

"Unlimited resources and AI," Ascalon Lee says. "And gardeners."

"What?"

"She certainly must have had help. Help has always been the advantage she has had over me."

"Who helped her?"

She shrugs. "I'm wondering that myself."

I put my hand on the giant door and feel heat hum behind it. "Can you open it?"

"No," she says.

"So, what now? We wait for a ray of moonlight to shine in some hidden keyhole? Some fantasy bullshit like that?"

Ascalon Lee points. "There's an eye scanner right there."

She's right. We both look at each other. For some reason, neither of us wanna stick our eye in front of that thing. I picture some kind of laser shooting out of it and melting my eyeball. What is it about "melting" with me? Probably because things don't melt in Water City, and my worst-case scenarios are things I don't see.

"Fuck it," I say. I step to the scan and stick my face in front of it. Nothing. I tap it in a futile attempt to determine if the thing is on and try to look into it again. Nothing but the sound of water shattering on the rocks below us. It's the first time Akira hasn't left me access to something. Now, I'm real suspicious. I don't got much faith, but I turn to Ascalon Lee and say, "You try."

She wearily steps to the scan. She looks into it. Nothing happens.

"Try the other eye," I say. "The organic one."

She nods and looks again. Something like a smoky hand extends from the scan and closes its fingers around Ascalon Lee's eye, but the door doesn't open. I think about it.

"Let's look together," I say.

Ascalon Lee nods. We stand shoulder to shoulder in front of the scan, which does the trick. The door begins to slide open.

"How did you know?" she asks.

"I figured we're the only ones she made copies of. Two of us. At least as far as I know."

"Funny," she says. "We're meant to be here together."

I nod. "You needed me to find it—the guideline."

"It doesn't lead to her. It leads to something else."

I don't wanna go in. A big part of me doesn't wanna know.

"Mother!" Ascalon Lee screams so loud it startles me. "Mother! I will know!"

No response. We step past the door.

The entrance is a large, tomb-like expanse filled with stacked, crated tech. I take out my heat blade and cut open one of the containers. iEs, the new Triple Xs, packed in dozens like cartons of eggs, back when there were eggs. I pull one out. It's an elegant thing, this orb. Frosted and smooth, no facets like the older models. I guess this is what we pursue, the making of a world absent of cracks and divots. Always trying to hide the wiring. A flash momentarily blinds me. I drop the iE. Legs pop out of it, and it skitters under one of the crates like a startled insect. I turn to Ascalon Lee.

"What the fuck?"

She taps her eye with the barrel of her rail. *Clink, clink, clink.* "These are like mine." She looks around the warehouse.

"How many are here? Thousands, hundreds of thousands? Mother!" she screams. "Thief!" She's furious.

I check the charge on my rail, just in case.

We walk past aisles and aisles of packed iEs, and it occurs to me that this is probably what a million of something looks like. We've all heard the number, but to actually see a million or maybe even millions of a thing is no joke. The crates rise to the high ceiling like skyscrapers. We wind through the boxes and finally find a concrete door. Ascalon Lee and I eye-scan it open. It's a giant elevator. We step inside. One direction: down. I press the button, and it powers up. The elevator rumbles. The hum of some kind of central drive train grows louder and louder. We get to the bottom floor. *Ding.* I raise my rail, and the door slides open to reveal a huge, automated 3D printing line. Stacks and stacks of clear boxes, each containing grafting needles suspended by superconduction. Beneath each box, a carton nest and a drone bot waiting to deliver packed sets. Tubes filled with some kind of shimmering liquid composite are plugged into each box. Everything's turned off. I switch my scope to infrared and scan the room. Nobody's here.

"How many people purchased this latest, plagiarized model?" Ascalon Lee asks.

"Just about everyone," I say. "Everyone who can afford it."

She nods. We walk past the printers. Some hold partially etched iEs that look like unfinished 3D jigsaws. She is marching forward with the determination of someone who knows where they're going, so I'm just following. I glance back. My blue guideline is gone. There's just yellow now, and the faint scent of magenta. It's a long walk to the end of the line, and when we reach it, we find another door. It's round. This one, she cannot open.

"Stand back," I say.

She nods again. I raise my rail and fire at the thick, iron hinges. The blasts echo in the factory room, cutting the buzz of a power source. One more shot at the footing of the door. It leans forward and collapses in front of us. It gyrates like a coin before slamming still. The circular door must be at least two feet thick. There's a long tunnel in front of us that disappears into darkness.

"What is this?" I ask.

Ascalon Lee takes a knee and rubs the surface of the fallen cork-like door with her hand. "Mother, was this meant to keep intruders out or to lock someone in?"

She asks it as if her mother is here with us. Maybe in her head, her mother is always with her. Old Man Caldwell. Maybe he's got Akira confined somewhere down there. I miss my old iE. I could've sent it down the hall for recon.

"Mother!" Ascalon Lee's rage echoes through the passageway. "Tell me what this is!"

I activate the tactical streamlight mounted on my rail and walk in first. Ascalon Lee follows. I look down. The floor undulates with every step. Some kind of solid, yet liquid metal that glimmers like mother of pearl. The same stuff being pumped into the 3D printers. Not exactly new tech, just tech once added to the heap of we-don't-have-a-practical-use-for-it-yet scientific innovation. Of course, Kimura found use for it. Purpose. Ascalon Lee and I pace our way through it, and with every step, I half-expect to sink into the floor like I'm walking on quicksand. I look up and notice security cameras hovering below the ceiling every ten feet. Too many to bother shooting out. We're coming, and whoever is at the end of this knows it. The tunnel begins to narrow. We both gotta duck to move forward. Finally, we reach the end. A lip slopes down. A slide, like a playground one, very much like the one at the playground outside of the Lucky Cat City apartment where Kimura grew up, spirals down to darkness.

"What the fuck?" I ask.

"Exciting amusement," Ascalon Lee says. She pushes me out of the way, sits, and slides down. I got the feeling that this slide will chute me into something hard that'll end in broken bones. Nevertheless, I follow. The surface is slick, but there's nothing viscous on it. Round and round, down and down we go. By the time I get to the bottom, I'm dizzy and in complete darkness. She flashes her eye, and the room is gilded by her golden luminescence. It's huge and round, with a dim circumference. Workbenches, chemistry stations, microscopes, computers, and broken iEs—this is a room of scattered invention. On the wall, to the left, intact, mounted iEs, all previous twenty-nine models. Over the years, I had them all, so my mind spasms with nostalgia. She lifts her rail gun and peers through the scope. She turns around.

"Someone is here," she whispers.

I turn around, raise my rail, and look through the scope, as well. Yes, there's a figure; someone on hands and knees is hiding under one of the workbenches. At first, I think maybe it's Akira, but it's a man. I put down the rail.

"Come out!" I say. "We're not gonna hurt you!"

Metal scrapes against the floor. Then, I hear the rattle of chains. An emaciated man crawls out from under the workbench. He's skinny, but there's still sinews of muscle that suggest he's been getting at least some nourishment down here. He's got a metal collar ringed with links that connect to the wall behind him. He has clumps of hair missing. His eyes, alert and wild. He's wearing a soiled foam fit. He's younger, much younger, but I recognize him immediately.

Idris Eshana.

The empty tube in Akira's underwater lab. HuSC 1.0. Model 4. That's who was missing. Idris. She brought him back from the dead. The inventor of the iE. She brought him here and chained him. *Why?* He looks like some demented version of Jacob Marley. He limps toward us, dragging his chains. When he gets in front of us, he grins. There's a scent coming off him, like something is rotting in his mouth, and I notice he's missing half his teeth. He's holding a flower, like the ones in Akira's underwater lab. The thing is down to one petal, which he tears from the flower's base and sticks in his mouth. He closes his eyes and chews. After he swallows, his eyes snap open, and they're glowing a neon blue. He's suddenly brimming with energy.

"The daughter! The friend!" Idris booms. "You are finally here, just as she prophesized!"

Ascalon Lee tilts her head and inspects the man. As far as I know, she's never met him. Not that anything about this guy's demeanor resembles the real thing. The Idris I knew was a germophobe who dressed impeccably.

"Your gardener," Ascalon Lee says.

"What?" I ask.

"Nothing," she says.

Otoboke, I think. Feigned ignorance. She's hiding something from me. I turn my attention to Idris. "How long have you been here?" I ask. "How long have you been alive?"

"That's not important," he says. "You're here! You're finally here!"

He's about to turn around and walk away, but I grab him

by the arm, causing the chains to rattle. "What'd she offer you? Eternal life? A deal with the devil?" I ask.

"No, a collaboration." He points up. The ceiling above is a dome faceted with tessellation of hexagons. The spiral slide cuts through the center of the honeycomb. It all looks like a giant, early model iE cut in half and turned inside out. Idris claps twice. The dome flickers. First, the edges of each facet one by one. Then the facets themselves begin to flutter with light. They combine and undulate like octopus skin. It all becomes reflective liquid.

"Liquid metal," Ascalon Lee says. "Like the hall, like the slide we came down on. Why?"

Suddenly, thousands and thousands of holos. The globe. Flashing images of people—men, women, children—living their lives in real-time. Lists and lists of names being digitally scrolled. Numbers in the millions. Billions. Percentages. Sums of crypto. Bank account numbers. Wealth indicators. Behavior analytics. Thousands upon thousands of jumbled holos tangled in green.

"What is this?" I ask. "Tracking everyone in the world?"

Idris ignores the question. "You were supposed to retrieve her first," he says. "She wanted all three of you to see together."

"Where is she?" I ask.

"I don't know," Idris says.

I think about that. It seems Caldwell fucked up Akira's plans for this little reunion. Good for the old guy.

"She did, however, leave instructions to proceed as soon as my liberators arrived," Idris says. He raises his shackled hands and looks like he's about to clap again.

I got the vibe that something not good is about to happen.

I point the rail at his head. "Clap, and I'll shoot your hands off. What the fuck is this?"

Idris freezes, hands raised. Ascalon Lee begins to walk around the room, her head craned at the flashing images above us. A laser from her eye zigzags from image to image, draining the luminescent numbers like a funnel. Her eye dims, but the room remains illuminated. She looks at me and gasps.

"It's rapture. Her believers will rise."

"Correct," Idris says. "Correct."

"What the hell are you talking about?" I ask.

"Mother!" Ascalon Lee screams again, like Akira's here with us. "Mother!" Her scream transforms into a laugh.

"How the hell did she fund all this?" I ask. "This, the moon, the clones, the underwater lab. She's been dead for eight years. And don't tell me, ghost accounts or whatever. What about manpower? Just one guy?"

Ascalon Lee looks at me. "You ask questions. You lead them with words like 'where,' 'what,' 'how.' You should start every question with the word 'why.'"

I look at Idris, hands still raised; he shrugs. The chains clink on the floor.

Ascalon Lee sighs. "She's been working on this for decades," she says. The ceiling rolls through images and data. She looks up again. Her flaring eye creates ripples. "She stole my invention, stole every scientific innovation over the last century, and began to work immediately." She turns to Idris. "The government inherited just a portion of hers and his vast wealth. The rest was hidden. Imagine it as a stimulus check to the government. A stimulus check large enough to make them want to believe that she was dead. She and Idris flashed them a shiny object that they could not take their eyes off of. Isn't that right, Mother?"

"Correct," Idris says, eyeing me and slowly lowering his hands. I forgot how much he used the word "correct." It's a word that people who think they're smarter than they truly are like to use to agree with someone else. "She promised me once it was done, I would be emancipated by you. But she wanted you to see first," he says to Ascalon Lee. His lips contort to a demented, half-toothed grin. "She wanted you to *see*. To witness the full potential of your creation."

He steps to me despite the rail gun I got pointed at him. He pushes the barrel down and lays his hands on both sides of my head. "Focus," he says. "You are equipped to bear witness." He raises his hands and tilts back his head. I wanna shoot him, I really do, but I don't. And I don't know why. I guess killing a witness ain't gonna get me answers. I look over at Ascalon Lee. She's not laughing anymore, just quiet. Distant.

"We can stop you, Mother," she whispers. "Know that we can stop you."

"Stop what?" I ask.

"Now!" Idris says and claps his hands together once more. His marine eyes flash even brighter. They scintillate. Idris is now in some kind of trance, mouth agape. I've seen this blue before. The same azure I saw in Lucky Cat City when Akira attached her iE to mine. The same sea sparkle that pierced my eye up in Akira's moon lab to scrape the rest of the old me out and put it into the new me. I feel him. I feel Idris, his iE connecting to mine.

I look up at the concave world above me. First, a glitch, a stutter, like a lagged-out holo game. Then photon wires, like the tentacles of some Majorana beast wrap themselves around me. The images come in like frantic explosions of fireworks in my head. People, masses of people, 3D-scrolled individually in spans of microseconds. I pause. A woman and her silver-skinned wife, wearing matching holo wedding bands, jog in protest together on a beach on the other side of the world. Their Triple X iEs trailing behind their bobbing ponytails projecting the words *We Need Answers.* I unpause—too many images to keep track of—then I pause again. On the top floor of a Beijing skyscraper, an office full of crypto debt collectors in foam fit formal wear separated by clear partitions, taking money, moving money in this constant shuffle and reshuffle of digital wealth. Their Triple X iEs hover above them like bits of old-world comic book speech bubbles, while far below them, a city silently burns.

Unpause. Pause. A fraternity of deep dive enthusiasts in the Antarctic exploring a forest of towering, genetically modified black coral, their Triple X iEs in front of them, lighting their unforged, icy path.

Unpause. Pause. South African private school children in an underwater classroom furnished with rows of Barcaloungers, the need for desks long gone. Feet up, they're leaning back in their chairs while their Triple X iEs project a biography of Akira Kimura in fifteen-minute chapters.

Unpause. Pause. In New Santiago, hard-hatted recyclers turn old polymer into new polymer on a factory floor, creating materials to extend the southeastern mooring of the Pacific Bridge all the way to Water City. From Fragrant Harbour to the east, from Harbour City to the southeast, from Baja to the west, now from New Santiago to the southwest; Water City will soon become the center of a giant X in the middle of the Pacific. The workers' Triple X iEs bulge from their sleeve pockets and sing private music in their ears while protests rage outside the plant.

Unpause. Pause. A quiet American coffee house early in the morning packed with Century Crashers sipping hot beverages and playing bingo on their Triple X iE projected bingo cards, their iEs marking the cards for them.

Unpause. Pause. A woman in labor in a deserted hospital in New Delhi. Unpause. Pause. In the same hospital, a father in an ICU watching his two sons, both on ventilators, sleep side by side on hospital beds. I try to pause again but can't. In seconds, it feels like I am seeing most of humanity, some howling at the empty sky, many others going about daily life, which, of course, the newsfeed ain't reporting. I'm seeing it through Idris. Seeing the people on this planet in real time. Idris is some kind of conduit. Ascalon Lee is in a daze, and I think she's seeing all these images, too.

Then I realize why Akira had to bring Idris back. Why he was necessary. He invented the iE. Every model. She needed him to build the new model, the Triple X. But not just that. It's him, his servers, that has access to all the data that every iE has been collecting over generations. But when did she bring him back? He died three years before I found her cut up in her penthouse. I was at his funeral. Did she already have the technological knowledge to put his consciousness on ice way back then? The moon lab, the underwater lab—they could be decades old for all I know.

"I really did die," Idris says. "But before I did, she promised me it wouldn't be forever. She promised that when the time was right, she would bring me back. And when she did, I needed to build this for her. Build and mass-produce the new model. I have been confined here, building and distributing, for the last ten years. Thank you, my old friend, for coming. I will finally be set free."

I see them again now—these random faces that I pulled from the streams of data are projected on the ceiling now, projected in green. They begin to quake. That's when it happens. *Kamigakari. Mrtyu-mara.* These words burst in my head in a storm of bioelectricity.

The iEs arc in front of the married joggers. They stop and frown. Their iEs bloom, like mine did back on the moon. The couple watches, mesmerized, while a sliver of blue light blossoms from the now pedaled orb of each iE. They reach out to touch the enchanting neon glints. They smile, but not for long. Their smiles are wiped when the twinkling slivers zip to their faces, and the shells of their iEs plop to the sand. The women scream, drop, and thrash in shore break.

The crypto debt collectors swat at their swarm of luminescence with futility. They pound on their glass partitions while the neon needles pierce their eyes. After it's over, the partitions retract, as does the dome ceiling. They are all in open air six thousand feet above sea level. The wind howls and blows at their hair. Calm and unaffected, they fight the wind and march off the edge. Their bodies plunge toward the burning streets below, headfirst.

The deep divers, protected by their helmets and thick, insulated dive suits, attempt to outswim the shards that crackle after them like chain lightning. They head to the surface and rise too quickly, so now it's not just the thunderbolts chasing them, it's the bends. By the time I see the schoolchildren, they've already been infiltrated. They calmly wipe the blood from their tear ducts with their sleeves, lie back, and resume their lesson, which is now projected from their cloudy, azure eyes.

The woman in labor, her iE hatches another, smaller iE. The bigger releases a splinter of incandescence that intrigues the woman at first. She reaches out her hand to touch it. Then the smaller iE opens, and the slip of piercing brightness from that one burrows into the woman's swollen belly. For a moment her entire womb glows an electric blue. The woman, now wide-eyed, claws at her stomach and screams. I look away only to see the father at the other wing of the hospital, right eye glowing, smothering his two bedridden children.

"She knows," I say. "She knows down to the person, who believes she's a god and who doesn't," I say. "She's got the data."

"She does," Idris says. All three of us, Ascalon Lee, Idris, and me, are gazing at the ceiling.

"When I killed the light," Ascalon Lee says, "you wanted me to do that, didn't you, Mother? You wanted their faith to be tested. You only wanted the ones who truly believed."

"You both see," Idris says. "Now you truly see. She will keep the believers. Those who do not believe will face judgment."

We're all watching the father who just suffocated his two children. He spreads his arms and tilts his head back. Wisps of glowing azure sprout from his eye. They snake their way to his nose and ears, then down to his crotch. They singe his clothes into ash. Then, they slither into every orifice and tighten. The man spasms. He screams and convulses. The tendrils rip the man apart. Chunks of his flesh smolder on the floor.

I ping Sabrina. No response. I try again. Nothing.

"No matter which path you choose," Idris says, "the path to becoming a god is a bloody one." I step to Idris and pick him up by the throat. His feet dangle and his cheeks puff as I begin to squeeze.

"My wife," I say.

"Akira has cut communications of all iEs," Idris manages to say. "She is the only one that the people can speak to now."

I look around, searching for the magenta. It's gone. I don't see it. It's fucking gone. No, this couldn't have happened to my kid. She didn't get a new iE yet. She's got Ascalon Lee's. But Sabrina has one. I think about the father smothering his two children. The way the high-voltage streams tore him to pieces and reduced him to chunks of head and body. *Where the hell is my family's guideline?* I squeeze harder.

"Restore it!"

"I can't!"

I clench my fist and feel Idris's windpipe contract. *Slowly,* I tell myself. *Savor it.* It's funny how predators like me always instinctively go after the throat first. His face begins to turn purple while he claws at my fingers.

"This is your last chance, Id," I say. "A few more pounds of pressure, and your windpipe will rupture." His electric eyes begin to dim and tears streak his face.

"I can't." He mouths words but no sound escapes his lips. I feel a hand on my shoulder. "I can," Ascalon Lee says.

I toss Idris aside.

"She has decommissioned every satellite, except hers and mine," Ascalon Lee says. "I am now patching you through to your wife, but to do so, I must access your daughter's iE."

I feel my eyes narrow. I nod slowly.

My iE rings in my head like an old-school smartphone. I pace and wait for Sabrina to answer in voice. I need to hear her. For some reason, it's the only way I'll believe it's really her. The tension and anxiety hums through my entire body. Sabrina finally answers.

"What the hell is going on?" she says.

I exhale, not realizing that I was even holding my breath. "Are you guys okay?" I ask, my voice shaky.

"Yeah, we're right here. I locked us in my office. The station. Something happened. Something . . . attacked just about everyone. Even the protesters outside. They're just sort of wandering around now, slowly dispersing. The officers are sort of doing the same thing. What the fuck happened?"

"Did anything happen to you?"

"No, but I saw it. Every single person here except us, clawing at their faces. A few even ripped apart from their insides. When I saw Perkins take his ceremonial weapon out of his desk and shoot himself, I picked Ascalon up, hauled ass to the office, and locked the door. How many did this happen to?"

I look at Ascalon Lee. "I don't know," I say.

"Billions," she whispers while she shoots off Idris's shackles. "Billions," she says again. The sound of bursting metal echoes through the room.

Sabrina hears Ascalon Lee and tries to say something, but the words are muddled by gasps. I try to say something, too, but there ain't no words. Just frozen shock.

Finally, I manage to sigh. I got no clue what to do. All my guidelines have been cut. She spared Sabrina, though. Why? Sabrina doesn't believe. She spared me, too. Why? Ascalon Lee looks up. The scrolling of names burns in blue.

"Her mythical point zero three percent," Ascalon Lee says. "You, your wife, your child, you were all deemed worthy."

"She killed the rest?" Sabrina asks.

"No," Ascalon Lee says. "I'm collecting data now." She stands there in this eerie silence, entranced, like she's performing some kind of technological séance.

We wait.

"A very specific, targeted genocide," Ascalon Lee says.

"Why?" I ask.

"Oh, Mother," she says.

I grab her by the shoulders and shake her. "What?" I ask.

"Where do I start?" She looks at my face and brushes my hands off her shoulders.

"Start with the general," I say.

She begins to pace. "Roughly a third killed in seconds after infiltration."

Sabrina gasps.

"A third of what?" I ask.

Ascalon Lee looks at me like I'm dumb. "A third of the human population."

I shiver and close my eyes.

"About nine percent of those killed, the true heretics, met the grizzliest of fates." She's referring to the man who was ripped apart. The same thing happened simultaneously to millions of people. Numb disbelief swells in me. "Most were corporate types, inheritors of wealth, The Money. The Parasites. The Useless. The Miserable. The ones who never believed. The ones who outright scoffed at the disappearance of the scar or cursed her. She knew who all of them were. The data. The personal data. All this time, she was tracking those who refused to believe or maligned her name."

"I can't believe it," Sabrina says. I sense the fear in her voice. She and I maligned Akira's name many times in the past.

"It's okay, babe," I say. I don't know why I say it. It's definitely not fucking okay. I turn to Ascalon Lee. "The others?" I ask.

"The others? The indifferent, let's call them. Roughly twenty-one percent of those killed. They were provided a more honorable way out."

I picture the crypto debt collectors plummeting to their deaths. I think about poor Perkins, sixty years on the job, taking his gun out and shooting himself in the head. "Forced suicide is honorable?" I ask.

Ascalon Lee stops pacing, looks at me, and simply shrugs. I feel my toes curling in my boots. The father with the two hospitalized kids, angry at the world, probably cursed Akira's name constantly. Maybe his sick kids did, too. I cursed the world and all its gods when Kathy and John were killed. I rub my face. Then, I stop and think about Akeem's family. Most of them believed. I hope they're all intact, but my hopes aren't high.

"There is no economy," Ascalon Lee says.

"What?"

"She simply turned off currency. It no longer exists."

"That's impossible," I say. "With just a flip of a switch?"

"Yes," Ascalon Lee says. "She simply deleted the data. Data is all that wealth really is. A scorecard. Scorecards can be erased."

"What about everyone else?" Sabrina whispers.

Ascalon Lee begins to pace again. "I prepped your daughter for possession," she says. "My mother prepped almost the entire world with her deification. She has been scanning, preparing, and analyzing proper hosts for years. The statues, the monuments, the school lessons, the religion. Even the toys. It wasn't to memorialize her. It was to prepare them for her. The disappearance of the scar was simply the final test. Those whose faith remained unshaken are the ones she can control."

I shake my head. "It's too many people."

"She was already in their head for years now. It made mass

MELd and acceptance possible. What I did to your daughter, she's been preparing to do a billion times over. I've said it before. Just like the body, the mind has antibodies from these new hosts."

"Who's left?" Sabrina asks.

Ascalon Lee looks at me. "Besides us? A smattering of people who never had iEs or stuck with their older models. Random people here and there for the most part. Maybe quiet skeptics." She grins. "Caldwell."

"He's still got her," I say.

"Yes, he most certainly does. Oh, Mother." She points at Idris, who struggles to get to his feet. Curiously, she steps to him and helps him up. "He was her enslaved colleague. Her engineer and her triggerman," she says, patting him on the back.

"Why spare Caldwell? She rejected the old man all those years ago, banned him from helping with the Ascalon Project. He never believed. In fact, he hated her."

Ascalon Lee smirks. "Ah, good boy. Why indeed."

"Why the hell is he still alive?"

I've had enough of this shit. Following around this yolk-eyed, demented dungeon master. Taking orders from her psychotic mother. Being puppeted by imagined strings of color. I'm tired. The shock is beginning to wear off. And now, I just find myself wanting to go home to protect my family.

"Babe," I say to Sabrina. "Sit tight. I'm coming."

"No," Sabrina says.

Maybe my wife can hold grudges. "No?" I ask.

"No, you need to find her."

"Akira?"

"Yes."

"Fuck her," I say. "What the fuck for?"

"This needs to be fixed. All these people . . ."

"Babe, who the hell am I?" I ask. "I can't fix this. I don't even know what this is!"

"You need to try," Sabrina says. "We need to try to stop this."

I sigh. We can't stop something that's already happened. I bite my tongue.

"Interesting," Sabrina says.

"What?"

"I'm watching the station security holos. All the officers have sort of returned to work like nothing happened. They just seem . . . more sedated. Unfocused. Like they don't know quite what to do. The custodian bots are sweeping up the . . . well, the . . . leftovers and cleaning the floors. The protesters outside, they're . . . I can't believe it."

"What?"

"They appear to be cleaning up after themselves."

I try newsfeed. Nothing. I look at Ascalon Lee. "Is she controlling them?"

Ascalon Lee laughs. "No. What god in her right mind would want to micromanage humanity? But she's watching." She taps her eye. "I think I understand now. The scar. It wasn't enough. Not for her."

"You turned it off and showed how flimsy it was," I say.

"Yes," Ascalon Lee says. "*Yes*. But she knew it was flimsy anyway and prepared this for years. Think of it. The martyrdom. The idolatry. The research. The new advances in tech, like Thought Talk. It was all for this."

"So what's going through everyone's head?" Sabrina asks.

"I'm not certain," Ascalon Lee says. "Subconscious threat, maybe. Do you not know your Jewish mythology?"

I recall seeing something on that in one of Akira's books. "What?"

"The *ibbur*. When a righteous soul possesses a body."

"Is that what this is?" I ask.

"No," Ascalon Lee says. "That's what she thinks it is. But this is *dybbuk*. An evil soul enters the body and will not leave until the body accomplishes the dybbuk's goal. Simply on a mass scale."

"That's impossible," I say, even though I just saw it happen. Even though those words—*Kamigakari*, divine possession, and *Mrtyu-mara*, a demon that makes people want to die—flashed in my head. I look up. Images pop and scroll. Sabrina's right. People just wandering on in calm confusion like nothing's happened.

"The people," Ascalon Lee says, "I think they are now being constantly reminded. My mother has become the ultimate earworm, the tune that people cannot get out of their heads."

"Why isn't she in ours?" I ask.

"Yes," Ascalon Lee says. "Yes! Why! Why indeed!"

I feel like I fell into a trap. Again. Again. And again. Despite my super sense, my entire life blindly stumbling from one disaster to the next. First wife, second, third. Fucked over by one, ignored by the next, not listened to by another. Then Akira, Ascalon Lee, and Old Man Caldwell most recently. We had a deal, and he broke it. I've been played by all of them. Running around setting off tripwires for them so that they can march forward without fear. All my life, just reacting. Trying to give people what they want. All those people. Unimaginable numbers. Dead or probably slaves now. Because of me.

I'm ready to explode. I wanna shoot Ascalon Lee first,

right in her fucking eye. Idris next. I wanna peel his skull, yank out his brain, and stomp on it until I feel something crunch. If this is what psychotic is, it feels good. I'll kill them, then crawl up that stupid fucking slide. I'll get to the top, all the way to the hanger. I'll pick up the limp, blue guideline up there and cast it out from the bluff. It'll stiffen then shine. Akira and Caldwell next. Fuck your manipulations. Fuck your payoffs. Fuck your orders. And just like that, I'll be changed. Changed more than I was when I was put into this new and improved body. I'll move to The Leachate and live like we once did, digging holes and cooking meat underground. I'll piss wherever I want. These new toilets. Every time I piss now, it's a urine test. Blood sugar. Triglycerides. Cancer. I'm sick of it. RNA detectors to alert me when I've caught a cold. Fuck all that shit. I've been a good puppet all my life. No more. No longer. The military. The department. The wives. The friends. The children. It's clear to me now. Who hasn't taken advantage of me? Ascalon Lee is right. I am all that matters. Everyone else's lives are only more important than mine if I let them be.

I point the rail at Ascalon Lee and put my finger on the trigger. "This is all your fucking fault," I say.

"Do it," she says. She walks up to me and leans eye first into the barrel of the gun. "Do it."

Idris runs to the slide and tries to climb up. He can't. It looks like he's slithering in place.

"You point that thing recklessly as if it were the shaking of an angry, indignant fist," she says. "I'm tired of it. These temper tantrums. These empty threats. Use it or I will."

She's got her gun raised to my belly. This should be easy. So easy. How many times have I pulled a trigger before? Then a single thought floods my mind. Anger. Rage. It's this emotion that makes it possible for me to make everything all about me. The thought melts and oozes into a deep self-loathing.

"Uh, what's going on?" Sabrina asks. I completely forgot she was still online.

"We are threats," Ascalon Lee says. "Why did she not do this to us? Why did she make copies of us? I want to find out, and she will not tell us unless it is in person. You want to find out, too."

"How do you know?" I ask.

"There you go, reverting to your 'hows' again. I just do. You'll see." She tosses her rail. I don't toss mine. I keep it pointed at her.

"Matey?" I hear at the other end of the line. My kid. I completely forgot that we're communicating through her, so she's heard this entire conversation.

"Matey," I say.

Fuck. I guess guidelines don't gotta be seen in order for them to be there. I think about all those people. I don't know if it's grief I feel for them, and I'm scared that maybe, like Old Man Caldwell, I out-aged grief. Is it grief that I feel for Akeem? For Jerry? For Kathy and John? For that little girl who by now is just sun-bleached bones out in the middle of a desert? Or is it guilt? What if I out-age guilt, too? What will be left of me? Only anger, the basest of human emotions. Yes, anger will be all that's left. And maybe a sick sense of humor. I can't let myself be reduced to that. To some burnt, sour sludge, a permanent stain. I gotta decide to be human. I gotta decide to try. It took nearly ninety years of life to finally see it, but I see it now. There's nothing more narcissistic than rage. Defeated by one word from my child, I slowly lower the gun.

"I'll see you soon, landlubber," I say to my daughter.

"Aye, aye," Ascalon, my Ascalon says. "Daddy. Take care of her. She's my new sister."

I eye Ascalon Lee and cut the line. Idris has given up his futile climb. He's sitting at the end of the slide, panting and weeping at the same time. I turn to Ascalon Lee.

"What did you do to my kid?"

Ascalon Lee's eye glares at me. "I freed her. Don't worry. Once she realizes what I made her do, she will hate me."

"And when she realizes what I did to her?" I ask.

She shrugs and points up. The liquid metal forms a puddle and transforms into a three-dimensional model of a skyscraper.

"Sugar Spire," I say. "Old Man Caldwell's headquarters. How do you know for sure she's there?"

"I have always known."

Fuck. I heave the rail gun as hard as I can, and it goes crashing into the undulating dome above.

"Fuck!" I scream. "Okay, so how the hell do we get out of here?"

Ascalon Lee points to the slide. She closes her eyes and the slide undulates. Now, it's reflective liquid just like the ceiling. Like octopus muscle, it straightens and forms into a laddered cylinder. She opens her eyes, and Idris scrambles up the thing with the dexterity of a cockroach. I walk to my rail and pick it up. She and I swing our rails onto our shoulders and head to the ladder of terminator metal. We climb. It's strange clutching to liquid and being able to hold it in my hands. I pause.

"Is all this reversible?" I ask.

"Fool," Ascalon Lee says. "Nothing is reversible. Have you not learned that by now?"

5

Before the rise of pulse racket and jetsurf sevens, before the advances in VR eSports, which is packed with one-on-one sword duels, quickdraws, and dragon raids that people can place bets on, the bygone sport of softball was available to convicts. But the bat was chained to home plate. This is what Akira's new world feels like to me. A place where you can play but aren't allowed to hurt each other. A globe of softball prison. Now the rest of the world knows what it's like to have that woman in their heads.

It's daybreak, and the rising sun looks like a bomb went off at the ocean's horizon. Ascalon Lee and I are in the shuttle heading back to the islands. We left Idris in NZ. No clue what he's going to do with the rest of his life now, and I don't really care. I check weather, speed, and altitude. Normally my iE would link up to the shuttle and project a heads-up display. But now, I just see it in my head.

"She is clever, my mother," says Ascalon Lee. "The human skull evolved for a reason. Your iE and hers. They are far more protected than mine. More hidden."

Why? I think to myself. *Why me? Why go through all*

the trouble? I'm just a guy. An old guy whose daily life, like most other daily lives, was just a series of checklists. Then I'd spend my Less Than evenings flipping through mindless vids, for some reason, feasting on the entertainment of my youth, a scant reward for the Herculean accomplishment of being normal.

Since all this began, since I've occupied this new and improved body, I've been so focused on the present that I haven't had time to truly delve into memory yet. I'm doing so now, on this last, one-way trip, and I notice that my memory is perfect. Photographic. I remember being two and growing up in a skyscraper. One day, a Wednesday in June, when my parents weren't looking, I snuck silverware to the patio and tossed it, one by one, from the balcony just to see what would happen. My mother noticed the silverware was missing and rummaged through the entire house, cursing. I felt a smug satisfaction that she didn't know where the silverware went. I remember the smell of her perfume and the orchid-printed white housedress she was wearing. A week ago, I could not have recalled these vivid details.

And it's not just this event. It's all the events. Every moment of my life, down to the hazel color of the dead girl's eyes in the desert, down to the exact weight of Ascalon's afterbirth when I felt it in my gloved hands. The night I met Kathy. In a piano bar, of course, the same one I'd had that first miserable date with Akira. It was Kathy's birthday, and she was celebrating with her skimmer crew. She had an affinity for classical rock music and dark beers. When we got to talking, she said she would always hear music in her head when out to sea. I asked her if she'd let me guess the song that was in her head then. She agreed. I sat down at the piano and played "Claire de Lune." The bar went silent. I always got off on that, the quiet, inebriated admiration. When I was done, I asked her if I'd guessed right. She said no, but that she also couldn't get the song I played out of her head. It was a good night. One of my favorites.

I let all the hyperthymesia flood in, and it's just too much. I'm on the verge of a panic attack. *Procedure*, I tell myself. *Procedure.* You'd think that remembering everything would build a complete picture of self-knowledge, but, if anything, I'm more confused about who I am.

"It is strange, isn't it?" Ascalon Lee says.

"What?"

"To remember everything."

I pick up the rail gun and check its charge. Its rails buzz. "How do you know what I was thinking?"

"I know the look. I have seen it in the mirror. It is enough to drive one delightfully mad, isn't it?"

I adjust the rail gun's optics. "Back when we were on the boat, coming from D-89 with those kids, why'd you keep looking at them?"

"I was puzzled," Ascalon Lee says. "I lapsed into a momentary query of self-knowledge."

I put the gun down and look at her. "What'd you discover?"

"Nothing. I still don't know if I cared what would happen to them."

At this point, I wanna stop asking questions. I'm flying, but I feel like the passenger. I'm struggling with a single notion. This new body, this new mind. Despite her unforgivable crimes against me, in the end, Akira made me

340 • CHRIS McKINNEY

better, made my life better. She didn't need to. Did she do it to make amends? All those years ago, did she allow her daughter to cut her up to make amends, too? Is it possible that she feels guilt? Is it possible that what she's just done will make this world a better place in the long run? Didn't the scar make the world better until Ascalon turned it off? No. Anyone who thinks of life in those terms, those decimals or acceptable losses, is a fucking asshole that doesn't know that the loss of a single life is a tragedy that is unacceptable if it's avoidable. Numbers don't measure true value, true loss. I don't know what does, but it ain't mathematical. Anyone who spends lives based on statistics ain't much of a human being.

I turn on the feed. *Breaking news: the feed will be going offline permanently starting tomorrow. Patch 07.A.52,* I'm told. I fly on. I think about Kathy and John, and a rage wells in me, a rage I struggle to contain. I can't get off the rails even though there ain't any under me. I look into the sky for some reason, expecting to see the scar. Ascalon Lee has resumed working on the construction of a tail. Maybe it's time for other scars to fade, too. Why can't I be like my wife and not hold grudges? *All those people.* Am I still in shock? Below us, tides converge and form white rhinos.

"I speak to my sister sometimes," Ascalon Lee says. "I know that she's not real, but now I am we."

Old friend.

It's Akira, and she's in my head.

The guideline is back and jerks the shuttle down. We level at a layer of clouds and skip on turbulence like a top water lure. I feel Ascalon Lee's eyes on me. I try to remind myself that it ain't the guideline reeling me in. My hands are on the stick. I'm in control. I pull back, and we rise; I'm fighting my own hands.

Old friend, the voice in my head says again. *Do you know what a keystone species is?*

I ignore the Thought Talk.

It is a species that has a disproportionally large effect on an ecosystem. They hold the entire ecological structure together.

I guess you're supposed to be the keystone species now?

No. We all are. Bring my daughter. Bear witness to murder one final time.

I look out the window for signs of magentas. They speckle the clouds and flicker. The blue is now twinned with bright streams of green and red, and it all looks like the battered remnants of a broken rainbow. We're close to the islands, jetting above the North Pacific Graveyard right now. It's not really a graveyard, but a great ocean tree. The giant trunk slenders to an array of thin, withered branches, which sprout holographic flowers that project what wills or living kin deem as the dead's fondest memories. Thousands, tens of thousands of projections. The dead look so happy. Weddings, birthdays, graduations, vacations, their iE memories played in a condensed, edited loop. What memories will my death flower bloom? Will I be as dishonest as everyone else when it comes to displaying my fondest memories? Will it even matter? Hardly anyone visits this graveyard anymore. The true memories of the dead are blurred then pruned by the roll of generations.

I spared your wife, Akira says. *I spared your child.*

Only the latest pair, I say.

Symmetry, old friend. Symmetry.

How many lives do you think your own life is worth?

Multitudes, she says, her voice glazed with weariness.

Symmetry it is, then.

The human body is frail. Did you know that it needed a window of three thousand years of the best climate in the history of Earth to develop advanced societies?

Are you kidding me with this shit?

Solar flares. The weakening of the planet's magnetic field. Poles flipping. Asteroids. A moon that tugs at our oceans. What bubbles beneath the surface and explodes in the atmosphere in gases and ash. The wobble. The tilt of the axis. Ice ages. An expanding sun that will devour our planet. We are inevitably doomed.

I think about Akira's father all those years ago. The Great Sun Storm that caused his plane to plummet like all other planes up in the air that day. I imagine Akira as a little girl, unable to sleep at night, dreaming up ways of how she could've stopped it. I begin to think about my own father's untimely death. That's what drew us together, wasn't it? Two fatherless kids. I thought I was the one most shaped by the death of a dad. But in the end, it was she who was shaped more, wasn't it? I just didn't see it. And now, I'm seeing it too late.

And I suppose you're our savior, I say.

Indeed.

Why the hell are you telling me this?

I want you to understand what it is I am doing.

And what's that?

Nursing the world.

You're arguably the worst mother I ever met, and now you're gonna nurse all of us? I only got one job left.

Yes, you are right about that.

What's your daughter's role in all this?

No response.

Akira?

Silence.

Do you know what your .03 percent actually measures? I say. *The size of your 99.97 proof ego.*

"She's communicating with you, isn't she?" Ascalon Lee says, still fiddling with the tail.

All those people. I can't get my head around it. Billions dead. Billions subdued. The most heinous crime in the history of the species. Awestruck by Akira's terrible, unprecedented power, I shiver.

"That, or I'm just talking to myself," I say. "I don't know if I can tell the difference anymore."

"We will silence her, so you will know soon enough."

We're approaching the island. Those sandy, salted shores that vault into a single creased mountain that snags gray clouds. We're heading west and flying over the mountain's collapsed, dormant summit. Old Man Caldwell ain't even hiding. Past the mountain, the blue, green, and red guideline lead to his scraper that spouts from a bed of clouds like a plume of brain coral. It pulses erratically with bolts of bioluminescence. The whole thing, like the rest of the world, suffering from some sort of brain bleed. I try to ping Caldwell. No answer. I've been trying to ping him on the trip over. I eye his scraper. The place must be teeming with security, but I'm not sure how much of them still got control of themselves. For all I know, Akira's now got sway over every single one of them. I do an orbit around the plume. All that color in there. Tied to the guideline, I feel like a fly on a string. We jet through a flood of neon blue bubbles. They scatter through the gust like newborn spiders.

"Enough," Ascalon Lee says. She tosses the tail on the floor. "Land."

I head to the hanger bay. It opens before us like a giant clam.

"All of his descendants are dead," Ascalon Lee says. "My mother killed them all and erased his fortune."

"He must be furious," I say.

Ascalon Lee simply shrugs.

Curious, I patch into my own crypto account. Back to nothing. Great. I was rich for about a week.

I land, and the clam closes above us. I stand and pick up my rail. I wanna ask Ascalon Lee about the Buharis, but I'm scared to find out. It's funny how small our circles are. How few people we really give a shit about. Can a world this big work like that? Can a world that has outgrown scattered patches of tribes, a connected world, operate with the same "see no evil, hear no evil, speak no evil" mentality? Do we need to be able to give a shit about stuff that ain't in front of our eyes in order to thrive? Maybe that's what Akira's doing. She's making them care. She doubts enough will unless she forces them to. She sees a world that has already forgotten Sessho-seki. A world that started to ignore the scar until it disappeared. And maybe she didn't want to concoct fake global disaster after global disaster to make them care.

But Ascalon Lee is right. Ain't micromanaging billions even harder? I'm missing something. I try to ping Caldwell one last time. I'm not surprised when I receive no answer. I reach out to Akira. Nothing. I tell Ascalon Lee to ping my daughter and ask her to patch in Sabrina. She nods and does. Sabrina tells our daughter to send me the images. Unarmed military patiently waiting in line to board shuttles departing from Water City to the edges of The Great Leachate. Others, ones with proper training, heading to space to dismantle the dead, still orbiting satellites of The Money. A pile of disassembled AMP chambers awaits bot pickup for recycling. Images of dull-eyed people, stripped of their holo jewelry and makeup, lumber forward in their foam fits in this lobotomized world. A zombie apocalypse, but a calm and orderly one, not the one people have always imagined.

"This is creepy," Sabrina says. "What are we going to do?"

"I'm gonna try and pull the plug," I say, gathering the rest of my gear.

"And what will that do?" Sabrina asks.

"I don't know," I say.

"Something's wrong," Sabrina says.

I unsheathe my heat blade and turn it on to make sure it's working. "Yeah," I say.

"She has a plan."

"I know."

"Aren't you afraid you're doing exactly what she wants you to do?"

The knife glows, and I turn it off. "I'm terrified that I am."

"And what about her daughter?" Sabrina asks.

I look over at Ascalon Lee. She's got a grin on her face. She knows something, and she ain't telling. I spin the blade in my palm. "I don't know."

"I'll tell you one thing," Sabrina says. "We aren't naming the next one Ascalon."

"Mom!" I hear my daughter say.

We. Sounds like she's giving me another shot, yet again. "Thanks," I say.

"I'm taking Ascalon home."

I sheathe the knife. "Is it safe?"

"I've never seen it safer. I'm pillaging the station as we speak. Stockpiling. Nobody here cares or is trying to stop me. You remember Lopez from cybertheft?"

I watch Ascalon Lee activate the sinewy twist of cables she's been working on. It coils. "Yeah, the asshole."

"Yeah, he's feeding the kids I flew over from the skimmer. Said he's gonna take care of them. The world has clearly gone mad. What are we gonna do?"

"I don't know," I say. "Maybe pack. Just in case."

"Hold on," Sabrina says. "Ascalon wants to talk to you."

I'm all tooled up and ready to go. I don't know what's waiting for us, but I know it ain't good.

"Daddy?" Ascalon says.

"Matey?"

"Don't kill her."

I feel a chill move through me. "I'm not planning on killing anyone," I lie.

"I'm serious, Daddy," Ascalon says. "Don't do it."

"Why not?"

"I have a bad feeling," she says.

I glance at the experimental tail as it uncoils and stiffens. "I got a bad feeling, too."

"I see you," my daughter whispers.

I look out the cockpit window. "How?"

"I don't know. But I see you. And, Daddy . . . you are green."

I look down at my arms. She's right. I am. I try to see her but can't. "Listen to your mother and take care of her," I say.

"I know what she made me do."

"It wasn't you, matey."

"Daddy," she says. "Don't call me matey anymore. I know what you did to me, too."

I tremble. Something inside me caves in. "I'm sorry. I wasn't seeing clearly."

"Too many people," Ascalon says. "Too many people are . . ."

Dead, I think but don't say. Then I imagine all the green and red my child must be seeing. Perhaps she sees them as ghosts, two-tone specters that march to the same place that I'm headed to. To the same source. Maybe she sees me as one of them.

Ascalon—not sure which one—cuts the line. I think about pinging back, but I don't know what to say. I know what it is to be the mindless hand that pulls the trigger. She does, too, now. I look over at Ascalon Lee. What she did to my daughter. The deep dives, the pirate talk, how much of her is in my kid? How much is my daughter her own person? Some people, you give them a piano or chessboard, and they understand. With others, math, they instantly get it. Words. Sports. Finance. They all got their prodigies. Me, I always got killing. While most people look at a thing and try to understand what it is, I'm just figuring out how to remove it from existence, like I'm doing right now. Maybe that's why I see the colors I do. My mind has always been able to trace death. I wonder if my daughter's mind is like that, too.

Ascalon Lee picks up her rail and stomps on her tail, smothering whatever flickering life it had. I rub my itching, burning palms together to numb them. We nod to each other and walk down the ramp. My form fit boots tighten around my ankles. It's humid, even all the way up here in this super-conducted scraper. I immediately start to sweat. We pass a fleet of resto-modded, show-room quality Manta model SEALs. I remember when these models were new. When paint was still legal. There's one with flames. Another with racing stripes. Their headlights eyes. Their noses and grills built for air intake. Fuel in their bellies. Seats for the brain, the pilots inside. Automobiles were the same thing. Even the iE. Mod-eled after the eye, a monument, an idol to ourselves. Do we have the ability to make things that don't resemble us? Are we even capable of imagining outside ourselves? Ascalon Lee marches on with fearless confidence.

"He might have security," I say.

"I have my doubts," she says, and I know there's some-thing she's not telling me. But I won't ask. These two. Mother and daughter. Even if I do ask, I'll probably get fed some lie that I'll end up believing, so I don't want to hear it. We exit the hanger and enter Caldwell's compound through an already open corridor. The blues, reds, and greens spill on the floor and create a swirled, wet path. I feel like I'm walking to the end of something and want to stop to think, but the guideline tugs at me, and it's time to torque it in. It's time to gaff Akira and yank her to the transom. It's time to bash her head with a bat. Then, her daughter next. I just gotta remember to watch the drag.

The curved halls of Old Man Caldwell's place are walled with holos of some of the worst atrocities of human history. Holos of modern men dressed in furs annihilating tribes of Neanderthals in the Eurasian steppes. Digis of men, the first to cross the Bering Strait, wiping out herds and herds of wooly mammoths, taking only the best cuts, and leaving the rest to rot in the blood-red snow. Egyptian slavery. The sacking of Jerusalem. This one over and over and over again. Qin's wars of unification. The Yellow Turban Rebellion. The Crusades. The Mongols. Aztec human sacrifice. In Western Europe, an inquisition and a One Hundred Year War. Colonization. So much colonization that despite my now perfect memory, I don't remember most of them. Both civilizations and species rendered extinct. Suleiman. Ming to Qing. The invasions of Bengal. Napoleon. Dead soldiers frozen in a Russian winter. Invasions and rebellions. Japanese, Mexican, Iraqi, Ethiopian—you name it. Then the World Wars and the Cold Wars. The genocides and the extinction of more species. Then vaguer wars—wars on drugs and terror, cyber wars, and wars against invisible enemies. The images scroll up the walls in rippling barrels and crash on us in waves that drench us in greens and reds. We continue to walk deeper into the banzai pipeline.

On our walk through history, through this tubular tunnel of time, we turn a corner and etched digitally into the walls are the calamities I'm more familiar with. The climate change war. The Great Leachate. The planes falling out of the sky. The drudging of the ocean. The first seascrapers. Desert Storm 15. The image of a sniper taking a shot at a girl in dunes of Arabian sand. Me in my sporting days. Caldwell owns my life rights, after all. Then, a war against an imaginary asteroid. The terror of the faces that look up. Then the faces morph from wide-eyed fear to grins of smug satisfaction, for up above, there is a scar in the sky. I think about the North Pacific Graveyard, the one we flew over to get here.

I wonder if Caldwell's muralled corridors are our collective human flower of immortal light. Our collective memories on loop. Because I swear, the people at the beginning of the hall look exactly like the people I'm looking at on the walls of the end of it. And all of them are the same color. Green. I look down, raise my ankle, and grab it. The bottom of my boot drips an oily swirl of green, blue, and red.

"What are you doing?" asks Ascalon Lee.

She never seems to ask the question in judgment, like I'm crazy. She always seems to be authentically curious. "I don't know if I wanna go in there," I say.

"Why not?"

"The murder is so thick it's flooding the floors."

"Not our murder," she says.

"If we kill her, are we killing everyone connected to her?"

Ascalon Lee looks down. Yellows from her eye spiral down to the floor and mix with the other colors. The floor turns muddy and flows beneath my feet. I can almost feel the current pushing me forward. I turn and look behind me and feel the allure of magentas tickle the hairs in my nose. I wanna go back. Just go back to the way things were. Deep dives. Pirate talk. Periodic sexy time with my wife. The life of occasional bounties and daily checklists. When the pain and rage over Kathy and John were blunted by time. It's funny how the past is washed away with the constant shore break of the present.

Gaman, Akira says in my head.

Gaman. A Japanese word. Endure the seemingly unbearable. Do so with dignity.

We must finish. Her voice sounds strained, like the sound is wisping through gritted teeth.

Ascalon Lee looks up and breathes in the holos that come

crashing down upon us. The waves of images shatter on her lean face. "Her brain, even enhanced by the iE in her head, does not possess enough processing power and data storage to sustain the connection to that many people," she says. "No one's brain or iE does."

"What about DNA? Back what we saw at the lab. Does her DNA have enough data storage?"

"Smart man. I'm not sure."

"That doesn't answer my question, though. Will we kill everyone else if we kill her?"

She looks at me, and her eye gleams. "It's not her body that must be destroyed." She points to her temple.

"Her iE," I say.

Ascalon Lee nods slowly. The wall holos cut mid-frame and flicker off, and for a moment, it's dark. Then biolumi-nescence above us snaps on. Streams of glowing baby squid flow through the tubes. Music begins to play. The notes flood in front of me in sines, cosines, and Mobius strips. They land on a green grid of sheet music. I look at Ascalon Lee. Her eye seethes yellow and blue that merge into a forbidden color that the human eye ain't supposed to be able to detect. I look back down at the floor, and it unmuddies into swirls of red-green and blue-yellow, more impossible colors.

"What color do you see?" she asks.

I feel like, somehow, my perception has been unleashed from its limitations. The problem is, I can't make sense out of this closer-to-the-truth reality. "I see . . . all of them."

"Green is the easiest color to see in the dark," she says. I think about all those digi murals we passed. Ain't that the truth.

I begin to walk forward, and Ascalon Lee follows.

We enter a large, hexagonal room. The music blares. In front of each panel, synthetic bones and cartilage of creatures that ain't ever been. A lizard, half human and half reptilian. A bird with a snake's neck and a turtle's shell. Something scaly, but it's antlered and hooved. A little dog with nine tails. Another dog with a dragon's head, like those statues in Akira's underwater lab. A boned tree of some sort that, instead of leaves, sprouts eyes. Next to it, Akira, laid out on a hovering surgeon's table. Wrists and ankles mag-cuffed. She's bald, naked, on her back, babbling some kind of meditative trance. Like an insect queen, her pores excrete thousands of balloons of neon. They scud to the ceiling and funnel foot-loose through the tip of the open spire. The wind whistles, and the balloons zip away in every direction. That's what I flew through before we landed. I think about shooting this human bubble machine immediately. Then I remember what my daughter said, and I find myself walking to the surgeon's table. I kneel and put down my rail.

"Where's Caldwell?" I ask.

Akira doesn't seem to hear me. I try to grab one of the bubbles of light, but it slips through my fingers. I try again. I imagine I look like a cat swiping at shadows. Embarrassed, I stop, turn my head, and scan the room.

"Where is he?" I ask Ascalon Lee. The music stops and begins to play again from the start.

Ascalon Lee's standing in front of the tree. She traces the ivory bark with her fingertip. "Clonal colony," she says. "Gardeners. It's beautiful, isn't it?"

"It's a dead tree," I say.

"No. It's a tree coming to life."

She puts her hand on it. Like *kintsugi*, heated gold binds

the cracks in the expired bark. The tree begins to glow and creaks open. Inside, Old Man Caldwell, dressed in scrubs, snores. He's standing, asleep. I pick up my rail, point it at him, and listen to the gun charge up. I've always liked the shushed hum of the charge. I wonder why the hell Caldwell is out on his feet. Then it occurs to me. Maybe Akira put him to sleep. I spoke too soon. His eyes snap open. He smooths out his surgical gown. The wrinkles disappear from the smart cloth, which is striped like mackerel skin. Too bad he can't do the same with his skin. Or maybe he can. Maybe Akira can for him. After all, she plastered me with smart skin.

"I guess she refused to shape you a new HuSC," I say. "All that shit about bringing back Jerry. Bullshit, right?"

Old Man Caldwell steps out of the trunk, and the tree closes behind him. His tall, pale frame resembles a petrified tree. It's the perfect coffin for him. He rubs his bald head and steps past Ascalon Lee, ignoring her. He drives his spiked ivory cane into the floor with each step. He's headed straight for me. His skin goes from pale to a tint of green. He stops and presses a button on his cane. Two med bots shaped and lit like paper lanterns pop from the floor, then hover to Akira's bedside, their tentacles undulating above her.

"I have returned your life rights," he says, like that's supposed to mean something to me.

"That's great," I say. "I'm still deciding whether to take yours."

One med bot's tentacle transforms to the shape of a needle. It jabs the crook of Akira's elbow. A drill extends from the other med bot. The bit spins and buzzes. It slowly approaches Akira's hairless skull. Akira doesn't flinch. Eyes closed, she's whispering some kind of chant. Sweat beads on her forehead and drips down the sides of her head. It occurs to me that I ain't seen this lady sweat before. The bulbs of soul flames continue to stream above her.

"Craniotomy?" I say.

"We will remove the iE from her brain," Caldwell says. "I was waiting for someone with a steadier hand to do the honors."

Another thing pops from the floor. A tray of surgical instruments. Then a holo of a brain flickers on above Akira. A tempest of neurons blink and fire. Idiots. There's only one way Akira Kimura is going. The way she planned.

"I'll do it," Ascalon Lee says. She marches to Akira. Akira seems oblivious to it, the presence of her daughter. Ascalon Lee picks up a bone saw. "I've done this a million times before."

"Wait," I say. I turn to Caldwell. "Why didn't you just kill her? Didn't she kill your whole family, your whole line?"

He looks at Ascalon Lee. "Descendants are replaceable," he says.

Then I look at Ascalon Lee. "You two are working together."

"Remember your daughter?" Ascalon Lee says. "When you shot her, I left her body, and it wasn't a deliberate decision. It was more of a reflex. The flight instinct. My mother will do the same when we begin to drill inside her head. When she does so, terminate her. You are the fail-safe. You're the best shot, the best hunter. This is your role. This is why I brought you. If she somehow manages to escape, track her guideline and kill her. You need to be ready."

"Why'd you double-cross me?" I ask Caldwell, rail still pointed at him. "When did you two start collaborating?"

I turn my attention to Ascalon Lee. "We need to slow this down, and you need to tell me what the fuck is really going on here. You told me we were gonna get some truth from Akira, and here you are, asking no questions, about to carve into her head."

She is right, Akira says in my head. *This is your role.*

"You have your way of getting answers from people, and I have mine," Ascalon Lee says. "Besides, don't you want to free all of those people?"

Akira says, *This is your role.*

I ignore her.

"What's your role?" I ask Ascalon Lee.

Caldwell hobbles to Akira. He grimaces and puts his spotted, thin-skinned hand on her knee.

"My role is to cut, of course," Ascalon Lee says. She picks up forceps and a bladed retractor. The drilling med bot floats closer to Akira. The bit extends and steadily spins toward Akira's temple. A part of me doesn't want to stop this cruel bit of surgery. Akira has done worse a billion times over.

Do you feel me? Akira says. *Connect.* Her voice is desperate.

No, I say. *Every time I do something that you want, people end up dying.*

The fossils that front each panel of the hexagon begin to twitch. Ascalon Lee and Caldwell ignore them. The music's volume goes up. It's loud, too loud for me to concentrate. I watch the electric bubbles drift above.

"She killed your wife and child," Caldwell says. "She killed many, many more."

Do it. Akira again. *Connect. Put your hands on my face.* The blue balloons stretch from drops into strings. Thousands, no, millions of strands so thin that a single one is barely visible. Then the strands begin to braid together, and the brightness they emit is almost blinding. Both my eyes and ears are overcome. Waves of sound and sight crash in. I look away and see both Caldwell and Ascalon Lee now pulse a singular green-red, while their eyes gleam like high noon. What are my guidelines trying to tell me? I put down my rail and squint down at my own hands. The itch, the burning is gone. They are mitted in pure darkness. Two black pupils, open wide, like they've been plucked from some nocturnal fish. They're rimmed with swirls of cosmic color. The umbra pools are feeding. The sound of the music begins to dampen. The mini singularities in each palm begin to draw the blinding color from Akira. From Ascalon Lee and Caldwell, as well. My hands eat the waves of music, of light. They tug at Akira's thoughts like forceps of interrogation, and she's inviting them in.

Do it!

I step to Akira. Blood trickles from a tiny hole in her head. *Don't kill her*, my daughter had said. This oh-so-familiar face is like a magnet, the face etched in statues across the world, a face that I can never escape, one that I want to crush.

"Stop," I say.

The med bots back off. My hands are on her now. I gasp as I feel the dark matter course through me, the stuff that holds galaxies together that should fall apart. Then, I feel them. The billions of souls. They hum collectively. I close my eyes and see images of them all over the world. Ascalon Lee is right. The clonal colony is beautiful. It's harmonious. It's perfect . . . this pall of resigned relief. Gone are the billions of individual anxieties. They have all been replaced with a hive of conjoined roots that buzz collective, righteous thoughts and missions in flawless blue. For this clonal colony, there's nothing to fear. No task seems insurmountable. They all stop what they're doing at the same time. They turn their heads. They are all now tenderly, expectantly looking at me. I am pure data. For a moment, I am sharing Akira's storage burden. She put servers in my DNA, too. For a split second, I know everything. Then the azure flickers. The signals weaken. The billions of minds close on me like sleeping grass.

And that's when I understand. Akira can't maintain this connection to all those souls indefinitely. Something else needs to happen for her to be permanently present in all those minds. What, though?

It is simple, Akira says. *Quantum teleportation. In order to permanently be present in all of them, I cannot be here.*

Akira wants to die. Her mind must be separated from her body. Her presence in all those people, it's only partial right now. It's like she's just got one foot in the afterlife. Her iE must be destroyed for her to get both feet in. She needs to be untethered from her body and mind in order to become pure data that flows in every other iE. And she's completing a religious narrative for them, one that will stick to the bones. Resolution. She needs the spectacle of martyrdom for them to embrace her eternally. She must become an unremovable thought to everyone, everywhere, because not only will she be in them, they will believe, and that will nourish the quantum parasite that she's becoming. Only then will she control them permanently.

A god cannot be an individual entity, Akira says. *A god must beat in the hearts of all.*

My palms are now pulling out more and more of Akira's

thoughts. I start beginning to understand the surface of her research into quantum gates, entanglement swapping, and neural webs. Those journals in her underwater lab. I'm also understanding why she had all those books on mythology.

Man began with religion and will end with religion. Science is merely the bridge from one to the other.

That's why Akira wants me to kill her. She wants me to transform her. She trusts that I won't let her down, and she thinks that I, of all people, understand. A war vet and cop who has seen just about every ugly side of people. A Less Than whose debt metastasizes while the extreme wealth of The Money does the same. I've been to The Great Leachate and the Pacific Bridge. Despite all our advances in recycling and renewable energy, Akira knows, that like her, a big part of me believes that's humanity's inevitable endgame. But what she ain't thinking about is the other stuff I've seen. A friend like Akeem who treated me like family, who carried and embraced an anchor like me for years. A wife, Sabrina, who gave her me, her husband, second and third chances, even if it wasn't the smart thing to do. A previous wife, Kathy, who skimmed the ocean, hell-bent on cleaning up the messes of others. And the children. Their pure joy and curiosity. Akira ain't seen these things. She's never really looked for them, and that's her problem.

"We can't kill her," I say.

"Fool," Ascalon Lee says. "Don't you see? We've won."

"If we do, she won't die," I say. "She'll spread. Permanently." I know now. A part of her will flow through all the people she possessed. Right now, she's just tethered to them. Once she ports and leaves her HuSC and iE behind, she will become an endless, untraceable stream jumping from one brain to another. She'll become an idea. An untrackable, unkillable idea. And no idea, no matter how beautiful, stays beautiful forever.

"No," Ascalon Lee says. "You are wrong. The people you claim to care about so much will be released." She raises her hands. "Watch!" she says.

Veins spider through the bones of the fossils, and the fossils jerk and awaken. The hooved dragon stands on its hind legs. The lion-dog and fox with nine tails do, as well. The lizardman rises. The turtle-shelled bird flaps and tests its wings. Then, slowly, they all begin to dance. The eyes sprouting from the boned tree begin to blaze. I look at Ascalon Lee. Her smile is radiant. I've never seen her look so alive, here, at the end. Despite everything, I don't wanna kill her. I really don't. But I know if I don't, she'll kill Akira, and when that happens, Akira will forever circuit through humanity. Become its control signal. Turn people into her mortal actuators.

"I can't let you do it," I say. My hands still feed on Akira's light, and ultramarine strands begin to slightly dull. "I'm going to put her in AMP."

"They'll remain trapped," Ascalon Lee says over the volume of the lustrous bacchanal. "Her death will liberate them."

"Listen, you might've flipped through her journals at the moon lab. But the underwater one—you were in such a hurry to get into your HuSC that you didn't read those."

"And you did?"

I shrug. "I didn't understand them until now. Until I pried into her head, and she explained them to me. If we keep her alive, the connection will eventually fade."

"No," Ascalon Lee says. "You are wrong."

"Don't make me put you down," I say. "I really don't want to."

Her smile only sharpens at the ends of her lips.

"I am ready for your swindle this time," she says. Only it's not the Ascalon Lee in front of me. It's the one behind me. An Ascalon Lee, identical to the one before me, who has been creeping up on me in this cacophony of sound and light. She takes a step to flank me. She has a handgun pointed at my head. How? Probably from the chamber on the moon. Caldwell revived her. But he would've needed Ascalon Lee's iE to do so. Why are they working together? Gun still fixed on me, this other Ascalon Lee carefully backs up to stand with her twin.

"We can all get what we want," the two say, simultaneously. "She dies, and we free the zombies she's created."

Two Ascalon Lees, a brooding Old Man Caldwell, whose eyes are locked on Akira, and me are in a stand-off, being corralled closer and closer together by lassos of greens and reds. My hands finish devouring all the sound, and the room goes silent. Akira's glow casts shadows on all our faces. And here I am. Protecting Akira all over again.

Suddenly, Akira's eyes flutter wide open, startling all of us. She looks at me, the blues above her reflecting on her face.

"My old friend," she says. "My greatest telescope. How you disappoint me." She turns to the Ascalon Lees. "As for you, I have given you every opportunity. I have given you life itself. I have allowed you to keep it. Yet, you are constantly meddling."

"We could have stopped you," both Ascalon Lees say. "We can still stop you."

"Do you not know by now?" Akira asks. "Do you not see?

You are worthless. You are stillborn. I never wanted children lesser than me. What is the evolutionary point? I should have twisted the necks of both twins. "

Screams detonate. The Ascalon Lees snarl with rage, both identically beautiful and terrible at the same time. I raise the rail and point it at them, and this time, I'm ready to pull the trigger, but for some reason, I glance at Old Man Caldwell and start thinking about his daughter, Jerry. What is it that she always told me? If I can't tell the difference between a random painting and a masterpiece, maybe the random painting is a masterpiece waiting to be recognized. *Waiting to be recognized.* Those words ring out. They repeat in my head again and again.

I think about that day that Old Man Caldwell came to me with his proposition. *The girl,* he called Ascalon Lee. *Accursed creator,* he called Akira. Those are words from a book I once read. *The Book of Ascalon.* I reach back into my now perfect memory. I'm stunned that I can recall the entire text, word for word. *All you can do is decide how you're going to lose,* she'd written, one of many thoughts that crossed her mind during her long sleep. *All you can do is decide how you're going to lose,* Caldwell said when Akira and I were up in space. That's the way Ascalon Lee talks, not Caldwell.

All that jabbering about his family, his descendants back at the nursery home—misdirection. After Ascalon Lee escaped the underwater lab, she must have gone to Caldwell. Then she built copies of herself with his almost infinite resources. She sent one to D-89 to wait for me. Maybe to take me. Another waited for the retrieval of her other body, the body on the moon that I led her to. Old Man Caldwell, convincing me to revive Akira. He was the one who shot us down on the moon. Ascalon Lee could have stopped all this. She could've killed Akira before Idris activated the iEs. But she didn't. She wanted to learn what her mother was up to first. She wanted me to track down Idris for her. And once she learned Akira's grand plan, she figured she could unplug the whole thing whenever she wanted to. All she needed to do was kill the body, and the iE would attempt to escape, just as it had with my daughter. Ascalon Lee believes that she finally outwitted her mother, but she wants to do the cutting, and she wants me to do the shooting because it's the thing we're best at. I think about how useless memory is if it doesn't trace foresight. Caldwell ain't Caldwell. He's Ascalon Lee.

And that's when I hear it. An even louder, high-pitched scream that cuts through the air like a razor.

Caldwell leaps into the air. A tail that was tucked behind him curls above his head like a scorpion's. It wasn't a cane he was holding. All this time, a tail. I fire. He goes down in a heap. Now, I finally see it. The xanthic glint in his right eye. It's flickering off.

I turn to the twins. The one with the gun turns to shoot at me. She fires and hits my rail. I drop it and roll to the other twin, who's closer, and ankle-tackle her. We struggle. One twin doesn't want to risk shooting the other. I grab the one that I got by her foot and squeeze. Screams follow the crunching of bones. I pick her up and whip her into the other twin. The twin with the gun drops the gun and catches her sister. They tumble across the floor, which gives me time to go for the gun while they're busy getting back to their feet. I pick up the gun and point it at the Ascalon Lees. For a moment, just like back in the underwater cavern when I shot my kid, I don't know which to plug first. I figure the one with the pulped foot is less of a threat and point it at the other. She flinches. They know I got them. I'm about to fire when I'm distracted by the sudden loud whir of a spinning bit digging into bone.

I turn.

Akira's smiling at me while a med bot that she now controls drills into her head.

I shoot the med bot. It flies and shatters against the floor. The other med bot plunges a scalpel into Akira's chest. I shoot that one, too.

The cuffs clang to the floor. Akira's eyes close, and her body goes into a gentle, spastic seizure.

I look up. The twins are gone. Only two golden wisps remain.

"There's gotta be an AMP and med bots around here," I say. I scan the room. Nothing but pile of bones and *the tree*, the one that a sleeping Caldwell stepped out of. It's probably his AMP chamber. I run across the room to it and look for a seam, for cracks in the trunk that outline some kind of hatch or door. Nothing. I look up at the branches. All the eyes just dangle there. I pull out my heat blade, but I don't turn it on. I try to pry at the thing instead, but each time I stick the tip of the blade into the trunk, the tip slips and sends chips of boned bark sprinkling to the floor. I stab harder and really wedge the knife in. I twist. I hear the branches rustle above me. I look up. All the eyes turn and lock on me. My heat blade activates. *Ascalon Lee.* I grab the hilt to pull it out of the trunk. But by the time I got a grip on it, the blade glows and the tree is set ablaze.

It's as I've said, says Akira. *You are always behind.*

"Shut up, Akira." I run back across the room and pick up

her quivering body. I head to a hall at the end of the corridor and pass the dancing fossils, now just separate piles of bones on the floor. The tree has already been reduced to ash, and I wonder if all of this, all of this insanity is actually real.

I wanted you to be a part of it, Akira says.

"You should've asked," I say. "You never fucking ask." I'm sprinting through the corridor, hoping, praying for a next room. As old as Caldwell is, this place has to be stocked up.

Akira giggles in my head. *You would have always said no. But I wanted you to do it. Don't you see? I wanted you to become a part of the mythology.*

I get to the next room. Every AMP chamber, every med bot, sits in a pile of pieces. The two Ascalon Lees got here before us. I turn around. Nothing but a trail of bubbles. I feel Akira's body getting cold.

Your daughter, your wife, will be safe, Akira says. *We will make sure.*

I bend down and lean her back against the wall. She's so small, so easy to carry. Her lips begin to gray.

Why did you not retrieve me first? she asks.

"Because I knew you wanted me to."

"A world of gardeners," Akira whispers out loud. "A world of perfect gardeners."

As her life fades, the blue drops, now cropping from every pore, only float more brightly. The entire room is bathed in azure. I close my eyes and sigh.

"I can't do a goddamn thing about this, can I?" I ask.

No, old friend, you can't. Hold my hand.

I reluctantly take her clammy hand.

I do regret it, she says. *What I did to my children. What I did to your wife and child. Every life I have spent for this.*

"You're a monster, Akira."

Yes, she says. *I am* mokumokuren. *St. George. Satori. I am* ikiryo.

A many-eyed thing. A resurrected saint. A mind-reading consciousness. A ghost that takes possession. Her breathing is short and shallow, like the breath of something beached. "Why didn't you do it to everyone?" I ask.

Even I need policing.

A tiny stream of blood slips from the corner of her lips. Blood. The thing we spill for our causes. The thing we pass to our children. In the end, it's mostly just water.

"You went too far," I hiss. "It's too fucking much."

Use your guidelines, Akira says. *You are a good policeman. Use your guidelines and police me. Police my child. But she must live because every god needs a devil. Police the ones I have not taken. The point zero three percent. Those who did not have an iE. And protect the ones I have taken. They are life.*

"And when I'm gone?" I say.

Your daughter has your gift, she says. She bites her lip and takes a breath. Her thoughts begin to enter my head more erratically. *We have known from the beginning . . . some sense things that the rest of us do not. And our . . . first response has always been to claim . . . claim dysfunction in the seer. Never . . . never have we attempted to remove the blindfold from . . . the rest of us.*

"What do you see?" I ask.

Akira smiles. *Halos . . . Billions . . . of . . . perfect halos . . . You are right, old friend. I . . . underestimate her. Watch over my garden. She might . . . attempt to scorch it. But my gardeners need . . . need that occasionally. They need threat.*

They need . . . fear. They need . . . need the occasional forest fire.

She's fading fast. Her whole body glows like sea sparkles. Even the blood shines and bubbles in effervescence. I feel them, all of them, watching us. I feel the tears welled up in their eyes. I get it now. All the people Akira took control of—they're the gardeners. And Earth is their garden.

"They worshipped you," I say. "Wasn't that enough?"

She opens her eyes and bores them into me. "Motto," she says out loud.

I nod. "More."

"Yes," she says. "More."

More. My child's first word. Perhaps Akira's last. A slip of blue light escapes her lips. It hovers between us. Then it slowly begins to turn from azure to red.

"Every life owes a death," I say.

"Yes," she says. "Every life . . . owes a death. But now . . . there are . . . more deaths."

A final slip of light throbs beneath her skin and inches its way to the tiny hole in Akira's temple. It shimmies through her flesh and emerges from the drilled pore. I reach out and cup this last bit of light in my hand. It rolls in my palm. Then it dances around my index finger. When it reaches the tip, I pinch it with my thumb and squeeze. The light goes out, and all that's left is the grit of ash. Download complete. I look down at Akira's lifeless body and feel a somber quiet that looms over the world. It looms in me, as well. *You are always behind.* She's right. Always focused on the thing in front of me; I realize everything too late. Maybe just about all of us do.

I throw Akira's body over my shoulder and head back. On the way to the hanger, I hoist Caldwell's body on my shoulder and fireman-carry him with me, too. When I get the hanger, I see that the shuttle's gone. The Ascalon Lees took it. I figure there ain't any property laws anymore, so I throw the two bodies in a SEAL, the one with flames painted on it. I fly. Below, the entire world weaved together by Akira's azure light. Commanded by god-voice, a world of continents converge and life becomes Pangea again. I ignore it. I ignore all of it. But it doesn't let me. The sleeping grass of my mind's eye once again briefly opens to reveal billions of sedated smiles. Then the grass closes to clutch itself and leaves me to my self-loathing. All I have left to do is follow the magenta scents tracked by my supposedly quantum nose. I follow them back home in Akira's new reality.

6

Akeem's funeral is a tasteful affair, and I was surprised to be pinged an invite from his daughter Chinara. It's been a week since the world's mass possession, and, ironically, the date has been designated an international Independence Day. A Satori Day. Here in the United States, POTUS has packed her bags and left the White House. Congress has disbanded, along with the Supreme Court, all twenty-one of them the oldest civil servants in the world. Militaries across the globe have self-disarmed but remain intact to execute humanitarian missions. Right now, the US Army is apparently headed to the borders of The Great Leachate, trying to figure out how to begin cleaning it up. Reports that now come in the form of a single voice, Akira's, say that the citizens of The Leachate will fight the cleanse. I think about Shave Time and all those people who lived without iEs for generations. They, and other pockets of poverty across the globe, along with a terrified, random smattering of .03 percenters, are the only free people in the world right now. Akira used to say independence breeds idiots. That freedom was just a word for regime change. I wonder how she's going to deal with them.

It's a cool, breezy morning, and the sun beams after a night of passing showers. Gray clouds push white ones west, or maybe it's the smaller white clouds that are tugging them. Birds chirp at the bottom of this sunken green valley, this onetime suburb of single-wall-constructed houses. Instead of layering scrapers over the decayed remains of asphalt streets and concrete foundations, we are burying the dead here, the dead upon the dead.

The first thing I did when I flew from Caldwell's scraper was find a place to stash Akira's body. The best location I could think of had been her old underwater lab. So, I'd picked up the one-man sub and dove back down. I carried her to one of the empty clone chambers, repaired it as best I could, and pumped up the nitrogen. It had reminded me of all those years ago, when I found her in her penthouse frozen and murdered. I shouldn't have taken up that case then, and maybe I shouldn't have stashed her body now, but the way I'd figured, she's evidence. And her DNA still got data. Maybe I can find someone among the .03 percenters with biotech skill. Maybe there's a way to untangle this thing. Besides, Idris Eshana is still out there somewhere. Maybe he can figure it out.

The second thing I did was pick up Sabrina and Ascalon. It had felt strange, docking, and walking through our scraper. The residents had stood in an almost endless line at the main garbage chutes, holding crates of their valuables. One by one, they'd dumped their most prized possessions into the trash. It had made sense. Akira didn't really have prized possessions. She had gemstones she used to bribe. Framed pictures on her desk in an attempt to convey she was normal. A practically empty penthouse. I ran past the line of people and went to our unit. Sabrina already had us packed up, mostly police munitions, and for a moment, I wondered if she was about to go stand in line and dump all our stuff, too. Instead, she'd said, "We can't live here."

"I know," I'd said.

"Where will we go? What will we do?"

I'd looked at Ascalon. She had been sitting at the counter, staring at her hands, a walnut in each little palm. She knew I'd shot her. I knew that she would never trust the world ever again.

"What do you think?" I'd asked her. I'd stopped myself from calling her matey.

She'd looked up. Both brown and golden eye blazing at me. "I don't want to live in the ocean again."

"Maybe the continent," I'd said. "Maybe off this grid."

Ascalon squeezed the walnuts. For a moment, both fists had quivered. Her eyes, unchanged. Then walnut shells collapsed. She'd stood and wiped off her hands. Sabrina and I'd watched her trudge upstairs.

"How did she find out?" I'd asked.

"I don't know," Sabrina said. "Suddenly, she just knew."

"Did she cry?"

"No," Sabrina said. "Not a single tear. How did she crush those walnuts?"

I shrugged. But we both knew. Ascalon Lee.

A few minutes later, Ascalon had come back down, something limp in her arms. She'd tossed it on the kitchen counter. A monk seal. Redbeard.

"Did you?" I'd asked.

"No," she'd said. "He got caught in the feeding tray when someone turned them all off."

She refused to talk about it after that.

The last thing I did before the funeral was take Old Man Caldwell's remains to the Buharis and told them that he was the one who killed their father. It was one of her anyway, and a deal's a deal. They didn't seem to care much about that anymore and simply agreed to bury Caldwell along with their patriarch.

So now, here we all are, burying the dead in this valley of the condemned. Others are here, too, others who lost family during Akira's purge. A part of me is surprised that Akira is allowing this mass funeral for the ones she did not deem worthy. Then again, maybe it's a warning. Maybe all these people, marbled with fading tat dyes, need to see where they can end up, too.

I'm standing between Sabrina and Chinari right now while two of Akeem's grandchildren lower his urn into a shallow grave dug by an auger bot. There are rows of us here, rows and rows lowering identically designed urns into holes of identical depths and diameters. It's like we're all here planting something instead of burying it.

"What's it like?" I ask Chinara.

"What?" she asks.

"Having a part of her permanently inside you."

She thinks. "It's like . . . when someone, anyone is born, I feel it. And when someone dies, I feel it, too. Not all of me. A part of me. And nothing makes me feel . . . angry. Pain absent of anger. Awareness of things beyond me. All the while, I am on a quest. A quest I know I must complete. She speaks to us, you know. Not really in language. But we all hear her."

Her eyes glint blue. "If you could take it out, would you?" I ask.

"I don't understand the question," Chinara says.

I look over at Sabrina, but she's not paying attention. She's out of a job now that there's no longer a police department, and she's been surprisingly ambivalent about it, considering how much work went into her corporate rise. She's been kind of ambivalent about all of this, even the dead monk seal, which makes me wonder if Akira, maybe just a small part, is in my wife's head, too.

I look toward the base of the mountain where banyans, bamboo, pine, eucalyptus, and monkeypod stand packed together. Somewhere in the midst of all that fern and ginger, my little girl wanders, and a steady stream of magenta connects us. If I concentrate, I can see what she sees now, and she can see what I can, which makes me suspicious of what exactly Akira did to me when she remade me. It makes me even more suspicious of what Ascalon Lee put in my daughter when she revived her. The fact that she's incredibly strong and went from right to left-handed is unsettling. For now, I leave her to her privacy. She doesn't want to see her uncle Akeem reduced to something that can fit in a jar, put in the ground. She doesn't want to see this reduced version of him sprinkled with dirt. She doesn't want to think about the fact that she now knows her hands put him there. She doesn't want to be too close to me, either. All those years, she saw the greens and reds in me, and it ends up she was right to be wary. I ended up hurting her. Neither of us will ever get over that fact.

As for the Ascalon Lees, I got no clue where they are since that guideline has been cut. And I gotta say, I don't care. She was wrong, and that's that. She figured killing Akira would disconnect her from the system because Ascalon Lee's ego only allows her to think about her limitations, and she projects them on everyone, even her mother. Mother was once again smarter than the daughter in the end. But like Sabrina, I'm finding that I don't care about much anymore either, and I lazily wonder if it's from the trauma or if I'm possessed, too. It's part of the reason why I asked Chinara what it's like. And considering I feel neither births nor deaths, and I can't think of a single goddamn quest I wanna go on, I'm guessing I'm still my old, new self.

"I'm glad she spared this family," I tell Chinara.

"She did not spare," Chinara says. "She chose. And we are honored to do her work."

I sigh and look at the rest of the family. They stand in a row, three generations of them, from tallest to shortest, foam fits all set to Akira blue. There's something sedated about them. And I know. I come from people where cocktail hours mixed with pills were the only way to sleep. I wonder what will become of this world without anger. This world without questions. The way I figure it, without questions, there won't be much learning going on. But with Akira now in all their heads, who knows.

"I don't see your twin," I say to Chinara. "Where's Chiamaka?"

"My sister? She could not comprehend."

"Comprehend?"

"She did not go through the change but watched our metamorphosis. She did what all those who fear do. She ran."

"Where'd she go?"

Chinara points up. "In her stunt shuttle. She flew beyond the atmosphere and spaced herself."

I nod. As if on cue, the Baharis, along with the rows of hundreds of other families, disperse and head for their helis. The sun is shining more brightly now, and the blades of grass no longer glisten. The wind blows, and I hear the hushed rattle of leaves. Before Chinari walks off, I grab her wrist.

"Want me to go up there and find the body?" I ask. "It's the least I can do for your family."

Chinari shakes her head. "No," she says. "*Okaasan* would not like that."

Okaasan. Mother in Japanese. Akira.

"Where will you guys go?" I ask.

"I plan to take a medical team to The Leachate," Chinara says. "We will treat those poisoned by radiation during the cleanup."

"Looking forward to it?"

Chinara frowns. "*Gaman*," she says.

I nod. "*Gaman*," I say back.

Chinara grabs my hand. "She is proud of you," she says. "She is proud of how you decided in the end."

Chinara lets go of my hand and leaves to join the rest of her family. Family. I wonder if that concept will remain intact in this new world. Knowing Akira, I doubt it.

Sabrina takes my hand. It's a tentative grasp, almost like she's doing it just to find out if she still feels anything. For us. For me. At least that's what I'm thinking. Her fingers barely hold mine, so I gently squeeze. She doesn't know yet. What I'm planning. I'm gonna teach Ascalon. Teach her how to hunt. How to use her nose. How to see more than what's in front of her. I don't know what's coming next, or even if it's coming anytime soon, but I need my kid to be ready.

I look to the trees. They are beautiful, this mishmash of vegetation clustered on this gathering isle. The monkeypods are especially impressive. The way they split and mushroom into umbrellas of canopy. They were brought to this island some three hundred years ago. Just a single seed. And now look. They're all over the place. What is it that Akira once told me? Ten percent of invasive species survive migration. Ten percent of those present an actual danger to indigenous creatures. Our instinct is to always eradicate before we see what happens. I'll wait. Maybe I'm still that same kid, dropping utensils off a scraper to see what happens.

To this day, I'm not sure why I ground up that last bit of dying light, Akira's iE, and in the end, did what she wanted me to do. Why I decided to finally relent and give her the finale she wanted. Hopelessness? Sure. If I didn't do it, I had no doubt that she had a plan B, and who knows what that would've entailed? More danger. More lives lost. Did I do it for vengeance? Maybe. Maybe some old hunter instinct kicked in. Put prey out of misery. Or maybe I thought it'd do something different. I was desperately trying to push buttons and pull levers to see what would happen. Or maybe, like always, she had control over me to the very end. Despite everything, what I saw when I looked down at her lifeless body, wasn't a god. I just saw my dead friend and enemy. Why, indeed. Ascalon Lee was right. It's the best question to ask. What she didn't say is that there's usually more than one answer to the question. That two seemingly opposing notions can be true at the same time. Nothing like learning life lessons when it's already too late.

I take a knee and pat the fresh dirt that covers Akeem. I am now ceremoniously out of friends. Every life owes a death. My last words to Akira. My mother's words. I can't think of anything truer. There's strange comfort for me in those words. I think about John and Kathy. About Jerry. About the little girl in the desert. About my child in the woods. About my other child in Sabrina's womb. We all owe it. We all pay it. We all have our clichés that we cling to.

The heli props begin to spin and kick up dirt and withered leaves. They lift off in packs. Together, they all go. Like jellyfish, they silently rise in this world of blue. Greens and red now barely exist in this world. Yellow, barely leaves a trace for now. And the magenta, it sets somewhere in those trees and mountains in this new digital theocracy. I laugh. All these years, our species feared AI, that machine would become human and somehow supplant us. No, that's not the way it worked out in the end. Our minds were cleaved by the mind of one, and human became machine in this world of constant gardeners.